When We Meet Again

Two Stories of World War II

By Carla Kelly

Kenmore, WA

CAMEL PRESS

A Camel Press book published by Epicenter Press

Epicenter Press
6524 NE 181st St. Suite 2
Kenmore, WA 98028.

For more information go to:
www.Camelpress.com
www.Coffeetownpress.com
www.Epicenterpress.com

Author website: www.carlakellyauthor.com

Design by Rudy Ramos

When We Meet Again: Two Stories of World War II
Copyright © 2022 by Carla Kelly

ISBN: 9781684920167 (trade paper)
ISBN: 9781684920174 (ebook)

Printed in the United States of America

In memory of Harold W. Suess, a dear friend from a later war.
I will always treasure your letters.

Books by Carla Kelly

Fiction

Daughter of Fortune
Summer Campaign
Miss Chartley's Guided Tour
Marian's Christmas Wish
Mrs. McVinnie's London Season
Libby's London Merchant
Miss Grimsley's Oxford Career
Miss Billings Treads the Boards
Miss Milton Speaks Her Mind
Miss Wittier Makes a List
Mrs. Drew Plays Her Hand
Reforming Lord Ragsdale
The Lady's Companion
With This Ring
One Good Turn
The Wedding Journey
Here's to the Ladies: Stories of the Frontier Army
Beau Crusoe
Marrying the Captain
The Surgeon's Lady
Marrying the Royal Marine
The Admiral's Penniless Bride
Borrowed Light
Enduring Light
Coming Home for Christmas: The Holiday Stories
Regency Christmas Gifts
Season's Regency Greetings
Marriage of Mercy
My Loving Vigil Keeping
Double Cross
Marco and the Devil's Bargain
Paloma and the Horse Traders
Star in the Meadow
Unlikely Master Genius
Unlikely Spy Catchers
Safe Passage
Softly Falling
One Step Enough
Courting Carrie in Wonderland
A Regency Royal Navy Christmas
Unlikely Heroes
A Hopeful Christmas
The Necklace
Her Smile

All My Love

To Arsula Shumway and her parents.
"No Greater Love."

Chapter One

Veronica Green blamed her impulse on the recruiting poster, the one showing a young woman in uniform, looking more valiant than Prince Valiant, with the same steely-eyed determination. An American flag fluttered behind her, a fitting sight for the caption, "Are you the girl with a Star-Spangled heart? Join the WAC now!"

Right there in little Ponca City, Oklahoma, where no one ever came except on purpose, it hung next to another, more practical poster with an equally determined lass in brown and khaki and the words, "The Army of the United States has 239 kinds of jobs for women."

As Ronnie walked by the recruiting center where men of her acquaintance had been enlisting since December 8, 1941, she reminded herself that she had a job. Since 1941, the plea for soldiers had sprung up like mushrooms after a downpour, posters mainly of a warlike Uncle Sam pointing his finger. None of *them* mentioned 239 jobs, not when the only job that mattered for men was defeating Hitler and the empire of Japan.

For two years since Pearl Harbor, she had walked the mile to work at Ponca's five and dime, where she had finally graduated from stocking shelves to the cash register. That happened when the owner's son heeded the call to duty and marched away to war. She knew Bill Bower, Jr., had suggested her to his father because Bill told her, "Ronnie, you're the man for the job. I know you can work a cash register was well as me. That's what I said to my father."

Certainly I can, you dolt, she wanted to say, but didn't. She knew there would be a slight raise and a girl has to get ahead somehow. She knew she was pretty enough without being a distraction to men who shopped, or an irritation to their wives. Mr. Bower, Sr., hadn't included a raise, however, muttering something about "patriotic duty," which indicated a lapse in logic, but who was she to tell the boss that?

As it turned out, being sufficiently pretty made no difference. It was January of 1943 now, and all the boys were gone except the ones with flat feet, bad eyes, and parts missing. Most of her high school friends were either suffering dengue fever in the South Pacific, sweating in North Africa, missing in action, or resting somewhere in early graves. Too many families had received The Telegram, the "We regret to inform you" telegram that sent some to the floor in a dead faint, and others to grim silence.

Why was that day different, the day where she stopped, read the poster again, and reconsidered? Ronnie asked herself that on the train ride to basic training in Daytona, Florida, which wasn't a bad place to be in February of 1944. She could have gone for training to Hunter College in New York City, but Ronnie Green was nobody's fool. Florida in February had far more appeal. Even now in September, as she sat in the Greyhound bus after compassionate leave for her father's funeral and frowned at surly clouds that Okies know, she had no answer.

She did, actually, but it was silly to mention, even in this time of heightened patriotism. Ronnie knew in her bones that she *was* the girl with a Star-Spangled heart. Throw in this superficial notion: She yearned to travel, and the U.S. Army recruiter had milked that longing. "WAVES and Spars don't typically go overseas, but WACs do," he coaxed as he held out the fountain pen. "You could be on your way to England after basic training. Sign here."

She signed, wondering what she would tell her father after work and her walk home to the house he shared with his spinster sister, Ronnie's Aunt Violet. She had saved the news until after dinner, when Aunt Vi rose to clear the table and Pop leaned back to light his pipe.

"Pop, I joined the WACs today."

Ronnie wasn't one to beat around the bush, and there was no telling how soon an official letter would arrive. She was twenty-one – just barely – and possessed all her wits. She knew she could pass the physical and she wanted to see more of the world than Ponca City, Oklahoma. Why not do it on Uncle Sam's dime in England?

The Greyhound slowed. Ronnie recognized the skyline of Topeka, Kansas – well, the slightly taller buildings and more grain silos by the railroad depot than in Wichita – and slumped lower in the seat, dissatisfied with herself. Uncle Sam's dime hadn't gotten her any farther than Kansas City, Kansas, where she had to return to duty, back from burying Pops and ready to paint a smile on her face because the U.S. Army, Lt. Colonel Phillip Dignam in particular, expected it.

The bus driver stood up and cleared his throat. "Fifteen minutes here. If you're changing to points west, this is the place. Fifteen minutes."

Ronnie looked in her brown leather, regulation U.S. Army pocketbook for a quarter, which she knew would get her pie a la mode and lemonade. Five days ago, that meant cherry pie. Maybe it still did, and hopefully not the same pie. She knew it wouldn't be banana cream pie. No one had seen bananas since Pearl Harbor.

"Bananas are for our boys overseas," the grocers explained with a shrug. It seemed a fair apology when she was still working at the five and dime in Ponca City. Eight months in the service had turned her cynical. She still hadn't found a banana in the U.S. Army.

The choice this afternoon was apple pie or apple pie, so she took apple pie. There wasn't any a la mode because of the boys overseas – although how vanilla ice cream would keep on Guadalcanal was anyone's guess – but the lemonade had little flecks of ice in it. She savored the moment.

"Say, miss, are you in the army?"

Ronnie put down her fork and took a closer look at the counter girl. She sat a little straighter, hoping she didn't look too travel-worn. "Yes, I am," she said. "I'm Private Green. Are you…"

"Hey you, how about some more java down here?"

The counter girl said, "Excuse me," and hurried to a man holding out his mug, looking impatient to be away. Ronnie recognized all the signs. One of her jobs, above and beyond the all-encompassing title of clerk-typist, was checking off manifests from truckers. Whether it was ball bearings or widgets, everyone had miles to go in a hurry. The war waited for no man, woman, or widget.

Speaking of which…Ronnie glanced at the clock. Five minutes. She picked up her fork and briefly inspected the crust. She knew it wasn't made with pork lard, which was the best. Mystery ingredients had come along with war, too, and this looked questionable. Her crust was better because for all her grumbles about the hand God had dealt her, Aunt Vi knew what made a good pie, and how to pass the secrets along to her niece. Down went the pie anyway.

"Miss, I was wondering…"

Brown eyes looked into brown eyes. The skin was different, but Ronnie had skill in finding the sisterhood. "…if maybe the U.S. Army has a place for you?"

The counter girl nodded. "When's your day off?" Ronnie asked.

"Half day tomorrow."

"Find the army recruiting depot and ask."

"They'll take me?"

Ronnie knew what she was really asking. "They will," she said quietly, "providing you're healthy and can read and write."

Counter Girl's head went up. "I am and I can." She leaned a little closer, but not too much to appear uppity. "I sorta hanker to see what's out there."

So did I, Ronnie thought, amused, and pleased that after eight months, the matter no longer rankled too much. *It got me all the way from Ponca City to Kansas City*. "There's a world outside of Topeka," she said, hoping it was true for Counter Girl, as she put a nickel tip beside the plate. "But trust me here: you'll probably still be working in a kitchen."

"I don't mind." The nickel went in the girl's apron pocket and she cleared the counter. "It'll still be a change of scenery, and there isn't much of that in Kansas."

The clouds looked even more ominous, with fitful puffs of hot air scudding them along. The bus driver stood by the door looking at his watch. He gave her a small salute. "General, you've got some interesting company this leg of the trip."

Ronnie smiled, wishing she had a nickel for every time some wise guy called her a general. What was it about a woman in uniform that made her fair game? She had already fended off two sailors and a Marine with an eyepatch by sitting down next to an old lady, who from the looks of her, was still asleep. Ronnie sat next to her again and glanced to her right across the aisle, then glanced again.

No one could overlook the black band with MP in white lettering on the sleeve of his uniform. Three rockers and three chevrons told her she was looking at a master sergeant and the sort of man who would have no trouble keeping order on a Greyhound with a few other uniforms and more people like the old woman snoring beside her.

He caught her second glance and nodded to her. "Private," he said with a nod. She assumed that likely constituted all his conversation. She had no burning urge to speak to someone adept at billy clubs, even if they were in the same army. There had been enough strikes at Pop's John Deere plant in Ponca and she had seen rough justice up close.

"Private Green, sir," she said, pretty sure that would constitute all of her conversation.

Except it didn't, to her surprise. Why was he smiling at her? She had to admit that the smile did remove some of his awesomeness. She had seen military policemen in action in Daytona, wading into a crowd of drunken soldiers and sailors with billy clubs in motion. She glanced to his side. The seat's armrest didn't quite obscure the pistol and holster, which she knew outranked a billy club. Still, why was he smiling? And my, didn't he have nice teeth?

"Master Sergeant Brown," he told her. He held up his right arm and brought with it another arm manacled to his. "And this is Helmut Schwarz. Black, plus Brown and Green. We're a colorful lot."

She laughed in spite of the sight of two men handcuffed together, something she had never seen before. "I suppose we are, sir," she said, mostly to be polite. She tugged out *McCall's Magazine*, letting it be known that she preferred to read. End of conversation.

Sergeant Brown got the message, which made Ronnie feel small inside. Maybe he wanted to talk. Maybe his obvious prisoner spoke only German, and he was bored. She knew it wasn't her place to resume a conversation she had nipped in the bud, especially since he was far superior in rank and truth be told, intimidating, whether he meant to be or not.

As the bus pulled away from the depot, Ronnie turned to an article on serving turnips and why they are good for us, and scolded herself for being a ninny. Maybe a side glance wouldn't be noticed. She decided that Master Sergeant Brown was worth more than a side glance, with blond hair and blue eyes. She knew it wasn't padding filling out his uniform.

His knees touched the seat in front, so she also knew he was tall, probably the sort of man Uncle Sam had in mind when he pointed that finger and said, "I want you." *Thousands must want you, Sergeant Brown*, she told herself, which was her first cheerful thought since saying goodbye to Aunt Vi, who now had to rattle around in a house minus her modest brother. The mere pleasure in a happy, entirely irrelevant thought made Ronnie smile.

Her frown returned, tempered with some emotion wavering between pity (although something told her this was not a man to pity), and concern.

When the sergeant turned his head toward his prisoner, she saw a raw-looking scar running north from his uniform and well into his closely cut hair. It appeared recent enough to make her wonder if seeing the world was such a good idea, after all. She wished she hadn't shut off conversation so thoroughly.

Over the whine of the Greyhound's engine, she tried to listen to the conversation across the aisle, only to discover it was entirely in German. *Who are you, Sergeant Brown?* she wanted to ask. With a small sigh, Ronnie turned back to turnips, at least until the bus started to sway and the sky darkened almost to dusk. Wind shooed dust across the highway and the Greyhound slowed down.

Ronnie closed the magazine and tried to see out the window. The woman next to her woke up and gasped. She pointed. Ronnie took a deep breath and another. Long acquaintance with life in Tornado Alley America sent her heart into her throat. *All right, Mr. Bus Driver,* she thought, her hands on the seat back in front of her, primed for flight. *It's time to bail out.*

Chapter Two

The bus came to an abrupt stop as Ronnie leaped up, which sent her staggering backward onto Sergeant Brown's lap. He grabbed her around the waist, put her on her feet and leaned toward her, giving her a whiff of Old Spice. When he winced, she knew that neck wound still pained him.

It didn't stop him. "Everybody up and out!" he shouted, in a voice of absolute command. "Follow Private Green here into that ditch." He pointed to the two sailors a few seats behind them. "Open the exit door and get those people off. I'll bring up the rear with my prisoner. Move!"

Almost before he finished, the Marine with the eyepatch who sat farther back yanked down on the exit handle. He put his shoulder to it. When the door flew open, he jumped off and held out his hands to a little boy pushed toward him by the boy's mother. He carried him away as the sailors ushered the back half down the aisle and away from the bus.

Energized, Ronnie motioned the others forward and out as the bus started to sway from the force of buffeting winds. She snaked down the aisle toward the front, leading the way as if she knew what she was doing. She realized with a pleasant start that she did know what to do. She wasn't a Ponca City girl for nothing. Pops had his own hidey-hole beside the farmhouse, a haven they had crouched in many times in her childhood, safe from tornados.

Others on the bus knew what they were doing, too. She hesitated by the bus driver, who had jerked forward when he brought the bus to a halt, which pushed his forehead into the front window. A crack widened as she watched, but the glass did not break. As she debated whether to help the driver, two old farmer types behind her grabbed him and hauled him along, his heels thumping down the steps after her.

She looked around to make sure her seatmate had followed her, and saw the formerly placid old lady give her a thumbs up, her expression resolute. "I saw you sit in that nice soldier's lap," she joked as she hurried down the steps and into the ditch. Ronnie blushed and motioned everyone to move away from the swaying bus and further into the ditch. "Everybody down!" she shouted. "You know what to do."

They did. She sank down, too, mindful that her khaki summer uniform was about to get dusty and probably wet when the rain came. The wind tugged her tidy hair out of its regulation-approved snood. As the bus continued to sway, she looked around at her charges, relieved to see them all hunkered down, hugging the sloping side of the ditch like an old friend.

Here came Sergeant Brown with prisoner Schwarz, his own constant companion, whose terrified eyes and open mouth suggested to Ronnie that he didn't see too many – or any – tornados in the Fatherland. "*Hinlegen!*" the MP commanded, then gave Herr Schwarz a push, in case he had any doubt.

"You, too," he said over his shoulder to Ronnie as he lay down against the slant of the ditch. "Burrow close to me. I'm not going anywhere."

She did as he said, thankful for his broad back, even if he was connected to a German prisoner. She pressed her cheek against the M.P.'s back and closed her eyes, unwilling to watch how close the tornado passed. She heard the unwelcome sound of a train where there were no tracks, heard the bus groan some more, and listened to the rush of leaves suddenly yanked from the shelterbelt's trees.

Silence for a brief moment, then came a patter of hail that mercifully turned to rain. Ronnie squinted into the distance, relieved to see the bus still upright.

"*Gott im Himmel, was war das?*" the prisoner asked.

"*Der Tornado.*"

"I'm happy to kiss *der tornado* goodbye," Ronnie muttered. She stood up, brushing sodden leaves from her skirt, wondering over what county her kepi sailed now. She knew her hair was a wreck all around her face – it wasn't her fault that it curled in such a non-regulation way when it was wet – and wondered why Sergeant Brown kept staring. Maybe she had a leaf plastered against her cheek. She touched it. No.

Ronnie shrugged and looked at the others, who were getting to their feet, talking to each other. She heard nervous laughter, then a baby cry.

The two men who had dragged the bus driver with them were looking down as the driver sat up. Blood ran down his face, but the rain sluiced it away, leaving a gash that appeared far from fatal. As Ronnie watched, a farm woman in a flowery dress with her hat mashed to one side pressed a handkerchief against the gash that only oozed now, gestured, and soon had someone's necktie knotted against the wound.

The men helped the driver to his feet. "Can you drive?" one of them asked. The driver shook his head.

"I can," said another farm woman, her dress not so flowery, her shoes more sensible. "Can't be worse'n a grain truck." The others laughed and everyone headed for the bus.

"Just like that, and it's all sorted out?" the M.P. commented.

"Just like that," Ronnie replied, amused. "You must not be from the Midwest, sir."

"I am, though," he said. "Rantoul, Illinois." He pulled his prisoner along. "We don't see as many tornados as you do." He appraised her in a way that made her feel sorry for his prisoners. Nothing seemed to escape his notice. "You knew what to do. You from around here?"

"Ponca City, Oklahoma, home of John Deere," she offered promptly. "Or at least, one of Mr. Deere's factories."

"And you're going to…"

"Kansas City, where I'm stationed," she said. It pleased her that he matched his stride to hers, even though he was much taller.

"So you joined the Army to see the Midwest?" he teased.

She made a face. "You should have heard everything the recruiter promised me!"

He laughed at that, and she felt better, because it wasn't a mean, point-your-finger-at-the-gullible-girl sound. It was more of a that's-war-and-duty sound. Or so she reckoned. She had heard the other laugh, too.

He didn't laugh long. His face turned serious and he frowned. "Private Green, Europe's not much fun right now. Trust me."

She nodded, and wondered some more about the healing scar on his head.

He must have wanted to change the subject, because he did. Who could blame him? "What'd your folks say when you joined up?"

"My mother died when I was young, but Aunt Violet – she helped Pops raise me – wow, she was startled."

"Not your dad?"

She didn't want to talk about Pops, but apparently she had to. "He knew I wanted a change." Should she say more? Why not? Would she see this man again? "I've just come from his funeral in Ponca City."

"I am so sorry," he said quietly. "It's never easy, is it?"

She shook her head, hoping he would overlook the way her eyes filled. Without a word, he handed her his handkerchief. She wiped her eyes, enjoyed that Old Spice again, then handed it back. "Thank you. He was a good father."

"Then we were both lucky. So was mine." He moved forward, after a meaningful look at his prisoner. He said something pithy-sounding in German and Schwarz frowned.

"I hope there aren't any live wires down," the sergeant commented as they queued up behind the others to board again.

"What would you do if there were?" she asked.

"Find a board and move them," he said. "Stuff has to get through. *I* get it through."

She heard the determination and something more. She didn't think it was pride. A glance at his eyes told her he had seen too much. She thought of the MPs who directed traffic now and then around the aircraft plant. This was something more, some anxiety for the safety of others, and probably none of her business.

She reached out on impulse and lightly touched her forefinger to his wrist. That was all. He sighed, and then he was back to business, taking a good look at the jury-rigged bandage with the striped tie as he stood next to the driver.

The driver must have felt his manhood was on the line. With a gingerly tug of his own on the tie, he sank into the driver's seat as everyone piled back in. Mrs. Sensible Shoes glared at him and plunked herself down in the seat behind. "In case you feel faint," she said.

"Lady, I…"

"Don't argue with me."

The M.P. caught Ronnie's eye and grinned, which threw a few years off the old look in his eyes, the look she was already familiar with after a mere eight months in the U.S. Army. She smiled back, content with that. She never had been the sort of woman who looked for the grandiose. She preferred capability, which was what smiled back at her.

To her delight, the little boy that the Marine had handed down tapped on her arm and held out her kepi, battered but in her possession once more, thank goodness. On her first day of work in the office of North American Aviation's aircraft inspector, Colonel Dignam had stressed the importance of losing no government property. His example was his own father's tale from Indian wars days of being haunted by the regimental quartermaster over the loss of a candlestick. "From the time my father was a second lieutenant until he retired as a major general, that quartermaster never gave up," Col. Dignam told her. She smiled at the memory.

"What's so funny?"

Sergeant Brown's gaze didn't miss much, she decided, unsure whether to be flattered, or to be grateful that she would likely never have to undergo an interrogation. Ronnie told him the candlestick story and he laughed.

The bus driver motioned to Sergeant Brown and he went to the front, tugging Herr Schwarz with him because he had no choice. Ronnie sat down next to the old lady again, whose face wore a more pleasant expression. As tornadoes go, theirs may not have been much, but it seemed to have left the busload of survivors happy and triumphant, as though they had bested a terrible force of nature singlehanded.

"How did he go and put himself in charge?" the woman asked, of no one in particular.

"Military policemen are like that," Ronnie said, her eyes on the sergeant and his prisoner. *Good ones, anyway,* she thought. *He probably thinks we're his responsibility.*

A few moments later, the sergeant looked back down the aisle and raised his hand. To Ronnie's amusement, everyone stopped talking. "We're going back to Wichita for another bus driver," he announced. He stared down the few protests. "Would you rather he passed out and we crashed?"

There endeth any mutiny, Ronnie thought, impressed.

They were back at the depot in a half hour, cooling their heels for an hour, then on the road again, as night came on. During the break, Sergeant Brown commandeered the Marine to come with him to the men's room. "I'd rather two of us watched outside the stall when he's uncuffed," Ronnie heard him say to the Marine in passing, and decided that her miniscule service to the U.S. war effort was considerably less bother than Sergeant Brown's. At least she needn't monitor lavatory stalls.

Supper was frankfurters and macaroni and fake cheese, eaten at the counter with her seatmate. Another hour passed in the dreariness of a bus depot that smelled of stale food, motor oil and travelers in need of shaves and showers. Ronnie stood by her duffel, wondering about the hurry up and wait she saw around her. If this was war… Well, it was her war.

They were on the road in darkness, finally, with fitful rain, and lightning to the east. Everyone sat where they had before, even though the depot swapped out both the bus and the driver. In minutes, Ronnie's seatmate wrapped herself in the solitude of a raincoat and was soon snoring. Ronnie leaned back, eyes closed, free to think about her father, free from pain finally, and Aunt Vi carrying on alone in a shabby farmhouse on the outskirts of Ponca City.

She smiled into the darkness. Maybe now, with no disapproving glares from Pops, her aunt's beau of fifteen years would work up the nerve to propose. Or not. Maybe he was set in his ways for Sunday dinner and the occasional peck in the cheek when Aunt Vi thought no one was watching. *I hope to goodness I find someone braver than that*, Ronnie thought, and not for the first time.

"You awake?"

She was. She had been hoping the M.P. might need some distraction to keep his eyes open. Was she nosy to want to know more about him? Probably, but what of it? In Kansas City, she would go one way, and he would probably transfer to the Fort Leavenworth line, prisoner in tow. That would be that, so why not ask some questions?

"I am, sir," she said, leaning across the aisle. "Is your prisoner not good company?"

"The worst. He's asleep, and doesn't like to talk to me anyway," Sergeant Brown said. "Um, look. Call me Ernie, will you?"

"If you'll call me Ronnie." It seemed brazen. After Mama died, Aunt Vi had taken her mother's last request to heart to raise Veronica right. Her aunt took no duty lightly. Ronnie's manners were good, even if based on an etiquette book from a previous century. Too brazen? "If you want to," she tempered.

"I do. I need to stay awake," Ernie said. "Looks like you're elected." He chuckled. "How'd a nice girl like you end up in Kansas City?"

With a smile of her own, she leaned closer as the 'Hound swayed around one of the few curves in an otherwise straight road. "I told you about that dratted recruiting poster."

"You did. Where'd they send you for basic training? I know there aren't too many options yet for women."

"Daytona Beach," she said and leaned back, remembering sand and seabirds so foreign to a girl from the Midwest who had never been anywhere. "I liked learning to drill and march, and I especially like the classes," she said. "I wanted to go to college, but we never had money like that."

"You and most of us. I joined the army in 1938, because Rantoul wasn't too promising. Since I had muscles and height, I ended up in the Military Police. What do you do?"

"Clerk-typist," Ronnie said and sighed. "I had the misfortune to be the best typist in the class on the day that my boss Lieutenant Colonel Dignam sent a telegram to an old West Point friend, pleading for a clerk-typist at the aircraft plant where *he* had been assigned." She leaned out again. "Imagine. Colonel Dignam was born on the frontier and retired after the Berlin Olympics – he was head of cavalry during the Twenties. Back in harness again, for the duration."

"And probably glad enough. Who wants to sit out a war?" Ronnie heard his sigh. "I don't, but here I am."

Was this where she poked around in this stranger's business? She decided it was. "It doesn't look as though you have been sitting out a war," she ventured.

"No, indeed. My battalion landed on Omaha Beach in the third wave and went to work directing tanks off the beach, evacuating the wounded, and wresting order out of chaos," he said. "I was directing traffic off the beach when I got this." He touched the back of his head. "I woke up in a hospital in Plymouth, England."

She heard no plea for sympathy. "I'm sorry," she said simply. "Why are you here, though?"

"I suppose my story bears some resemblance to yours," he said. "After a few weeks recuperating, one of the battalion officers saw me, did that Uncle-Sam-I-Want-You pose, and sent me stateside to direct a different kind of traffic." He cleared his throat. "You may have noticed that I speak German."

"And rather well."

"It was my first language."

"Ernie Brown?" she asked, mystified.

"Try Ernst Braun," he said. "Rantoul has a sizeable German population, many of whom changed their names when the Great War began." He leaned closer and whispered. "This gent was trying to steal secrets at one of Wichita's aircraft plants. I'm escorting him to Fort Leavenworth, where he will sit out the war, courtesy of Uncle Sam."

He stretched his legs into the aisle, after looking around and seeing no movement from anyone. "That's better. I'm biding my time here Stateside. I'll go over again, and soon. Plenty of prisoners to interrogate."

"And I'll stay safe and bored in Kansas City," Ronnie said, trying not to sound bitter and shortchanged.

"I'd rather you did," he said, his voice quiet but compelling in a way that made her breath come quickly. "I really would."

What could she say to that? The dark settled in and the 'Hound bounded along, taking her back to her Olivetti-Underwood and all those filing cabinets. Still, it was nice to chat with the MP. Since she knew she wouldn't see him again and he needed to stay awake, Ronnie told him about Ponca City, and her mother's death, Aunt Violet's arrival, the five and dime where she dusted knickknacks no one bought. Once it was dark – she knew her chatter was aiding the war effort by keeping this MP awake – she admitted to Master Sergeant Ernie Brown that she sometimes imagined she really was the Star-Spangled girl from the recruiting poster.

"I wanted to do something great for the war," she admitted. "I file charts and correspondence in a factory building big planes."

Silence. Maybe Ernie had drifted off to sleep. She glanced over him at Herr Schwarz, who was snoring. "I will watch over both of you," she whispered, certain he slept.

"I believe you would," Sergeant Brown said without opening his eyes. "Thank you. I need a little shut-eye."

Surprised, then amused, she watched his shoulders lower as he relaxed and slept. His trust humbled her in a way she hadn't thought possible. She barely knew him. *Maybe this was what I joined the army for*, she thought. *A chance to help out someone.*

To her dismay, Kansas City came too soon. Sergeant Brown woke up Herr Schwarz and they left the bus first for the transfer to Fort Leavenworth per orders, he told her over his shoulder. There was no time for her to say goodbye, or thanks for listening, or good luck when you are reassigned to Europe. There also wasn't time or opportunity for him to get her name or barracks address, or even the name of the factory where she worked. There were several in Kansas City, after all. Then again, that probably had never been his intention. He was a busy man, working in dangerous waters. She doubted all spies were as simple and compliant as Herr Schwarz.

The sergeant looked back at her once, though, and she smiled. No sense in showing off her disappointment for all to see. There wasn't any dismissing the hollow feeling that made itself comfortable again, not when she got off the bus and saw soldiers and wives and sweethearts saying goodbye next to another 'Hound, this one loaded and quivering, ready to leave for war.

Ronnie returned her gaze to the M.P. and the prisoner, looking as though they walked hand in hand. She shook her head, grateful she didn't have to be handcuffed to someone who didn't mind sabotaging aircraft.

For the smallest moment, she pretended she walked hand in hand with the military policeman. A girl wouldn't ever have to be wary of mashers or wolves, not with someone that capable. Maybe there would even be an opportunity for that MP to slip his arm around her waist. "In my dreams," she whispered, and turned away, because the night wasn't getting one bit younger. Come to think of it, neither was she.

War, you passed me by, she thought, as she held up her hand for a taxi.

Chapter Three

Ronnie decided to forget Master Sergeant Ernest Brown, not because he wasn't memorable to her, but because she knew the world was full of people you see only once, even if that's a crying shame. That's what she told herself on the taxi ride to Kansas City's northeast corner and North American Aviation, where she was one of thousands: workers turning out B-25 bombers, and a WAC clerk-typist filing reports that she doubted anyone read.

He didn't ask for your address or a telephone number where you could be reached, she reminded herself as the cab bumped along with dimmed lights. *He was kind to you, but nothing more.* She diverted her attention by thinking – not for the first time – that a nighttime blackout in the interior of a country as large as the United States of America bordered on the ludicrous. Only a month ago, an early-morning fog had snarled traffic to the plant and two workers died in a crosswalk by the highway. She had seen the accident report – also filed it – which blamed their deaths on the fact that they must not have seen the car with the low lights as they started across the road.

"Which way, lady?"

"Turn left here at Constitution Way, then right in two blocks on Marshall," she said. "Stop at the first door."

Two turns and a stop and she was home, or at least in front of a massive wooden barracks that housed other WAC stenographers, switchboard operators, clerk-typists like herself and civilian women machinists, welders, and riveters, all lumped together as "Rosies," after the poster that popped up everywhere. She shook her head over the driver's offer of help with her duffel, handed him a dime tip, and let herself into the barracks.

The door was never locked. North American Aviation ran three shifts seven days a week, with women coming and going. She sniffed. The cafeteria did close between midnight and three for perfunctory cleaning. If she hurried, there was food and she was hungry. She sniffed again; she knew that smell.

The others rolled their eyes at her, but creamed chipped beef on toast still tasted better than anything else. True, when she wrote home about the delicacy, carefully writing S, followed by three dashes, then, *on a Shingle*, followed by "That's what the soldiers call it," Aunt Vi had been aghast. Or so Pops had said in a letter. "You know what a stickler your aunt is," he had written, then eased the blow by adding, "I thought it was funny. Make me some next time I see you."

Oh, Pops, she thought, *I wish I could*. She left her duffel by a chair, got a tray and a fork and lined up behind two women in coveralls, their hair wrapped in bandannas, who did look like the stereotypical Rosies. Who knew women could grow muscles like that? Amazing what war was teaching everyone.

This batch of SOS might have been left over from the last shift, but the chipped beef went down easily. Even though she knew it was too early, by habit she looked around for Mrs. Dobbs, who ran the kitchen, and usually came on at six for her 12-hour shift. Ronnie didn't remember her own mother, but she had decided after her arrival here from basic training, followed by a week of homesickness, that her mother must have been like Mrs. Dobbs, capable and hardworking. Pops had never wanted talk about Mama and her asthma, so Ronnie was free to substitute Mrs. Dobbs.

She never told Mrs. Dobbs, of course. It was enough to watch her overseeing the production of food bought at least expense during wartime rationing, and turn it into, well, S***on a Shingle.

Still hungry, she followed the SOS with a monkey dish of canned peaches. Everything else had been devoured and she was finally feeling the effects of a long ride, a tornado, and more riding. She knew she had to be at her desk right outside Colonel Dignam's office at seven. Her duffel seemed heavier now when she shouldered it and climbed two flights of stairs to the room she shared with three other WACs.

The others might wonder, but Ronnie still felt satisfaction from sharing a room with only three other women. Maybe they hadn't grown up in a three-room house, where one bedroom was Pop's, the other Aunt Vi's, with the sofa in the front room for Ronnie. As good as her aunt was to drop everything and move in with Pops and her after her sister died, Aunt Vi was a stickler for privacy, her privacy. "It's the price of having her with us," Pops had explained when she was old enough to question why there wasn't room for her with Aunt Vi.

She unlocked the door and tiptoed in, hoping to disturb no one. In minutes she had shucked her uniform, hanging it carefully in her designated corner of the closet, set aside her battered kepi, and found her nightgown. She quietly settled herself in the prized bottom bunk, hers only because she was the second arrival in the room six months ago, and not because she was persuasive.

"Ronnie, that had better be you." The sleepy voice belonged to Private Millie Sturdivant, who slept above her.

"No, it's your fairy godmother," Ronnie started to whisper, then reminded herself that the other two empty beds belonged to late shift WACs, one of them a switchboard operator, and the other a nurse in the plant's infirmary. They would drag in around seven in the morning, promptly collapse and resurface in early evening for a few words with the daytime crew. It was no way to develop friendships, but that was war.

"If you're my fairy godmother, Ronnie, I wish you would send me letters from Bob."

Ronnie's eyes were closing of their own accord, but she knew Millie. "I promise you will get four or five tomorrow. 'Night, Millie." She knew what would happen in the morning, as the two of them followed their morning routine in the little room, which involved avoidance choreography to get dressed. Millie would demand Ronnie's sympathy that she had not heard from her husband Bob with Patton's Third Armored Division, located somewhere vaguely north of Italy.

Ronnie knew there would be no questions from Millie about Pops' funeral, no commiseration, not because Millie was heartless, but because Millie counted no one's losses worse than hers. Pops had told her a few letters back, when she complained to him, that some people were built that way. It wasn't personal. Still, it would have been nice to casually mention a military policeman who was tall and blond and helpful. Just a mention in passing, nothing more.

Morning brought the unwelcome alarm clock, which Ronnie ignored. Let Millie scurry around first then make her way down the corridor to the communal lavatory. This was the best time – to have the room all to herself, to stretch, to think about yesterday and then remind herself that nothing monumental had happened. She had met a man she wanted to know better, but the matter had come to nothing.

This morning she could be practical. It was mid-September. The army dictated that summer uniforms were put away, even though Kansas weather didn't cooperate with wool or even gabardine yet. She reminded herself that her shoes needed a quick brushing, after stumbling down into a ditch to avoid a tornado. "Rise and shine," she said out loud, and began her day.

She had the usual for breakfast: toast with grape jelly, oatmeal with raisins and half an apple. She didn't care for coffee, but there was always Postum, a humble hot drink never rationed like coffee to one cuppa. She breathed in the molasses flavor and resolved to file better this day than any other WAC in the service of her country.

She smiled to see Mrs. Dobbs, who liked to make the rounds of the tables, stopping to chat, wiping up spills. Maybe Mrs. Dobbs would come this way. She might even remember her.

Ronnie knew it would be a good day when the cafeteria supervisor sat down. "Ronnie, you're back," she said simply. "I hope you had time for the necessaries."

"I did," Ronnie told her. "Aunt Violet made all the arrangements. Some of the ladies even brought flowers to the church."

"Mums this time of year? Maybe some zinnias and asters?"

Mrs. Dobbs knew what to say. She never failed. Was my mother like this? Ronnie asked herself as she set down her cup and told the supervisor about the service, and the singing, and the testimonial from two of Pops's friends from the John Deere factory. "They said he was the best man they knew, someone who never shirked his duty," Ronnie finished.

"Did it help?"

How did Mrs. Dobbs know? Ronnie nodded, her heart full. "Pops was quiet and good," she said, after a moment to compose herself. "He gave away a lot of food to bums, but we never went hungry."

That was the way of it, when your house came within half an acre of the railroad at that spot where the trains slowed down as they approached Ponca City. The smarter men and women who rode for free got off then, to avoid the bulls with their Billy sticks and flashlights in the train yard. Aunt Vi fussed about her brother's generosity, but after a while, she just added more beans to the pot.

"Quiet and good," Ronnie repeated, as her eyes filled. "My father."

Mrs. Dobbs leaned forward and dabbed at Ronnie's eyes with that same cloth that wiped tables. She found a clean corner. Maybe she made sure there was always a clean corner.

"I would say the apple didn't fall too far from the Green tree." Mrs. Dobbs always knew what to say.

Ronnie knew how to return the favor. "Mrs. D, have you heard from Chaz or Tom?"

"Got a two-page letter from Tom last week," the woman said. It was her turn to find a clean corner. "A'course, the censors blotted out half of it, but I know they're somewhere in the Pacific Ocean."

It was her little joke, and Ronnie smiled, because she knew what to say. "Why then, he could be in San Francisco any day now."

"When he comes to see me in Kansas, you can meet him. I wrote him about you, remember?"

Ronnie remembered. She wondered now and then how often Mrs. Dobbs had told both sons – Chaz was based in England in a bomber crew – about one or another of the factory girls and the WACs she thought might make good wives someday. It was harmless conversation, the kind of chit chat that made life seem normal when it was anything but, and young men could just show up to visit their mothers anytime they wanted, and meet some girls.

"You tell him from me that I hope he isn't seasick anymore," Ronnie said as she stood up. "Have a good day, Mrs. Dobbs."

"I will if you will, dearie." This was their usual exchange. Today, it buoyed up Ronnie beyond mere words. Everyone said the war was winding down. Maybe someday Mrs. Dobbs's boys *would* return and meet the legion of girls their mother had promised were precisely right for them.

As she waited for the shuttle to take her to the other side of the massive acreage that comprised North American Aviation, Ronnie wondered why the day seemed better than she had hoped for. Even Mr. Jackson's cheery "good morning, chile," seemed even more friendly than usual, just as Mrs. Dobbs' kind dab at her eyes put the heart back into her body where it belonged.

She shaded her eyes with her hand and squinted east at the row of shiny new B-25s lined up on the runway, ready for their test flights with the Women's Air Force Service Pilots, women at home in the air who chafed for combat, something that would never happen in a million years. But there they were in cockpits, listening to the hum of Pratt and Whitney engines. Ronnie easily imagined the WASPs on the alert for a cough or sputter that didn't belong, determined to deliver the best aircraft to Allies that darkened German skies with bombs, or flew low-altitude raids over oilfields in Romania, happy to deprive the Luftwaffe of aviation fuel.

Now *that* was glamor. Ronnie nodded to Mr. Jackson, who unfailingly delivered her to the right door. He knew where everyone belonged, and he knew his place, too, although he had confided to her once with great pride that his oldest son was a Tuskegee Airman. "Mark my word, chile, that boy is going places."

We all are, she thought, cheered by Postum, Mrs. Dobbs's kindness, her driver's optimism, the sight of all those bombers ready to roll, and, if she wanted to admit it – she didn't of course, because it was foolish – the memory of a capable military policeman, even if he did have his mind on his work and not on her.

Chapter Four

Ronnie steeled herself before she opened the factory door, wondering how anyone on the floor still had any hearing left. She knew most of the workers sported ear plugs, but was that enough?

She stepped into the noisy world of war. Up one open flight of wooden stairs, and then another, she had a moment to look across at the amazing sight of America's secret weapon: raw materials, factories and the will to win. She knew the numbers, but she counted the rows of B-25s in various stages of production anyway, proud at the sight, even though she was the smallest cog in the vast machinery of destruction.

"My goodness, Pops, but I wish you could have seen this," she said out loud, knowing that her words were tossed into the sea of sound. Silently now, she thanked the Lord God Almighty for her part in the struggle to free the world from tyranny. Fifty-eight dollars a month, uniforms and shoes, room and board were nothing to anyone but her. *But I am not selling things no one wants in a five and dime*, she reminded herself. *I am part of this.*

She knew no one was watching, so she gave a small salute, squared her shoulders, did an about face, and opened the door into the office of Lt. Colonel Philip Dignam, her boss and the man who had kept her out of England, a place she mightily wished to see.

She knew he was already at work behind that closed door. He had assured her early in her assignment that he would always be the first person at work, no matter how early she thought to arrive. No morning lark, Ronnie had never been tempted to try him on the matter. Ten-hour days, six days a week were enough to capture her attention.

At least she wasn't afraid of Col. Dignam anymore. On the train from Daytona Beach to Kansas City, she had nursed a grudge until the Tennessee border, before her usual cheery outlook had pointed out that her future, less-then-glamorous employment was due entirely to her own secretarial skills. If she had typed sixty words per minute like the others in her unit, her eighty w.p.m. wouldn't have stuck out like a prairie dog still looking around, when all the others had vanished at the sight of a hawk's shadow overhead.

She learned soon enough that she wasn't the only person dragged into an unwanted wartime billet. When Col. Dignam was hauled out of retirement because of war, he had gulped over his future assignment and called in a chip from a fellow West Point graduate of the same vintage (Spanish American War) who happened to be overseeing the sprawling WAC training facility in Florida.

"I told him I needed the best typist he could send me on short notice," Col. Dignam had informed her on her arrival at the enormous North American Aviation plant. "You're it. I assume you know your ABCs and you can file, too."

She could and did, squirreling away letters, memos, inspection reports, top secret blueprints, for all she knew, of the B-25 Mitchell bomber. It was the medium range workhorse of a bomber that in those earlier, darker days, Colonel James Doolittle and his squadron flew off the deck of the *Hornet* and over a surprised Tokyo. Every piece of paper that the hand of man could devise, relating to North American Aviation, Private Green immortalized into the rank of filing cabinets in her outer office.

That became Ronnie's war, no-frills secretarial labor that would never have induced her grandchildren to beg for more stories of Gran's war (providing she had children, or even a husband). It hadn't helped that as she was leaving Daytona, word came that her fellow WACs had orders to four different army airfields in England, some bound for secretarial work, others to staff control towers (the job she had wanted), or to change oil in motor pools.

The light was already on, so she set down her purse, removed the cover from the typewriter, sighed at the amount of filing that five days away from the office could produce, straightened her uniform jacket, and knocked on Col. Dignam's door.

At his grunt, she stuck her head in the door. "I'm back, sir," she said simply.

"I'm glad to see you, Private Green," he said, looking at her over what she suspected was his second or third cuppa. She knew he was seventy years old because his wife in St. Louis had visited and brought in a cake overburdened with that many candles last spring. His eyes were bright behind their spectacles, and she saw the sympathy, too, not so much as to make her cry, but enough to comfort. "I wish the U.S. Army could have allowed you more time at home. Blame it on Hitler, but by Gadfreys, I'm glad to see you."

He gestured behind her to the mound of paperwork on her desk, then leaned back in his chair as much as an old cavalryman would have leaned, which wasn't much. "Private, 242 of our bombers rolled out of here last month. You'll find a commendation signed by FDR himself in that mound on your desk. See if you can find us a frame somewhere. That's not going in any old file folder, no sirree."

He held out his empty cup. "Get me a refill, Private, before you start."

And so it went, back to work for a retired lieutenant colonel dragged away from his favorite Missouri fishing hole and ordered to Kansas City as the army's liaison with North American Aviation, the man who signed off on every new plane, from rivets and sheet metal to Wright Cyclone engine, the man whose father had fought rebels in the Civil War, and Sioux and Cheyenne warriors at Rosebud Creek. The others may have called Col. Dignam a relic, but Ronnie saw devotion to duty, even duty he didn't precisely savor. She could do no less herself.

She didn't tell the other WACs how she felt about duty. They already thought she was corny and square, an Okie from the sticks who went to church when she could, and blushed when the girls asked her to join them barhopping in Kansas City. They didn't ask her anymore, but that was all right. They had their war; she had hers.

She wanted to tell someone about Master Sergeant Brown, though. To her surprise, it turned out to be Colonel Dignam. She stayed a little later than the usual 5 p.m. closing, because she was only up to the Ts in her filing. She thought the Colonel usually left shortly after she did, but she tapped on his door to let him know she was staying until six to finish up. "I can lock up," she said.

"You could," he agreed, looking up from a stack of his own papers, "but I'll see you out."

She smiled to herself, amused and wondering if he had been as territorial about his regiments of mounted troops as he was about his one clerk-typist. She came to the bottom of the stack before six, but as usual, there were odds and ends to file somewhere. One caught her attention, a letter from a Major Mathers, Military Police, Fort Leavenworth. The envelope was stamped TOP SECRET so she didn't look inside. She went to Colonel Dignam's office and knocked.

When he gave his usual entry grumble, she held out the letter. "How do you want me to file this, Colonel?" she asked. "Under M for Military Police or Mathers, or L for Fort Leavenworth."

"Leavenworth," he said. He hesitated. "You can keep a secret."

"Yes, sir."

"It took a while, but the Krauts finally found our factories." He pointed at the letter in her hand. "Apparently in my copious free time, I am to corner every department head and tell them to be watchful for operatives."

"Goodness." It was her turn to hesitate then, but she wanted to tell someone about Sergeant Brown. "Sir, on my way back from Ponca City, I sat across from an MP who was handcuffed to a German spy."

"Well, that's a fine howdy do," the colonel said, his eyes bright. "Did you learn any secrets?"

She knew when she was being teased. "No, sir! They both spoke German."

Colonel Dignam was on a roll now. "Worse and worse, private. Maybe they were both German spies. You only thought one was a prisoner."

She must have looked surprised at that, because he laughed. "Oh, sir!" she exclaimed, and laughed, too. "Sergeant Brown took charge of the whole bus when we had to get off because a tornado was headed toward us."

"They do that," he said.

"Tornados?"

"MPs," he replied, and they laughed again.

He seemed relaxed. Maybe she could slide in an offhand question. "Would someone like Sergeant Brown be stationed at Fort Leavenworth?" Ronnie asked.

"More than likely. If he speaks German, I'm surprised he's not in Europe now. I hear the troops are taking a lot of Kraut prisoners."

"He was at D-day and was wounded bad enough to end up back here temporarily," she said. Could she slide in another question without being too obvious? "He said he directed traffic off Utah Beach. Uh, is that dangerous?"

He looked her in the eye then, and he almost didn't have to say anything. "I'd shudder to do it, private," he told her quietly. "Try that in rain or snow, with Krauts shooting at you and commanders barking orders, and you, Private Green, have to stand there and take it. I don't think the shelf life of an MP trying to direct troops and tanks off a beach is very long, but by all that's holy, I watched MPs stand and take it at Belleau Wood on the Marne in 1918. There weren't just Marines at Belleau Wood."

Why would that make her tear up? Was it because Pops' death was still so fresh in her mind? That must be it. She turned away. "I…I'd better go file this, Colonel," she said.

"Then call it a day, private," he replied. She went to the door. "And private…"

"Yes, sir?"

"Did Sergeant Brown get your address and a telephone number where you could be reached?"

Was she that obvious? Obviously. Her face felt red hot, but oh well. "N..no, sir."

"I didn't know the army was so backward, kiddo," he said.

He had called her that once before, when the girls brought in a slice of cake for her twenty-second birthday. Ronnie knew he had daughters with husbands in the Pacific and in Italy. She felt a little less sad. Pops was gone, but she could file letters for Colonel Dignam, who called her kiddo when she needed it.

"Oh, well, sir," she said, her mind clear again. Maybe it helped to talk about disappointment now and then. "I expect I'll survive."

"Sergeant Brown, you say?"

"He's a master sergeant, sir. From Rantoul, Illinois. Said he's seen tornados, too, and he knows he's headed back to Europe."

"I don't doubt it. That's a pretty common name. Does he have a first name?" he asked, and his eyes had a distinct twinkle this time.

"Ernie."

Colonel Dignam nodded. He held out his hand. "Let me hang onto that letter, private. I can file it. You go on now. It's late."

Chapter Five

Colonel Dignam didn't resume the conversation the next day. Ronnie would have been startled if he had. She took a moment over oatmeal and toast that morning at the barracks to tell Mrs. Dobbs about Master Sergeant Brown. The cafeteria supervisor listened in that wholehearted way of hers, which was far more satisfying that Millie Sturdivant's "Hmm," and "Oh, my."

Millie was still sulking because the mail had failed to produce a letter from Lieutenant Sturdivant. "It's been two weeks now, Ronnie," she complained. "Sometimes I envy you because you don't have to worry about a husband, or a fiancé." She laughed, but Ronnie heard no humor. "Or even a boyfriend. Count yourself lucky. You don't have to wonder if he's behaving himself in those villages they are liberating."

It had been a relief to leave the miniscule quarters they shared and go to breakfast where she knew Mrs. Dobbs had a more sympathetic heart. Ronnie knew Millie was right, as unfeeling as it might seem. She *was* lucky not to have the burden of a husband in the army, or even a sweetheart. She never had to dread mail call because she never had any mail. The only letters she dealt with were government documents to be filed, nothing that would injure the heart.

Routine settled over Colonel Dignam's office, as Ronnie knew it would. She wrote home to Aunt Vi that second evening back, which pained her. Usually, her letters home were addressed to Bart Green. With Pops gone, there was no one in the world who knew her except Aunt Vi.

It was a daunting thought that made her wonder if she could become more outgoing. Something told her she should; the question was, could she? Newspaper ads went on at length about that Pepsodent Smile, and how halitosis could extend a curse, yea, even unto the third and fourth generation of potential suitors, or so it sounded in overblown ad copy. The next question was, Why bother? She used Pepsodent and Listerine, but neither did anything to produce someone handsome her age, or even just someone her age. Most of the factory workers were older men not eligible for the draft, or young men with flat feet and poor eyesight, or something that kept them out of the crosshairs of a Mauser rifle. She felt a little sorry for those workers, in a time when women tended to ignore men not in uniform. She had always been quiet and shy. Could she change? Might it seem artificial? She had no glib answer.

It didn't help that the one WAC she struck up a friendship with at boot camp was now in England, writing glowing letters about all the servicemen stationed at their various bases, men from all over the United States happy to give them the time of day when a flight was done, or other duty tucked away. In her last letter, heavily censored, her friend had written about a possible change of duty station. Somehow the censor missed "Ooh la la," which suggested France to Ronnie. And why not? Paris was in Allied hands now, and everyone seemed to need file clerks and typists.

She wanted to tell Colonel Dignam more about Sergeant Brown, but realized she didn't know anything beyond that afternoon and evening, when the sergeant had to be far more concerned with duty than the WAC seated across the aisle in the Greyhound. The matter of a capable man who took an interest in Ronnie was obviously over and done.

She was ready to resign herself to a boring war when something changed, something so marvelous and unexpected, something she knew she could thank Colonel Dignam for. Two weeks after her return from Pops' funeral, she found a letter on her desk with a memo from her boss that read, *Private Green, arrange for Master Sergeant Brown's billet in the NCO guesthouse this Friday night. Get meal chits for him at the same location. Mark this letter Sabotage Instruction and file under Leavenworth, Fort.*

She read it again then looked up, surprised to see the colonel's door open, where he watched her with a smile. When he motioned to her, she went into his office, letter in hand. Still grinning, he leaned back his usual minimal amount.

"I've been thinking about what you said, private. The other old geezer retired-guy a step above me in St. Louis approved a visit from someone to give all my department heads the hot poop on spies and saboteurs. I might have mentioned Sergeant Brown's name." His chair came down. "He complimented me on my forward thinking. Private Green, I owe you."

"I owe *you*, sir," she said before she thought. "I…I don't mind seeing him again."

Oh, glory, how unprofessional was that? Ronnie put her hand over her mouth.

He laughed. "That's a relief, seeing as how you're in charge of him pretty soon for two days."

"Me, sir?"

"You, private. Correct me if I'm wrong, but I think he'd rather have you show him the ropes than a bald lieutenant colonel. You do the honors."

Who wouldn't smile at that? "I assume that's an order, sir?" Ronnie asked, not worried for once if she said the right thing, or if it was proper.

He answered her smile with a rare one of his, then gave her the appraising look that had probably frightened a generation or two of young lieutenants, but which had never bothered her. "You're very good at what you do," the colonel told her. "I know you will do exactly what I ask, and in a way to represent the best of the Women's Army Corps."

How kind of him. "Thank you, sir," she said simply. She realized with a start that Colonel Dignam reminded her a little of Pops. How, she wasn't sure. He looked at her as though he wanted to know more. Well, why not? This was now officially a morning of surprises. "I..I get teased sometimes because some of the other WACs think I have patriotic stars in my eyes. I do, though. What we WACs do matters for the war effort." She smiled. "Even typing and filing, I guess."

"I'll let you in on a secret, Private Green," her boss said. "I get corny, too, and it's OK." He stacked some papers that were already stacked and straight. "I want to see Sergeant Brown, too." He smiled down at those papers. "Maybe he'll work up the nerve to get your address this time."

"Sir!" She had to smile because it was funny.

"More smiles, private, more smiles. The war doesn't need to grind us totally into powder."

"No, it doesn't, sir," Ronnie agreed. Should she? Why not? "I do want to see Sergeant Brown again. I…I liked him."

The colonel chuckled. "This visit, however brief, should give you a better notion." He sat up straight again, back in charge, back being a colonel and not someone who just possibly might be an ally. "Truth to tell, we need the sergeant's information, Private Green, and your experience on the Greyhound reminded me of that." He gestured to the humming factory through the wall and down two flights of stairs. "We all know these aircraft factories were planted here because we're remote from either coast. It also stands to reason that we shouldn't let down our guard, eh?"

Perhaps I can let down my guard a bit, Ronnie thought that afternoon when she put the cover on her typewriter. She had never known her grandparents, but Pops and his sister Violet had always stressed circumspection. They must have learned it from their parents, and passed it on to her, whether it was a good idea or not. In the main, it was. From the time she was small, Ronnie knew better than to stray far from them when they were in a town even as small as Ponca City. She had turned down a high school date from the boy on the neighboring farm, because Aunt Vi said she saw him driving his deathtrap of a pickup forty miles an hour, and that was dangerous.

Did I listen too hard to their caution, she asked herself, as she waited for the shuttle. She smiled to think of her one impulsive act, which was stopping to listen to the sergeant who staffed the recruiting office in Ponca City. Even worse, she believed him when he promised a glamorous overseas assignment.

As she rode home, Ronnie realized that her disappointment over not receiving that billet in England had drawn her back to her quiet side again, the side that let caution guide every thought and deed. *People are risking so much, Veronica Green*, she scolded herself. *You can at least be brave enough to smile at Sergeant Brown when he shows up. And didn't the colonel sort of make it an order?*

She did smile. There he was, standing outside her office door three mornings later with a leather carryall instead of a duffel, and no prisoner attached to him anywhere. "Well, Private Green," he said, after they exchanged salutes. "Do I have you to blame for this particular assignment?"

"No sir," she assured him, then knew he was teasing. "Maybe a little. When I got back to work, I told Colonel Dignam about you and Herr...Herr..."

"Herr Schwarz," he reminded her. "Remember? He's black, you're green and I'm brown. I'll have you know that Herr Schwarz now inhabits cell 53, block A15, in Building 2A. He seems content to wait out the remainder of this war in a cell in Leavenworth." He indicated the door. "I was just going to knock."

"No need," she opened the door for him, pleased with his fragrance of Old Spice, uncluttered this time by a humid afternoon and dust from the ditch beside the Greyhound. He was more handsome than she remembered, and this time, his uniform hadn't suffered the indignity of a day too long on a Greyhound. His capable air remained the same, set off by the exact knot of his tie and the crease in his trousers. A professional must have shined those shoes.

She knocked on the colonel's door, ushered Master Sergeant Brown inside and introduced them to each other. Coffee came next, and she returned to her desk to file and try not to eavesdrop. She should have closed the colonel's door.

"Private Green, get this man over to the NCO billet, would you?"

"Yes, sir."

She knew Jeeps. She also knew when someone was admiring her legs without appearing to – just a little side eye and a smile.

"What's that building, private?" he asked, pointing, his face a little flushed. Too much side eye?

"That's the high bay, sir," she said. "It was built for the production of B-29s, but that shifted to a Boeing plant in Washington, and another in Wichita."

"The one where I collared that saboteur," he said, as calmly as another man might talk about expected rainfall. "What's in there now?"

"More B-25s on the grow," she said, doing her own side eye because she liked broad-shouldered men. "It's the wartime workhorse, or so we've been informed."

He nodded. "What're my chances of taking you to lunch in the NCO mess, if there is one?"

She couldn't help her smile. She also decided to take a chance. "I thought you were going to ask me about monthly production, and number of workers on the payroll. I'm ready for those questions, sir."

He chuckled. "I studied this place before I left Leavenworth. I know those answers. I'm assuming you like to eat."

"I do, but there isn't an NCO mess." She pulled into a parking place in front of a two-story building that looked as ordinary and temporary as everything else at North American Aviation. "We're not an army base. Just a B-25 incubator." She pointed over her shoulder. "The employee cafeteria is big and noisy, but that's it."

"Fair enough. Are you game, after this morning's workshop?"

Was she? Oh absolutely. "I am," she replied and took another step forward in her quest to know this man better before he disappeared again. "I can probably even find a quieter place to eat such a lunch."

"You're on then," he said. "Along with lunch, I expect an honest critique of my morning's work." He looked at her directly, no side eye. "I'm good at apprehending and cuffing, but not so much at talking about it. I doubt you could say anything but the truth, even if it hurts."

You don't even know me, Ronnie thought, flattered. She handed him the papers for his billet and meal chits. "This'll get you settled, sir. I'll wait and drive you to the classroom where you're speaking."

He took them. "Would you have lunch with me in a big noisy place then?"

"I would, sir."

She turned off the motor and watched him walk into the guest house. She admired the swing in his walk. Funny how a day that started out on the cool side could warm up so quickly. She smiled to herself. She couldn't ogle *his* legs, but she bet they were symmetrical, at the least.

Ronnie leaned back in the seat. "I'll file that under *what a pity I can't see them*," she said softly.

Chapter Six

The sergeant came out a few minutes later, minus his baggage but carrying several file folders. He turned back for a good look at the guest house. "Be it ever so humble," he murmured as he climbed aboard.

"The place I'm taking you now is a cut above, sir," she said as she started the engine and backed out. "The hoity toity – the brass – stay there, and there is a large conference room. I'll drop you off and go get my colonel."

"Stay with me long enough to make sure I have a blackboard and chalk." He cleared his throat. "Stow the *sir* and call me Ernie, when no one else is around."

With pleasure, she thought, remembering that bus ride with the handcuffed prisoner sleeping, as they rode toward Kansas City and her boring job. "I'm still Ronnie."

"I was hoping you were," he said, then his words came out in a rush. "Look, I was a stupid chump on the bus. I wanted to get your address and maybe a phone number. When my captain got the letter from your colonel and assigned me, well…."

He seemed to run out of words then, which made Ronnie think that maybe, just maybe, he wasn't any better at this socializing business than she was. It gave her heart a boost. "I told my colonel about you," she said, and resisted the impulse to let her words pour out, too. And there was that darned building already. Why hadn't North American Aviation built it farther away? "Ernie," she added, which made him laugh.

She went into the officers' billet with him, pleased to note that he matched her shorter stride. There had been a fellow senior in high school, now serving in the Central Pacific, who had asked her out a few times. He never thought to walk with her, but always strode ahead. Their last date had been a double date with taller friends to "The Devil and Miss Jones," starring Jean Arthur, her favorite actress. Everyone walked ahead, talking. She hurried along as far as the bus stop before the theatre, climbed on the bus and left. She couldn't help laughing out the window as the bus pulled away and her date and his friends looked around, wondering where she was. Aunt Vi hadn't thought it funny at all, but Pops laughed.

She went to the receptionist's desk, explained the situation, and left the sergeant to her tender care. Hmm. The receptionist seemed to be eyeing Sergeant Brown, too. And why not? He was handsome enough for general purposes, young, not disabled or old. By 1944, outside of a naval base or an army garrison, that was an oddity on any street in America.

And here I leave again, she thought, as she said goodbye and turned to go, her part in this day's work done.

Or not. "Private Green?"

She stopped, quietly pleased, hopeful. "Yes, sir?"

"Would you ask Colonel Dignam for me if you can attend the workshop and take notes? I've done this a few times, but I'd appreciate your feedback." Sergeant Brown leaned closer, him and his Old Spice. "That is, unless you'd rather stay in your office and file stuff."

"I will certainly ask him," she said promptly, then took another, longer look at the MP. "Besides, you've promised me lunch, haven't you?" That was bold, but she didn't want him to forget.

"Yes, ma'am," he said promptly. "See you soon. I have confidence in the ingenuity of the Women's Army Corps."

Back in her office, Ronnie hesitated not a moment in addressing the matter. "He...he wants my notes to make sure he's covering the subject," she said. "That is, if..."

"I wouldn't have it any other way," Colonel Dignam said. "Your notes will also prove useful here, if NAA's division heads want to share them around – discreetly, of course. We wouldn't want any Nazi operatives or cleaning ladies to get a look, now, would we?"

"Oh, sir," she said and laughed. "Thank you."

"It's all for the good of the war effort, Private Green," he replied. "I mean, that's why we're doing this, isn't it?"

"Certainly."

Ronnie was used to being the only woman in the room, so the presence at the workshop of the women who ran the lunchrooms did surprise her. She patted the empty seat beside her for Mrs. Dobbs to join her.

"Is this the MP you told me about?" Mrs. Dobbs whispered when they sat down after the Pledge of Allegiance.

"Yes," she whispered back, all business with a steno tablet on her lap. When she crossed her legs, Sergeant Brown looked her way and – my goodness – he winked. Just a small wink, but she knew a wink.

"Bring him around for breakfast tomorrow morning," Mrs. Dobbs said, then took out her own notepad.

Ronnie had been prepared for the usual dry meeting – this wasn't her first time taking notes – but Sergeant Brown had an undeniable gift for educating his audience about espionage. In a quick stroke he took them through a catalog of spies on American soil from the American Revolution to the present, holding his audience where he wanted them, pausing only for a sip of water, and the occasional question. She knew these division heads because she had done this sort of thing before. She knew who would start to wiggle and shift around first, or mutter to his seatmate. These were active men not used to conference tables.

Not this time. Sergeant Brown had them where he wanted them, and he wanted them to feel the nation's concern for safeguarding the bombers they built. "That's the task, gentlemen," he concluded right before noon. "We need every one of you to be alert for anything out of the ordinary. Nothing is too small to question, not when the lives of your workers and the men in the air are on the line. Thank you."

No one ever applauded at these meetings, but this was the exception. Then came questions, and comments, no one in a hurry to leave. Ronnie stared down at her barely legible squiggles, wishing for a stenographer's course, proud of this man she barely knew, wondering why *he* wasn't on a recruiting poster. By the time the division heads left the room, she was exhausted from notetaking, but beaming inside, happy for the first time since Aunt Vi's telegram that she should prepare herself for the worst because Pops was sinking.

She sat back, struck by the idea that she had spent most of her life preparing for the worst – Mama's death, Pops' disability, his death only weeks ago, a childhood in the Great Depression, her disappointment at her unglamorous part in the war. Maybe it was time to prepare herself for the best.

It was a beguiling thought that she would ordinarily have poo-pooed away. But not now, not with Sergeant Ernie Green standing there so casually now, not stiff as during the first few minutes, but relaxed because he knew his subject and he understood the matter. *You're a natural-born teacher*, she thought, and added that to her notes. If she felt bold enough, she could really add that to his notes, and he could laugh about it later, when he was back at Fort Leavenworth. She could do that.

After the final question and the last lingering comment, the sergeant erased the blackboard while she waited, uncertain. Doubts returned; maybe he really hadn't planned to have lunch with her. *No, he did*, she thought. But there was her colonel, coming toward her now, probably ready for a ride back to his building. She reached in her purse for the keys to the Jeep.

He waved away her gesture. "I can get a ride with Manwaring, Jones and Archibald," he said, then chuckled. "That sounds like a law firm, doesn't it?" He glanced at the sergeant, who had set down the eraser. "Take him out to lunch at our fair cafeteria," he told her.

"He did invite me, sir."

"Well, then, private. Drop him back here for the afternoon session, and you go back to the office. Answer my phone, take messages, and write up your notes." With a smile, he left her there.

It was too much to hope she could spend a whole day listening to Sergeant Brown, or even just watching him. He had an animated expression when he lectured, leaning forward as if to turn his audience into co-conspirators. *I had a half day*, she thought, determined not to feel disappointed, because she wanted more time to chat, to listen, to observe, to be in the orbit of someone who interested her.

There he was, alone finally. She took a deep breath. "Sergeant, are you hungry?"

"I'll say. My bowl of oatmeal and black coffee eaten in a prison gave out hours ago." He dusted off his hands. "May I meet you outside?"

She nodded, crossing the lobby, happy her visit with Sergeant Green wasn't over yet, glad the sun was shining, pleased with her reflection in the glass door, certain there was no finer-looking WAC in the vicinity – well, there weren't any WACs in the vicinity – and wishing the employee cafeteria she knew so well could turn into a temple of fine dining. *Probably better than a federal prison*, she thought.

Mrs. Dobbs stood outside with her counterpart from that fine-dining establishment, waiting for the shuttle that would return them to duty. Ronnie took another deep breath. It wouldn't hurt to ask.

"My dear, that's your sergeant?" Mrs. Dobbs asked.

"Not *my* sergeant," Ronnie said, "but yes, he's the one handcuffed to the prisoner that I was telling you about." She hesitated only a moment. "Mrs. … Mrs. Creighton, is it?"

"Yes, dearie?"

"He's escorting me to lunch in *your* building. Is there a quiet place where we could talk?"

The two lunchroom managers looked at each other. "There really isn't anything going on," Ronnie insisted, feeling her cheeks grow hot. "I hardly know him. But it sure would be dandy to chat without all the racket."

Mrs. Creighton nodded. She waved goodbye to Mrs. Dobbs as the shuttle pulled up, and took Ronnie's arm. "You know that side door by the cashier?"

Ronnie nodded. "That leads onto the assembly floor, doesn't it?"

"Sure does." She patted Ronnie's arm and let go. "Find yourself a nice quiet B-25 fuselage, dearie." Mrs. Creighton looked up. "There's my shuttle. Go to the closest cashier to that door. I made some pie just for the staff today. There'll be some for you, too. Tell her I sent you."

"Thanks, Mrs. Creighton." She should explain herself. "I really don't know him well at all, but…"

The lunchroom lady shrugged. "It's war, dearie. Take what you can get."

Chapter Seven

Wh at she got was a tray of tomato soup, a sandwich with meat of unknown origin, and apple pie, which made Sergeant Brown's eyes light up.

"It's been a while," he said, raising his voice to speak over the lunchroom chatter. He nodded his thanks when the cashier slid a piece of pie on his tray, too. "Now if only we could find a quiet spot to talk."

I will owe Mrs. Creighton until I die, Ronnie thought. She gestured with her head toward the door. Ernie juggled his tray and opened the door for her. He looked around and smiled.

"The heart of operations," he said. "It's so quiet I can hear a rivet drop."

She laughed. "Pick your poison, Ernie."

He looked around at the giant assembly room, which was far from silent, since the workers ate in shifts, but quieter than a noisy lunchroom. "Over there," he said, leading her to a row of half-built B-25s where nobody was hammering, or riveting or polishing. "I guess they're at lunch."

Perfect. She followed the MP to a row of flight chairs, waiting to take their turn inside the warplanes, waiting to hold pilots crossing the English Channel, or maybe flying from Benghazi to low-bomb the oil fields at Ploesti in Romania. But no, the war had moved on. Maybe the crew in this B-25 would bomb Berlin itself.

"Wooden," Ernie said, as he set down his tray on an upturned keg of bolts and pulled another one around for her.

"Metal is too heavy," Ronnie said, thinking of letters she had filed. "The lighter the load up front, the more the payload in the back."

He sat down in one of the chairs, a contemplative expression on his face as he looked around. "We GIs getting shot at on the ground wonder what it's like in the air." He shook his head. "I'll stay on the ground."

"I would, too," Ronnie said. She picked up her mug of tomato soup, wishing it would turn into something really good. She took a sip and made a face. "My Aunt Vi would never serve you something like this. Too watery."

He smiled, and took a sip himself, then shrugged. "I've had worse. What would you serve me if I came for Sunday dinner in Ponca City?"

"Fried chicken and green beans," she said promptly, touched somehow in that deep place where she barely dreamed. "We have chickens, so the survivors of the Saturday night massacre would furnish eggs for deviled eggs. There would be hot biscuits, too, and honey, because Pops has hives." She frowned, wishing she hadn't mentioned Pops. "He did. I think Aunt Vi will give them away now."

Oh, gracious, this was no time for tears to well up and spill out. She dabbed at her face with a paper napkin, appalled at herself. "I'm sorry. I miss him," she said simply.

"That's no crime," he said. "It hasn't been that long, although I can tell you time is not always the ally." He seemed to give himself a little mental shake. "It's awfully easy to forget that anyone besides soldiers, airmen and sailors die. I'm sorry for your loss." He leaned back in the pilot's seat. "It's just you and Aunt Vi now?"

She nodded. "So far." She managed a smile. "My aunt has a boyfriend who has come to Sunday dinner for as long as I can remember. Maybe he'll work up his nerve one of these years."

He laughed at that, but it wasn't really a laugh, to Ronnie's ears. "Time is a luxury few can afford. If I've learned anything since Pearl Harbor, it's that time runs out." He took a bite of the sandwich and made a face. "I'd like a fried chicken dinner."

"Wouldn't we all?" she said, on more sure ground now. She knew fried chicken. "I'd coat it in buttermilk, dredge it in flour, and fry it to the perfect golden color."

"Oh, stop!" he exclaimed. "You know, this war can't wind down fast enough. Call me shallow if you want, but I'd like a really great chicken dinner, and gobs of butter on those hot biscuits you're tempting me with. Then maybe an afternoon in a porch swing, with no particular place to be immediately."

"Play your cards right and if it's August, there'll be corn on the cob, too, for dinner. My, don't I sound shallow."

It was so lighthearted and so silly, but there they sat, nearly knee to knee. She knew then that their conversation was far from shallow. It was getting-to-know-you conversation in a strange setting with the future too cloudy to contemplate. It warmed her heart.

"It's not shallow, it's fun," he contradicted. "You're reminding me of some Sunday dinners in Rantoul."

"I think if we couldn't remember how things used to be, we'd be so unhappy."

"I believe you're right." He took another bite. "Tell me something: I've been thinking about that Serviceman's Readjustment Act – you know, the one everyone is calling the GI Bill – and wondering if I could be a teacher." He looked down at his soup. "Did I make any sense at all this morning? Mind you, I'm not fishing for compliments. I want to know."

"Oh, you were organized and made plenty of sense," she said. "I can see you being a teacher. What would you teach?"

She could tell this was something he had been thinking about. "I like history." He seemed to read her mind then. He touched the black MP band on his sleeve. "'You're a healthy-looking farm boy,' the recruiter told me when I signed up in 1938. 'Can you fight?' he asked me, 'knock heads together?' I told him I could, but I like history. I didn't tell *him* that because all he could see was height and muscle. I'm more than that, Ronnie."

He gave her a long look, one that might have worried her on the Greyhound, before she knew his name even. She knew Aunt Vi would consider him a stranger – how many times had they even seen each other? This was only the second time, snatched between duty. She looked back and liked what she saw. "I know you are," was all she said.

He smiled at that and finished his sandwich. "I'll appreciate your notes, when you transcribe them," he told her. He eyed the tomato soup and shook his head. "I think the wiser choice now is that apple pie." He took a bite and nodded. "Should've started with this."

Ronnie took two bites of hers and handed it to him over the small space separating their pilots' chairs. He gave her a questioning glance, then ate it, too. "Better," he said when he finished.

The silence between them was brief but not uncomfortable. "What about you and the GI Bill, Ronnie?" he asked. "I know it's for women, too."

She nodded. "I've been thinking about it. Does anyone in your family have a college degree?"

"I was the first to finish high school," he replied. "College is for rich kids, or so I thought."

"Same here. Tuition, books and a stipend, though. I could go to college."

"And study what?"

"Maybe nursing." Should she say any more? Workers were starting to filter back onto the assembly floor as the riveters in the far corner stopped their work and walked into the cafeteria.

Soon enough, someone would want their spot. She knew the sergeant had to return to the conference room. He would be gone tomorrow, and suddenly it mattered to her that he know her better. One breath, two breaths. "I wish I could have been helpful to Pops during his illness," she said, those words coming out in a rush, as his had earlier. "Oh, I know I'm in the army and I couldn't have gotten leave for anything like that, so it's mere wishful thinking. Maybe I want to help others."

"Nursing school for you, then," he said. He looked away. "You have an aunt. I'm alone. My father died when I was in second grade and Mom last year. There's nothing holding me to Rantoul, but it's next door to the University of Illinois in Urbana. Anything holding you to Ponca City? What'll you do when your aunt's beau finally works up his nerve and pops the question?"

He said it with a smile, but it didn't feel like casual conversation. She glanced at the big clock. Time was everyone's enemy now. Build those planes, fill them with bombs, move troops here and there, file faster, type with greater speed and accuracy. Get to know someone worth knowing in jig time. Could it be done? She could try. "I expect I'll be alone, too," Ronnie said quietly. "I'm not so certain Ponca City is where I want to live anymore." Another breath. "Sergeant Brown, I believe you just made me decide on college. I owe you."

"I told you it's Ernie," he said, his expression so serious now. His eyes went to the clock. "Let me take your tray. Time's up."

She felt shy walking back into the cafeteria past the cashier, who gave an inquiring tip of her head in Ernie's direction. And there was Mrs. Creighton to thank for a moment's peace in a time of war. That was easily done with a nod.

The cafeteria was crowded and noisy and the exit a long way off. Ronnie noted with some gratification that everyone gave a wide berth to an NCO sporting a Military Police armband. His hand went automatically to her waist to steer her closer when four welders blundered by. "Sorry, sergeant," one of them muttered.

I'm not alone now, she thought, as a feeling of relief calmed her. She had barely passed the army's five feet requirement for hopeful WACs. How nice to know that a nice man would steer a path for a shorty. She glanced at him, thinking how handy he could be in a kitchen with tall cupboards, or even walking along an aisle in a market where something she wanted always seemed to reside on a top shelf. She liked Old Spice, too.

But there was the Jeep and Ernie looked at his watch again. "Duty calls," he said, in joking tone of voice, but he frowned as he spoke.

She drove him back to the officers' guest billet and the conference room where division heads milled outside the closed door. Two of them headed in their direction, men wanting answers to their own particular questions.

Ernie stopped. "May I meet you for dinner?" he asked, one eye on the approaching men.

"Oh, yes. I suppose it's the cafeteria again," Ronnie said. "I'll have my notes typed up by then. When should I come by for you?"

"Six?"

"Six, it is."

One of the department heads standing nearby cleared his throat. "Excuse me, Sergeant, for interrupting you. One quick question before we reconvene."

"Six tonight," Ernie said, and turned away to speak to his questioner. "Yes, sir?"

She watched him for longer than she needed to, a tall man of commanding bulk. She didn't even know his age, his favorite food, or if he preferred the St. Louis Cardinals to the Cincinnati Red Legs, or even his religion.

She knew enough.

Chapter Eight

Ronnie had the office to herself all afternoon, while Colonel Dignam attended the second session. Her boss said he wanted two copies of Ernie's morning talk – one for Ernie, and one for the ubiquitous files – but she put in another piece of carbon paper for her own copy.

If only there were someplace better for dinner than a cafeteria that never closed and overflowed with too many diners. She didn't know Kansas City well, and was pretty sure she had no authorization to take the Jeep off North American Aviation's grounds, anyway, even if she did know one of those one of those hole-in-the-wall places for Kansas City barbeque.

Millie Sturdivant had told her about one joint called the Watering Hole, where black men, probably turned shades darker by all that hickory smoke, presided over an open pit, located somewhere between bliss and paradise. She and her husband Bob had spent a messy, finger-licking evening there. But, as Millie liked to remind everyone, Bob was a lieutenant and could go anywhere.

As she typed, Ronnie decided a quiet walk would be better, and more easily found, even here at North American Aviation, where 23,000 people worked in shifts to build B-25s. The place was never still, but a runway was a good place to walk. It wasn't too much to ask.

It was four o'clock when she finished her notes. She stashed her copy in a bottom drawer and looked at the original with a critical eye. Too bad mere words couldn't convey the intensity of what Ernie told the department heads about keeping the plant safe from sabotage, the way he leaned forward to caution them, and the emphasis of his held-out hands urging them to never overlook the smallest things.

"You are a teacher," she said, "and there is a GI Bill. I'm glad for you."

Four o'clock turned into five. She cleared off her desk of more filing, stopping a few times to wonder if, when the war ended, all of her hard work would be trundled to a dump. Who could possibly care about how many pounds of rivets passed through NAA, or employee disagreements? Everyone would be intent upon getting their lives back to normal. Mrs. Dobbs would welcome her sons home from battle, and Millie and Bob Sturdivant would return to Cleveland and save up for a house.

What will I do? She asked herself. *I owe nothing to anyone, and my future is my own.* She looked at Ernie's words, too shy to even ask herself what it would be like to hear someone, maybe Ernie, come home every night with a kiss and a honey, what's for dinner? She did know fried chicken and cream gravy. She didn't care for ironing, but she would make an exception for Ernie. *Or someone like him*, she hastily amended in her thoughts. She barely knew him.

This wasn't getting the filing done. Five thirty, and then the phone rang. "Colonel Dignam's office, Private Green speaking," she said.

Ernie sounded different on the telephone, but it was his hesitancy and urgency that made her frown. "Ronnie, I can't take you to a delicious dinner in the cafeteria, or even stay the night here."

"That's all right. I know you're busy," she said, trying to sound professional. Wow, it hurt, though. "Thanks for letting m..."

"No. No. It's nothing like that. No, Ronnie," he said. "I got a telegram from Leavenworth. I have orders to France."

That's not fair, she thought. Tears started in her eyes, even as she wished them away, reminding herself that she didn't even know this man, and it was too soon to cry over him. "My goodness," was all she could think to say.

"I got a ride over to the NCO billet, and luckily I hadn't unpacked. Colonel Dignam said you have his permission to drive me to the railroad depot. If we hurry, I can make the 6:15 to Leavenworth."

"I'll be right there, Ernie," she said and hung up. She was halfway down the hall when she remembered her uniform jacket and the notes. She ran back for them both, trying not to cry, hoping for calm collectedness.

"It's Master Sergeant Ernest Brown," she said out loud as she goosed the Jeep up to twenty-two miles per hour, which wouldn't attract the attention of NAA's military police. "He's from Rantoul, Illinois, he's an orphan like you, and he's going to teach history someday. That's all you know, Private Green. Don't be a chump."

He was waiting for her in front of the billet. He stowed his duffel in the back and climbed in. She nodded to him, calm now. She took her foot off the gas when he held out the telegram. She glanced at it: *Embarking 0600 hours, transport train, destination New York City.*

"Well, let's hope you don't have any library books overdue at 0900 hours tomorrow morning," she joked, which made Ernie chuckle.

She knew how to get to the Atchison-Topeka-Santa Fe Depot. "Maybe if I get you there fast enough, you'll have time for some French toast in the dining room. It's awfully good, and they serve it anytime of day," she said as she drove as fast as she dared, her eyes on the road because she didn't want to look at Sergeant Brown. There he was, though, in the edge of her vision, a tall, capable man she would like to have known better.

"All I know is that I'm going to France," he said. "My lieutenant thinks I'm heading to Belgium, because that's where the trouble is right now. Don't repeat this, but rumor has it that a lot of Krauts are surrendering and the army needs interpreters more than ever." He smiled. "And also tough guys like me."

She found that encouraging. "Sounds like good trouble, when people surrender."

"I agree." At a stoplight, he turned toward her. "The war is winding down, Ronnie. I won't be there long."

She looked at him then, and saw enough concern in his eyes to make her breathe faster. *You don't want to miss the train*, she thought. That's all it was, even though she knew it was more. How she knew she couldn't have said, but she knew. This was nothing she learned from Aunt Vi. Pops would have been too shy to speak of it. Her mother might have talked to her, but her mother was long dead. She felt something inside her change and strengthen. Who could she talk to?

The light changed, the car behind honked way too fast, and she turned her attention to the road. Out of the corner of her eye she saw Ernie pulling out a notepad – maybe it was a citation book – and a pencil.

"Tell me your address," he said. "Better give me the office telephone number again, too."

She smiled inside and gave her address to him, plus the office number. "I always answer the telephone, Ernie," she said. She laughed. "And if that is your citation book, for heaven's sake don't get me in trouble!"

"Wouldn't dream of it," he said. "Get in that lane and pull off."

Puzzled, she did as he said, raising her arm to signal then edging the Jeep onto a quiet side street.

"Turn off the motor."

Her heart pounding, Ronnie obeyed. When the engine was silent except for the usual tick tick, she turned to him as he moved toward her with no hesitation. He took her in his arms, pulled her close and kissed her. There was nothing forward or presumptuous about his kiss, because it felt like the most natural consequence of what had begun so oddly only weeks before on a Greyhound bus. She had never dated Sergeant Brown. Their only connection had been the bus and today's conference. She knew she didn't play a fast and loose game, and suspected he didn't, either. Whether he ever kissed her again, she knew this was a kiss for the ages.

Who teaches anyone how to kiss? Ronnie knew she had no guidance, beyond the fact that this good man was leaving her orbit and she wanted to let him know that she would miss him. She wouldn't do anything else that might betray her modesty or manners, but as they kissed, she wanted to. Thank goodness for railroad timetables and the timetable of war.

When their lips parted, he didn't say anything. The sky had darkened even more, but not so much that she couldn't see the way his shoulders relaxed. He tipped his head back against the seat and finally spoke. "I have wanted to kiss you since Herr Schwarz and I slid into that ditch beside the bus," he said. "Now I'm leaving, and I didn't want to waste another minute."

She laughed softly at that. not wanting to disturb the mood she could only describe as peaceful. He took her hand, held it, kissed it, then set it back on the gear shift. She started the Jeep and they drove in silence to the nearby depot.

He checked his watch. "No time for French toast in the depot, but I'll make the train," he said. He sighed. "Mrs. Creighton left me a note at my billet, telling me that there was a peach pie for us tonight. Would you apologize to her for me?"

"I will, Ernie," Ronnie said, not trusting herself to say more, not when tears threatened, but knowing better than to waste the seconds left to them. "Mrs. Dobbs already made me promise to bring you by her dining room at my dormitory for breakfast tomorrow morning. They're looking out for me."

"Then I won't worry about you, Veronica Green, not with those two busybodies so skilled in management," he said. He handed her a scrap torn from his citation book. "Here's my APO address. V Mail is the best idea. Please write to me. I won't be able to say much in reply, because of censorship."

"I know," she said. She leaned over and kissed him, just a peck on the cheek this time, because everybody in Kansas City seemed to be headed through the glass doors toward the tracks. She saw couples embracing, and felt monumentally cheated, she who answered her country's call to serve and ended up in Kansas. Kansas! Since the U.S. government owed her more than that, she turned off the engine and got out when he did.

He stopped her, a hand on her arm. "I mean it about mail. My parents are both gone, same as you. I sure would like to get a letter or two at every mail call." He looked away. "Usually there isn't anything for me."

"I can do that," she told him, touched to her heart's core, because she knew what it was to want mail and not get any.

"I suppose I'm being silly," he said, but she heard all the longing, mainly because she recognized it in herself.

"No, you're not. It's nice to know someone is aware that you're on the planet," she assured him. *I am*, she thought. *Maybe more than you know.*

She walked with him to the ticket office, standing to the side while he showed what looked like a pass, and earned a stamp and a nod in return. She heard "Platform Three," and walked beside him in silence. He shifted his duffle to the other shoulder and took her hand.

"Do you know anything about your assignment?" she asked, almost not wanting to know. She smiled at her presumption then took a step closer to commitment. "I mean, I intend to worry. Perhaps you should tell me how much."

"I'll be directing traffic."

"I'm sure there's more to it than that."

"A little."

Obviously that was all she was going to get out of him. And now the conductor was calling, "Aboard! All aboard!"

Ernie took her in his arms and gave her ample reason to know that their first kiss in the Jeep wasn't a fluke. The kiss was shorter because the conductor was practically shouting in her ear. To her embarrassment, the man with the lantern leaned closer. "Sergeant, get on the train and win the war. Then you can take all the time you want."

The conductor walked on, delivering a similar message to another couple and then another. Ernie watched him go. "Killjoy," he muttered, then he laughed. "He's right. Up I get."

A corporal stood in the doorway to the rail car, distress written all over his face, eyes searching the crowd. "Catch this, corporal," Ernie said, and tossed up his duffel. After he hugged her, Ernie followed his bag. He gave Ronnie a small salute and started down the aisle. She watched him until he sat down, the aisle full of soldiers and sailors.

The corporal stayed where he was until the conductor climbed aboard and gave him the stink eye. After one more futile glance about, the corporal slunk off to find his own place on a railcar already at standing room only. Ronnie watched until the locomotive, wreathed with steam, started to move.

"No! Wait!"

Ronnie turned around to see a girl probably not out of her teen years work her way through the lingerers on the platform, those people like Ronnie hopeful of one more glimpse. *You just missed him*, she thought. *He waited as long as he could*. The girl began to sob. "My watch stopped," she wailed to no one in particular.

The hours was late. Soon it was just the two of them on the platform. As she watched, the train started forward with creaks and groans because time waits for no one, especially a stopped watch. The sobbing girl left. Ronnie walked back to her Jeep. She sat in it until her mind cleared, reminding herself that she had never even gone on a date with Sergeant Brown, and it would never do to make a great symphony out of a tune barely whistled.

That's what she told herself. She didn't have to believe it.

Chapter Nine

Ronnie returned the Jeep to the motor pool and hiked to the cafeteria because she needed a long walk. It must not have been long enough. After she delivered Sergeant Brown's apology to Mrs. Creighton, the supervisor handed her a Kleenex, a slice of the peach pie and a bigger piece of advice. "Never mind, dearie," she said. "You'll meet some other nice man." Mrs. Creighton raised her voice to be heard over the dining room chatter. "It may not seem like it now, but they come and go."

Ronnie blew her nose and nodded. Mrs. Creighton was probably right. She knew she would certainly write to Sergeant Brown, even though she knew so little about him. If he saved her letters, years from now he could show them to his grandchildren and tell them about the clerk/typist he met on a Greyhound bus who saw him off to war. When they asked what had happened to her, he could shrug and shake his head. He might say, "I sometimes wonder what happened to that little lady, but then I met your grandma."

In the morning, after a sleepless night of wanting more than two kisses and with no guarantee of anything, Ronnie took her troubles to Millie Sturdivant as they walked down the hall to the shower. "He didn't even get to take me to dinner at the dreaded employee lunchroom," she said, trying to make light of it.

"Count your blessings, honey," Millie said. "If I'd known Bob was going to turn into such a poor correspondent, I probably wouldn't have said I do."

Millie, you're a ninny, Ronnie thought. *He might be busy.* "He's probably quite occupied. Didn't you say he commanded a tank company?"

"Yeah, they lumber around inside a metal box," Millie said. "He's not a glamorous flyboy." She turned on the shower and stuck her hand in

51

until the water warmed. Ronnie had to give Millie credit. She tried to be interested. "What does what's-his-name do?"

"Master Sergeant Brown," Ronnie said, wishing she hadn't bothered Millie with anything resembling a detail. "He's an MP. He said he mostly directs traffic and rounds up prisoners."

Millie rolled her eyes. "Now *that's* an exciting war." She sighed and shook her fist at the showerhead. "Lukewarm is the order of the day, I guess. At least you don't need to worry about Sergeant Brown complicating your life. You only saw him once or twice."

Well, yes, but…she wanted to argue, but for what purpose? No one could accuse Millie Sturdivant of empathy. Maybe Ronnie Green needed her bracing comments, the kind that took a person right back down to earth.

Mrs. Dobbs lifted her spirits, Mrs. Dobbs who probably served as a sounding board to many a woman in the barracks. Ronnie had never needed her special brand of cheer before, but she did now.

She tried for a casual tone. "Mrs. Dobbs, Sergeant Brown wanted me to tell you he was sorry to miss breakfast here this morning, but he was called back to Fort Leavenworth. He's…he's shipping out to Europe."

"You didn't want him to leave so soon, did you?"

All Ronnie wanted was sympathy, and there it was, accompanied by a cinnamon roll as big as the plate. "For *me*?"

"You were supposed to split it with your sergeant," Mrs. Dobbs said. "Since he's not here, you'd better eat it all." She spoke to her second in command, then ushered Ronnie into her office with the cinnamon roll. She closed the door and Ronnie burst into tears. "Oh, honey, he'll be back," the cafeteria's Iron Lady manager said. "What happened?"

Through her tears, and between bites of a heavenly cinnamon roll, all yeasty and well-iced, Ronnie said that he was called back to Fort Leavenworth immediately. "And…and he's on his way to New York and then Europe."

It was hard to eat and cry at the same time, and Ronnie was hungry. The roll went down so well, accompanied by orange juice that was probably well-watered, but so what? Oranges seemed to have gone to the same place as bananas. "He told me to write to him as often as I could."

"Better get yourself a packet of those Vmail letters," Mrs. Dobbs said. "I write my boys every day, never fail."

Ronnie heard the longing. "Let's see, one is in the Pacific and the other in England?"

She also heard the pride. "Tom is a mechanic on the *St. Lô* – it's an aircraft carrier – and Chaz is a radioman on a plane based in England somewhere. They both joined up the second they could."

Ronnie observed the cafeteria manager, this time seeing more than the no-nonsense lady with fierce eyes who struck fear into her staff. She wondered how many of the other older woman had sons in the service. "Does everyone have someone they worry about?" she asked.

"All my staff does," Mrs. Dobbs said. "I doubt many of you young girls are aware of that."

"I am now."

"Then you're the exception!" Mrs. Dobb said, her eyes kind. "You can talk to me about your MP anytime you want."

"He isn't my MP," Ronnie argued, even though she had spent half the night reliving his two wonderful kisses.

"I believe he is," Mrs. Dobbs replied. She looked twenty years younger when she smiled. "Too quick, you say? He never got to sit in your parlor in Oklahoma and meet the folks?" She shrugged. "If you know, you know."

I wonder, Millie thought, *I wonder*.

She had equally good luck with Col. Dignam, who greeted her with a shake of his head, and the comment, "I was hoping he'd be able to stay longer, Private Green." He gave her a wink. "Hopefully, you took the long way to the depot."

"Not for a 6:15 train," she said. Her boss didn't need to know about that brief and memorable stop. "I just...I just hope he'll be safe."

She wanted a smiling confirmation, a he'll-be-fine-don't-you-worry, but she knew Colonel Dignam wasn't someone to gild a lily. "Nobody's safe in war," he said, "except maybe us." He chuckled. "And you be careful crossing the construction floor!"

"Oh, colonel..."

He tapped her report on his desk. "He did a fine job. I could have said the very same thing to the staff here, but maybe it takes a capable-looking man with an MP armband to help it sink in. He educated us all."

The colonel didn't seem too busy. Maybe this was the time. "He told me he wants to teach history when the war is over. He plans to use that GI Bill of Rights."

"You should, too."

"He said the same thing," she replied. She went into the outside office, her office, but left the door open.

"Why not?" Colonel Dignam asked, before he turned his attention to a stack of correspondence that she knew would end up on her desk by the end of the day to be filed.

"Colonel, I'm the first person in my family to graduate from high school."

"All the more reason."

After Ronnie put that cover back on her typewriter at the end of the day, she took a thoughtful walk to Building C, a.k.a. US Post Office, and spent fifty cents on a packet of Vmail letters. There wasn't anyone waiting in line behind her. "How does it work?" she asked. "I've never written to anyone overseas."

The postmistress leaned across the counter. "Write your letters in pretty heavy ink and mail them. A censor will black out anything inappropriate."

"Inappropriate?" Ronnie asked, hoping she could write "Love, Ronnie," if she got up the nerve.

"You know. Don't say anything about the plant here, or the B-25s."

"Oh. That's it?"

The woman was patient. Maybe she saw something in Ronnie that needed to know just how a letter written in Kansas to a soldier going overseas was going to get there.

"Honey, then your letter is photographed and put onto something called microfilm – I know, I know, whatever that is. A whole roll of letters goes to the boys overseas that way. Someone on the other end develops the film, but not as large was the one you write, and prints them on paper again. It goes into an envelope and eventually ends up in your sweetie's hands."

"That's amazing."

"Isn't it?" The postmistress gave her a stern look. "No kissing the original Vmail. Lipstick just gums up the works."

"I wouldn't do that," Ronnie assured her. *I would kiss him again in a minute,* she thought, *but that's my business.*

"And no perfume on the page. The microfilm doesn't carry any scent." She straightened up and looked at the clock. "You'd be amazed what some women do. Honey, it's time to go home."

Ronnie walked slowly to the shuttle stop, wondering what she could possibly find to say in a letter each day. Maybe Ernie Brown wouldn't mind learning about their little farm near Ponca City. She could write about Pops' beehives, or tell him she was thinking about nursing school. Or maybe that she had worked in the library one summer, and when a single copy of *Gone with the Wind* came in, how she promised the librarian she would read that monster overnight and get it back so one of the 250 patrons signed up could check it out. He might find that amusing.

I will tell you about myself, she thought as she rode home. She had never minded the shuttle's stops and starts, because she had free time for her mind to wander, and this was such an occasion. Her life so far had been a modest one, frugal, even, because life in Oklahoma in the Dirty Thirties had never allowed anything else. She could write about when Rural Electric lit their home, and Pops scolded her for turning the light on and off and on and off. Simple stuff. Her life.

Chapter Ten

I *will tell you about my life*, she wrote in her first Vmail. *It's not very* *exciting. Will you tell me about yours, if you have time after directing* *traffic all day, and aren't too tired?*

It looked stupid on paper, but Ronnie Green wasn't one to tear up a letter and start over, not when each page cost a penny. "Here goes," she said.

She filled the single sheet with her early life, then reread what she had poured out. The realization that no one else knew these homely details – she had so few living relatives – humbled her. She sat there, struck with another fact: She knew every single word was going to be read and savored, even though she was not really more than an acquaintance. She knew each Vmail letter brought home close, no matter if anything came of it.

"I can live with that," she said, her face close to the page, careful not to leave any lipstick on it. Just as wearing a WAC uniform and working in an unglamorous aircraft factory added her mite to the war effort, so did Vmail.

The only person she mentioned her commitment and resolve to was Mrs. Dobbs, who nodded her approval. Theirs was a brief chat as Mrs. Dobbs passed down the row between tables, carrying a coffeepot. It turned into more when the cafeteria manager whispered, "I'm always here by 5 a.m. Just so you know."

Ronnie set her alarm clock a little earlier, to Millie Sturdivant's groans, and had the pleasure of a quiet moment with Mrs. Dobbs in her small office, going over invoices and menus. A few minutes only, and Ronnie understood better that concern of a parent for a child – two sons, actually – in harm's way. "I read their letters over and over," Mrs. Dobbs said. "I do my part by seeing that everyone here is fed." She squeezed Ronnie's hand. "It's our war, too. You write those letters, hear?"

Three days later, she had barely reached the colonel's office when the phone rang. Setting down her PB&J sandwich and apple, she answered it to hear a scratchy voice indicating long distance. These came often enough for her boss. "Colonel Dignam's office," she said. "May I tell him who is calling?"

Scratchy Voice said, "This call is for Private Veronica Green."

She held her breath in surprise, so hopeful, then let it out. "This is she." "Go ahead, Sergeant."

Scratchy Voice sank an octave, maybe more. "Ronnie? Ernie Brown. We're shipping out in a matter of minutes, and I pulled a little rank to speak to you. Hear that?"

He must have held out the telephone receiver. She chuckled to hear a loud chorus of lamentation, obviously from outranked privates and corporals.

"I'll make it quick. Our destination is Europe, of course, provided the U-boats are looking the other way."

What could she say to that?

"Ronnie?"

"Be careful," she blurted out. "Wear your life jacket."

"Yes, sir!" he teased. "Write to me, please, well, if you want to."

"I do. I will. I already mailed a letter."

"Ronnie, you're a wonder," she heard, something no one had ever said to her before; she knew she was too ordinary to be a wonder. "I have to hang up before this mob tars and feathers me." Silence a moment, then, "I wish I could kiss you now."

"I wish you could, too," she replied, not caring what she sounded like.

"Don't repeat this." A smaller silence, then one word. "Bastogne." Click. She stared, squinty-eyed, at the receiver as though it were a low-achieving riveter on the assembly floor. *I wanted to tell you I love you*, she thought, then discarded the silly notion, knowing better than anyone how short their acquaintance was.

"Was that your feller?"

She blushed and went to Colonel Dignam's office. "It was Sergeant Brown," she said.

"Your feller," he replied, and she heard all his satisfaction, which reminded her of Pops.

She sat down without permission. "Sir, he said one word and told me not to repeat it: Bastogne."

"And you just repeated it! The O.S.S. will never recruit you to spy for them," was his comment. "It's a major city in Belgium, not far from the French border. A bunch of roads converge there."

"He'll be directing a lot of traffic," Ronnie said, even though she was well aware how naïve she sounded. She knew better.

"A lot," Colonel Dignam agreed, but kindly. He seemed to be composing himself, which touched her heart, because his concern made him more than a boss. "You needn't repeat this, but if the Germans weren't retreating, I would swear that's where they would push back."

"Then thank goodness they are retreating," Ronnie said.

He nodded, seemed to make a mental correction, and handed her a sheaf of papers and her orders for the day, a lieutenant colonel again.

Her chief consoler remained Mrs. Dobbs, even when all Ronnie had to say about a day without any mail was, "I wish I could hear something." She was guaranteed a "You'll hear soon," from the cafeteria manager.

Ronnie had tried that approach with Millie, who scoffed and reminded her that she should count her lucky stars that she hadn't even had a date with – what as his name again? "Sergeant Brown," Ronnie said, but Millie was already off on another track.

"Nothing yet?" Mrs. Dobbs had asked a week later. It had become her replacement for "Good morning," when Ronnie continued to make her way downstairs early enough to catch the cafeteria supervisor still in her office, and not pacing around the steam tables, barking out orders.

"Nope, but I sent another letter yesterday," which had turned into Ronnie's replacement for "And good morning to you," in reply.

"What in the world are you finding to say?" Mrs. Dobbs asked as she divided her cinnamon roll and forked it to Ronnie.

"More than I would have thought, Mrs. Dobbs." Ronnie took the fork. "I've been amazing myself."

True enough. Her evenings were never busy, so it had been easy to stake out a corner of the reading room, with its newspapers from all over, and a few well-read novels. She had quickly determined that women who inhabited the reading room appreciated silence as much as she did. She had never been prone to gab, being more of an observer. Still, she had surprised herself with written accounts of life and work at the five and dime, high school graduation, the way the morning sky turned sunflowers toward the east and how they tracked the light all day, a disastrous blind date that still made her chuckle, the anticipation of those first little potatoes, real butter.

Mrs. Dobbs didn't laugh at her homely subjects. She nodded when Ronnie – embarrassed and wondering if she was prideful – said that she copied her letters into a Big Chief tablet, thinking someday, provided she ever married and had children, her offspring would like a look at a supremely ordinary life in Oklahoma.

"It's a good thing you're doing," Mrs. Dobbs assured her.

Ronnie always left time for the cafeteria supe to mention her own letters from her boys. "They never say much, but I don't care. All I'm looking for is Dear Mom," Mrs. Dobbs said. "It's been me and them for most of their lives. I save their letters, of course."

So, nothing from Europe for Ronnie. She made a conscious effort not to think about Sergeant Brown, up to and including a movie date with a one-armed farm boy. A corn picker had neatly picked *him* when he was six, he told her. He had found work in the aircraft plant as a bolt collector, and segued into junior payroll clerk when the civilian manager asked for someone, anyone who could add and subtract.

The movie was *Mr. Lucky*, the story of a debonair gambler and a socialite, and had nothing to do with the war, which suited Ronnie. The newsreel even reassured her, with stirring tales of the tide turning in Europe and the Pacific. No fool, she managed to sit on her date's side with the missing arm. He was nice enough, but she didn't want someone's arm around her that wasn't Sergeant Brown's.

He was polite; she was kind. There was no second date.

When she had almost given up on a letter, one came. It was lying on her desk, squared away, which made her look through the open door to Colonel Dignam as he flashed a V sign and returned to his own correspondence.

She opened the envelope and drew out a small sheet with painstaking printing, shrunk down and microfilmed then reconstituted, as she had been assured was the fate of her letters. She sighed to see several dark lines drawn through whole sentences, but the censor had generously allowed, "Imagine my delight to find ten letters waiting for me here at *black line*."

Nice try, Ernie, she thought, amused. "It's good to be back with my friends again," he wrote. "I won't wish you were here, but please know I am thinking of you. Have you gotten information about the GI Bill? I'll nag you until you do."

He signed it, "All my love, Ernie," which made Ronnie wonder and blush over just how much love that was. She thought it might be a great deal.

His P.S. touched her heart and told her she was on the right track. "Your life sounds much like mine in Illinois," he printed. "I notice those sunflowers, too, dear heart."

Dear heart. Oh, my. She sailed down to breakfast with Mrs. Dobbs the next morning, still drifting along on dear heart, and willing to share that with the cafeteria lady.

There was no cinnamon roll to share that morning, only Mrs. Dobbs frowning at the day's Kansas City *Star* as though it had committed a misdemeanor. Ronnie looked over her shoulder at "Fleet action near the Philippines." Her eyes went to the world map Mrs. Dobbs had found somewhere. She located the islands and sat quietly beside her friend.

Mrs. Dobbs looked up. "It mentions Leyte Gulf and something two weeks ago." She gave herself a visible shake and folded the paper. Ronnie kept her news to herself. What was Ernie Green to a widow who had raised two sons though a Depression, waiting tables and surviving on tips? She waited for Mrs. Dobbs to right herself and turn into the practical woman. It didn't take long.

"Chaz likes to tease Tom about taking the easy way out and joining the Navy," Mrs. Dobbs said. "I don't like to hear about antiaircraft fire over Berlin, but I keep getting Dear Moms from that APO address."

They smiled at each other. Mrs. Dobbs turned the conversation to Thanksgiving in two weeks and the promise of turkey and gravy. Ernie could wait.

Chapter Eleven

Dear Heart received another letter by the end of the week, this letter with complaints about the cold, limited supplies and monotonous food. Her heart warmed at "the one bright spot on my too-long day is a stack of mail waiting for me at Mail Call. I am the envy of nations."

She showed it to Mrs. Dobbs, who presented her with a sliver of apple pie this time. "Whatever is the occasion?" she teased, already looking forward to Thanksgiving next week.

"Everyone wants pumpkin pie, of course, but apple pie even more." Mrs. Dobbs leaned closer. "Don't tell anyone, but this recipe contains no apples. Can you tell?"

Ronnie took another bite, savoring this one in her mouth for a moment. "There's something else but... No. It's fine. What's the substitute?"

"Ritz crackers and the usual apple pie spices. Fooled you?"

Not really, but Mrs. Dobbs was so pleased with herself. Even better, the worried crease was gone between her eyes. "You fooled me," Ronnie said, perjuring herself without a qualm. "Hopefully, there is pumpkin enough."

"Yes, indeed. No shortage there. Just a dab of whipped cream should do it for my apple." Her eyes shone with pleasure. "I got a letter from Tom, 'somewhere in the vast Pacific,' as he puts it. I'm so pleased when they are both accounted for."

Ronnie looked at her own letter from Bastogne (only she never said Bastogne out loud). "Ernie had four letters from me at mail call," she said.

Mrs. Dobbs nodded. "This is how we fight," she said, her voice soft, almost reverent.

"Millie Sturdivant thinks I am lucky I never had a chance to develop any feelings toward him."

"She's probably right," Mrs. Dobbs said, disappointing Ronnie. She patted Ronnie's hand. "Just keep those letters going to Europe."

Between typing and filing and running errands for Colonel Dignam, she had no time to consider the matter. By the evening shuttle ride home, she had almost convinced herself that no one falls in love so fast. End of problem.

Millie Sturdivant was on the boil when she got back to their shared, crowded quarters. "One letter in three weeks!" she said in a flat voice, that made Ronnie wonder how Lt. Sturdivant liked the sound of *that* coming at him.

"I'm sure he's busy."

"Not too busy to leer at little French girls, I imagine," Millie said. She threw herself down on the bunk that creaked in protest, and turned her face to the wall. "*You* don't have to worry about that," she added, as if blaming Ronnie for….something.

Ronnie had her own letter to consider, not one from Ernie this time. She took it down the hall to the reading room, this letter from a new Aunt Vi, one full of hope and love, no longer ground down with the greyness that seemed to cover so many years during Ronnie's childhood in the '30s. She read it again with a smile. *Dear Veronica, Bill finally proposed. After all this time, he said he was ready!* Ronnie couldn't help a laugh, remembering years and years of Bill Vance sitting with Vi in the living room, and then on the porch swing in summer, never saying much, adoring her aunt with his eyes.

The wedding was going to be a quiet event, nothing more than a visit to the courthouse. Ronnie frowned over the next paragraph, even though she knew what Pops would have her do. *Veronica, he wants to buy your house,* she read, noticing how the words blurred a little. *Even here in Ponca City, housing is so scarce. He wants to put down new linoleum in the kitchen and pipe in water. Once there is water, he has plans for an indoor privy.*

"All those things Pops could never afford," Ronnie whispered to Aunt Vi's neat handwriting.

He'll pay you fifteen hundred dollars, Ronnie, she read. *Isn't that generous?* Yes, it was, considering it came with twenty acres. She could bank the money and when the war ended, go where, and do what? Ponca City held no particular attractions, but what else was there? She thought about Sergeant Brown, and Rantoul, Illinois, and the GI Bill.

She stared at Aunt Vi's letter and knew what to do. It only took two or three crumbled attempts before she created a letter of love, congratulations, and permission for Bill Vance to buy the only home she knew. When that letter was done, she wrote another to Ernie Brown, so far away in Belgium, telling him what she had done. Somehow, seeing the words on paper gave them meaning.

She didn't sleep well that night, feeling suddenly insecure, even though she knew Bill Vance, if shy around women, was a man of his word and would deliver fifteen hundred dollars into her possession. Whether he was aware of it or not, Mr. Vance was also severing her connection to everything she knew.

By morning's light, she knew that lessening her tie to Ponca City turned the GI Bill into reality. Ernie was right; maybe she could be anything she wanted. Maybe the world needed another nurse. She repeated it softly, careful not to wake up Millie. She, Veronica Green, the family's first high school graduate, was going to the Information Office to ask for the GI Bill packet. Mrs. Dobbs would be the first to know.

Something felt different this time. She felt it in her bones as she walked down the hall flanked with memo boards, and the time clock for cafeteria workers.

She saw no welcoming light under the door. She knocked, fearful. "Mrs. Dobbs? Mrs. Dobbs?"

After far too long, she heard, "Come in."

Her heart in her throat, she opened the door. The only light came from the little window, with its blackout curtains barely open. She saw Mrs. Dobbs sitting in her usual place, but there was no fragrance of coffee. She turned on the light, looking first at the cut-out Thanksgiving turkey that seemed to leer at her this time.

Head down, Mrs. Dobbs sat behind her desk as usual, but with the Kansas City *Times* in her lap. Wordless, Ronnie came close enough to see the banner headline. *Battle of Leyte Gulf!* the thirty-point headline screamed. *Allied victory! Jap Defeat!*

"Mrs. Dobbs?"

The cafeteria supe looked up, her eyes and nose red. Ronnie knelt by the chair. "Please, what happened?"

Mrs. Dobbs made a pitiful attempt to pull herself together. Wordless, she pointed to a paragraph far down in the article. Ronnie read it to herself,

"At a climactic point in the engagement, a Jap dive bomber crashed into the deck of the carrier *St. Lô*, setting it ablaze. The mighty machine of war sank in thirty minutes, taking with it some 100 sailors killed or missing, out of 900 men."

Ronnie put her hand over Mrs. Dobbs' cold fist. "You don't know if Tom was among them," she said in a low voice, hoping she conveyed conviction and confidence, when she felt only distress. "Please, please focus on the eight hundred still left."

"No, I don't know," Mrs. Dobbs said after a long, long pause. "Maybe he is safe."

"I think the odds are in his favor," Ronnie said, acutely aware that she had nothing to base her words on. "I mean, look, there are 800 men left on that carrier. Let me get you some coffee."

Coffee helped. Mrs. Dobbs seemed to perk up. By the time Ronnie had to leave to catch the last shuttle before she would be officially late, Mrs. Dobbs was back to her recipes and numbers, to all intents normal, except for the occasional deep shudder.

When she got to work, Colonel Dignam was looking at his copy of the *Times*, his feet propped on his desk, his swivel chair enduring punishment as he leaned back. She didn't ask permission but came into his office and sat there until he looked up.

"Sir, Mrs. Dobbs' son Tom is on the *St. Lô*," she said, not certain why she sat there – there had been no invitation – but not wanting to be by herself.

He lowered his feet from the desk and indicated the paper with a nod. "It happened October 25, almost a month ago, and we here in the States went on blithely as though no one was swept from a burning deck." He stared at the calendar over Ronnie's shoulder, seeing something besides numbers in small compartments. "Now we wait to know more. For some, it's not going to be a good Thanksgiving." His glance wandered to the open door. "Maybe not for Mrs. Dobbs."

His words chilled her. They also made her brave, she who seldom revealed much about herself to anyone, let alone her superior officer by many ranks.

"Colonel Dignam, do you ever feel puny and inconsequential?" she blurted out, then wondered what she was saying. "I mean, well, you're a lieutenant colonel, but what does that mean when armies march and navies sail?"

What was she saying? She sounded unprofessional and afraid. She sounded like a twenty-two-year-old girl masquerading as a member of the Women's Army Corps. She brought this officer coffee every morning, handled all correspondence and filed and typed. It was so small.

Bless the man, he understood. "We don't amount to much, do we, Ronnie?" he asked in turn, using her name for the first time.

She shook her head, miserable, seeing Mrs. Dobbs staring at the newspaper, her dread almost a living thing. She thought of Sergeant Brown in Bastogne. Better not think of Ernie. Writing a letter a day to a man everyone would say she didn't know at all had changed her. She was sharing her life with him, something she had never done before.

"I write a letter every day to Sergeant Brown," she told him. "I type and file. It's so small."

Colonel Dignam smiled for the first time. "I'd be willing to bet it doesn't seem small to the sarge."

"Do you think, sir?"

"I'm certain of it, Private Green. Ask him when he comes back."

She nodded, shy again. Should she say more? She had to. She cleared her throat, ready to tell him that Mrs. Dobbs and Millie Sturdivant had assured her how fortunate it was she hadn't invested too much of herself yet, that Sergeant Brown was a man she barely knew and hadn't dated. She was ready to tell her superior officer – a grandfather with sons-in-law, serving in the army and air corps – that she was in love with Sergeant Brown; she was certain of it.

The telephone on her desk rang. She became a clerk again, and not a hesitant woman of little experience, with doubts and worries about a man who had somehow attached himself to her heart. She answered in her cool professional voice and patched the call through to Colonel Dignam.

The moment passed. Tonight, she would write another letter to Sergeant Brown. Thanksgiving was nearly here. She could keep Mrs. Dobbs company, a woman with real concerns, far bigger than hers.

She heard the colonel hang up. "Private, you were about to tell me something."

"It's not important, sir."

Chapter Twelve

Everything changed two days later on Thanksgiving, when chickens came home to roost.

First of all, Thanksgiving was a holiday. Even in this time of shortages and sacrifice, not one rivet was going into a single B-25 today. The novelty of a silent production floor almost – almost – made Ronnie want to go there for a look.

She allowed herself a luxurious stretch, a yawn, and the realization that she could do as much or as little as she wanted today. She began by taking out Sergeant Brown's Vmail, his second, from under her pillow, this letter telling her about motor pools and patching tires, subjects that had never struck her as even remotely interesting. Now, through some alchemy she accepted without question, they took on new depth because this was Ernie and she cared what he thought and did.

She looked at the bottom of the letter first, as she had done with yesterday's initial reading. He had written *All my love* again. Nothing had changed overnight; it was still there. She stretched and settled back in her warm nest, determined not to leave it too soon. Mrs. Dobbs had said the breakfast line would extend to nine o'clock today in honor of those pilgrims who probably never allowed themselves such a luxury, and would have wondered about moral degenerates who so indulged.

Ernie knew enough about censors to not tempt them with anything that might bring out the black marking pen. It was an ordinary letter with complaints about food and rain and the discomfort of wet socks. He included a drawing of a little girl in a too-big coat, wearing broken shoes and holding out a bowl and captioned "We share," which made her mind take a leap of fancy and imagine what kind of a father he might be.

The censor had saved his black mark for the last sentence, whatever it was. Ernie had written, "Snow is coming," followed by "It's too quiet," and then, "I'm…"

I'm what? Ronnie asked herself. Bored? Worried? In love? Thinking of spring? Glad you write so often? Afraid? Wondering what the Germans were up to? She dismissed the last thought, especially since even Colonel Dignam said all signs pointed to an end to the fighting in Europe, maybe by Christmas. "They're beaten and they know it," her boss had said only yesterday. She decided things were too quiet because a surrender was coming.

The warming thought carried her down the cold corridor to the bathroom, where – oh bliss – there was hot water for a change. She soaped up in the shower, allowing herself the added luxury of wondering what it might feel like to have a husband scrub her back. The thought turned her face warmer than the water.

Back in her room, Millie only muttered something, and pulled her blanket higher. So much for company at breakfast. When she went to open the door, Ronnie watched the other two roommates, the ones on the night shift heading toward her.

She stepped aside to let them into the room, but the shorter one took her by the arm.

"Ronnie, something bad has happened. Your boss went into Mrs. Dobbs's office, and he was carrying a telegram."

Not that, please not that. Ronnie nodded and hurried down the hall and down the stairs. Running by the time she reached the double doors, she stopped, out of breath, maybe out of courage. She opened the cafeteria door to see the usual diners crowded in one corner, and Mrs. Dobbs and Colonel Dignam sitting at a table by themselves. No one was talking. There was no holiday banter, no chatter about football scores, or ration woes, or any normal chatter. Everyone stared at the breakfast before them, some eating, others simply staring.

Unsure of herself, she went to the line where the servers waited, all of them glum and looking down, too, as if hashbrowns and scrambled powdered eggs held some unexpected fascination. Even the toast looked withered. When the hashbrowns went down with a thump on her plate, Ronnie leaned closer. "What happened?" she whispered, even though she knew.

"Her son in the Pacific," the kitchen girl whispered back. "Ketchup?"

Ronnie shook her head and moved on to the eggs and toast. And there was prune juice. Wouldn't you know it?

Coward. She wanted to keep her head down, too, didn't want Colonel Dignam to see her and call her over to share the sorrow. She knew he delivered such telegrams when the doctor was off duty.

"Private Green."

Caught. She turned toward the table for two, where her boss motioned her closer. "Sir?"

"Would you please get a cup of coffee for Mrs. Dobbs?"

"Yes, sir."

Two cups of coffee went on her tray. Sympathy in her eyes, the cashier totted up the meal and checked off her name on the list. She knew Mrs. Dobbs took two lumps of sugar and a little cream, so that bought her another moment for her to think of what to say. Then there was nothing to do but join Mrs. Dobbs and Colonel Dignam, dreading every moment.

She reminded herself that she was Mrs. Dobbs's friend, the lady she shared early morning coffee with, and who read her portions of letters from her sons. She sat down beside Mrs. Dobbs, taking in the emptiness in her red eyes. Mrs. Dobbs took the cup of coffee and held it to her cheek, seeking warmth or perhaps the consolation of familiar objects that never changed.

"It's Tom," she whispered. She pushed the telegram toward her.

Ronnie didn't want to touch it, either. She looked at the cool, formal words that by 1944 had found their way to thousands of mothers and fathers. *We regret to inform you...missing in action and presumed dead... please accept our sympathy...your sacrifice will not go unnoted...your country mourns with you...*

She looked at her boss for help, for some indication of what she should do, but his eyes were as lost and helpless as Mrs. Dobbs's. *Why is this my burden?* Ronnie wanted to scream, but she didn't.

She had never known her mother, who died of asthma when Ronnie was three, but she did know what Aunt Violet would have done. Without a word, she dipped her napkin in the glass of water on the table, squeezed it a little, and wiped the bereft woman's face. "This will feel better," she whispered, as she dipped the cloth again and gently dabbed at the cafeteria manager's forehead. Her eyes were next, and then dip again, and her temples, all the time humming low in her throat.

Ronnie looked up when Colonel Dignam quietly left them, looking older than he had yesterday afternoon. "There now," Ronnie said and held out the coffee cup. "Drink some of this."

Mrs. Dobbs dutifully did as she said, then set down the mug. "What on earth will I tell Chaz?" she asked.

"That Tom was brave to the end and gave everything for his country," Ronnie told her.

Mrs. Dobbs sobbed. "He probably died in a ball of flame! They were probably refueling the planes!"

Ronnie shuddered inside, wondering at the agony, the cries, the metallic screech of a ship groaning in death, the smell of machine oil. "Then it was quick, and his suffering is long over, Mrs. Dobbs," she said instead. "He is at peace with the Lord." It was an Aunt Vi answer, all Ronnie had.

"He is, isn't he?" Mrs. Dobbs said. "Poor boy. Poor me."

Ronnie took the older woman in her arms, rocking with her as she wept, grateful suddenly for the cakes and pies she had taken with Aunt Vi to houses of mourning in Ponca City, because Aunt Vi ran the town library and knew everyone. Ronnie had resisted and complained, but only inside her heart, because Aunt Vi would have been so disappointed in her. As she held Mrs. Dobbs close and crooned to her, she thanked her aunt in silence and gratitude for that lesson in neighborly kindness, Ponca City style.

Oddly enough, she thought of ration books. Nowhere had she seen any rationing of tears. Unlike bananas and gasoline and nylon stockings and a gazillion other wants and needs, there was no limit on grief. The thought shook her to the depths of her soul as she mourned along with Mrs. Dobbs.

Hours later, Ronnie dragged herself upstairs, Thanksgiving over and done, the turkey eaten, the powdered mashed potatoes and gravy a memory. Mrs. Dobbs had dried her tears, given herself a shake, and carried on, assisted by more than her usual crew as word spread in the way it did, in times like these. All the pie makers, Ronnie among them, crossed their fingers and assured the steely woman with the hollow eyes that no one would ever suspect the apples were Ritz Crackers.

After the last dish was washed and put away, the kitchen workers conferred among themselves and assured Mrs. Dobbs that she could take the rest of the week off. "We got this, honey," the big woman who usually worked the later shift told her. "We can do it, never you worry."

Hugs and more hugs, and they finally turned Mrs. Dobbs loose. Ronnie took her by the hand and walked her to her little apartment off the kitchen, where the cafeteria manager went directly to her bureau in the bedroom and picked up the framed photo of a smiling man with light hair and eyes and dressed in navy blues.

"He gave this to me before he shipped out," Mrs. Dobbs said. With a steady finger, she outlined her son's face and smiled. "He was going to use the GI Bill to become a mechanic," she whispered, as the bleakness returned to her face. "He loved airplanes." Her expression hardened. "And now they have killed him."

They sat together in silence for another hour. Finally, Mrs. Dobbs looked at her almost as if seeing her for the first time in the long day, the Thanksgiving that Ronnie knew she would remember forever. "Thank you," she said simply. "I can manage now." Her hand went to her forehead. "I'm tired."

"Everyone is going to do your job for the rest of the week," Ronnie reminded her. "Beulah said she would bring you breakfast tomorrow and handle your shift and hers. I'll check in before I go to work."

"And when you return after the day's work is done?" Mrs. Dobbs asked hopefully.

"If you'd like."

"I would." Mrs. Dobbs took her hand. "It's a hard business, my dear." She gazed deep into Ronnie's eyes. "It's better if you don't think too much about Sergeant Brown." She patted Ronnie's hand. "You can get serious after the war is over, if you're so inclined."

Almost before the door closed, Ronnie heard deep, wracking sobs from a woman who had already cried every tear there was. Listening to the agony on the other side of the door, powerless to do anything because there was nothing she could do, Ronnie realized how little she knew about the power of love, and the utter devastation, as well.

Was that true? She thought about Sergeant Brown ordering her to pull over the Jeep and how he took her in his arms and drove out every fear, every dread, because he was there and he was strong, and nothing could possibly happen to him. And because he was strong, she could be, too, even though an ocean and many miles separated them.

There was no one in the corridor between the apartment and the kitchen. Ronnie leaned against the wall and sank down until she was seated with her chin on her upraised knees, exhausted. "It's too late, Mrs. Dobbs," she murmured. "I am already so inclined."

Chapter Thirteen

Curious how Millie Sturdivant had nothing to say about the deadly telegram. Even more curious was her ferocity when Ronnie tried to mention the matter the next day as they were dressing for work.

"Don't you dare say another word!" she had warned Ronnie. "It's bad luck and I will not allow you to breathe a word of this."

"But Mrs. Dobbs is hurting," Ronnie said in protest. "We have to help her!"

"I mean it," Millie replied, managing to look both tight-lipped and pathetic, which touched something deep and disturbing in Ronnie. "I...I'm going to stay far away from her."

"She's not bad luck," Ronnie snapped.

"I mean it," Millie repeated, her eyes narrow, her expression set.

There followed a strange week, one in which Millie was largely silent, and one in which Ronnie noticed others, those with loved ones overseas, avoiding Mrs. Dobbs when she returned to work. Her eyes red but her back straight, the cafeteria manager presided over a usually noisy dining hall that was hushed now, fearful almost, of more bad news.

"I hope she doesn't notice that people are avoiding her," Ronnie told her boss on that third morning. "It would break her heart."

"She knows," was all Colonel Dignam said.

And what have you done, she asked herself the following morning, stung by her own neglect. She reasoned that she didn't *always* stop in every morning to sit and visit, and then shook her head at her own folly. Yes, she did. She was as bad as the others.

Her remorse bullied her into that usual trip down the hall by the cafeteria to knock on the door of Mrs. Dobbs's office. She came inside after the manager's soft reply, and took her usual seat by the desk, where Mrs. Dobbs stared at invoices.

"There's such a stack of these," the woman said. "I hardly know where to begin."

"I can classify them by date, the oldest first," Ronnie offered, pleased for once to be a mere clerk/typist and a tiny cog in the machine of war. "I will do that while you drink your coffee."

Mrs. Dobbs looked at the mug with no steam rising from it. She took a sip and made a face. "This might even be left over from yesterday," she said, then shrugged. "Maybe the day before."

Saddened, Ronnie arranged the neglected invoices. "I will get you a hot cup," she said when she finished.

"You'll be late for work," Mrs. Dobbs protested, but there wasn't any muscle behind her admonition.

"Doesn't matter. What'll the colonel do? Fire me?" Ronnie delighted in the returning smile, a small one, her puny joke inspired.

Mrs. Dobbs was stamping the invoices when Ronnie returned with steaming hot joe. "Just what I needed," she said after a sip and another.

"Mrs. Dobbs, I'm sorry I haven't been in here for...for a few days," Ronnie began, wondering if she should say anything.

"Don't worry about that," the cafeteria lady said.

"I didn't know what to say," she admitted.

"No one does, once it happens to them," Mrs. Dobbs said. She folded her hands on the desk. "They avoid me because they see themselves in me."

Ronnie nodded. It was true.

"I could tell them that bad luck...bad luck like this doesn't rub off, but who would believe me?" She touched Ronnie's sleeve. "Scram now. You'll be late."

Another week, and the cafeteria slowly returned to normal, people laughing again, after looking around to make sure they weren't overheard, then relaxing. *Our lives are going on*, Ronnie thought. *We're leaving Mrs. Dobbs behind.*

She said as much to Colonel Dignam, who nodded. "I was with Pershing's Expeditionary Force in France for the Great War," he told her. "I was on his staff. Nothing seemed to faze him. I asked one of his older officers about it. You know what he said?"

Ronnie shook her head. The death of Mrs. Dobbs's son had set the two of them on a different course. Her boss didn't mind a head shake now, instead of a "No, sir."

"He told me that Black Jack Pershing's wife and two daughters died in a house fire when he was stationed at Fort Bliss."

Ronnie gasped. "I had the same reaction," the colonel said. "The officer told me that Pershing told him, 'What else can happen to me?' Somehow, death lost its power. Maybe Mrs. Dobbs feels that way."

As Ronnie got out pen and Vmail paper that night for her next letter, she debated long and hard whether to mention what had happened. After all, Sergeant Brown was surrounded by war and mayhem, even if things were quieter in Bastogne than in Leyte Gulf. She told him, then added something Pops had said once when they put flowers on Mama's grave, the mother she didn't remember. 'Ernie, he told me that death turned him into a rock in the stream. He remained immovable, but life kept flowing on around him.'

She looked at the words, thinking of the Pops she knew – the quiet man often given to sitting in silence on the porch and gazing across the field – and wondered what he had been like when her mother was alive. She wrote that next, curious to know if the censor would think she was too glum. She gave herself a mental shake and finished the letter by telling Ernie about the time she and Pops made raspberry jam, let it boil over, and spent hours scraping it off their wood-burning stove, and eating little crispy bits. She went to bed hoping the censor would at least smile over the crispy bits.

The air turned cold in the following week, which meant something else to write about when it snowed. Mrs. Dobbs even smiled a little now, but it never lasted long. At least she didn't neglect to drink her coffee while it was still hot.

To her utter delight, Ronnie received two letters on the same day from Sergeant Brown. The postal clerk, an earnest young man who wore thick glasses, delivered them right to her desk with a flourish. She stared at the envelopes, wanting with all her heart to open them, but knowing the door between her office and the colonel's was wide open, and he always seemed to know what she was doing. She set them aside.

"Private Green, you'd better read those, or you know you'll be worthless until noon mess call," her colonel said.

She laughed and opened the older of the two, pleased to see that Ernie had sketched that same little girl with the broken shoes. "She comes by when we eat, just hanging around the edges, carefully not watching us. There always seems to be a little left over for her," he wrote. "I wish you could send me a Raggedy Annie doll for her, but I doubt the War Department would consider that vital to the war effort. It is, though. All my love, Ernie."

"All my love, Ronnie," she whispered back. She couldn't say, but she thought, *You will be an excellent father of daughters.*

In the more recent letter, the one dated December Fifth, only ten days ago – imagine! – Ernie complained of the cold. The little girl, her name was Madeline, had missed two meals and they were all worried. "She showed up for breakfast this morning," he wrote, "and everyone heaved a sigh of relief. She looked a little worn down, though, so our medic found some cod liver oil from somewhere. Whoowhee, I used to hate that stuff! She took the teaspoon and wanted more. I hope I'm never that hungry."

He asked about any Christmas decorations in the dining halls. "I don't suppose your colonel will let you decorate your office," he wrote. "Any mistletoe?"

She looked closer at the tiny writing and saw a date two days later. "Must finish. It's getting colder here and Madeline hasn't been by. We're worried. Besides that, it's too quiet in..." Word marked out, so Ronnie whispered, "Bastogne." She squinted at what remained. "I'm..." she read, and the rest, what looked like nearly a paragraph, was blacked out.

You're what, she asked herself. *Tired? Ill? In love? Worried about trouble from the Germans? Everyone says they're retreating.*

"Colonel Dignam, what do you think?" she asked, as she came into his office without being called there.

He took that letter from Ernie when she handed it to him, wanting reassurance. He read it and leaned back. "'I'm what?'" he asked, and sat up, looking her in the eye. "Private Green, I get info through some odd back channels. I've been hearing stuff."

"What stuff, sir?" She didn't want to know. No, she wanted to know everything, even the worst.

"That maybe the Germans aren't retreating." He raised his hands in a helpless gesture. "That's all I know and you can't repeat it."

She wrapped her arms around herself, the room suddenly cold. Funny about these temporary buildings – the heat could be so unreliable.

"Sir, you said you were there during the Great War."

"I was. Hard times, kiddo," he told her. "All roads lead right to Bastogne, for better or worse."

She tried to make light of it, even though the room seemed to grow colder. "So…so he'll be standing at the corner of Bastogne and Elm Street and directing traffic?"

He must have smiled because he sensed she needed it. "More'un likely."

She was far from reassured when his smile faded so quickly. He looked at the calendar. "Here we are," he said. "It is December 15th, one week to Christmas." He tried to smile again, but he knew her better than that, because he stopped the pretense. "How long until we actually know something?" He handed her a stack of documents to file. "What I learn, I'll share with you because I trust you. As for now, get to work, private, and that's an order."

Chapter Fourteen

Ronnie got to work, shaking her head over her own folly. In an effort to cheer up Millie a few nights ago, she told her silent roomie – she hadn't heard from Bob Sturdivant in days – that she decided to be the U.S. Army's best clerk-typist. "I have resolved that every little bit counts in the war effort."

Ronnie knew that would bring down Millie's scorn and make her a target for jibes about "nobodies who think filing even matters," but she did it deliberately, trying to distract the wife of a husband in a tank battalion from her irritation, because the man did not write much. Ronnie decided that when Lt. Sturdivant came back, he should thank her. She knew better than to mention *that* to Millie.

Her letter to Ernie that night included that bit of folderol, and the comment that her roommate thought her a simpleton even imagining for a moment that filing mattered. Already she could envision hulking crates jammed with paperwork being dumped into landfills after victory in Europe and Japan.

She took more time over her decision to go to college when the war ended. *You've convinced me I should use that GI Bill. I think it will be nursing school. I'm not the teacher that I already know you are, but I like to take care of things,* she wrote. The sentence didn't satisfy her. After all, keeping clothes ironed or sweeping for dust bunnies also constituted taking care of things. It was late; she was tired. She counted on him being pleased to get a letter, no matter how inane.

The next sentence was harder to write, even though she knew it was true. Bill Vance, Aunt Violet's husband now, had sent her a check for fifteen hundred dollars, which she had banked immediately. He had written that a contract for the farm would follow next, for her to sign here and there and return. *When the war ends, I will be an heiress of vast wealth, but officially homeless*, she wrote to Ernie, then added *Haha! You were right; I needed a plan. Thanks to you, I have one.*

She nearly decided against going to breakfast that morning. It was Sunday, and she had created a warm nest of blankets. A chatter against the window heralded the arrival of sleet and ice chips. She lay in bed, allowing herself to woolgather and think how nice it might be if someone brought her breakfast in bed and a newspaper. She wondered if Ernie could cook, then blushed at her thoughts.

Her lifelong practicality took over. Likely, future mornings would mean an early shift at a hospital and venturing out in all sorts of nasty weather. Or not. She snuggled down deeper. What was to stop her from moving to Texas, San Antonio maybe, and never seeing snow again? She could do what she wanted, but not in Ponca City. What did she owe that tired old town anyway?

This would never do. She wasn't a sleep-late kind of woman. Twenty minutes later, she headed down the hall to the cafeteria manager's office. Mrs. Dobbs had asked her opinion yesterday about a paper Christmas wreath she knew she could finagle from December's budget. The idea had brought back a modest bit of color to her friend's cheeks and a smile less fleeting than usual. If they couldn't get one, Ronnie knew she could make one out of newspaper.

"Mrs. Dobbs?" She knocked again. "Mrs. Dobbs?"

"Come in, Ronnie," she heard finally. She also heard something else, a hesitation. *Please please*, she thought in sudden panic. *Not her other boy. The Eighth Air Force? Based in England?*

The Kansas City Times lay on the desk on top of menus and invoices. The headline in its two-inch glory stared back at Ronnie as if daring her to do something about it: *Massive Kraut attack overwhelms GIs.*

She came closer, scarcely breathing, and sank into the chair by the desk, seeing nothing but that dark type. The slightly smaller subhead gave no reassurance. *Allied Forces Reel from Blow.* Even worse was a separate article: *Malmedy Massacre.* Then, *Is Bastogne the Target?*

"Everyone said the Germans were retreating," Ronnie managed to say.

Mrs. Dobbs shook her head. "Ronnie," was all she said, her voice quiet and soft, almost soothing.

Ronnie picked up the newspaper, holding it with thumbs and forefingers on the edges because she didn't want to touch it at all. Barely breathing, she read of German forces slamming into thinly stretched American units in the forest at Ardennes, tanks firing at point blank range, tanks with flame throwers – all of it payback for D-day and Normandy in June.

Tightly coordinated forces under Field Marshal Gerd von Rundstedt… Ronnie put down the paper and sighed, then picked it up again. "…appear to be converging on Bastogne," caught her eye. She put down the paper and covered her face with her hands. She wanted a dark and quiet place, but this wasn't one. It felt more like that moment when the lights went down in the movie house and it was dark for that fraction of time before the newsreel started. In her mental newsreel, she thought she saw Sergeant Ernie Brown directing GIs running and dodging everything the German army was throwing at them.

"Ronnie?"

She shook her head. "Give me another moment, Mrs. Dobbs."

The cafeteria manager left the office, quietly closing the door behind her. Ronnie kept her hands over her eyes, breathing in Jergen's Hand Lotion, calming her heart. She took her hands away and looked at the Christmas wreath on the desk. Mrs. Dobbs had found one after all. Despite her own sorrow and mental turmoil, Mrs. Dobbs knew what they needed and found a wreath. Ronnie knew it was a brave gesture from a grieving woman and took heart.

In the quiet, Private Green reminded herself that she had no ties to Sergeant Brown. She had heard other WACs and cafeteria workers joke with each other about kissing the boys and sending them to war. She had done that, too, when Sergeant Brown told her to pull the Jeep to the curb and took her in his arms.

In that deepest part of her heart, she knew it was not just kiss and tell. He had begun it, not her. No one else knew that, though. Her acquaintances would think her foolish if she sobbed and worried. What was a kiss or two? Some letters? Thousands of women wrote letters. She was one of many and nothing more, to all appearances.

She was far too practical to believe in love at first sight, a favorite plot of hack short story writers churning out fodder for *Saturday Evening Post* or *Redbook*. The notion was something nice to think about, in the here-today-gone-tomorrow world of soldiers on the move and lovers not wasting a moment, was how realistic was it?

She opened the door, managing a smile for the cafeteria manager. "I really do hope the GIs get themselves out of this mess," she said, which sounded calm enough to her.

Ronnie's studied air of normality seemed to relieve Mrs. Dobbs. "So do I," she said almost eagerly, as if relieved Ronnie wasn't taking the news too hard. "I'm pretty sure my boy with the Eighth Air Force will be bombing that bunch of Krauts and showing them what for!"

"I don't doubt it for a minute. Mrs. Dobbs, that's a wonderful wreath. Where are you going to put it?"

"I think by the clock," she said, then held her hand up as if measuring off words. "I've asked the girl who makes the salads to letter something like 'Peace on Earth,' on a banner below it. What do you think?"

"Great idea," Ronnie said, breaking her heart as she thought of all the days ahead during what was going to be a terrible battle, striking a note of concern for "our boys" – easy to do – but trying not to think too hard about *her* boy, even if he was her boy and no one knew.

"Mrs. Taylor in the Hampton Hall Dining Room is organizing carolers to go around to the various offices," Mrs. Dobbs said.

"Wonderful."

She had to know more. She wanted more than just a few moments with Colonel Dignam, who knew something about the Ardennes, but he was getting ready for two weeks at home in St. Louis with his wife, who hadn't thought much of moving to Kansas City for the duration, and didn't. What he told Ronnie brought no peace.

"Von Rundstedt has Panzer divisions and they move fast," her boss said. "I'm afraid they've caught us with our pants down."

"But will the Eighth Air Force bomb the living daylights out of them?" she asked, wanting to clutch his arm like a toddler and demand his attention as he looked around his office, perhaps wondering if he was missing something he needed to take to St. Louis.

"Private, weather reports aren't promising. My backdoor sources say it's too cloudy for them to take off, and that gets no better over Belgium. Getting colder by the minute, as well." He paused, as if remembering her concerns, when from the looks of things, all he wanted to do was get home. "If memory serves me, General Patton and his tanks are roaming around there somewhere. It's gonna be tight, but I'd put my money on the GIs, if I were you."

He took a closer look at her. "We're not going to lose this war."

I don't care about that, she thought, with a sudden flash of anger. *I want to know what's going to happen to Bastogne and Ernie.* "It'll just take a little longer?" she asked, trying to hit that tone between concern and wistful without sounding needy.

He nodded. "Seems like in every war since cavemen first threw rocks at each other, Ug and Og Neanderthal always think they're going to be home by Christmas. Not this year, either."

She smiled because she knew that was what he wanted from her. "I hope Sergeant Brown is as resourceful as Ug and Og," she said, keeping her tone light.

"If he's an MP, you can count on that. See you in the New Year, Private Green. Keep that filing and correspondence down to a minimum, you hear? It's Christmas. Enjoy yourself."

She laughed for his benefit and waved him off for St. Louis, surprised how easy he was to bamboozle. "Yes, sir!"

Chapter Fifteen

Ronnie wanted to avoid the newspapers, but she couldn't; no one could. Bing Crosby could croon, "I'm Dreaming of a White Christmas," on the public address system, but that didn't fool anyone, either. Even after three, almost four, Christmases of war, there was something about the pummeling that Germans delivered to the GIs now besieged in Bastogne that seemed to touch a nerve with everyone.

Ever observant, Ronnie noticed that even the rat-a-tat of the riveters made some on the production floor start and look around. Maybe because it was Christmas, when other years had shown them newspaper photos of GIs lined up for Christmas dinner, the headlines screamed starvation in Bastogne. The news of no hope of food drops by air turned everyone more solemn than usual. Even worse was no opportunity to bomb the living daylights out of the Germans surrounding Bastogne.

Millie fretted as usual, but gone were the digs and jabs at her lieutenant, a faulty correspondent in better times. Ronnie's own hopes rose when the postal clerk delivered her a Vmail, then to her irritation, hung around to flirt for a few minutes because the colonel was gone. She was kind, she was polite, she rejoiced when he finally left. She tore open the envelope.

Her heart sank to see *AML,* and nothing else. She fumed a moment until she realized AML had to mean All My Love, then worried even more because he hadn't time or energy to spell out the words. In a terrifying mental flash, she saw a tank trundling up to him and opening fire, ending his correspondence forever. *Oh no*, she thought. *You're tougher than that.*

Christmas dinner in the cafeteria might as well have been mystery meat and more Ritz Cracker apple pie, for all the attention anyone paid. Bastogne was surrounded by veteran Panzer divisions. A makeshift hospital in a hotel had taken a direct hit. More GIs were cut off even from Bastogne. A doctor operated with cognac as an anesthetic and a serrated knife. When another article mentioned GIs frozen to death in foxholes she worried about little Madeline, ill and without even cod liver oil, wearing broken shoes, her toes black from frostbite.

Since she had the day off, Ronnie found a quiet corner in Colonel Dignam's office, sitting there in the silent dark until seven o'clock and the last shuttle back to the dorm. Aunt Violet had sent a Christmas card, news of Ponca City, and an embroidered handkerchief with her initials, VLG. Mama's name was Louise. She cried into the gift, wanting as never before a living mother who would have comforted her. She cried for doctors operating with nothing, for Madeline of the broken shoes, and for Ernie, cold, hungry and too tired to write more than AML.

To everyone's infinite relief, the weather lifted in Bastogne two days after Christmas. England-based warplanes – Mrs. Dobbs beamed with pride – bombed the Krauts and others dropped needed food and medicine. Just as good, maybe better, was the article about General McAuliffe's simply worded "Nuts!" to the demand for surrender from General von Luttwitz. Even Millie laughed at that.

The news gradually improved after everyone welcomed 1945 like a long-lost cousin. When he returned, and with real flair, Colonel Dignam spread out the *St. Louis Post-Dispatch* with the single word NUTS!!! in all caps and spanning eight columns. "Have you heard from your feller yet, Private Green?" he asked, by way of greeting.

"Sir, he's not my feller," Ronnie replied.

"Maybe not, but I know you like him."

"Haven't heard a word, sir."

"He's busy. My back door sources say the MPs are rounding up whole regiments now." He rubbed his hands with, if not glee, something approaching it. "I'll wager Sergeant Brown is directing a whole lot of Sherman tanks toward Berlin."

Maybe he was. It was just enough good cheer to keep the tears at bay, at least until that second week in January when she arrived at work to see a handful of War Department telegrams like the one Colonel Dignam had given to Mrs. Dobbs at Thanksgiving. Struggling to keep her heart beating, she hung up her coat and took them in to Colonel Dignam's office, ready for him when he returned from the weekly department head meeting.

She started typing letters the colonel wrote longhand after she left the office at six each evening. She yearned to look through the telegrams, until she reminded herself there was nothing for her and never would be. Letters were for the next of kin.

Colonel Dignam came back from the meeting in his own blue funk. "Dr. Weinberg said he divided the next-of-kin letters, Private Green," he said, as he picked up the telegrams. "And here they are. Helluva way to start the new year. The Bulge was a bad business. Three of us are delivering telegrams."

He closed the door behind him. Ronnie stared at the door, grateful to be a private and nothing more. Command came with prestige, higher pay, and telegrams destined to ruin lives.

"Private."

Ronnie looked up from the contemplation of her fingers as Colonel Dignam opened his door and held out a telegram. After a moment of terror, she knew it couldn't be Ernie. Even worse was the unescapable knowledge that if something happened to him, she would never know. She had no idea who his next of kin was.

She took the telegram and gasped. Corporal Millicent Sturdivent. Trust the U.S. Army to misspell Millie's last name.

"Please come with me," Colonel Dignam said. It didn't sound like an order, but she didn't think it would be wise to refuse. "I'll drive."

"Quality Control?" he asked as he released the brake.

"Yes, sir. This isn't going to go well."

"It never does," he replied, his eyes straight ahead. He drove slowly, partly to follow the speed limit and partly because she knew he didn't want to do this. "We discussed her case in our meeting. Corporal Sturdivant will be offered a release from service."

She looked down at the three telegrams in her lap. So now Corporal Millie Sturdivant, WAC, had become a government case, probably with a number for some other clerk-typist to deal with. Ronnie thought of the times that spoiled, exasperating Millie Sturdivant had been no one's idea of a roommate, and felt sympathy well inside her, something she would not have thought possible before right now. "These other two telegrams, sir?"

"They're to parents. We'll offer them two weeks off and the consolation of a European cemetery."

She heard the sarcasm but didn't see it in his bland expression. He seemed to understand her glance. "My brother is buried near Verdun," he said. "It's a huge cemetery."

Silence. They came to Quality Control, located inside the newer aircraft plant. Colonel Dignam turned off the engine. "What is Corporal Sturdivant like?" he asked.

"I honestly don't know how she will react," Ronnie said. "She...she complains that he doesn't write enough, but... I don't know."

"I suppose no one knows until it happens," he said. "C'mon, Private Green. Let's do this."

They walked down the hall toward the offices. He held up the telegrams. "I have two to deliver here," he told her. He managed a slight smile. "You know, I could be fishing."

"Not now, sir," she reminded him. "It's winter."

"Are you always so practical?"

"I suppose I am, sir."

Everyone in the front office knew what those telegrams in the colonel's hand meant. Her face pale, the front office clerk motioned to a door. Ronnie watched her sigh with relief when the colonel whispered Millie's name. *It's not for you*, she thought. *I'm glad. I will never know if something happens to Ernie.*

Her boss knocked, then opened the door without waiting. Millie looked up from her paperwork in irritation. "I'd rather you'd wait until I..." She stopped and stared at the telegram. "No. That's not for me."

Colonel Dignam came a step closer, and Millie backed her chair up. "I said it's not for me," she repeated, her voice louder this time.

"Corporal Sturdivant, I am so sorry to be the bearer of this," he said. He took the unwanted telegram from its envelope and set it on her desk.

"No!" Her voice was no louder. Ronnie flinched at the intensity, as disbelief and denial clashed with fact. Millie Sturdivant, Battle of the Bulge widow, stared at the first words, *We regret to inform you.*

Humbled and saddened, Ronnie thought how often Millie had irritated her during their months of sharing a crowded room. Millie had teased her about her prudent social skills, her small-town ways. She flaunted her own good fortune to be the wife of an officer, someone with plans to move to southern California when the war was over and buy a car and a bungalow. "He's a man with a future," she had boasted on more than one occasion. Not now.

Months ago, Ronnie had told herself after one of Millie's arguments about something trivial that she'd probably send her one or two Christmas cards, but that would be all. Watching her roommate's face turned pale as she pushed away the telegram then sobbed, Ronnie felt only pity and sorrow at such loss.

Only last week, Millie had complained that they had only been married for eight months, and he had been gone for six of them, as if it was his fault. Poor Millie. Ronnie knew Millie well enough to doubt much introspection, but she regretted that her thoughts had too often not been kinder. Surely Lieutenant Sturdivant hadn't wanted to be in a tank, when his future after college had pointed toward civil engineering. Damn Hitler, anyway.

Unsure of herself, Ronnie pulled up a chair next to Millie. "What do you want?" Millie snapped.

"To sit with you and cry," Ronnie said quietly. In a second, they clung together and wept.

Colonel Dignam left to deliver the next telegram to a sheet metal worker on the floor. When he returned, Millie remained in Ronnie's close embrace, her face calm now, her eyes deep pools of misery.

"Ronnie says I can leave any time, and with an honorable discharge, sir," she said. "I want to go."

"You can, corporal," he replied. "I'll initiate the paperwork and Private Green will see you back to the barracks."

Millie stood up, staggered, and straightened herself. She looked down at the unfinished work on her desk, shrugged and turned away. "Someone else can do this," she murmured. "It's not my war now."

She was gone by daybreak after a sleepless night, an eastbound train to catch. Ronnie packed Millie's duffel bag, her ready tears falling at the little photo of a quick justice of the peace wedding, the wartime special. She wrapped it carefully in Millie's extra nightgown, the silky one she never wore in the dorm that had probably made Lieutenant Sturdivant's eyes light up and reach for her.

Eyes puffy, face set, unwilling to go anywhere alone, putting off the moment when everything would be done alone, Millie Sturdivant made Ronnie accompany her to the admin building. She signed document after document, signing where the clerk pointed and reading nothing. Without a word, she took her travel voucher and stuffed it in her purse. She would have left her duffel behind, so Ronnie shouldered it and trailed after her to the foyer, where the chief medical officer and his driver waited to take her to the depot.

The driver took the duffel. Ronnie shivered in the sleet, the sky grey, even dawn reluctant: perfect worse-than-bad-news weather. Millie was headed to Cincinnati, home to her mother and father, people to cry with and share the sorrow.

"I suppose I didn't even know Bob all that well," Millie whispered to her as they stood together for the final time.

You never had an opportunity to know him well, Ronnie thought, reminding herself of the years her brand new Uncle Bill Vance had sat in the front room of Pops' house in Ponca City, the house that belonged to him and Aunt Violet now. It could be years, or it might be mere months. War had definitely speeded up most courtships, apparently, including the Sturdivant's, now minus one member. Or it might be that man who came into her life on a Greyhound bus, and visited her once before duty called him back to Europe. Life was strange.

"You brought him joy, Millie," she said simply. Maybe, maybe not. Did it matter now? It was what Millie needed to hear. "I know you did."

Millie's face brightened. "Do you think so?"

"I'm certain of it," Ronnie replied, she who knew nothing of the kind. She knew this was the moment for the kind thought, the reassurance that Millie Sturdivant craved.

They hugged. Millie kissed her cheek, then held her off, looking into Ronnie's eyes. "I'm so glad *you* don't have to go through this. It hurts."

"Yes, it would," Ronnie said.

Millie's eyes filled with tears. "Count your blessings that you haven't fallen in love yet."

"But I did," Ronnie told the sky as the car roared to life, and drove away. "I did."

Chapter Sixteen

Mid-January began the mighty Allied offensive, revealing to all that the Wehrmacht's sudden and fearsome attack in the Ardennes was the last gasp. Six weeks of surprise and death surrendered to the hard slog of relentless warfare that turned more Germans into prisoners, at least the hardened *soldaten* in the Bulge. Newspapers showed photos of other prisoners, some barely out of their childhood and others too old for anything except a chair by a fireplace. The Third Reich was scraping the bottom of the barrel.

Those dreadful six weeks became the Battle of the Bulge, as reporters on the scene pieced together a sequence of events for their American audience hungry for information. News came of a fearsome massacre of surrendering GI infantrymen at Malmédy on December 19, two days after Ernie's last letter containing only *AML* had been written. Recalling his own time in the Ardennes during the Great War, Colonel Dignam remembered Malmédy as a crossroads village. Now it was everlastingly to be notorious as the place where surrendering GIs were mowed down with cool ferocity, and Belgians likewise. Desperate men did terrible things.

Ronnie knew crossroads required MPs directing traffic. Had Ernie been directing army units fleeing toward Bastogne, soon to be surrounded and besieged by Germans? She knew he would never shirk his post, but would point tanks and infantrymen in the right direction. All he had time to write was *AML*. All my love.

The only peace she found during the endless days of typing and filing came at noon, when Colonel Dignam made his way to the mess hall, leaving her alone. After he closed the door, she covered her face with her hands and sat in absolute silence, craving the darkness and the fragrance of Jergens on her hands. When she thought she could paste a smile on her face, she went to the mess hall, too, eating whatever there was without complaint, and letting the talk swirl around her. Gradually, she began to converse again, and even joke a little, because she hadn't lost anyone, had she?

Spring came, and with it no news, which, Ronnie had ample time to consider, didn't necessarily mean good news. Quite the opposite, in fact. Her last two Vmail letters, the ones from early December, ended up on her desk in March with North American Aviation correspondence, marked Whereabouts Unknown, Return to Sender.

Colonel Dignam saw the letters on her desk and sighed. "It's chaotic right now, Private Green," he reminded her (as if she needed reminding). "Even if it weren't, I have no clout or channels to find out what you need."

"Would they know anything at Fort Leavenworth?" Where was her persistence coming from? She had always been a most biddable human: eager to work, anxious to please, not one to rock a boat.

"I'll ask," had been her boss's reply, which warmed her heart until the next week, when he shook his head at his lean information. "They told me Sergeant Brown had been on temporary loan to them because of his German language skills. They did mention the 518th MP Battalion."

She waited for more from him. She knew her boss well enough to know when he was hedging. "Sir?"

"All I learned is that there were no rear lines. Everyone was in the thick of it." When she continued her polite stare, he spread out his hand on his desk and spoke with reluctance. "I do know that the Krauts took some prisoners east of Bastogne. He could be stuck in some *stalag*." He let that sink in. "Patience, private, patience. We can do no more."

And that was that, except drat the man if he didn't say what Millie had said, as if it should be a comfort for her. "I, for one, am grateful you didn't really have a chance to get to know Sergeant Brown."

But I did, she thought, as sure of the fact as she was certain that every year there would be a tornado or two in Oklahoma, and that the sun always rose in the east. Maybe no one understood that. She didn't intend to batter her heart any further by grieving noticeably. After all, what were pillows for after lights were out, and the two other women she shared the room with were on the night shift? She could cry all she wanted then. Tears weren't rationed, were they?

In her sorrow, she remembered something told her once by the lady whose house she cleaned in Ponca City during high school. Her husband was the new manager of the local John Deere Plant, and they had settled in the nicest house in town.

"Here's one way you can always tell if it's a house you want to buy," she told Ronnie as she waited patiently for the woman to pay her the weekly two dollars. The lady looked around at the marvelous Queen Anne house built in far better times. "I walked into this empty house and immediately started mentally arranging my furniture in each room. That's when I knew I would buy this place."

The idea had struck Ronnie as remarkably pretentious at the time, even a little cruel, especially since most folks in Ponca City in 1938 were happy to have a roof over their heads. She understood it now, and on a far deeper level. Somehow, some way, a too-brief time in Sergeant Brown's company had allowed her to move inside his orbit. Everything fit. He was the man she wanted. No one knew.

She knew it would have to remain that way, especially when there was more agony ahead in the following weeks for the 23,000 workers at NA Aviation. Everyone on every shift in every building felt keenly the death of both sons in Italy of Jasper Griffin (night crew-Upper Bay Assembly). He took some time off until the middle of February, coming back to work with hollow eyes and a nervous tic.

The next telegram came for Florence Layton, day shift sheet metal worker in the main assembly bay. Her only son, Private Jack Layton of the 4th Marine Division, died in the carnage that was Iwo Jima. The main assembly bay was a cavernous and noisy structure. A riveter, shaken to the core, told Ronnie they could still hear Florence's screams over all the building.

And the next telegram, and the next telegram. They began to blur together. Her heart hollowed out, scooped like a cantaloupe, Ronnie did the paperwork required of her and filed it away.

She spent more time with her new best friend, the thick packet explaining the Servicemen's Readjustment Act and its lengthy application forms. First, she had to assure herself that the GI Bill was for men *and* women, because, well, because she was a realist. There it was: women who had served at least ninety days were as eligible as the men.

The colonel was away at an always-lengthy staff meeting. She closed the door and propped her feet up on her desk. *Well, that's not comfortable,* she thought after a few minutes, and put her legs down, feeling foolish and amused at the same time. *Why do men do that?*

Encouraged for the first time in ages, she learned that she could get a low-cost mortgage – *My word, a house of my own someday?* – and a low-interest loan, should she decide to start a business or go into farming. No. No. She turned the page and sighed with true pleasure. There it was: five hundred dollars a year for tuition, books and fees for college or vocational school. And look, fifty dollars a month for subsistence. If that wouldn't buy room and board in some boarding house, then she wasn't smart enough to go to school.

Encouraged, she began to fill out the forms. The packet came with a huge list of colleges and universities, as well as major trade and vocational schools. She considered the Oklahoma schools, but in a moment of blinding assertion, she informed the college-bound freshman looking at her from the mirror across the room that she didn't much care for Oklahoma and never had.

Then where? With no hesitation she turned to the Illinois schools. She ran her finger down the list until she came to the University of Illinois, Urbana-Champaign. There was a set of encyclopedias in the reading room that she turned to after work, settling into a leather armchair that hissed and sighed. A quick and disappointing perusal told her that a nursing degree was available at the Chicago campus only.

A teaching degree was listed at the Urbana campus. Hmm. That may have been Ernie's goal, but it wasn't hers. Her finger stopped at the College of Business. She couldn't help her smile, thinking of all the typing and filing she had done in the past year. Why not? She knew she was good at it. *Whatever I want*, she thought. *Maybe even accounting. I don't mind numbers.*

By the end of the week, with the Russians racing to Berlin and everyone on edge, Ronnie mailed the forms to the proper office in Washington. She could have listed two other colleges, but Sergeant Ernie Brown had said he would go to the school in Urbana. Maybe she was being silly. Certainly she was, but did it matter? If Ernie never was allowed to fulfill his dream, then she would do it for him.

The news got better and better from Europe as the Allies raced the Russians toward Berlin. Nothing slowed the production of North American Aviation's Mitchell bombers which went from sheet metal to warplanes in a month, and roared into the sky. Almost as if in defiant agreement with the Allied push to Bastogne and beyond, January was the best production month of all: 315 B-25s. This distinction earned North American Aviation a certificate, plus doughnuts and coffee. The clatter, rumble, and high whine in the main production factory did not slack during the brief ceremony.

Ronnie never heard from Millie Sturdivant, not that she had expected to. The only thing they ever had in common was a shared room in the barracks. Mrs. Dobbs withdrew inside herself, found it a comfortable place, and stayed there. Colonel Dignam spent time rocking back and forth on his heels, staring at the world map in her office, one son-in-law safe enough in Cairo, but the other was somewhere in the Pacific with Bull Halsey, kamikazes, and the hard slog that Okinawa promised.

Then it was over in Europe. German forces surrendered in one fraught week in May to Russians, to Allies, probably to privates on KP duty in kitchens. They were hungry, muddy, beaten, and done. Colonel Dignam joked that the B-25s produced that week should be carefully examined by Quality Control. "No one is paying attention," he explained, exulting over the news proclaimed over the plant's PA system.

Not thinking to ask permission, Ronnie went out of the office to the landing overlooking the production floor. For a blessed moment there was silence as the news penetrated, following by a roar of approval. Some of the Rosies stopped riveting and wept. One older man fell to his knees, whether in anguish or exultation she had no idea.

She looked down at the papers in her hand, signed by Colonel Dignam and approving of her increase in rank to corporal, with its fifteen dollar a month raise. She thought of her GI Bill packet somewhere in Washington by this time. She considered the life ahead of her without Ernie Brown in it and fought back her tears at the moment when the nation was erupting in joy.

She knew if she pressed hard enough with her tongue on the hard palate of her mouth, she could keep tears away. "Pops, I did my part," she whispered, when she could speak. "Ernie, now I will do yours."

Chapter Seventeen

Everyone knew the war wasn't over yet, not until the Japanese surrendered, but everything had changed. The air itself seemed charged with long-missing energy. It changed even more by the end of May, when the Army Air Force cancelled its production of short-range aircraft not suited to the vast expanses of the Pacific Ocean, that remaining theatre of war. Fifteen hundred workers were let go, but the long-range B-25s kept the production floor almost as busy as ever.

Colonel Dignam was one of those let go, as he put it with a smile. He held out the telegram to Ronnie when she arrived at work. "Here are my walking papers, Corporal Green," he said. "I'm now retired again. I'll still have time to drown a worm or two in the Buffalo River before winter comes."

"What will happen here, once you're gone?" Ronnie asked, feeling suddenly adrift. How dare he bail out and leave her alone in this office with years of papers filed away?

"I've already taken up the matter with Mr. Raynor," he said with a grin. "Be on your best behavior, corporal! You'll soon be working for the real boss, the guy who runs this place."

His looming departure didn't feel right. "Sir, I was hoping I'd be working for you until the end of the war," was the best she could do in protest, considering how monumentally he outranked her. Still, they had acquired a certain camaraderie she was going to miss.

His expression, generally serious anyway, grew more so. "Corporal Green, I requested this, and I'll tell you why. My wife is not in good health. I need to be in St. Louis." His eyes assumed that distant look she saw on other veterans' faces. "When I think of all the years she waited for me here, when I was out roaming the world…" She looked away when his eyes misted over. "I owe her."

Ronnie understood. "You do, sir. Colonel, I won't complain."

And she didn't, even though she cried when she said good night to him a week later, knowing he wouldn't be there in the morning. They had spent the last day going over an ever-lengthening list of tasks destined to keep her busy for months, if the government was really serious about archiving documents, bills, invoices and correspondence she doubted anyone would ever look at again.

She walked him to the Jeep which was taking him to the depot, the Jeep that had taken the two of them with death telegrams all around the far-flung production buildings, the same Jeep she had used to drive Ernie to the depot. One of the mechanics from the motor pool sat in the driver's seat this time.

Colonel Dignam returned the best salute Corporal Green had ever given anyone, then shook her hand. He followed that with a grandfatherly hug that dissolved her into tears. His voice was none too steady when he grasped her hand again. "Ronnie, we're in St. Louis. Stop in, maybe when you're on your way to Urbana, Illinois?"

She nodded, not certain that she would. As much as she admired her boss, she could already feel the door closing on ration books, boot camp reveille, highly polished pumps, war effort posters exhorting her best, Uncle Sam pointing at her, and maybe even on Sergeant Brown. To visit a civilian Colonel Dignam, might be a reminder she didn't want.

She steeled herself to go into work the next day and found it not so wrenching. She knew what to do when banker's boxes materialized from some distant warehouse, and she began to transfer files.

Only days later, eyes wide, her hand to her throat, she read the colonel's *Kansas City Times*' dispatch about the dropping of two super-secret bombs on Hiroshima and Nagasaki, a naval port. The surrender of the empire of Japan to Allied forces in the middle of August ended it all. The production floor erupted in joyful pandemonium as metal workers banged on aluminum sheets and a row of riveters started an impromptu conga line that wound around the partially completed aircraft. Tears in her eyes, Ronnie watched from the landing, shaking her head but giving them a thumbs up when they gestured for her to join them. She scanned the rows and rows of partially finished B-25s, wondering if they would even be completed, or tossed onto the scrap heap of history. History. That would have been Ernie's major at U of I.

Mr. Raynor sent them all home early that day to a more subdued and more than half-empty dorm. It was all so hard to bear, even as she joined Mrs. Dobbs in a beer toast, and laughed when the cafeteria manager shook her finger and said, "Just you wait. Next week we will have bananas again!"

"Chaz will be home before Christmas, I imagine," Ronnie said.

"I wish it were both sons," Mrs. Dobbs said quietly. She took Ronnie's hand. "I owe you an apology."

"For what?"

She wasn't prepared for what the cafeteria manager said. "I have watched you since Christmas become so silent, so…pensive." Mrs. Dobbs looked her in the eyes. "You loved him, didn't you? And here I was, congratulating you to be spared of great loss. Maybe I even envied you."

"Don't," Ronnie said, as tears filled her eyes. "I'm reconciled to it."

"No, you're not. You love him still."

Drat that Mrs. Dobbs. She saw through it all. Ronnie nodded, speechless. Mrs. Dobbs put her arm around her, and they stood in silence until the moment passed and calm returned.

"You told me you're going to college."

"Yes. I haven't been accepted yet, but…but…it'll be Ernie's school, the University of Illinois."

Mrs. Dobbs understood. "You'll do him proud."

"I owe him," she said to her reflection in the mirror as she prepared for bed.

Matters moved right along for North American Aviation. The morning after the surrender – Ronnie had already drawn a most unmilitary circle around Wednesday, August 15 on the office calendar – the PA system crackled to life with the first four notes of Beethoven's Fifth that had caught their attention for four years. Ronnie set down the 1941 files in her hand.

Mr. Raynor, the plant manager, cleared his throat and began. "'Men and women of North American Aviation. This day we have been fighting for since December 7, 1941 has come at last.'" She knew Mr. Raynor was not given to emotion, but she heard it in his voice, and remembered his three sons in various parts of the world. "Beg pardon. 'The world is finally free. We can now go back to our peacetime pursuits.'"

"Ponca City's five and dime?" Ronnie asked out loud. "Not on your life. What would Ernie say?"

She got up from her desk and went onto the short landing overlooking the production floor, where all work had stopped. She looked down two flights and saw the little figure of their boss, surrounded by workers. She leaned her elbows on the railing and knew she was witnessing history. They all were. The war was over.

He continued. "I've been directed to tell you that our B-25 contract is terminated." He looked around at his employees, already numbering far fewer than had worked here only last month. "Your department heads will direct what you will finish. By the end of next week, you will be given your last paycheck plus two weeks of severance." He looked beyond them all to the planes in their half-finished state, their war fought here in Kansas City. "What can I say. You have built…"

"Nah, it's we, Mr. Raynor. You made it happen, too," came a good-natured voice, which made everyone laugh.

He looked at them, really looked at them, visibly moved. "We did," Mr. Raynor said quietly. "We built nearly seven thousand B-25s. No one could have won without us."

It was the right touch. Ronnie looked closer at the workers around Mr. Raynor: the mail clerk with his Coke-bottle glasses and terrible vision that kept him out of the service; the young man on his pegleg, the result of an earlier farm injury that no recruiter could overlook; the Black Rosie the Riveter who never turned down overtime, because her husband was a galley cook on a carrier and they had California plans. They had all carried their own war to the Axis powers.

"The Ponca City girl eager to see the world," Ronnie whispered. "You needed me, too."

Mr. Raynor perked up visibly; he wasn't done yet. He tossed aside his papers and grinned. "We're still negotiating, but it looks like General Motors wants to lease this complex and build automobiles, starting this fall. I'll have application forms next week!"

The crew erupted in cheers and back slaps all around. Their top boss held up his hand. "I have no doubt that those of you who want work will still find it here. You've been well-trained. You can hold up your heads and work anywhere." He looked around. "Just tell the man who hires you that you trained at North American Aviation." He laughed. "Who knows? He might have piloted your plane over Berlin. You're a shoo-in!"

He left them laughing. Ronnie watched as they chatted in small groups then without any orders, returned to work, as she started toward her office. But here was Mr. Raynor beckoning to her, then puffing up the stairs. She waited.

"Was that the right touch, Corporal Green?" he asked, his eyes lively.

"Yes, sir," she said. "They'll all be employed again in no time."

"Indeed. Once the boys come home, this country will be on the grow." She felt a pang. Not all the boys.

"And you? What are your plans? I imagine a pretty girl like you has some."

She had to stop him before he asked if she had a sweetheart in uniform, she simply had to. "I'm going to college on the GI Bill, probably sometime next year," she said quickly.

"May I?" He followed her into the office and looked around at the already labelled boxes. "How much longer will it take you to finish up in here?"

"I could be done by the end of next week, sir."

He held out five letters to her. She looked closer to see the government stamp and felt that indescribable chill. "I...I don't think I can hand out death notices, sir."

"No, no," he said with a smile. "These are addressed to you five WACs still here, from your own Uncle Sam. I know it's something about termination, too. Hand them out for me, will you?"

She took them, seeing the letters for two nurses, the quality control corporal who had replaced Millie Sturdivant, a corporal who ran guest housing, and Corporal Veronica Green. "I will, sir."

He wasn't through. "I've been given permission by the powers that be to ask if you will give me a few more months of your time. I have a powerful lot to do – you know, those nuts and bolts and tidying up of loose ends." He held up his hand. "If it interferes with college, feel free to say no."

"I haven't been accepted yet," she said. *And no one else needs me*, she thought. "A few months?"

"That's all. You're good at what you do, and efficient. Finish up here next week, and pack your duffel. The barracks and mess hall are shutting down. You can move to posh digs in the guest house and help me until around Thanksgiving."

He gave her an inquiring look and Ronnie nodded. "Good! I'll put that in a memo to the next guy up the chain of command in my department."

He left with a wave of his hand. "Thanks. Those loose ends are calling my name."

She smiled and put the letters on her desk. *I have no loose ends to tidy up, Mr. Raynor,* she thought. *No one needs me. I can suit myself.*

The thought brought her no joy. All my love, Ronnie Green.

Chapter Eighteen

Ronnie finished up her war at North American Aviation the week of Thanksgiving. She eventually joined Mr. Raynor's voluminous files to the ones from her office, and sent them off to points unknown, probably to some gigantic warehouse with two keys that would eventually be misplaced, and no one would mind. Stuff has to go somewhere, but once that happens, who cares? She didn't.

Since the barracks was already being dismantled, she asked for and received permission to move her belongings into Room 11 of the NCO guest house, the room Ernie was going to occupy for one night, before orders from the 518th Battalion sent him back to Europe. The first night, she cried herself to sleep in the bed where he may have at least laid down for a nap. Maybe it was even the same pillow.

Mrs. Dobbs had stopped by Mr. Raynor's office before she left. "Chaz will be home before Christmas," she confided. "I got one Vmail with not a single *anything* blacked out. He's in London now, waiting for a transport."

Before Mrs. Dobbs left the office, she handed Ronnie a banana and they had a good laugh. "Maybe my boy can tell me if he ever saw one of these in England. *Someone* was eating them somewhere!" It was satisfying to laugh with Mrs. Dobbs, who would forever have one gold star in her window on Trinity Street in Newton, Kansas.

One of the WAC nurses decided to stay in the Army. She was already on her way to Letterman Hospital in San Francisco, and a full-to-overflowing rehab floor of men from the Pacific war with missing limbs. The other nurse, looking forward to working in a doctor's office in Cheyenne, Wyoming, teased her about finding a veteran with enough parts to keep her entertained.

The guest house coordinator was headed back to her father's tobacco farm in North Carolina. The corporal who had replaced Millie in Quality Control had complained loud and long about Millie's inattention to the details of her job. "I don't know where she's filed *anything*," was the lament, which only made Ronnie shrug.

The best moment came in early October, when she received an official packet from the University of Illinois Urbana-Champaign, welcoming her to the 1946 spring semester. She stared at it long and hard. Pops had never even finished the sixth grade. She hoped that in heaven he knew his only child was going to become a coed at a major university, thanks to the United States government, and maybe even thanks to a war that had turned her world – everyone's world – upside down.

Aunt Vi invited her to Ponca City for Thanksgiving. *'We're eager to show you all our plans for the place,'* her aunt wrote. *'Maybe the next time you visit, we'll even have a guest room for you!'*

It was a kind letter, even as it reminded Ronnie that she had no home of her own. She knew Vi and Bill would always welcome her, but she didn't live in Ponca City anymore.

Only days later came her separation papers from the U.S. Army, more forms to sign and return, and others to squirrel away. Maybe if she was lucky and found someone who delighted her heart as much as Ernie Brown had, she could tell her children and grandchildren what she had done in World War II. *The dustbin of history*, she thought, amused. *It wasn't glamorous, my lovelies, but it was my war.*

Saying goodbye to Mr. Raynor was easy. As kind as he was, even with the monumental task of running a factory of supreme importance to Allied success in overcoming the Axis powers, she still felt a pang every morning not to open the door on Colonel Dignam. She thanked Mr. Raynor for the extra few months of work, and wished him well at his next assignment, something about managing Beechcraft Aviation in Wichita. "We'll be manufacturing crop dusters and small planes," he said as he shook her hand. "Beating swords into plowshares and pruning hooks, eh? Major in accounting at that school of yours and I know I can find a place for you."

And that was that. Before Mr. Raynor's other secretary took her to the bus depot, Ronnie took a last look around her temporary quarters in the guest house. She touched the pillow one more time, this time for Sergeant

Ernest Brown, and closed the door on North American Aviation and the Women's Army Corps.

Everything she owned still fit in her duffel bag, which was heavy on her shoulder until another returning vet helped her with it on the Greyhound from Kansas City to Ponca City, Oklahoma, by way of all those same sleepy towns humbled by the Dust Bowl and Depression. She sensed a certain energy this time. Other vets, no WACs among them, sat here and there. Somehow, they gathered into a group of seats close by. Everyone introduced themselves, which meant the trip wasn't the drag she had dreaded.

Of course, everyone had many more adventures than she could ever claim. Despite this, she discovered something wonderful when she introduced herself by apologizing for being a mere clerk/typist at North American Aviation. One of the GIs let out a low whistle. He eyed her rank. "Corporal Green…"

"I'm just Ronnie Green now," she interrupted.

The GI – he must have been the life of any party – raised his voice. "Hey, how many of you sad sacks ever visited Berlin or Cologne, or maybe Tokyo courtesy of this little lady's B-25s?"

Ronnie looked around, startled, to see several hands go up. As she saw the smiles of recognition, the relief even, she sat up straighter, at the same time wishing with all her heart that Sergeant Ernie Brown, 518th MP Battalion, could see this, too.

A lieutenant in the seat in front of hers stuck out his hand. "Shake, little lady. I wouldn't be here if someone at your factory had slacked off on the rivets. Ted Reardon, Eighth Army Air Corps, headed home to my wife in Wichita." His face clouded over. "I mean it. I owe you."

Something happened when she shook his hand, something that changed her life forever. She could have protested and said he should thank the Rosies who riveted, or the electricians or the sheet metal men, but she understood finally what Ernie had tried to tell her earlier about wartime service. To Lt. Reardon, *she* was the Mitchell bomber. To these fellow servicemen, united in a hard slog, *she* was that WAC on that poster, stars in her eyes, flag waving behind her.

"You're welcome, lieutenant," she said simply. "I'm glad my B-25s did you proud. I imagine you'll be happy to forget all of this."

"Whaddya think, guys?" He grinned at the others, those who might have also seen the same view from his office thousands of feet over Berlin.

"I'm no prophet, but I'll make you a prediction. Give us thirty or forty years, and you'll see sky jockeys like me finding and refurbishing those old warbirds." He motioned with a placating gesture to the hoots and eyerolls. "Not today or tomorrow, guys, but someday we'll fly our B-25s and B-17s again at airshows. Mark my word. All right. All right," he said, cheerfully. "Give it a few years, ok?"

He turned his smile on Ronnie, even as she laughed inside to think there was an eager wife waiting to see *that* look trained on her. "And you, little corporal, can come to those airshows and tell your grandkiddies about *your* war." A chaste kiss to her cheek, and he turned around and bowed while the others clapped and cheered.

So it went all the way to Ponca City, with its changes, and stops and starts, and layovers as more and more vets got on, then got off, as the Greyhound stopped at their own little towns. From bustling Topeka to little Miller, to even smaller El Dorado, the returning veterans stopped at wide spots in the road that they must have dreamed of during low level bombings of Ploesti oil fields, or in malarial New Guinea, or even – she understood now – from prosaic stateside induction centers at Fort Drum or Fort Lauderdale.

She watched them throw their arms around wives and bewildered children. No matter where their duty took them, they had won. She knew as never before they were all equal in the sight of Mars, the god of war, even her. And thus Ronnie Green's war ended, too.

Two days later at dusk, weary, frowsy and a bit stale herself, she dragged up the two steps to the house Pops had built outside of Ponca City for his new bride, the mother Ronnie never knew. With a cry of delight, Aunt Vi pulled her inside, calling for Bill to get Ronnie's duffel bag. In mere minutes, she was seated in Pops's old chair, her shoes off, her stockinged feet on the hassock, and a sandwich in her hand.

The only real difference was new wallpaper and a better carpet underfoot, plus she got to sleep in the room that had formerly been Ant Vi's, instead of on the sofa. The other difference was much sweeter.

Aunt Vi was pregnant. Aunt Vi who had always seemed so old-maidish and proper had a rounded belly. She even blushed when Uncle Bill left the room for something, and Ronnie, swallowing her own sudden envy, blew her a kiss and asked, "When?"

"Probably around Easter," Vi said, her eyes on the door to the kitchen where Bill had gone. "I know I'm too old for this..."

"Obviously not," Ronnie replied, enjoying the moment.

"Ronnie, I'm forty-one," Vi whispered, then giggled. "My brother would be scandalized."

She thought of Pops, a quiet man who had lost so much when his wife died and never recovered, or cared to. "He would be delighted and so am I."

Thanksgiving followed the next day, their table graced by an overlarge chicken with stuffing. Uncle Bill promised that things would be back to normal by 1946 and there would be a turkey, and sweet potatoes gooey with marshmallows, marshmallows having disappeared along with bananas.

Neither of them understood why she had decided on the University of Illinois, and not an Oklahoma school, until Aunt Vi sat with her in the porch swing although it was too cold, and Ronnie told her about Ernie.

"It's something I want to do," she said, toeing the swing along, something she had done with Vi since she was a little girl and they Needed To Talk about stuff that would have embarrassed Pops. "He can't be there, but I will. I can't explain it better than that."

"You loved him, even though...." Aunt Vi let the thought dangle.

Vi didn't quite get it. *Loved him?* Ronnie thought. *Love him.*

Chapter Nineteen

Over the protests of Vi and Bill, Ronnie packed her duffel life into a suitcase that had been her mother's and left for the University of Illinois the second week after Thanksgiving. Her few civilian clothes went into the suitcase, too, looking dowdy and out of place.

She would have stayed longer, but a letter from Colonel Dignam in St. Louis changed her plans. He began by telling her he had no news about Sergeant Brown, but he could put her in touch with someone in Urbana, a cousin, who might have a spare bedroom. *Corporal Green, you should read the nightmare stories in the Post-Dispatch about no housing large enough for church mice, let alone people,* she read.

Truth to tell, it was time to leave Ponca City. Beyond new wallpaper in the parlor, Vi and Bill shared their plans for two new rooms on the house, and a garage to replace the barn – it was falling down – where Pops had kept a cow and a car in equanimity. It was no longer her house, anyway. She sent a telegram to Colonel Dignam, visited her parents in the cemetery, promised Vi she would send an address when she had one, kissed them both and left on the morning bus.

She wore her uniform again, and her military overcoat, because her civilian clothes were too shabby, and her civvy overcoat not even warm enough for Oklahoma. How had she managed, all those years? She enjoyed the camaraderie on the bus and then the train, listening to others' war stories, sharing her own shyly at first, and then with more assertion because everyone loved her B-25s.

The Dignam's house was a delight, decorated inside and out, because Mrs. Dignam believed in wringing every last ounce of fa-la-la-la-la out of Christmas, especially one with her retired-again husband there, and not in some dusty outpost or airplane factory.

St. Louis was lit up and ready to enjoy the first Christmas without rationing and bad news. True, there were still shortages and nylons were just as hard to find, but Ronnie threw herself into the holiday shopping frenzy at Stix, Baer & Fuller and its eight floors of everything a person needed. Her wardrobe improved beyond her wildest imaginings. Bolstered by her house sale, her GI Bill vouchers, and her last few months of corporal's pay, she shopped without a qualm.

"You'll find some handsome aviator in your new dresses," Mrs. Dignam assured her, as they ate French onion soup and black raspberry pie at nearby Famous-Barr. She put her hand to her mouth and giggled. "I didn't mean it like that!" They laughed together, happy that Colonel Dignam had bowed out of accompanying the ladies downtown, and Mrs. Dignam felt well enough to shop.

I needed this, Ronnie thought that night as she packed her new clothes in a new suitcase. She decided not to tell Mrs. Dignam that her favorite purchase was two pairs of wool trousers that would match her more-practical Army brogans. She hoped the University of Illinois wasn't a stuffy place, and didn't mind ladies in trousers.

Her last night in St. Louis – the Dignams insisted she stay for Christmas, but she demurred – found her comfortable in bed, staring at the ceiling, and going over her usual ritual of assuring Ernie that she would do her best in college, even as she wished he lay beside her. She thought of the servicemen returning home, sighed this time without tears, and slept.

The train took her to Chicago – too cold, too big, too windy – and then down to Urbana-Champaign on Christmas Day. She was a woman on her own, not through choice. A cosmic hand had shuffled the cards for millions of women like her, and she was ready to make the best of a bad hand. She knew it could have been a worse hand, and settled for that scrap of wisdom.

She didn't mind Christmas Eve spent in Chicago's train depot, a drafty cavernous affair hung with wreaths and smelling of cider and cinnamon. All three restaurants gave out free hot cider. She ate turkey in one, and rare roast beef in another, and contented herself with a full belly as she watched people. She was by herself, and would be, until she found some man she loved as much as Ernie Brown, but the pain was gone. Even if no one ever knew how much she loved that man she never dated once, she knew she was in good company. Lots of houses in lots of small towns and big cities had gold stars in the windows. Ronnie stored hers in her heart.

The train heading south was late. She had all those wonderful clothes in her suitcase, and still the army uniform felt better. Habit gravitated her toward other GIs, especially since this group contained what looked like a Navy nurse and another WAC, still relatively rare. Her shyness had left her back in that Greyhound in Kansas. Soon she was telling her little war story about North American Aviation, confident there would be at least one airman in the gathering.

Sure enough. Maybe she needed that appreciative nod, that testimonial in someone's eyes that the B-25s would always reign supreme. She settled in to listen to other stories going on between two groups.

"That's what they called it, the Battle of the Bulge," she heard, and knew which group to join. "Don't let anyone tell you it was just a catchy name. We suffered." She sat, scarcely breathing, listening to a firsthand account of cold, frostbite, starvation, surprise and terror. *Good God, good God*, she thought. The others were silent, too, listening to this former 101st paratrooper describe all the misery and mud that turned into snow and blood.

"Didya ever corner a hungry dog?" the paratrooper asked them at large. "That was us. No way were we going to be captured and die like those poor guys at Malmédy." He shook his head a little too vehemently. The Navy nurse put her hand on his arm and kept it there, which took away some of the wildness from his eyes. Not all.

Ronnie thought of Colonel Dignam's eyes, suddenly solemn, when she told him her last Vmail had been dated December 17, two days before Malmédy, followed by nothing more. "I remember Malmédy from the Great War. It's a crossroads, Private Green," he had said, before they had even heard the worst. "That's where you find MPs."

"Malmédy?" someone asked in the group.

"More than one hundred dogfaces were surprised by a Panzer division and had no choice but to surrender." Ronnie heard all the bitterness. "Trouble was, it was an SS division. Mowed down in a field like wheat, so we heard. A few escaped. I hope somebody pays for that at Nuremberg. You know, those trials that just started."

Were you there, Ernie? she asked herself. *Will I ever know?*

The talk turned to other theatres of war, other equally charged moments in someone's war. Soon, she was able to slip away to sit quietly with her own thoughts until the call for Illinois Central Railroad and points south sent her to the right platform. She enjoyed a nice moment then, when two girls – sisters from the look of them – tried to be unobtrusive as they stared at her uniform. Amused, she watched them whisper to their mother then approach her.

The older of the two held out her hand. "Thank you for your service," the child whispered, then ducked her head, overcome with shyness.

"I would do it again," Ronnie said. She smiled. "Maybe someday you might want to enlist. Women are always needed." *That poster in Ponca City said 239 jobs for women*, she thought, remembering without sorrow this time.

"I might," the little girl said, then hurried back to her mother.

Rain turned to snow when they approached Rantoul, slowed and stopped to let off Christmas shoppers laden with presents from the big city. As the train chugged away, she admired the town's tidy streets and other shoppers, uniformed men among them. She knew there was an airbase at Rantoul because Ernie had mentioned one. She wondered how many of those bases would begin closing, winking out like streetlamps at morning, now that America's great national emergency was over.

A matter of minutes brought them to Urbana, where it was her turn to disembark with her two suitcases, bulging now (thanks to St. Louis and the Dignams), with a college wardrobe any coed would envy. Even though he used a cane and struggled, a sailor helped her to the street. On the curb and eyeing a cab, she took out the address and asked, "Do you know Urbana? I'm looking for this address."

"Fifty-five Elm? Mrs. Dignam. She's a dragon." He grinned. "We never soap her windows on Halloween." He motioned to the cab. "Ride with me and I'll drop you off. Mrs. Dignam's place is a few blocks before my home." He pointed to his own duffel, much smaller than Ronnie's had been, except that there was a strange sword attached to it. "A kamikaze took out our destroyer at Okinawa," he told her. "I lost everything except this sword I, uh, found on Ie Shima. No way I was leaving that behind when the ship sank!"

He introduced himself in the cab. "Are you going to the university, Corporal Green?" he asked, after she gave her name and after he eyed her uniform.

"Yes. I'm just Miss Green," she said, then smiled. "It's harder than I thought it would be to stop wearing khaki."

"Or Navy blues," he added with his own smile. "Maybe I'll see you on campus."

"Maybe you will. Thanks for the lift," she said when the cab slowed in front of a modest-looking two-story house.

He winked, which made Ronnie smile inside. Sailors. "See you around campus?" Then she saw his pride. "I'm going, too."

"You never know." No. She could do better. "I'd say the chances are good. Merry Christmas."

Contrary to what the Navy said, Mrs. Dignam was no more a dragon than her cousin, Ronnie's former boss. Yes, she did have that extra bedroom, and it was hers for the renting. True, Mrs. D (as she preferred to be called), had fended off four other potential renters who had heard through the grapevine about a spare room. Things were like that in Urbana, now that GIs were heading to college in huge numbers.

"Phil told me you'd be a good tenant, so yes, let's make a deal. It's twenty-five dollars a month, plus ten dollars more, if you'd like breakfast and supper, too." Her chin went up and Ronnie saw the pride. "I'm a good cook."

"I would love that, Mrs. D," Ronnie said, laughing inside to think that anyone on earth called the dignified Colonel Dignam Phil. Perfect. Thirty-five dollars a month, and her voucher allowed for fifty.

The room was ideal, the armchair comfortably lived in, the bed soft, with a serious-looking desk and empty bookcase. She liked the padded window seat most of all, knowing she could spend a lot of time reading there.

Between Christmas and New Year's Day, she walked around the Illini campus, snow-covered and buttoned up for winter. "I'm here, Pops," she whispered. She wanted to say, "I made it, Ernie," out loud. Maybe later, after she scrubbed away another layer or two of sadness.

On the day before official class registration, she took the Illinois Central north for the short journey to Rantoul. The high school was already in session, so she went inside for no particular reason, except that Ernie had attended and more than likely walked up these steps many times. There was a trophy case in the main hallway, looking remarkably like the one at Ponca City High School – nothing overly flashy, no state football or basketball teams. She looked closer at the 1938 football team. There he was: Ernest Brown, senior, on the back row, second from the left, looking determined. She could imagine the photographer telling them to look determined for posterity. She could also imagine, if Rantoul were anything like Ponca City, that the Depression already assured that. No one needed to tell anyone to look determined, or stalwart.

"Weren't we all," she murmured, then left the building.

After lunch at a cafe on the main street, Ronnie asked the cashier where the cemetery was located.

"Honey, if you're looking for Catholics, go to St. Malachy," the woman said. She shrugged. "That's mostly everyone."

She hadn't asked Ernie what church he attended. Everyone in Ponca City was either Baptist or Assembly of God, so the Catholics remained mysterious and vaguely pagan. Ronnie had been on a few dates in her life, and a few more in those last few months before she left North American Aviation, but religion never came up. That must be something that waited until much later in the dating life.

"Where is St. Malachy?" she asked.

The cashier pointed. "You can't miss it." Maybe there was something in Ronnie's expression that softened her own. "You looking for someone in particular, honey?"

"Not really," Ronnie said. "Well, are there any Browns around here anymore?"

"Just in the cemetery," came the kindlier answer. "Father Groening has gone to Chicago for the holiday, but you'll find a little gatehouse with a list of names."

She found the gatehouse as snow began to settle on her army overcoat. She ran her finger down the list, stopping with an intake of breath at Ernst Brown, then letting it out when she noticed February 15, 1926. She wondered if that was Ernie's father, the man who had changed his family name during World War I. Right underneath that name was Helen Brown, with a death date of four years ago, Ernie's mother. *You dear ones*, she thought, thinking of her own.

The instructions were easy to follow. She found the right row and walked down it slowly, seeing some Brauns, and then Browns. She stopped at Ernst Brown, noting his place of birth as Dresden, Germany, a city she knew had been terribly fire-bombed only two years ago. And there was Helen next to him.

Someone had placed a Christmas wreath on each grave. She admired the wreaths, wondering if Ernie had any living relatives nearby, then righted the one on his father's grave. The wind must have blown it over. Maybe she would come around Easter and leave flowers.

Yes. She would return with flowers.

Chapter Twenty

Class registration was an ordeal all its own, reinforcing, as nothing else could have, the lowly life of a freshman at the University of Illinois. "I'd rather hit a beach in the Marianas," Ronnie heard one ex-Marine mutter as he stood behind her in the Freshman English 101 line.

The best she could do in that line was Monday, Wednesday, and Friday at 8 a.m. in Harker Hall, where she also had American History, ditto days, place and 10 a.m.

The Marine knew more about the university than she did. She also liked the fragrance of his aftershave when he looked over her shoulder. "Room 24. Everyone calls it the Harker Snake Pit," he said, as they stood in another line, the textbook one. "I hope you're not subject to vertigo."

"Meaning…"

He was joined by another veteran. They were everywhere. "You'll see! I was with the Tenth Mountain Division in Italy, so I'm fine," the new arrival said. "See you in the Pit next week."

• • •

Ooh. That's what he meant. On Monday, Ronnie stared down the row of steps, the Ilini version of an amphitheater. It was hardly something she wanted to face at 7:55 in the morning on the first day of class. A child of the Great Plains, she knew towering mountains would intimidate her. Apparently, so did deep valleys.

The Pit filled rapidly, so she joined the throng in the descent to higher education, turning in at a row halfway down with a seat or two left toward the middle. Her row was close enough to see the professor without squinting, and far enough away not to risk falling onto his podium if she lost her balance.

She sat next to another coed on purpose. A few days on campus had already indicated numerous returning servicemen not shy about introducing themselves and asking her out, almost in the same breath. Touched and flattered at the same time, she had turned down two former GIs, then agreed to ice cream and a walk around the campus last night with a Seabee.

Over a malt, he had shared his work with her of building runways under fire at Guadalcanal, and declared maybe he could aim a little higher with an engineering degree. When she mentioned her more-modest goal of accounting, he nodded.

"You the first in your family to try college?" he asked.

"Pops finished the sixth grade," she told him.

"Farther than my old man got," the former Seabee said. "And here we are." He looked around at younger students, none of them old enough to have slogged through jungles under fire. "We don't look like them, do we?"

Ronnie had no trouble answering him. "We look better."

Here we are in the snake pit. She thought about that as she opened her notebook, smiled at the woman seated beside her, and introduced herself. *I will meet amazing people here*, she thought, after they shared names and smiles. She looked at the clock at the same time the professor raised his hand for everyone's attention, and shared *his* name.

"Welcome to this monstrous mob," he said, to good-natured laughter. "We knew there would be a lot of you GIs this second semester, but my goodness, who is minding the store?"

We are, Ronnie thought with pride. She sat back, suddenly wishing she could write a Vmail to Ernie, sharing this moment that he should have had. This was no time for tears, but her eyes welled up. She swallowed down the emotion and told herself that she could write a letter to Ernie every day, if she chose, sharing her college life. For the umpteenth time, she wondered if she would even be here, if he hadn't encouraged her. She owed him a bona fide letter every day, one that she could put in a binder and maybe read at the end of each semester.

Now was the time to pay attention. "…and as you know, this is one of many required courses we will inflict upon you." The professor put his hand to his eyes like a visor and looked up at what must have seemed like a sea of faces staring down at him. "Although I will say that if you are anything like the classes I taught last fall, when many of you started here, you already know what you want to do."

Ronnie saw other students nodding. She knew she was looking at a generation hardened by a depression and a world war, who had seen and done things no earlier classes at this university or any university had seen and done before. *We know what we want*, she thought, deeply aware that every moment here was going to be a gift, courtesy of the U.S. government. And Ernie Brown.

The professor juggled sheets of paper. "I have before me a roster," he informed them. "If I were to call attendance at every class session, there wouldn't be time for my lectures on sentence structure, the parts of speech, or diagramming sentences, now would there?"

General laughter. "Just for my edification, I'd like to know just how many of you are here on the GI Bill. Show of hands, please."

Hands went up, hers among them. They looked around at each other, and she heard a low murmur of recognition, perhaps not of people – who knew anyone in a snake pit? – but of a shared experience unlike any other. *I belong here*, Ronnie thought. Her heart lifted in an anatomically impossible way. She had started this journey as a tribute to the man she loved. It became her journey now.

The professor scanned the rows, nodding. "Men *and* women? This is a new generation of soldiers," he said. He adjusted his glasses and took a firmer grip on the roll. "Here we go. A raised hand is sufficient unto the day."

"Ainsworth. Appleton. Astle. Babcock. Barnes. Bletchley. Bowen. Brown. Buchanan."

Ronnie stopped drawing bullseyes, felt something in her heart between pain and longing, then reminded herself that there would be a lifetimes of Browns on lists. It was a name as common as Green. She rested her chin on her palm and continued the bullseye. She wondered what Mrs. Dignam had planned for dinner. Yesterday's Sunday pot roast exceeded all expectations.

"Fogarty. Franklin. Freund. Gaultier. Giddings. Grady. Green." The professor shuffled another paper. "I have here two Greens: Edward Green. Thank you, sir. Veronica Green."

Ronnie raised her hand and her life changed.

"Oh God!" she heard from above her in the snake pit. She turned around, stared up at Sergeant Ernest Brown staring down at her, and quietly fainted for the first time in her life.

The middle of the row in a snake pit is an awkward place to faint. She came around quickly enough as the man seated directly below her in the snake pit turned around, announced he had been a corpsman with the First Marine Division, and fanned her vigorously with the course outline, while placing an expert finger on the pulse in her neck. The GI on the other side of her gently helped her into a sitting position, while the woman seated beside her made sure her skirt was relocated modestly at her knees instead of above.

When the dizziness passed, she looked up to that top row again. It really was Ernie, much thinner, yes, but there was no mistaking that face so dear to her. He stared back and tried to say something, then leaned toward the student next to him, who nodded and helped him to his feet.

He needed help; she could tell that. She saw the cane. The professor did, too. With an agility belying more mature years than all of his students, he bounded up the steps to her row and motioned for her to join him. The corpsman in the row below climbed into her row and helped her thread her way to the aisle, where the professor put his arm around her shoulder. The corpsman took no hint and kept his grip around her waist.

"I think I'll be all right now," she told him, her face red. Ronnie Green had spent her whole life staying out of the limelight, and here she was, part of a scene that no one in this entire snake pit was likely to ever forget. "I'm sorry for this, sir."

"Do you *know* that man up there?" the professor asked in a soft voice.

"Yes, I do, sir," she assured him. "He owes me a huge explanation. I thought he was dead."

Maybe the professor realized that in a lifetime of pounding knowledge into fertile brains or otherwise, he might have finally seen it all. He rose to the occasion anyway. "Miss...Miss."

"I'm Veronica Green."

Sergeant Ernie Brown stood at the top of the steps now, leaning on a cane. Another word to the men helping him and they backed him away from the precipice. Veronica turned to the professor. "I will be all right now," she said, "and I'll be here Wednesday, but maybe not in the same row. It depends on the explanation I get from Sergeant Brown."

Chapter Twenty-one

"I admire your fortitude! I'll give you your Wednesday assignment right now. I want two pages with something about you, and why you're here." He coughed delicately. "In your case, I might wish for a few more pages."

"You'll have it, sir." *No matter what*, she thought, as she let go of the professor and started up the steps, the corpsman not loosening his grip, which relieved her, because she was more unsteady than she cared to admit.

"Wowsa, Miss Veronica Green," the corpsman said. "You'd better share this whole story with all of us."

"You're cheeky," she teased.

"I'm a Navy man," he returned with a grin, confident that explained everything. He handed her over to Sergeant Brown, the man she had never thought to see again, the man she knew was dead, the man she had loved and lost and quietly mourned, because she had no claim on him whatsoever: no dates, no promise, no ring, no anything. She had nothing but love at first sight, which everyone knew was improbable in the extreme, even her, until it happened. Here he stood, considerably worse for wear, and leaning heavily on a cane.

He looked so unsteady that she put her arm around *his* waist, saddened to feel his sparse frame where once had been that Military Policeman kind of muscle. The corpsman pointed to a sofa beside a bulletin board. "Slow and easy," was all he said, which meant Ernie flashed him that familiar grin and reoriented Ronnie's entire world.

Ernie sat down with a small sigh, giving Ronnie some idea how difficult his journey had been. Whether it was the journey from Belgium, or only the journey to Harker Hall, she wasn't certain, but she suspected both.

"Thank you so much," she told the corpsman, who grinned, gave them a salute, and returned to the snake pit. In another moment, she heard the professor continuing with the roll call.

Ernie put his arm around her shoulders, and she settled closer, relieved all out of proportion to any emotion she had ever felt. Her head went to his chest.

She felt him tense. "Ponca City," he said suddenly. "Ponca City! That's it! The doctors said it would come back to me, but Ronnie, I gave up." He rested his head against hers. "Forgive me."

"You mean, you mean, you honestly didn't *know*?" she asked, sitting up, the better to see him. The disappointment on his face when she left his embrace would have broken her heart last Christmas, before her heart had been broken over and over until nothing was left.

She reconsidered. Almost nothing. She took a good look at his eyes, seeing past the thousand-yard stare into the eyes of the Ernie she remembered. "What happened to you was that bad." It was not a question.

He nodded. His eyes on hers, he took his cane and tapped it against his right leg. She heard the hollow sound. "That was the easy part," he told her. "C'mere again."

She relaxed into his arms once more. "We could find a more private place to talk."

"I agree, but just getting this far across campus turned out to be harder than I thought it might be. I have a ways to go, but maybe not at this moment."

It was a small bit of droll humor, but she heard the old Ernie.

"Jergens," he said, as he brought her hand to his lips and kissed it. "After I was on a plane to England, the flight nurse's hands smelled of Jergens lotion, and I started to remember things."

Ronnie decided not to interrupt him, beyond a pat to his chest when he faltered in telling of standing at the Baugnez crossroads two miles south of Malmédy and directing tank traffic, as units fled toward Bastogne in a snowstorm. "I stood that post for hours," he said. He touched his temple and she noticed a scar.

"The Germans shot you?"

"Nothing that glamorous. One of the tanks threw out a rivet that glanced off my helmet. I woke up at an aid station. My right foot was frozen. Couldn't feel a thing." He tapped his hollow leg. "Still can't."

To laugh or not to laugh? Ronnie laughed just a quiet laugh, a testing-the-water-laugh. Ernie's grin relieved her heart.

Ronnie snuggled closer. "The last Vmail I received from you was dated December 17." She took a chance. "Do you remember what you wrote?"

His expression softened, and a smile played around his lips. "I do remember that. The corporal was waiting for me to give him that letter." He chuckled, and she felt his good humor returning. "I could tell he didn't want to argue with an MP. I was due at that road crossing in five minutes. AML, All My Love. Who forgets that?"

"I didn't," Ronnie said. "Better keep talking, Sarge. I don't mind arguing with an MP."

That did it. He laughed out loud and relieved her heart in places she hadn't known existed. "You, uh, plan to tell me what to do, Miss Green?" he teased.

"If you need it, Mr. Brown," she assured him, on firmer ground now. "Keep talking."

He was silent more than a few heartbeats. "The tank battalion had to bust out fast. Someone strapped me to a tank because I couldn't walk." He leaned his head against the sofa back. "We learned later that we missed Pieper's Panzer group by mere minutes, the ones that massacred the guys near Malmédy. I hope that man burns in a hot place someday." He sighed. "At least the Panzergruppen that stopped us just before Bastogne wasn't SS. All they did was capture us and send us marching to a *stalag*."

She knew the word, remembering one of the sheet metal workers at North American Aviation whose son was a prisoner of war in Germany, and allowed a letter home now and then, courtesy of the Red Cross.

"They stuck us in a boxcar. Two men froze one night while we sat at a sidelined track."

He said nothing more, only shook his head. Ronnie went to the drinking fountain she had noticed down the hall, complete with little cone-shaped water cups and filled one for Ernie. He downed it with gratitude.

"The Allies bombed the train another day. Those of us who survived were told to walk. I couldn't by then. The frostbite…"

"They left you there?"

"They were going to shoot me, Ronnie. The lieutenant had his pistol out. He stuck it in my ear." Ernie shuddered and she put her arm across his chest.

"What on earth changed his mind?" she asked.

"I did what I should have done from the beginning. I spoke to him in German. Told him if he kept me alive, I could translate for all of us. They had no English speakers, which was starting to tell on the lieutenant's nerves." He let out a gust of air. "He shouldered his sidearm and told the others to carry my stretcher. Twenty hard kilometers to that *stalag*, snowing all the way. I don't know how they did it."

"I didn't know what had happened to you and couldn't find out anything," Ronnie said into the quiet. To her surprise, other students were listening. The class had let out, and there they were, listening. "You had to be next of kin to know anything, and I was nothing."

"Not to me," he said quickly. "Never to me." He looked at the listeners. "This is where you folks move along. Nothing to see here. I'm not a former MP for nothing."

"Kiss her, Sarge," someone said, and they all laughed, including her sarge.

"I plan to, but without all of you around," Ernie replied. He returned his attention to Ronnie. "Should we humor them with an update on Wednesday, when this class reconvenes?"

She nodded, too shy for words. She felt the good-natured humor of the moment, contrasting so remarkably with the story of war and misery that Ernie still needed to tell.

In a few minutes, it was just the two of them. "Wh…what happened in the …"

"*Stalag*?" He tightened his grip on her shoulder. "Conditions were as you imagine. They had no food for us, or for themselves, for that matter. We all starved together." He took a deep breath. "I went to the infirmary and a week later, a visiting surgeon took off my leg about mid-calf." He started to shake. "There was no anesthesia, just him and me and a lot of screaming."

God forgive me when I whine. Ronnie kissed his cheek. Another class filed into the snake pit. Soon she heard the same professor begin his introduction. "How long were you in that *stalag*?"

"As near as I recall, from early December to the middle of April. At least I think so. I was already having trouble with my memory." His tone turned wistful. "Dear God, I was forgetting what I wanted to remember. I wish I could forget the *stalag*."

"But you interpreted?"

"*Ja wohl, meine fraulein.* I never left the infirmary, but I interpreted for everyone." He nudged her then. "It's nice to have an extraterrestrial power like Superman. What's yours?"

"I am constant," she said softly.

He kissed her and she clung to him. It was the kiss from the Jeep, so many months ago. It ended too soon, but it was a long-enough kiss – one that promised more, because everything had changed.

"You need to keep going," she said, breathless now, but agreeably so.

"Not here! I wouldn't dare," he replied. "Oh, you mean the explanation." They shared a look of good humor, until his expression changed. "We were turning into skeletons, and I am including the guards," he said. "In commandants, we were luckier than most. Lieutenant Friederik Schutz wasn't more enlightened, but shall we say he was more skeptical than others of his brethren in higher command."

"Had you any idea what was going on?"

"More than he did, I think. Someone had smuggled in a radio, so we knew the Russians and the Allies were both coming our way. That's where things got grim."

She stared at him. "I think it's already grim enough."

He gave her the look that an indulgent German shepherd might give a rambunctious pup. "Veronica, I can't promise you the moon and stars, but I will promise you that you will never know that kind of suffering."

She accepted that, but he needed to know. "I had my own suffering." She put her fingers to his lips. "I'll tell you about it….I'll tell you tonight, because you are going to take me on an actual date. You will take me to dinner – I don't care where – then we will find a quiet spot somewhere."

"It *would* be a good idea to have a date, wouldn't it, before I…"

"Before you what?" she asked, but she knew. She had always known.

"Before I ask you to limp through life with me," he said, his voice no longer tentative, but more like the self-assured military policeman she had met on a Greyhound bus.

With painful clarity, Ronnie remembered the dark days of January when she knew he was dead and she would never know more. Compared to the horror of his war, her own sorrowful uncertainty sounded puny to her. Still, it was her story, a woman's story. It would keep, as so many things did for women, because she knew this was his time to talk.

"Sarge, you'd better tell me how grim."

Chapter Twenty-two

Her permission opened the floodgates. "Since I had been interpreting and translating for *Leutnant* Schutz, we struck up an odd relationship. I could almost call it a friendship, well, a wary one." That far-off look returned to his eyes. "I wonder every day where he is."

"Please tell me what happened."

He held her hand. "You're an impatient one, missy. It's hard to talk about this, but three days before – well, before – he came to the infirmary, looking white about the mouth and beyond grim, as if he had been given an unpleasant duty."

He was squeezing her hand too tight, but she said nothing. "He told me that he had been instructed to kill all of us PWs. He and the guards were to join the few troops in nearby Koblenz for a final stand for the glory of the Third Reich. He took out his Luger." He shuddered, the memory too fresh.

When his silence went on too long, she squeezed his hand in turn. "You're here, so clearly that didn't happen. What *did* happen?"

"I talked him out of it." He managed a shaky laugh. "I was as fluent as…as… Goethe. I begged him to leave us alive. I promised him a letter signed by…I can't recall his name – the camp's highest-ranking PW – that we had not been mistreated, and there should be no retribution against Leutnant Schutz. I assured him that the Americans would look on such a statement with fairness, and we could tell our liberators that in person, if we were allowed to live. I couldn't promise him anything of the sort if the Russians got to the *stalag* first. I told him it would be the good thing, the Christian thing, to spare us."

"And he listened."

"I assured Schutz that whatever happened, his chances were far better

118

with the Allies than the Russians. I told him the war was over, but he could save his men if *they* left. I said there was nothing he could do for Hitler now, but he could save the lives of his own men, with such a letter."

They both jumped when the buzzer rang and the nine o'clock class climbed out of the snake pit. Ronnie held out her class schedule. "History 101 in the pit next, Sarge," she told him. "Back I go."

"I'm in here, too," he said, taking his schedule from his coat pocket. "The best I can do is that top row of seats."

"Perfect. May I help you up?"

She thought he might say no, but he nodded. "Just get me by the elbow. That's it. Up I go. I'm getting better."

She saw pain in his eyes. "Better than you were?" she asked.

He nodded as he concentrated on moving toward the snake pit. "I spent the last three months in Washington, DC, where there are a bunch of hospitals. Told'um I was enrolled here, and classes started the first week in January, so could we move this rehab right along?"

"In your best MP voice?" she teased.

"I'm here, aren't I?"

He managed well enough, after that first step into the pit, edging along the top row into the center, where he had sat before. He didn't object when she steadied him. Once seated, she watched the other students, noticing how many of them, like her sergeant, still wore their uniforms, or at least portions of them. She thought of President Franklin Roosevelt, that frail man, that giant of a leader, who had implemented the Servicemen's Readjustment Act, and hoped that he knew, somehow, that many Ernies and Ronnies were going to change the world because of it.

"I'd better hurry with this," Ernie said in a lower voice. "The next morning, I woke up and all the guards were gone. The others told me the gates were left open wide."

"And the lieutenant?"

"I have no idea what happened to him. I wish I did. I owe him my life." As others took their places in the snake pit and a different professor walk down to the front, he continued, "We starved for a few more days – nothing new – and thank God the Americans beat the Russians to us. The infirmary…"

He closed his eyes. Nothing else was needed for Ronnie to imagine a ward of dying patients with no dressing changes, no medicine, no food.

"The other prisoners were in no shape to help you in the infirmary, were they?" she asked tentatively, wanting to know, fearing that she already did.

"It was no better in the camp, I am told. They were maybe worse off than we were in that ward. Some GIs and Tommies had been there for three years. We only had the privilege of starving for four months, but at least they could make their way to the privies. That is all I am saying about what the tank company saw when they found us." Again the pause. She waited. "Well, found *me*. I was the only one alive in the infirmary when help came."

He leaned back. His expression softened when he described that first meal of K rations, followed by confiscated schnapps from someone's stash. He had been flown somewhere – was it Paris? – and operated on again, this time with anesthesia. The surgeon amputated higher this time, closer to his knee. "I surprised them all by living," Ernie said with quiet satisfaction. "I couldn't remember anything worth beans, but the doctors assured me my memory, most of it anyway, would gradually come back."

The professor raised his hand for order. Ernie turned to her and whispered, "But you. You're *here*. Ronnie, I sent you a letter in December, addressed to North American Aviation. It came back, Return to Sender. I didn't know what to do then, because I couldn't remember much more."

"The factory closed in September. I worked for Mr. Raynor until the middle of November. I believe General Motors is opening it up very soon to build Chevys. I spent Thanksgiving in Ponca City."

"Ponca City," he murmured, "Ponca City."

"Well, well, more GIs," the professor was saying. "I trust you intend to let me fight the battles in here! We'll probably start with Pontiac's War. I am Dr. Driscoll, and I drive a Ford, not a Pontiac."

"I'll keep," Ronnie whispered in Ernie's ear.

He gave her a searching look at that, which made her blush. "I maybe didn't remember Ponca City," he whispered in her ear, "but I never forgot you. Not once."

I never forgot you, she thought. *Not once.*

There was no class after theirs, so they stayed in that top row once the snake pit emptied of students headed to lunch or other classes. She shared the jam sandwich and apple in her purse.

"I still eat everything in sight," he said, when he finished half of her lunch, too, and eyed her uneaten half of apple. She handed it to him.

"I lay there in a hospital bed in DC long enough to mull around what a guy like me can do, and I still want to teach," he said, when he finished the apple. "History, in fact. I seem to recall you mentioned nursing. There's no nursing school here, is there?"

"It's in Chicago."

"Then why…why all the way to Illinois and Urbana? Especially when you assumed I was dead?"

"I suppose it's silly," she hedged. "No, it's not. I wanted to honor your memory by attending the school you wanted to attend." It came out in a rush. She hoped he would understand. "I'm majoring in accounting because I like numbers. To be honest, I don't think I would be a good nurse. Besides, Chicago isn't Urbana."

She told him about Millie Sturdivant, and Mrs. Dobbs, and other losses of loved ones on the production floor. "Everyone congratulated me that I didn't have to mourn the loss of a husband, a fiancé or even a boyfriend," she said, holding back tears. "'You never even went on a date,' they told me. 'You never had time to get serious.' 'You'll find another boyfriend, if that's what he was.' What could I say to that? I wasn't allowed to grieve. I hated it."

"North American Aviation was your war," he concluded. "Ronnie, I guess war is painful wherever it takes you."

She mulled that over, thinking through the year and a half, remembering her disappointment to have no more glamorous assignment than clerk/typist in the neighboring state, one as boring as Oklahoma. "I was ready to hate it there, but I didn't," she said. "It was my war and I met you." That was bald and obvious enough.

"Ponca City," he said again. "Ronnie, someone found me an Oklahoma road map and I looked up all the towns big and small, hoping one would jog my memory. Nothing."

"My letters? I talked about Ponca City a lot."

"I lost everything when we were captured, except the uniform I wore and my dog tags. I have no idea what became of my gear in Bastogne. I finally remembered Rantoul, Illinois, at least, which brought back my childhood. I visited Rantoul a few weeks ago."

So that was it. "Did you leave Christmas wreaths on your parents' graves?"

He started at that. "*Gott im Himmel*, I did. Ronnie, did you…"

"I was there. I wanted to know more about you. I saw two wreaths a few days ago in the cemetery of that Catholic church."

"St. Malachy."

"That's how you pronounce it? I decided right then that I would take flowers on Easter." She tried to keep her voice light and failed. "You know, since I didn't think you would be visiting them."

He bowed his head at that. When she put her hand on his arm, he tapped his prosthesis again, a little harder this time. "I'm not the man I was, Ronnie. I wish I could tell you different."

This was no place to tell this man what was in her heart, that he was precisely the man she wanted. She reconsidered. A modest woman, she thought she needed a private setting to explain her enrollment at the University of Illinois as a way of squeezing in one final connection with the man she loved. No. He needed to know exactly now how she felt, even if it was in Harker Hall with others around. When had they ever enjoyed a private setting? She acknowledged that whatever she said, was his to use as he saw fit. It would include her, or it would not.

Should she be gentle? Funny? Firm? Above all, whatever she said had to be right. Ronnie looked directly into his eyes, seeing – to her infinite relief – the same expression that had caught her attention on the Greyhound bus. So much had happened, but the war had not dimmed that expression, which gave her courage. She took a deep breath.

"Sergeant Brown, I've never seen either of your legs, but I am certain it was a very fine leg. That makes you every bit the man I remember. Excuse me for being forward, but we're going on a date tonight."

"Well, in that case…It was a pretty fine leg, but I have another one." His smile was genuine. Ronnie felt her shoulders relax. No one was going to call him back to Fort Leavenworth early, or send him overseas again. He was here and she knew right down to the depth of her being that he was hers. "There's an Italian restaurant not far from campus."

"Our first date," she said. "I hope you'll be a gentleman, Sergeant Brown. At least you don't have a German spy strapped to your wrist."

"And you don't have a curfew, Private Green."

"It was corporal before the war ended, Sergeant Brown. Where have you been?"

She knew where he had been. He had never left her heart.

Chapter Twenty-three

Theirs was a small wedding three weeks later in Rantoul, Illinois, Ernie's childhood home. Far advanced in pregnancy, Aunt Vi couldn't travel. None of Ernie's close relatives were alive, and his California cousins too far away for short notice. Both of their landladies attended, and to her delight, so did Colonel and Mrs. Dignam. Mrs. Dobbs came all the way from Kansas, accompanied by a handsome son in an Army uniform.

Except it wasn't a small wedding. To Ronnie's amazement, many in Dr. Driscoll's snake pit history class attended. There were also familiar faces from their English class. The first to kiss her cheek in the adjoining hall was the corpsman who revived her and helped her from the snake pit. She laughed inside, aware he had aimed for her lips, but was deterred by the potent presence of a former military policeman giving him the professional stink eye. Once an MP, always an MP, apparently.

St. Malachy was full, which thrilled Father Koenig, a priest used to celebrating Mass for a congregation of older ladies and newly confirmed youngsters. They were all amazed when the planned reception with cake and coffee for ten at most turned into a noisy, light-hearted bash with more than one hundred, young/old veterans like themselves, men and woman with linked pasts and promising futures. Most of the unexpected guests brought cookies and doughnuts. Water didn't turn into wine, but no Catholic Church in the Midwest was short on coffee, urns, and china mugs.

Ronnie and Ernie walked arm in arm (and cane) among the well-wishers. She had to smile when the guests subdivided into army, navy and Marines, army air corps, and nurses, everyone ready to share their stories with other veterans who understood. By the end of the impromptu party, Ronnie had promised the loan of her wedding dress to another WAC and a WAVE. She told them the story of the dress, courtesy of a boardinghouse friend of Ernie's in the 101st Airborne. It had begun life as a parachute, one of the later nylon ones. Somehow, he had spirited it home from Europe.

Ernie handed the parachute to her the day after he proposed in that Italian restaurant before the waiter even brought the menu. "Sergeant Gibbon – well, Dale Gibbon – is studying engineering here. He told me to tell you to use what you need. His mother volunteered to sew it for you." The result was soft, slinky, and comfortable. Colonel Dignam's wife brought along her veil, last used at West Point years ago. Ronnie didn't need to look in a mirror to know that she was going to be the season's most beautiful bride. She just knew.

Only days before the wedding, their landladies came close to duking it out over where the couple would live. Campus Housing had already assured them there would be no apartment on such short notice, or even *any* notice until next fall, when more married housing units would be completed. Even then, they would be on a lengthy waiting list.

The matter resolved itself peacefully; neither lady won. As it turned out, there were journalism majors in that eight a.m. English class. When a feature article about Ernest Brown and Veronica Green's chance reunion appeared in the *Daily Illini*, Ernie was approached on the QT by the head librarian. For fifteen dollars a month and a little light housekeeping of books, he offered them the use of the largely unknown apartment on the first floor, where, in the century before, the custodian lived because the boiler had to be fed constantly in winters like this one.

"You know this is an engineering school," he told his appreciative audience of two. "There's a well-designed central boiler now that serves the campus. A good cleaning and maybe a layer of paint will turn this into a great apartment." He leaned closer. "Nothing wrong with the plumbing." He laughed, a dignified librarian, but not too dignified for a discreet jab. "And if you two get really bored, there are books!" He peered at Ronnie. "My goodness, but you can blush."

"She's not planning to be bored, sir," Ernie said, with just a hint of the former MP in his tone.

And now they were married. Ronnie knew he was eager to get in bed. So was she, but she had one question. He helped her off with her coat and kissed her neck. Maybe the question could wait. No, it couldn't.

"One moment, Ernie."

"Only one," he said, but he smiled.

She went to the desk in the small parlor and took out the Vmails Ernie had sent. She handed him the third one, pointing to the last paragraph, which had been partially blacked out. She pointed at the first one marked. "I know the censor blotted out this one because you probably wrote Bastogne."

He took the letter from her, and read it. She saw recognition in his eyes, as if another piece of the puzzle was moving into place.

"Yes, Bastogne," he said, then gave her a look of real gratitude. "I'm remembering."

"Maybe you don't want to remember some of this," she said, wondering if she had done the right thing.

"I want to remember it all," he assured her. "Even the tough parts. It was my war." He moved his finger lower. "Now this one. 'I'm…'"

"Do you remember?" she asked. "Must've been a doozy. He blotted out the whole paragraph."

He kissed her cheek. "It was a homesick MP. Here's what I wrote." Ernie looked up, as if seeing the words, remembering them, another puzzle to those silent months. "'I'm so eager to get out of Belgium' – that's the magic censored word – 'and home to you. Yes, home.' I remember writing that!" He put the letter down on the desk and took her in his arms.

Whatever doubts she feared Ernie might harbor on their wedding night lasted no longer than sitting with her on their bed in the newly painted apartment. He took off his leg and set it on the chair next to the bed by his crutches. "I want crutches there in case I ever have to get up in the middle of the night." He looked at them. "Maybe a cane will suffice some day."

"I'd say it's still a mighty fine two-thirds of a leg," Ronnie said. She looked at the mighty fine leg, the one that ended about four inches below his knee. She thought about a rough surgery with no anesthetic, and more surgeries later, then decided not to think about it again. What was done wouldn't change. "You have your knee. What more could a man possibly want?"

She meant it as a joke, but he looked at her seriously. "You'll be amazed how much better off I am than a lot of other GIs. Here."

He took her hand and ran it down his thigh and past that valuable knee. She gently patted the end, running her finger along a scar. He kissed her then, that same wonderful kiss from the side of the road in Kansas City, and more times since they found each other in a snake pit in Harker Hall.

One thing most definitely led to another. A total newcomer to the deepest exhibition of love, Ronnie still had some inkling that much more was at stake on their first coupling. She sighed with relief at her husband's pleasure and couldn't help but think that two knees were far better than one. She held him close and felt his confidence. All was well; she would see to it.

He raised up on his elbows to watch her face below his. They hadn't bothered to turn off the lights. He searched her face, hopeful, cautious, as if wanting – needing – to know all would be well with her and a husband with a leg and a half.

She touched his face, gently outlining his profile with her finger. "When I knew you weren't coming back, I was mostly afraid that as the years passed, I would forget what you looked like. I had no photograph," she whispered in his ear, keeping their conversation private, even though no one else was in the library, and certainly not in their apartment.

"You knew I wasn't coming back," he said, then lowered himself back on her body, where she wanted him. "*Meine Geliebte*, when I didn't know how to find you, I …I finally hoped you would find someone else to marry."

She smiled and enjoyed the kiss that followed. Her hands tight across his back, she began to caress him. "I suppose I would have, eventually," she told him. She couldn't help that her eyes filled with tears. "I knew if I did, I would have to be awfully careful not to think of you too often."

She kissed his tears, or maybe they were her tears, amazed at the knowledge that terrible war had brought them together, separated them, and brought them together again, when peace returned and demanded her due now. It was too much unhoped-for goodness, rising out of horror, to ever ignore or take for granted.

When Ernie slept, his face and hands relaxed, looking younger than he did in daylight, she got out of bed, found her nightgown, and turned off the light overhead. She thought of Pops, and hoped that somehow, in a sweet theology she didn't know any preacher would understand, her father knew that she was married and probably going to be a happy wife and mother.

Maybe it was a kindness from heaven. She leaned against the door and admired her husband. For a small moment, she saw their path of life as it twisted and wound around obstacles and triumphs. She had never asked for ease, and she did not ask for it now. It was enough to be this man's wife in a post-war world.

She thought of that smiling, perfect WAC, the Star-Spangled Girl on the poster that had tugged her into the recruiting office to do something impulsive and out of character. Her ordinary war – in Kansas City, for heaven's sake – was her war. Never again would she downplay her role, small as she knew it was, because it was anything but small. Every report she typed, every bit of correspondence she filed, had taken her right to this room she now shared with her husband. "Thank you," she whispered, not certain if it was a prayer to God, or simple gratitude for life and more of it.

"You're going to get cold feet."

Ronnie laughed. So her man was a light sleeper? "Not a problem, Sergeant Brown, when I put my icicle feet on your warm leg."

She did precisely that, laughing when he flinched, snuggling close, ready to sleep and probably wake up a few hours later for more lovemaking. *Stamina, Ronnie, stamina,* she thought, and closed her eyes. When her sergeant was breathing evenly again, she knew she could surrender her personal watch and sleep, too. The war was over. "All my love," she whispered.

Yet I Will Love Him

To the people of Goshen County, Wyoming, who took in German prisoners of war and never forgot them.

Passing By

There is a lady sweet and kind.
Was never a face so pleased my mind.
I did but see her passing by,
And yet I'll love her till I die.

Her gesture, motion, and her smiles,
Her wit, her voice my heart beguiles.
Beguiles my heart, I know not why,
And yet I'll love her till I die.

Cupid is wingéd and he doth range,
My country, so, my love doth change.
But change ye earth, or change ye sky,
Yet, I will love her till I die.

Thomas Ford, 1607

Prologue

E ven now, nearly a year since his capture at miserable Wadi-al-Akarit, Gerd Gauss, fighter pilot with Rommel's air wing of Afrika Korps, still found sand on his pillow in the morning. He knew that was impossible. His head had been shaved close against lice after his months' long detention at a dreary seaport on the Tunisian coast, but some alchemy of war seemed to keep sand in his brain, if not on his scalp.

Why he even lived made no sense, not to his logical, Austrian mind. It wasn't his choice. Anyone with a brain and his load of recent loss would have simply pointed his Messerschmitt 109 toward the ground after that unlucky but not fatal hit by ground fire as he swooped in low over Allied forces. *Ach, nein.* Big Shot Gerd let his fighter glide to the desert floor because he could, and stop with a gentle jolt, testimony both to his expertise in the cockpit and his idiocy, because he had nothing to live for.

Truly nothing. That morning of his last sortie in North Africa, he had put on his black leather flight jacket. In the inside pocket over his heart, he put in the letter from his father-in-law, recently received, informing him of the death of his wife and infant son in one of the RAF's nighttime raids over Hamburg. In went his rosary as usual, and his Knight's Cross around his neck, because that was an order. Last of all, in went the only photograph he possessed of Hannelore holding their newborn son, Stefan.

He waited in his plane for the enemy swarm to approach cautiously, then more boldly. One of the Tommies ordered him from his plane. When he still sat there, cursing himself that he hadn't bothered with his sidearm so he could shoot himself in the head, they yanked him from the cockpit and picked him clean. The Knight's Cross went first – thirty-five kills and counting – followed by his rosary, and that letter and picture of his dear ones.

He told them in perfect English that they could keep the Knight's Cross and the rosary, but the photo meant something to him. Why did he *say* that? The result was a gap-tooth grin –British soldiers had terrible teeth – and the shock of the man tearing Hannelore and Stefan into tiny scraps and letting them float away on the hot desert wind. "Piss on that, you wanker." Oh, those foul-mouthed Brits. God curse them, please.

When the Tommies finally ended that particular torment, he was left standing in his light blue flight shorts, tawny-colored shirt, and flight boots, his leather jacket someone else's prized possession. Nobody wanted his white cap with the long bill, but someone slapped him hard with it, then placed it backward on his sandy hair, sandy in color and filled with sand because no one kept clean in the desert.

Even his goggles were a trophy of war. Until his desert tan faded, he was going to look like a freak, with pale skin circling his eyes. Someone called him a racoon, a word he knew only from a newspaper article years ago about fur farmers importing the odd creatures from America. *Ja*, a racoon. So he was, burned dark from the North African sun, with racoon eyes.

The desert tan faded. He and thousands of other PWs crossed the Atlantic in the reeking hold of an empty transport that had dropped off determined-looking, healthy American troops to speed up Germany's retreat from North Africa. So many troops, so much war materiel. Only an idiot or a fanatic still thought Germany might win; he was neither.

When he sat in the library of the PW camp in Veteran, Wyoming, he liked to lean back in the reasonably comfortable chair and wonder again why he hadn't just shot himself earlier in 1940, when informed that all Lufthansa pilots – captains, first officers, flight crew, whoever – were now enrolled in the Luftwaffe. There was only one right answer. Any answer besides, "Why, certainly, I was planning to join anyway," meant death by firing squad.

His decision in 1940 to submit and live was predicated entirely on the fact that he had married Hannelore, his dearest love, only weeks before the deadly ultimatum. He had even more to live for when she informed him through a letter months later that his last and only visit had proved fruitful; he was going to be a father. Had he known that wife and son would die in that raid over Hamburg when the building they lived in collapsed, he would have put the pistol in his ear and fired. He loved her and the infant he never saw.

Even now, he crossed himself at the thought. Suicide was a sin. That he was Austrian meant nothing to his British or American captors, and he understood. He spoke German, he wore a German uniform and that was sufficient unto the day for them. He accepted that, too. In appearance he was the personification of Hitler's ideal: blond, intensely blue-eyed, well-built, capable of giving the Third Reich sons like himself. No one in charge of him now cared that his heart broke after the *Anschluss* in 1938, when Germany essentially absorbed Austria, his homeland. Such was war.

On the other hand, it was also well that no one – hopefully – in the Veteran camp knew why he had been shifted from the main Scottsbluff PW camp so quietly. He came on a stretcher, the result of informing a camp guard that one of his fellow prisoners had that blood group tattoo below his armpit, identifying a member of Waffen-SS, the worst of the worst and feared by other soldiers.

Gerd took his chances, knowing full well that there were always eager Nazi prisoners willing to inform on the less diligent. After the SS prisoner had been taken away, two other such SS unknown to him had cornered him in the shower, thrashed him, and delivered a blow to his head before others intervened. His right ear still rang from the blow, but his ribs were less tender.

Now it was April, the fifth year of the war that began with the invasion of Poland. Spring was finally in the air in the southeast corner of Wyoming. At roll call, the camp commander, a U.S. Army captain grounded because of serious injuries, had informed them that soon they would be working in the fields, planting beet seeds for farmers whose own sons were fighting in the Pacific and Europe. "How will they treat us?" he asked one of his fellow prisoners over breakfast, a German from the Sudetenland who had been in this camp longer.

"No fears, Gerd," his friend said. "We're sitting out the war in a good place." He laughed and buttered another piece of toast. "With any luck, you'll land on a farm where the farmer wouldn't dream of sending you home hungry."

"I would like that," he said.

Chapter One

Nothing prepared Audrey Nolan Allerton for her father's announcement over dinner that in the morning he was taking the beet truck to the PW camp for a load of German prisoners.

Dad knew how much she loathed Germans. He understood her return home from Boston as a war widow. "Settle down, missy. They'll be in the fields. You won't know they're around. I promise."

Here was the difference between Audrey and her mother, a Boston lady who had never fit into life in Wyoming and severed her ties with Peter Nolan and her young daughter. Audrey knew she could let her brown eyes well with tears, Mama's favorite ploy. No man cared for tears. Or she could bow to the necessity brought about by manpower shortage because of war and make the best of a bad situation. She bowed to the necessity.

Still, she wouldn't be Audrey Allerton if she remained silent. "You know I'm willing to help in the fields."

"I know, Audie, I know. There's only one of you, though. And think how disappointed your boss will be if you don't show up to work."

It was a private joke between them. Walter Watkins, Goshen County Extension Agent, had a hard time remembering she even existed, being content to stack papers on her desk as he hurried off to another meeting somewhere, secure in the knowledge that she would organize matters in his absence. Apparently, her next-to-useless degree in English lit, from Radcliffe even, didn't hold too much water in the wartime working world. She typed. She collated. She fumed.

"Still, Dad…" What more could she say? One moment Lieutenant Ed Allerton was on his way to England with a well-known State Department official, ready to facilitate the inevitable American entry into the war. That was September 5, 1941. The next moment, a German fighter pilot from Fortress Europa ended all that, and whatever future with her new husband she had envisioned.

When she rose to clear the table, Dad took her arm. "I need the prisoners. We all do. You know how intensive planting beets is."

Audrey tamped down her unease at the news, remembering how hard he worked to raise her, after her mother bailed out. No one had any control over events. "I didn't mean to whine."

"You didn't," he said. "What happened to Ed was a damned shame. Trouble is, the world's full of damned shames now."

They never stayed up late, not with Dad rising early to follow the work of each season. Truth to tell, Audrey relished surrendering to her mattress. In the comforting solitude of night, she could think about Ed and their few months together, grateful they had never quarreled, thankful she sent him off on that trip to England with a kiss and a wave.

After the usual female ritual of wandering the house, wondering what else needed to be done, Audrey climbed the stairs to her old room, containing the mattress sagging in all the right places, and the armchair too decrepit for the sitting room downstairs, but ditto with the sag. Ed had teased her once about never throwing anything out. He was from old Boston money and had no understanding of the occasional vicissitudes of farming and ranching. In Wyoming, her furniture was just getting broken in.

Since April was only half gone, her bedroom was still cold, but not see-your-breath cold. One of Dad's little rituals, probably since her youngest days, was to put a hot water bottle between her sheets before he went to bed. She sighed with the comfort and lay there with her hands behind her head, deciding what to think of tonight.

She noted that it had been a month since she had cried over her miscarriage, a dreadful end to a terrible six weeks after Ed's death, when the State Department wouldn't say anything beyond his death. Her father-in-law had enough connections to finally pry loose a few details. Other diplomats on the same mission had traveled to England aboard a ship, perilous enough, what with U-boat wolfpacks on the prowl. Ed had gone by air. His body was never recovered.

She failed Ed then, unable to carry the baby inside her. At least he knew he was going to be a father. Whether that was better or worse, who could say? She felt all the guilt and sorrow. But now, three years later, even the precise details of Ed Allerton's face were starting to fade. At least she had photographs to remind her. Of her child, there was nothing. She patted her belly anyway.

She decided not to cry tonight. Tears changed nothing. She thought about German PWs working in Dad's fields, bending down and planting several beet seeds ten inches apart, back-breaking work. Maybe the days would be misty with rain, too, so the sandy soil would make the Germans slip and slide. That would serve them right.

Later on came the thinning, equally backbreaking after the beet seeds sprouted and branched out. Each row would be blocked, as the planters used a long-handled hoe to form a block of sprouts. The thinning itself was usually done by hand, with the extra sprouts removed so the most promising-looking plant could leaf out and turn into a shady spot for farm cats to lie under. The widely spaced plants had room now to leaf out in splendor and grow white sugar beets to be harvested and hauled to the Holly Sugar factory in Torrington. It was backbreaking and labor-intensive, just right for German prisoners.

The earlier Italians were not up to much work, especially not the kind that crimped the back until standing erect was an ordeal. Since the coup that deposed Mussolini in 1943 and in essence took Italy out of the war, they had been withdrawn from the Veteran PW camp to go somewhere else. It was a grudging thought, but she had to admit to herself that the Germans might be harder workers than the Italians.

Before she turned out the light, she glanced at the calendar and looked at the circled 15, her reminder to write dutiful letters to her Bostonian mother and mother-in-law. Mrs. Allerton could barely hide her relief to see Audrey gone after two years while she completed a useless degree in English literature, something Ed had encouraged, because it was refined, and suited the wife of a future diplomat. Scratch one dream.

The letter to her mother, now married to the distinguished and bland William Peabody, always took more time. That letter had to include a little about the weather and something about her former husband, Audrey's father. Audrey never understood why, since Mama had left him after one blizzard too many, and two orphaned calves in the kitchen that she seldom entered – what were cooks for, after all? Mother had met Peter Nolan in Chicago, when she and her father were visiting an old school chum of his who had gone into cattle-buying – how vulgar – and made a fortune.

Audrey had no doubt that Dad had impressed Mother. He was tall and handsome, with dark hair like Audrey's and kind eyes. In her own way, Mother learned how much money changed hands for those cattle. He seemed like a safe bet to an impressionable debutante who hadn't really sparkled during her own society come out.

Six years on a cattle ranch and beet farm had cured Mother of the romance of cowboys. A year of separate bedrooms – her idea – and a train ticket home to Boston on her breakfast plate one morning – Dad's response – sent her packing. Audrey could write Mother about the weather, and add a dig that Dad was looking splendid and healthy, and this promised to be a good year for crops. Love, Your Dutiful Daughter.

She turned out the light, enjoying the warmed bed, and the hint of spring in the fragrance of newly turned earth in the beet fields to the west. Maybe she would write those letters, and maybe she wouldn't.

There was one thing she knew for certain: She would stay far away from Germans on their knees planting beet seeds.

Chapter Two

In the morning, Audrey had no choice but to think about Germans. An early telephone call informed her that Mrs. Baysinger, the neighbor who usually dropped her off at the courthouse before continuing on to the high school, was ill with pleurisy and would be out that week. Gasoline rationing being what it was, she needed that ride to work.

"No problem, Audrey," Dad said as he sopped up egg juice – her childish name for fried eggs – with toast. "I'm to meet my Germans at seven. I'll take you to the courthouse after that." He grinned. "I'll pick you up at five, unless you want to play Claudette Colbert and raise your skirt and stick out your leg on the highway."

"Claudette Colbert? Oh, Dad," she said, knowing he wanted her to laugh and somehow still not think about a truck load of Germans coming her way, because Mrs. Baysinger had pleurisy.

Claudette Colbert was a tender point, but Dad didn't know. After Ed proposed and she accepted, they had sat close together on a stone ledge at his parents' summer home in the Adirondacks, shoulders touching in that delicious way that meant so much, because Mother had seldom touched her, and Dad was always circumspect.

As she held her breath with the wonder of love and stared at the diamond rock he placed on her finger, Ed had nudged her and whispered, "I had to propose, just had to. You have the shapeliest legs I have ever sneaked a peek at. I want to see all of them."

That was Ed, a big tease. She smiled at the memory – last year it would have brought tears – of Ed laughing, then snuggling her close, because he was a toucher. On their brief honeymoon in that summer home (he promised her Europe someday), he admired the whole length of those legs he liked and assured her that Claudette Colbert had nothing on her. Funny what memories popped into her mind. She could either like them or dread them. She chose to like them.

"You ready?"

"I'll get my hat, Dad. Rev up the engine."

When she climbed into the cab of the beet truck, wishing that she could wear trousers to work and not horrify that priss Walter Watkins, Dad handed her a clipboard. "I'm supposed to pick up ten PWs and one guard. If you don't mind, maybe you could write down their names."

"I don't want anything to do with them, Dad. I told you."

"Just this once. I promise." He turned the key in the ignition, heard all the protest from an old truck that had no business on any road, and shifted gears. "I won't have a beet harvest without Hans and Friedrich, and their Germanic brethren, and I'm not independently wealthy."

She nodded and read through the mimeographed page. "It says here they come with a sack lunch, but we…you… need to provide water."

"Can do," he said cheerfully. "Anything about rest periods?"

"Fifteen minutes, morning and afternoon," she read as they bumped along. "You pay the camp eighty cents a day, per prisoner, once a week. The camp commander turns it into scrip so they can buy things in the camp store."

"Hopefully not shovels to dig under the wire. Ow! I get no respect," he joked when she swatted him with the mimeographed instructions.

From Veteran to Torrington was sixteen miles, driven at a sedate thirty-five miles per hour, as mandated both by wartime regulations, and the truck's waning ability. There were still patches of snow, courtesy of the weekend's wintry squall, but the ditches ran with snow melt.

She wondered what the proper Mrs. Allerton, her mother-in-law, would think of her Wyoming life. She would be appalled, most likely. Mrs. Allerton – Audrey never had permission to call her anything else – lived in a world of tea in the afternoon, understated but expensive clothes, exotic perfumes, and many hats. Ed's suits were tailored just for him. Before he flew to his death, he had joined his father's club, the Somerset on Beacon Street.

I never belonged in Boston, she admitted to herself. She glanced at Dad, wondering what Mrs. Allerton would have thought of Pete Nolan's membership in the Boot and Bottle Club, where riders of some renown liked to hang out, drink, and swap lies. She smiled to think what Dad would make of a fox hunt, and riders posting in English saddles and red coats after a terrified animal.

"What's the joke, Audie?"

"Nothing much. I was thinking of you in a red coat, riding to the hounds with Mr. Allerton."

"On one of those skinny little saddles? Sheesh." After a chuckle of his own, he gave her a thoughtful side eye. "Do you miss that life?"

"Nope. I never belonged there. I…I think Ed would have liked it out here, though. He enjoyed his one visit."

They pulled into the parking lot at the armory beside other beet trucks as equally worn out as theirs. The farmers had gathered into a little bunch, no one moving any closer, until a soldier gestured to them.

Staying in the truck as Dad joined his friends, she saw two orderly rows of men wearing blue denim pants and long-sleeved shirts of the same fabric. Someone with more yellow paint than artistry had stenciled a large P on one leg and a W on the other. The sleeves received the same treatment. If they turned around, she suspected there would be a PW on the back, too. *Serves you right,* she thought.

Audrey looked at the prisoners again, noting deep tans on some, probably the most recent arrivals from North Africa. "Afrika Korps," she said out loud. Others had more sallow tans, suggesting they were from the same place, but not so recently.

None of them looked evil, but what did she expect? Mostly they looked interested, as if happy enough to end what she imagined was the boredom of camp life. Each day had to be pretty much like another. She smiled inside. *Probably what my life was like in Boston, once I finished school,* she thought. She had never been idle in her life, starting at four years old, putting a basket on her arm to head to the chicken coop. God bless Ed Allerton, but his mother, and those of her class, were remarkably idle. A tea here, an event there, perhaps some light volunteer hospital duty no more taxing than wheeling around a book cart. How did they stand it?

She looked again. Most of these men – prisoners, she reminded herself – wore an air of capability. Maybe it was the confident way they stood, or their easy conversation with each other. She saw they did not fear the guards close by, uniformed soldiers who carried their rifles so casually. She remembered one of Dad's friends scoffing at a photo of prisoners being transported across America in passenger cars with cushioned seats. "It's the Ritz for Fritz," he huffed, maybe thinking they should all be crammed in boxcars, shunted to a remote siding and forgotten as the war raged on.

"Dad says we need you," she said out loud. "I don't."

A door in the armory opened. To her surprise, her boss Walter Watkins walked out with an army officer leaning heavily on a cane. So that's why he sometimes pounded in just after her on Mondays, Wednesdays, and Fridays. Mr. Watkins must have some role to play here. She typed letters for him addressed to Captain Gleason, this wounded officer kept in service, heading the Veteran PW camp now. *Captain Gleason, you don't look too good,* she thought.

The captain raised his hand for silence. Interested, Audrey rolled down the window to listen. "Prisoners, I will name each farmer. When your name is called," – he indicated the farmers – "stand by that farmer. You'll be going with him to plant beets. He has a similar list of your names."

Audrey expected groans from the PWs. She knew how hard it was to stoop, drop in several seeds, cover them carefully, and make sure they were spaced ten inches apart and move on. Dad always bought more bottles of liniment during planting season for himself and his hired hands, those men who had vanished when war came, and Uncle Sam called. When she was little, Audrey liked to stick dandelions into empty liniment bottles. Maybe she didn't clean out the bottles well enough. The dandelions generally gasped and died.

Any conversation among the prisoners stopped abruptly when a German officer, impeccable in a field gray uniform, stepped out of the armory. He spoke to the men in rapid fire German, clipped and somehow intimidating. Audrey was not slow of wit. It was quickly obvious to her that the Nazi officer controlled these men and not the camp commander. The PWs snapped to attention and looked at him, not the American officer.

She noticed one-armed Mr. Petersen trying to juggle his clipboard and pass on a handful of papers to another farmer. He had lost his arm in the Great War. The son who was literally his right arm was serving on a destroyer in the South Pacific.

Out you get, Audrey, she told herself, as she leaned her shoulder into the truck door – it always required a nudge and a bump – and climbed out of the cab.

She hadn't expected to see more than one hundred pairs of eyes turn to her, at least until their uniformed leader said something in German that didn't sound kind. "Thank you, you nasty man," she muttered under her breath and joined Mr. Petersen. "I can fill in for Ron," she told him. "Want me to hold that clipboard for you?"

His farm bordered theirs. She had known him for years. "You're a sport, Audie," he said, using her childhood nickname.

"Nothing to it," she replied, then nodded to Walter Watkins, who peered at her through his thick glasses.

"Just check off the names here when that Kraut officer says them. They'll stand by us and their guard."

She waited with Mr. Petersen as the German officer cleared his throat and began. The list was alphabetical with the farmers' surnames. When their names were called, the PWs moved with a march cadence to stand in perfect order by "their" farmer. She noticed one of the prisoners carried a cardboard box. "What's that, Mr. Petersen?"

"Their sack lunches. They eat in the field."

Her father's turn came after a few other farmers received their quota of substitutes for their own sons fighting far away, and drove off. Dad nodded to her, indicating he'd wait for her. Audrey saw something else in his expression. Was it pity she had to be close to the men he had promised she would never have to acknowledge? Was it his own nod of approval that she hadn't hesitated to help Mr. Petersen, despite her misgivings? She decided that at twenty-four, she wasn't too old to bask in the warm glow of her father's approval.

She looked at Dad's PWs, the ones who were going to be part of her life for the foreseeable future, like it or not. Some were darkly tanned, some not. Some tall, some short, all prisoners and far from home.

Mr. Petersen's turn came next. The names were hard to understand, but the men certainly knew who they were. They did the same thing the other PWs had done, standing by her and repeating their names so she could check them off.

"Thanks, Audie," Mr. Petersen said when they finished, and took the clipboard from her. "I appreciate ya."

She felt suddenly shy, with all those eyes on her. "Happy to help. Tell Ron hi from me in your next letter."

She rejoined her father, stepping around the muddy spots, or trying to. She almost reached the truck when she slipped. She would have gone down, except for one hand grasping her elbow firmly and the other equally firm on her shoulder. She turned in surprise to look on a pair of seriously blue eyes in a sallow face. "Thank you," she managed.

He released her quickly and stepped back, focusing his attention again on the Nazi officer, who was eyeing him. He spoke to her out of the side of his mouth. "You're welcome. This is slippery goo."

Wonder of wonders. She didn't want to say anything else, but he *had* helped her. "Slippery goo? You're English is so good."

"It had better be," he replied, keeping his eyes straight ahead because the Nazi officer had taken a step toward him. "I was a first officer for Lufthansa. We had to know your language. We flew into Boston and New York."

Her father casually moved in front of the German officer. "We're fine here, sir. He was being helpful to my daughter, and I appreciate it."

The officer nodded, glared at the PW, then strutted off. Audrey let her father help her into the truck.

"We are not all Nazis, *Frau*," she heard behind her.

Chapter Three

The PWs and their guard climbed into the truck bed. Dad was starting the truck when Walter Watkins waved him down.

"Mr. Nolan, I can take Mrs. Allerton to the courthouse. I'm going there." He peered around Audrey's father to see her. "If she doesn't mind."

"Not at all, Mr. Watkins," she assured him, amused because he was too big of a priss to talk to her directly, even after working for him for six months. Hmm. Or maybe he was shy. Be kind, Audrey. "Thanks."

She climbed out of the cab again, aware of eyes on her once more, but not minding it so much, for some reason, maybe because that one PW was so polite.

They rode in silence for a few minutes. Mr. Watkins navigated carefully through winter's ruts. Sensing the conversational ball had dropped in her lap, she picked it up. "Mr. Watkins, I didn't know you came here before work."

He surprised her, even if he turned beet red in doing so. "I...I know you came back to Wyoming after your own loss. I didn't want to trouble you with this part of my job."

"That's nice of you, sir. I'll just have to get used to seeing the PWs around," she replied, touched by his kindness. "Why do you have to go there?"

He allowed himself the luxury of a smile. "Mrs. Allerton, you're obviously perspicacious enough to recognize just who runs that camp."

She was right. "The Nazi head officer, I think. Who is he?"

"The highest-ranking German officer in this batch of prisoners. His name is Helmut Rheinhold, and he is a major. Same title in their army as ours. I think he is Luftwaffe, their air force."

"You sound a little doubtful, Mr. Watkins."

"I don't understand his game."

"Game?"

"Just a feeling. At least he commands the prisoners and they obey. I believe discipline is a national specialty," he replied, as he pulled into his designated parking place, precisely between the lines, as she had noticed before. Mr. Watkins was a precise sort of fellow. "Still….I don't know."

"And Captain Gleason?"

Audrey heard his concern. "He isn't well, and I worry about his… his… ability to be in charge, with a bully like Major Rheinhold around."

She knew she was learning more than she had suspected, perhaps about the PW camp, or possibly about Mr. Watkins. She knew some of the courthouse secretaries called him Mr. Colorless. That might not be accurate. "I don't believe you think that's enough."

He turned off the ignition. "I don't." He turned to face her. "You are observant, Mrs. Allerton."

She could blush and deny, but why? "I am, sir."

He sat back, silent in thought. She knew he did that in the office, too, and let him think. "Would you consider something, Mrs. Allerton?"

"Depending on…" she asked, wanting more.

"It's this: I don't trust our Major Rheinhold. I don't think Captain Gleason can do his job." He reddened again. "But who listens to me?"

"As in, they are incarcerated and who cares what happens to German prisoners?"

"Yes, Mrs. Allerton. Out of sight out of mind in God-help-us Wyoming, far away from either shore."

It was food for thought, something she had never considered. Germans were the enemy and *she* wanted nothing to do with them. Still, that brief visit to the armory intrigued her. Life was dull enough; maybe that could change a little, depending on what her boss wanted. "What would you like me to do, Mr. Watkins?"

"Meet me at the armory every morning, at least during the beet season. I know you don't work on Tuesdays and Thursdays, but I can change that a little, if you don't mind."

"Doing what?"

"Observing." He touched his glasses frame. "My eyes have never been strong. It has kept me out of war, and I am not proud of that."

"That's hardly your…"

"My fault? No, but I wanted to sign up like every other man in Wyoming. Maybe this is my imagination. Maybe not. Would you stand with me and watch where the PWs go? They're supposed to be assigned to the same farmer. I want to know if that's what is happening."

She thought about the implications. "To do mischief with the field work?"

"No." He took a deep breath, as if wondering how much he should say. "To do mischief to each other. Nurse Stokes has told me about men in the camp infirmary with broken ribs and other odd wounds. When she asks how they got them, they clam up."

You could just let them kill each other, she thought. *They're the enemy*. She dismissed the thought, ashamed of herself. One of the PWs had steadied her when she nearly tripped. She saw it as a kind gesture. They were so far from home. She had come home, for the relief she knew she would find there. These men had no such recourse.

They walked into the courthouse together. He opened the office door and she followed him in, knowing she would see Dorrie Hatcher already hard at work, typing and filing and preparing for her day as the extension agent's assistant. Audrey noticed how she appraised the two of them coming in like that. She wanted to say something – what, she wasn't certain – but Mr. Watkins beat her to it.

"Miss Hatcher, I'm going to change the morning routine a little," he said, after setting down his hat and briefcase. "Mrs. Allerton came with her father to pick up some PWs for work in his fields. She is going to help me in those early-morning roll calls of the prisoners to the farmers. I've...I've mentioned my suspicions to you." He allowed himself a smile. "And you already know it's no mistake that our classmates called me Four-Eyes."

Dorrie smiled back. "They were a mean lot. They teased me, too."

"But, Miss Hatcher, you have the distinct advantage there. None of them ever graduated from the University of Wyoming." He chuckled. "Or ever will."

Audrey could tell it was a private joke between them, which made her feel like a little door was opening on an office that only last week had felt stifling and sterile. Both Walter Watkins and Dorrie Hatcher had been seniors when she was a lowly freshman. She did a mental back-peddle, hoping she had never joked about Dorrie's weight to her classmates.

As she considered, she remembered a time when Dorrie and a friend had been walking on the sidewalk just beyond the high school. Jimmie

Clancy drove by in his jalopy and yelled, "Tubba lard," out the window, then laughed with his buddies and roared off in a cloud of exhaust. So much for Jimmie Clancy. He was Torrington's first war dead at what came to be known as the Battle of the Coral Sea. Nobody wins.

"Do something else, Miss Hatcher," her boss said, and brought Audrey back to the moment. "You have a ration book pep talk at the Presbyterian Church today, don't you?"

"Yes, indeed. It's another variation on how to cook with food rationing and don't we like it," Dorrie joked, which pulled another smile out of their boss.

"Take Mrs. Allerton with you. You're on call so often for programs. Maybe Mrs. Allerton can learn about programs and give you a break."

"Sounds fine to me."

"And you, Mrs. Allerton?" Mr. Watkins said.

Why not? This morning had already been a segue from an office routine that was starting to bore her, because she liked variety, something obviously rationed in this office. "I'd like that, but on one condition, if you please."

Mr. Watkins froze, this man of routine. "Can we please call each other by our first names?" she asked, wondering at her temerity. "I got tired of all the formality in Boston. We're Westerners from the Cowboy State, and I prefer first names."

Silence. Maybe she had overstepped some extension agency rule. He thought a moment, then, "I have no problem with that, Mrs., uh, Audrey. How about you, uh, Dorrie?"

"It's high time, Walter." Dorrie smiled. Audrey already knew she had the loveliest smile. She was also a bit of a jokester herself. "After all, we live on the same block, and, ahem, weren't you salutatorian to my valedictorian?"

He laughed and went into his office. With a nod, Dorrie Hatcher invited her to come closer. "Thanks, Audrey. I believe you just changed this office."

"I'm not a very formal gal," she said, then went to her desk, where unopened letters awaited.

As she slit the first envelope from Washington, DC, Audrey decided to give the credit for this different day to the PW with the bright blue eyes who flew for Lufthansa. In explaining his command of English, he became more than a name on a clipboard. *There's always something below the surface*, she thought. *I think I was reminded of that today at the armory.* She looked toward Mr. Watkins's closed door. *And maybe here in the office.*

Chapter Four

To Audrey's delight, the day didn't drag like the ones preceding it. She went with Dorrie to the First Presbyterian Church, where patriotic church ladies provided a luncheon with deviled eggs and other goodies far exceeding any government-mandated ration list. Audrey enjoyed every delicious bite, and somehow managed to keep a straight face while Dorrie delivered the message of rationing choice items like eggs, butter and cream to help the war effort.

The church ladies nodded gravely in all the right places, took notes, and served marvelous, well-sugared doughnuts to send them all on their way rejoicing. One of them slipped her a pound of butter and whispered, "For Mr. Nolan. Your father is such a nice man, but he's too thin."

Once out of sight of the church, Dorrie pulled over and surrendered to a bout of laughter that Audrey was helpless against. When they were both wiping their eyes and only giggling at odd moments, Dorrie started the car. "Seriously, Audrey," she began, which set them both off again. "Seriously," she tried a minute later, "one could sooner stop the Platte River from flowing than try to convince farm women, awash in eggs, milk and butter, to obey the government. Why do I try?"

"If it's any consolation, I heard from some of the Boston Allertons, Republicans all and FDR-haters, that the White House bill of fare is terrible, and Eleanor doesn't care," Audrey said. "I suspect it's true, at least the White House food."

"And I must deliver these totally useless messages from the county extension agent," Dorrie said.

"Try this next time," Audrey suggested, wondering where all this wisdom came from until she realized she was echoing something Dad would do. "Have them ask around to find out who right here in the community could use extra cream and eggs."

"I'll do that," Dorrie said. "I know these ladies. I wish Walter would let me do more. Don't tell him this, but I know I could do his job, too. I've filled in on occasion, when his mother needs him."

"I don't doubt you could do any man's job," Audrey said. "I probably could, too, but that's not the reality, is it? Tell me this: is his mother really ill, or an excuse. Dad's heard rumors."

They had pulled into the parking lot. Dorrie sat there a moment. "She isn't well, and he does his best to satisfy a somewhat demanding woman, in addition." She threw up her hands. "I know, I know. People think he's a mama's boy."

"Is he?"

"That's his story to tell."

It was a story Audrey doubted he would tell, not one so proper as the extension agent. And yet, his kindness to her just this morning in not wanting to mention something that might make her sad, told her volumes about him. *We're all sad these days*, she thought.

Her afternoon work turned into something she enjoyed. The state had deemed it time to update an old manual on the correct time and way to plant flowers in this harsh climate. According to Walter, many such manuals were being updated throughout the state. "The updates are accompanied by a proviso."

"As in?"

"As in, we'll probably have to hold off on printing until the war ends."

"It's busy work?" Ooh, that sounded harsh.

He didn't seem to mind. "It's wait-and-see work, Audrey. You do this now, and it'll be ready when the times are right. I hope you don't mind."

"Mind? I love to edit."

He reached for his hat on top of the coat tree. "Now that you two are back, I'll have lunch with my mother."

"I hope she is feeling better."

His expression clouded. "Good days and bad days, Mrs. …Audrey." He paused as if wondering what to say, then, "She sometimes forgets to eat, so I go home for lunch."

"Then you have a bigger burden than most of us," she said under her breath after he closed the door. She knew she was an observant woman. In fact, that had caught Ed's attention, and became – according to him – the reason he paid special attention to her. ("Above and beyond the fact that you are simply lovely to look at," he admitted after their engagement.)

She had remarked on the color in his paisley tie during the first Christmas madrigals rehearsal, when singers from Radcliffe and Harvard practiced together, then commented again a day later on a different paisley tie. She smiled at the memory, and remembered Ed's laughter, after they married, when she said what she *really* noticed was the width of his shoulders, a feature that mattered to her in men she ogled.

Why did she feel so lighthearted? Audrey didn't want to credit the Lufthansa pilot, but something told her that he was an observer. His shoulders were wide, too. And eyes that blue weren't something ordinarily found in nature. Stop it, Audrey. Then, *and what, sir, did you observe about me?*

The afternoon went by without her once looking at the clock, something she did with regularity when she was typing or filing. Her desk was a mess of agronomy reports, helpfully provided by Walter, who might not know a daffodil from a daisy. To her editor's eye – hadn't she been feature editor for Radcliffe's *Etc*? – she knew she could create a pamphlet far superior to the one now cowering on the edge of her desk.

Walter Watkins startled her when he cleared his throat by her desk. "Quitting time, Audrey. Let's go to the armory for roll call."

"Oh, but it's only…" She looked at the clock, and chuckled. "…quitting time." She gestured to her untidy desk. "Excuse the mess."

"Some people work best, um, in a little clutter," he said generously.

Does he actually have a sense of humor? she asked herself. "I always manage to snatch chaos from the jaws of order."

He laughed. Out of the corner of her eye, Audrey noticed Dorrie staring, wide-eyed, at their boss. She shook her head and returned to work.

"It's like this," Walter said a few minutes later in the car. "Last fall, I never bothered with an afternoon roll call. As long as there were the same number of PWs in each group as went out that morning, I didn't care."

He looked over his shoulder and backed out of the parking space. In doing so, he rested one arm on the back of her seat. "Beg pardon," he mumbled, his face red again. "Old habit."

"My dad does the same thing. Don't worry," she said. She could cover his embarrassment quickly enough. "Why are you thinking about an afternoon roll call now?"

"Two deaths this winter," he said. "I am convinced they weren't natural causes, but Major Rheinhold signed off on them. They were his men, after all. I mentioned the scraps and abrasions the nurse noticed." He sighed. "And occasional broken bones."

"What did Captain Gleason do?"

"He signed off on those deaths, too, and the injuries. Gleason follows Rheinhold's lead."

At the armory, Walter parked his car but made no move to get out. He turned to Audrey. "There's this, too: Captain Gleason, the camp commander, was wounded in North Africa, which in my mind makes him someone I wouldn't put in charge of even a dishwashing unit of the Afrika Korps. He doesn't like them."

"A lot of people don't." She said it cautiously, admitting her own misgivings about Germans suddenly on the farm. "At least they didn't need to come into the house."

"I don't mean friendship," he said. "They're prisoners and we can't forget that. The Geneva Convention, which we two countries signed, is specific on how prisoners are to be treated. We're doing that part well."

"Some think the government is doing it too well," she said. "Fritz at the Ritz."

"They don't understand. Audrey, there are some 80,000 Americans in German *stalags*. Word gets back to the Third Reich via the International Red Cross and Switzerland about our treatment here of German PWs. The better the reports, the better we hope our own boys will be treated over there. It's simple."

Walter Watkins was starting to impress her with his knowledge of the camp. "Just what is your role here?" she asked.

"All agricultural extension agencies in most states coordinate PWs working in the fields. We need them badly and we treat them well. It's their leaders I worry about, the ones who are dyed-in-the-wool Nazis."

"You said there were suspicious deaths?" she asked, not sure she wanted to know more.

An official-looking car from the Veteran camp drove up, followed by empty camp trucks. "Tell you later. What I want you to do is stand by me. I brought along a clipboard for you." He chuckled. "You'll see old invoices on it just for show. I want them to get used to seeing you here morning and night with me."

"I don't do anything?"

"Not yet." He took a deep breath. "Next week, I'm going to insist on an afternoon roll call. I want to make sure that no one is going to the wrong farms in the morning."

"Mischief?"

"The fatal kind."

She considered that as he took two clipboards from the back seat. "Do they all look alike to you?" she asked, thinking of all that blue denim with PW painted on.

He touched his glasses again and gave an apologetic grimace. "Pretty much. To you?"

That morning, she would have said yes. This afternoon, she wasn't sure.

Chapter Five

She followed Walter's lead, walking toward the Camp Veteran car. She looked closer; it was driven by a prisoner.

"You remember Major Helmut Rheinhold from this morning," Walter said, speaking softly. "The officers wear their uniforms and they do not work. Sergeants – *feldwebels* – are to supervise the men in the fields, but some of them work, too."

The prisoner/chauffeur leaped from the car and opened the back door. Major Rheinhold stepped out.

"He'll ignore us again," Walter whispered. "He knows I'm not important. Oh, my. He did look twice." He grinned and threw ten years off his age. "He just spotted you. Uh oh. He's coming over."

The major was tall man, wearing all sorts of medals, including what she knew was a Knight's Cross directly at his throat. He stood too close and she wanted to take a step back.

"Mr. Watkins, who *is* this lovely creature? I noticed her this morning."

Audrey glared at the major. All he did was raise his eyebrows and take a step closer. She backed up.

"Major, this is *Mrs.* Allerton. I should have introduced you earlier. She is my office assistant."

My, my, I just got a promotion, Audrey thought, wavering between amusement and unease. *Does it come with a pay raise? Thank you for emphasizing the Mrs.*

Major Rheinhold held out his gloved hand. She stared at it, thought about the Geneva Convention, and held out her hand. She was not prepared for him to kiss it. She snatched her hand back.

"Mr. Allerton is a lucky man, indeed," the major purred.

"Mr. Allerton died over the English Channel, shot down by a member of *your* Luftwaffe," she said, biting off each word and looking him in the eye, which seemed to startle him. She doubted anyone in the camp looked him in the eye. The venom he returned set red flags waving in her mind, those red flags that any reasonably pretty girl learned to interpret.

"A pity, I am certain," the major said. She saw no sympathy in those eyes. He looked toward the incoming beet trucks, with their harvest of prisoners. "Here we are. The business at hand." With a slight nod at the two of them, he stalked forward, his hands behind his back, every inch the Nazi.

"You're a cool one, Mrs. A," Walter said under his breath.

"Have you ever hated someone on sight?"

"Not yet but almost," he replied, which stiffened her spine.

She watched as the trucks slowed, somehow relieved to see her father's truck and its German cargo. At least they hadn't murdered him when forced to plant beets seeds.

Walter leaned closer. "You're really not going to like this, but the Geneva Convention allows it. Focus on one or two of the PWs and watch what happens. It'll be quick."

Puzzled, she watched as the prisoners, ten per truck, stood at attention, their eyes on the major. *Almost* all of them with their eyes on their leader. Here and there, she saw men looking at her, the only female in sight. She glanced at the row beside her father to see Prisoner Blue Eyes looking at her with a smile. She nearly smiled back, but stopped herself in time.

"Watch now."

She turned her attention to the major. She covered her mouth in surprise when he raised his right arm and shouted, "Heil Hitler!"

"Watch."

Astounded, amazed, horrified, she watched as the prisoners snapped to attention and returned the salute, something she had only seen on newsreels, and not in the heart of her nation. Sick to her stomach, she scanned the rows and saw what Walter saw. And she worried.

Some of the prisoners had not given the salute as promptly as the others. She couldn't be sure how many, because the whole exhibition had shocked her.

"Some don't appear to be as enthusiastic as the others," she whispered.

"They're the ones I worry about."

"I think I understand."

"I thought you might. Stand by me now."

She stood there, hoping her fake clipboard made her look official. "I should hate them."

He shrugged. "Every man has a story."

The roll call moved right along, with the major calling each PW's name, and giving and receiving a *heil Hitler*, as the PWs formed into two orderly rows at attention. When the major finished, he got back into his car and drove away. The men left their rows and filed toward the other trucks, talking and laughing. PW Blue Eyes still chatted with her father. She waited, not wanting to interrupt a conversation, but curious to know what they were talking about. Dad gestured to her.

"Audrey, this is Feldwebel – did I say that right? – Gerd Gauss. He's supposed to supervise, but he works, too." Dad chuckled. "And his English is better than mine."

She nodded to the man with the blue eyes. She didn't want to say anything, but after watching Major Rheinhold in action, she had a question. "You told me this morning you flew for Lufthansa. You're an officer, aren't you? Why are you even standing here with my father?" She couldn't help herself then, just couldn't. "You should have stood with that awful man and *heiled* away."

He fixed a look on her then that she couldn't interpret. "It is a long story. Suffice it to say I am an Austrian." He lowered his voice, even as the intensity rose. "I told you I flew for Lufthansa. When the war began, we Lufthansa pilots were given the choice of joining the Luftwaffe or facing a firing squad. What would you have done?"

As she stood there with her mouth open, he nodded to her father, turned on his heel and left them. "I guess he told me," Audrey murmured. "I deserved it."

Dad put his arm around her shoulder. "For what it's worth, you got more out of him of a personal nature in ten seconds than I learned all day." He gave her a gentle push toward the truck's cab. "He's good with the other PWs and that's all I need. He watches over them, like a good NCO should."

He looked around in irritation. "Blast it, I think my dog has decided to become a PW."

"What?" she asked, happy for a different topic. "You know Gut Bucket isn't too bright."

"All the same..." Dad put two fingers in his mouth and whistled. Nothing. He did it again. "Where's my dog?" he hollered.

Most of the men were in three camp trucks now. Audrey heard laughter and then saw Gut Bucket, held in Gerd Gauss's arms. Dog in hand – and Gut Bucket was on the meaty side – he carried the struggling mutt toward them. "I cannot guarantee he will not follow us again," he said, as he held out Gut Bucket. "He likes baloney sandwiches."

Trying not to laugh, Audrey held out her arms. "He's a horrible mooch."

"I do not know that word."

"He will eat anything that isn't nailed down."

With a grin, Gerd handed her the dog. He was close enough for her to breathe in his healthy sweat, something she had never noticed about her husband, who worked in an office and had probably never even picked a flower, let alone planted beets. She didn't mind it. His arm touched hers and she didn't mind that, either. Gut Bucket started to whine. "Miserable mutt," she said. "Gut Bucket is a terrible opportunist."

"Gut Bucket? That's funny. We've been calling him Schmalz."

"Which is?"

A bigger smile. "Pig lard."

She laughed. She couldn't help herself. In went Gut Bucket/Schmalz into the cab. She started to climb in after the dog, wishing her skirt wasn't so short. Gerd put his hands on her waist and boosted her in as if she weighed nothing, which she knew wasn't the case.

Before Gerd closed her door, Audrey leaned toward him. "I ...I believe I would have made the same choice," she whispered.

"I also had a new wife," he whispered back. "What could I do?"

"What you did. Goodbye."

"See you tomorrow."

Chapter Six

She repeated Gerd's words to her father. "I suppose they all have wives and children," she said, knowing she needed the reminder that others had lives, too, not just her. Gerd had a wife.

Dad nodded, eyes ahead on the road with all its ruts and potholes. The usual road crew had gone the way of all road crews, drafted and sent to war. "It's amazing what happens when they turn into people, isn't it?"

"I haven't quite decided," she replied. She shuddered. "That major! Walter told me the Geneva Convention allows a *heil Hitler.*"

"He's Walter now?"

Happy to think of something else, Audrey told him about the First Presbyterian Ladies Guild breaking every single law, chapter and verse, in the Book of Rations. "Dorrie and I were laughing about it. I suggested we use first names in the office." She nudged him. "You know I'm not stuffy."

She didn't want to say anything then about Walter's observation and suspicions. She waited until after dinner and dishes, and before Dad lay down on the sofa, shoes off, with his latest library book, which she knew would put him to sleep in minutes.

"I'll be going with you to the armory each morning," she said, then explained Walter Watkins's fears. "He wants me to see if the prisoners are switching to other farms, to do mischief to fellow PWs with less-then-fervid love for Hitler."

"Could be we've all been underestimating mild-mannered Walter Watkins," Dad said, rubbing his chin.

"I know I have. Walter is serious about this."

"You'll be welcome at roll call, I am certain," he said. "Couldn't help but notice a few eyes on you this morning and afternoon."

"Dad, really," she murmured.

"Yes really," he replied, calm as always, but with that bit of fun she wondered if her mother ever missed, since current husband number three was rich but bland beyond belief. "Audie, you ever look in the mirror?"

She smiled at him then made a face. "I will not argue that dark brown hair will suffice." She could have added that a deep bosom was nice in its place, but destined to sag eventually. "I don't think about mirrors much," she said. Unsaid was her question, *Why bother? Ed's gone.*

Dad seemed to understand, choosing his words carefully. "It's been a long three years for you and all of us."

"I feel old," she admitted.

Trust Dad. "That'll change when you find another right man. Maybe it's time to move on."

Should she? Why not? "You didn't move on, after Mother left." It sounded cheeky and clearly something she shouldn't say to her own father, but there it was, all laid out.

"I should have, Audie," he said promptly. "I don't mind admitting I passed up some opportunities. I was wrong. Don't you miss out on life, my dear girl."

"Pickings are pretty slim right now," she hedged, even if it was true.

"The war won't last forever. The boys'll come home. Maybe you'll go back to Boston."

She shook her head at that. "Nope. I'm here for better or worse." She kissed his cheek. "Right now it's worse, but I have hopes."

She did. It was early, but she went upstairs to bed, happy when Gut Bucket traipsed along. "You should know better than to cozy up to the enemy, Mr. GB. That's called fraternization, and it's probably illegal."

Gut Bucket wagged his tail and wore that look of eternal optimism only found in *canis lupus familiaris.* She had no doubt that eons ago, a wolf had bellied up to a campfire of Cro-Magnon hunters and that was that. "Gerd called you Schmalz." She gave Lard a good rub and then a kiss because he was a dog.

She dressed for bed and did something she hadn't done in years – she took a good look at herself in the mirror. "I'm top heavy," she said to the mirror. "Can't do a thing about that. Wish I had some actual nylon stockings, but we'll blame the war." She looked into her eyes, those brown eyes that her hazel-eyed husband had thought so pretty.

Tomorrow she would go to the armory with Dad, taking along her superfluous clipboard. She had seen yesterday how Mr. Watkins simply checked off each PW going to each farmer. Would he mind if she made each one print his same on the roster beside his typed name? She knew it would slow down the process, but needs must, as Mrs. Petersen on the farm next to theirs said, when confronted with a dilemma.

This time, though, she would be returning with Dad and the PWs, because she only worked on Monday, Wednesday, and Friday. She thought of Dad's mimeographed instructions on the care and feeding of PWs, relieved that she didn't have to cook for them. *You will remain distant workers in the beet fields*, she thought.

She yawned and put aside her book. *Green Dolphin Street* was brand new, and it was her turn for the library's only copy. She promised to have the 500-page weeper back by the end of the week, but honestly, William Ozanne, languishing in frontier New Zealand, was a ninny to confuse Marguerite and Marianne and propose to the wrong one. It was enough to try even the most ardent romantic, which she certainly was not.

But there was Schmalz, looking ever hopeful and wagging his tail. She patted the bed. "We need to talk about your role in fraternizing with prisoners. It won't do."

Morning was usually such a rush, except on Tuesdays and Thursdays, when she could lie in bed and think. Now Walter wanted her at the armory.

Quite possibly Walter Watkins had overthought that whole matter of prisoner abuse, and so she told Schmalz a.k.a. Gut Bucket, who had remained at his post by her feet all night, managing to turn one foot numb. She reminded the dog that he shouldn't go around begging for food. It appeared to make no impact.

Breakfast was baked oatmeal with copious cream on top and a handful of raspberries left over from last year's bounty along the fence. The day was cool so she wore wool trousers and a light sweater, taking a little extra time with her hair. When had she last French-braided it? She turned around for a better look, satisfied.

Because the air was cool, she stuck her head out of the open window as they rattled toward town. Gut Bucket did the same thing on the other side of the truck where he sat on Dad's lap, something he had done since his long-ago puppy days. "I'm not sure which of you amuses me more," was Dad's only comment as they came to town and she pulled her head in, reminding herself that she was a grownup and a widow. Gut Bucket needed no excuse.

Walter waited for her by his automobile with Goshen County Extension Services USDA stenciled on the door. "A little casual, are we?" he asked, but she saw something close to appreciation behind those thick lenses.

"Nope. This is Tuesday and Thursday attire," she said. "Trousers won't scare the horses because I don't see any."

He laughed a full belly laugh, not a Monday-Wednesday-Friday laugh, and it did her heart good. He handed her ten typed rosters with farmers' names at the top and their prisoner crew. To her surprise, he pointed to her father's list. "See what you can find out about *Feldwebel* Gerd Gauss."

"Why? He seems nice."

Walter shrugged. "Officers are not required to work. He's a pilot, which means he should be an officer and not working. *Feldwebel*, as near as I can place it, is a staff sergeant. He can supervise."

"Dad said he worked with the others yesterday," Audrey said. "He told me he is an Austrian, not a German."

"It's a little strange. Why isn't he an officer? Should we worry about him?"

I wouldn't, she thought. *He likes my dad's dog, too.*

"Just keep an eye on him."

She stood with Walter as the camp's car roared up, with two men in the back seat. The German prisoner got out first, and then he helped out the second man wearing U.S. Army khaki and leaning on a cane.

At a command from Major Rheinhold, the PWs got out of the trucks. Audrey looked them over, those men of about the same height, many with blond hair, and all wearing the same blue denim. "It's going to be hard to tell them apart," she whispered to Walter. "There could be assassins in every group all bent on trouble, and I'd never know."

Walter chuckled. "I don't think it's that serious. Besides, this is only a hunch of mine. They're probably all choirboys and pure as the driven snow."

It was time to tell Walter her plan. "I want each man to print his name on the roster beside his typed name."

"What'll that prove? A check mark is quicker."

"If someone is pretending to be someone else, I bet he'll hesitate. He might even not know what to do."

"Go ahead. They'll get used to it."

He walked over to Captain Gleason and explained, then gestured Audrey over. She tried to skirt around the German major, but he managed to come close enough for her to smell his aftershave. What in the world were prisoners of war doing with aftershave? What kind of war was this? "You give me the creeps," she muttered quietly under her breath when he looked away after ogling her chest that suddenly felt two sizes larger in her modest sweater.

"Is this something new?" Captain Gleason asked Walter.

"New regulation from the Department of Agriculture," Walter lied, and gave a put-upon sigh. "It won't slow things down too much."

You're a cool one, she thought, feeling new admiration for her boss, who apparently could lie with the best of bureaucrats.

"Let me introduce you to Mrs. Audrey Allerton. She's Pete Nolan's daughter and works part-time for me as a clerk-typist."

They shook hands. Up close or farther away, Audrey decided that Captain Gleason didn't look too healthy. *You're probably relieved to turn the camp over to Major Rheinhold*, she thought, then scolded herself for such a silly notion.

"Very well then," Walter said. "Let's get started."

She tried to avoid Major Rheinhold, but she felt his eyes boring into her back as she walked away. *I didn't sign up for this*, she told herself. Come to think of it, she didn't sign up for Ed's death, or her return to Wyoming, or this PW camp full of Germans.

She looked at the prisoners. *None of us signed up for this. Not me. Not them.*

Chapter Seven

The roll call began smoothly. After the Heil to *der Fuhrer* that was always going to make Audrey shudder, Major Rheinhold explained something which must have been the new requirement to print their name on the roster, because all the PWs looked at her. *All right, Audrey, you brought this on herself,* she thought, and stood a little taller which backfired immediately when she heard low whistles of appreciation from somewhere among the PWs. *Oh mercy, bless me and my size 38.*

Major Rheinhold fixed his audience with a stare that would have melted steel. *Ha, you big hypocrite,* Audrey thought. *You were staring at my girls just a few minutes ago.* She did a brave thing in her mind – maybe it was foolish – and fixed her own stare on *him.*

She returned a proper gaze to the clipboard as Walter began the roll call. "I could use a good interpreter," he began. "Have I a volunteer?"

He did. A PW with an eyepatch stepped forward. "I learned at school in London," he said, sounding more British than Winston Churchill.

"Thank you. I will speak in short sentences," Walter said. "We are new to this business of farm labor." Pause and interpret. "When your name is called, please spell it on Mrs. Allerton's clipboard beside your typed name." Pause. "We want to get to know you. You are performing a task of vital importance. I will begin with Number One Farmer, Mr. Bower."

He called out the farmers in alphabetical order. Audrey gave the clipboard and pen to each PW for his printed name. Shy smiles were easy to return. No one ogled her, but she did get a wink or two, which reminded her, as nothing else could, that she was still a pretty woman. That fact had never died with Edgar Allerton. Maybe she needed the reminder.

She couldn't help laughing – quietly quietly – when Gerd Gauss came forward and printed his name. He held the clipboard a moment longer and drew a tiny bucket and printed the word *schmalz*.

"You are a rascal," she whispered.

"All pilots are," he whispered back, then stood in the line beside her father.

Down the list Walter went. The PWs were too polite to laugh at his mispronunciations, but Major Rheinhold smirked until Audrey wanted to smack him. As the PWs got into the beet trucks, she handed Walter the roster.

"We'll do it this evening, too. Morning and night," he told the major.

"This is a stupid waste of time," Rheinhold snapped.

Walter shrugged. "You, sir, may take that up with the Department of Agriculture. I'm merely following orders," he concluded, blander than bland.

Major Rheinhold turned on his heel and stalked back to the car, where the driver, fear on his face, had already started the engine. Captain Gleason, who had been leaning harder and harder on his cane, followed slowly, every step an effort.

"Sir, if we may help?"

The other beet trucks had pulled away. Only her father remained for her. Audrey turned to see Gerd Gauss and another PW leap down and hurry toward Captain Gleason. They walked along slowly on either side of the camp's commander, bearing him up. She glanced at her father, who winked at her.

"See you this evening," Walter said, with a jaunty tip of his hat, her clipboard tucked under his arm.

"Captain Gleason is in poor health," Gerd Gauss said as he and the other PW walked with her to Dad's truck. "Ah, my best friend in America," he exclaimed, as Gut Bucket leaped from the cab. Gerd rubbed him in all the right places, which told Audrey everything she needed to know about this Lufthansa pilot with a wife in Germany.

"You have a dog?" she asked.

"I did," he replied, straightening up. "My father-in-law wrote that they found him dead in the rubble of my apartment building in Hamburg, lying on top of my wife and infant son."

"Oh God," she said, and stopped walking.

"He thought to protect them, apparently," Gerd replied, his voice calm. He patted Gut Bucket again. "Dogs do that."

She heard no plea for sympathy, only a statement of fact. "I am so sorry."

He looked her in the eyes. "You cry your tears. I cry mine, *Frau Allerton*."

Accompanied by Gut Bucket, the two men climbed into the beet truck. Audrey looked up at the truck to see Gerd Gauss watching her. He put his hand to his heart. Impulsively, she made the same gesture, then wiped her eyes and climbed into the shotgun side of the old rattletrap.

Dad looked at her with concern in his eyes. "What happened a minute ago?" he asked. He started the truck. "You okay? Did he say something he shouldn't have? I hope not, because I like Gerd."

"Nothing like that," she said when she could talk. "He said he had a dog once." She swallowed back more tears and told him the rest. Wordless, Dad handed her his handkerchief when she finished.

"Audie, this war can't end soon enough," was all he said.

Probably for all of us, she told herself, *and I include the men in this truck.*

She didn't linger by the truck when Dad pulled into their circle driveway, but hurried into the house, wanting to be alone as an overload of sorrow landed on her shoulders. Relentless, it drove her into the quiet parlor. She curled up in her favorite armchair and cried. Silly girl, she thought she had cried all of what she called her sudden tears, tears that a word or glance let loose. Clearly, she hadn't.

After she blew her nose, she stood up and ran her hand idly across the top of the piano, dismayed to see the dust. Blame it on Wyoming's constant wind, or possibly, her slacking of household chores. She wasn't so busy today that she couldn't dust off the beast, maybe even play for Dad tonight.

She went to the porch and watched the men head toward the field, ten PWs and a guard who slouched along behind them. She counted nine prisoners, then heard some noise on the back porch. She opened a door to see one of the prisoners setting down a box of sack lunches. He smiled at her and gave a casual salute. He looked so young.

Audrey followed him off the porch, watching as Dad filled the barrel in the back with water, then got in the truck with Sack Lunch Man to drive it to a shady spot. He parked the truck under the cottonwoods and joined the others in the field.

She didn't envy them their stoop work. They had to plant several seeds together, just to be on the sure side, carefully spaced from the next small group of seeds. In another month, they would have to thin them, weeding out the smaller shoots by hand and leaving the strongest plant. More stoop work, then weeding until that big plant spread out its leaves and spent the rest of the summer turning into a sugar beet.

Maybe it was better here than in the camp, if the place was run by a martinet like Major Rheinhold. Only an idiot would imagine that the wounded army officer leaning on a cane could exercise much control. She wondered what the camp was like, surprising herself by hoping it wasn't too bleak. All because a pilot lost a wife, baby, and dog in a bombing raid over Hamburg.

She watched the men working and realized precisely what had happened to her. She knew the enemy suffered, too. This sudden knowledge made her realize she needed to reorder her thinking.

Weeding out the smaller shoots and leaving the strongest plant. She watched the men. She knew from sad experience that war was no respecter of persons. The strong succumbed as easily as the weak, when the force against them was awesome. What is a man to do when his plane is shot down and plunges into the English Channel? How can a wife and her baby cope when someone thousands of feet up in the dark releases a bomb? She dies, too.

"I'm not strong, but here I am," Audrey said. "And there you are, Gerd Gauss."

She turned around and saw the box of sack lunches, to be taken to the field, and washed down with water from a barrel because they were prisoners of war.

"We are all prisoners of war," she said, and in the saying, realized an enormous truth.

She opened one sack. It looked as basic as a baloney sandwich can be. No cheese, no mayonnaise, no lettuce, no pickle. There was a smallish apple and that was it.

That's not enough, she thought. *We can do better. I can do better.*

Chapter Eight

But what? Pie. She thought of the multiple pages of do's and mostly don'ts that Dad and all the beet growers agreed to, for the right to hire PWs. She also knew her neighbors, and doubted that any farm wife could resist the urge to be kind. The government might have no problem calling a bare sandwich and one apple a working man's lunch, but farm women did.

She hadn't much faith in the pantry, but several bottles of cherries and more of apples lurked just beyond the buckets of lard rendered last fall from Dad's pigs. She despaired a moment over the level of sugar in the canister, then remembered Dad's honey.

Mrs. Petersen in the next farm over had taught her the intricacies of pie dough when she was nine and old enough to pay attention. Audrey wanted to write precise amounts in her notebook, but that only earned her a frown from their neighbor. "Audrey, it's just a handful of this and that! Pay attention," Mrs. Petersen told her.

Audrey didn't remember the story, but Dad claimed that her response had been one repeated up and down the irrigation canal. "She said you drew yourself up like a duchess, and declared that your hands were a lot smaller and there wasn't a thing you could do about that!"

No duchess, a grownup handful of this and that worked fine. The measurements for honey versus sugar were iffy, but the crust was perfect, thanks to the lard. The pies went in the oven about the same time the guard returned to the house for sack lunches. Audrey noticed his muddy knees. "Are you planting, too?"

He nodded and flashed a shy smile. "We'd be doing this with cotton back home in Arkansas," he told her.

"And here you are, fighting the war in Wyoming," she said.

"Yes'm." He looked down at his feet. "Rickets kinda stunted me, so I'm staying in the States." He brightened up. "Maybe just for now, though."

"Do the prisoners ever give you any trouble?"

"No, ma'am. They do what Major Rheinhold tells them to do, and everyone gets along."

"And Captain Gleason?"

"He usually stays in his office. He's not well. Bye now." He hefted the box onto his shoulder and set off, moving a little faster. Maybe it was a subject the guard wasn't comfortable with.

She heated up last night's stew for Dad when he came in for lunch. He sniffed at the pie. "Change of heart, Audie?" he asked.

"They only get a skinny sandwich and an apple, Dad." He didn't question her. "Can you bring them to the porch a little early, so they can have pie?"

He nodded and reached for his hat. "Do we have any cream?"

"You like cream with your cereal," she reminded him.

"There's plenty. It's hard to argue with a dab of whipped cream on pie."

She couldn't dispute that, not since it sounded like permission. The eggbeater wore her out, but no one could fault the stiff peaks. All she had by now was honey for sweetener, but it didn't change the composition of the whipped cream beyond turning the white more tan. Into the refrigerator it went, a surprise dessert for hungry men.

She could ignore the parlor no longer. The piano looked better after a good dusting and some polish that the wood drank up like a thirsty plant. So did the writing desk and bookshelves. Soon the place smelled of linseed oil.

All this reminded her of that dutiful letter waiting to be written to Mother. She sat down at the writing desk and started out the usual way with her letter to Mumsy, politely asking about the weather and commenting on her job here with the county extension agency, which Audrey knew would never interest her mother in a million years.

Her next paragraph turned into sympathy over Mother's last letter, with its querulous complaints about Husband Three and her needy bid for consolation, now that the war had shut down most of her fun. Instead of her usual coddling of Mother, Audrey urged her to visit a library or perhaps find the nearest Red Cross facility and volunteer for…something. She signed her name, stuffed the letter into an envelope, addressed it to

Boston's finest street, stuck on a stamp and called it good. Could she even call it quits?

She heard distant thunder. Maybe the storm would hold off long enough for it to break at bedtime. She could lie there with Gut Bucket at her feet and enjoy the companionable clatter of rain on the roof. She might relish her last night with Ed, before he flew to London with the State Department bigwig whose name she had forgotten. She thought about him now, aware that he was never far from her thoughts.

They made love, then lay close together, talking about the expected baby, making plans. "The war won't last forever," he had told her, and he was right. His war ended three days later. She vowed to hate the Germans forever, which worked pretty well, until she met some.

Shaking her head over that, Audrey turned her attention to the next duty letter, this one to her mother-in-law, who never wanted to be addressed by anything except Mrs. Allerton. She found she just couldn't. "Very well then, don't," said the new Audrey Allerton. She waited for a guilty twinge that didn't come, closed the writing desk, and went back to the piano, to see what sheet music remained after years of neglect.

The sky darkened, so she turned on the lights, thinking of Dad's ecstatic letter to her at Radcliffe, telling her that rural electric had arrived in Goshen County. She turned the light off and on for fun. They had lights and a refrigerator, and indoor plumbing. True, the kitchen range was still a wood stove, but Dad promised to change that.

She opened the piano bench and pulled out a stack of old show tunes, exercises, and etudes she had cried over in music lessons Dad had insisted on. She sat down and began to run through the scales, limbering up her voice, as well, reminding herself that she was whole and healthy, there were pies on the range top, and a gentle rain would be a good thing.

To her surprise, she found the music for "Passing By." She remembered last seeing it in the box her mother-in-law had sent, after she left. She also distinctly remembered carting it to the burn barrel because the thought of even seeing the music, much less singing it, was impossible. It had become their song, this little madrigal of devotion, learned during the Christmas practices that introduced them. To his red-faced delight, she sang it to Ed during their engagement party, singing, "I did but see *him* passing by," instead of "I did but see her passing by."

Even now, Audrey couldn't look at the next words. She took the music between her fingers to tear it up. She couldn't keep that next plaintive line from her traitor memory, though. *"And yet I'll love him till I die."* Tear it up? Never. The little Elizabethan love song would always tie her to Edward Allerton, gone too soon.

She set it on the piano, wondering if Dad had rescued it. She found she could finger the notes, but singing, not yet. Back it went into the piano bench. She kept out some Mozart airs, a little Bach, some Brahms for beginners.

The clock in the kitchen chimed the one-note four fifteen at the same time the heavens opened and dumped out an extraordinary amount of rain. She ran to the back porch, looking for the PWs and Dad. She could barely see them through a sheet of rain.

She ran down the hall to the linen closet and pulled out an armful of towels. The lights flickered but didn't go out. She piled the towels on the porch swing and waited for the men to arrive. Surely Dad wouldn't make them stand outside in the rain.

He didn't, although he gave her a questioning look as he hit the front steps first. Audrey waved them all in, pointed to the towels, and stood out of the way.

After apologetic looks, the PWs reached the porch and grabbed the towels she held out, handing them around. She went back for more until there were enough. Lightning flashed, thunder rattled the windows, and the wind changed direction, soaking them again on the porch.

"Come inside," Audrey said. "We have room."

She saw their reluctance. Their shoes were muddy, and one towel apiece was barely enough. "Don't worry," she said, then looked for Gerd. "Gerd?"

He looked up from toweling his hair. She must have surprised him. Maybe she surprised herself. That was his name, wasn't it? Easy to remember. Gerd Gauss. Two syllables. Not like some of the lengthy names she had noted this morning, when Major Rheinhold called the roll.

"Please tell them to come in and not to worry about mud on their shoes."

"Can we leave our shoes on the porch?"

"Certainly."

He told them what to do. She wondered what else he said, because some of them chuckled. "I'll bite. What else did you tell them?" she asked.

He gave her a puzzled look. "I'll bite?"

"American slang. It means, well, that's hard to explain." Audrey laughed. "I don't think I can."

"I told them to line up their shoes neatly, so we do not get demerits."

"Demerits? In my father's house? Knothead."

"More slang? My English is Lufthansa English. Not up to American slang."

"Head them toward the kitchen. I have something for you all."

Dad was way ahead of her. He had set the pies on the table next to the plates and was rummaging for forks. Audrey started cutting, doing the math of twelve pieces, which covered PWs, a guard and Dad. That meant four pieces left over. Three maybe two. Gut Bucket was nosing in for his share.

As barefoot and ragged-stockinged men looked on, she cut the pie, plopped on a little whipped cream, put a fork on each plate and handed them around. The rain thundered down and then the lights went out.

"Well, that's inconvenient," she murmured, then stared as one of the prisoners sank to his knees and covered his head. Another man reached for him and held him close.

"He was the only survivor of an air attack on a bunker at El Alamein," Gerd said. "He has trouble when the lights go out at night."

"Poor man," she said. "Can I…can I do anything?"

"I saw the piano. Can you play something soothing?"

She hurried into the parlor, pulled out the Brahms and played his lullaby. There was enough light to play it over and over until the storm receded and the lights came on. Before she knew it, everyone was in the room listening, including the man who had cowered on her kitchen floor. She finished and put her hands in her lap. "I'm out of practice. Would one of you…"

"Heinz," someone said.

Another of the blond-haired, blue-eyed men came forward. She indicated the music, but he shook his head. He closed his eyes, then began to play something so lovely that Audrey thought her heart might stop.

"One of Bach's many lullabies," Gerd said. "He had a lot of children."

The pianist played a more complicated Bach invention next, still without music. "Who is he?" she whispered to Gerd.

"Who was he," he corrected. "Heinz Dorschel was a student at a music conservatory in Berlin, then duty called. That man to the right of the window? He was the best mechanic in the Afrika Korps. Before that, he designed automobiles."

"Everyone has a story."

"We do. Would you like to hear them someday?"

I have a story, too, she thought. *Silly me. I thought I knew what it was. I think it's changing.*

Chapter Nine

The storm let up too soon to suit Audrey. Dad joined her as the men gathered around Heinz and his magic fingers and sang along to a tune that sounded vaguely familiar. Some of the notes were too high for Gut Bucket, who started to howl.

The traitor clock in the kitchen chimed out five notes. Dad motioned the men toward the front door. She stood by the door as shoes went on amid what sounded like cheerful conversation. When they were ready to go, Gerd held up his hand.

"Mr. Nolan, Mrs. Allerton, let me express our thanks to you both for this lovely moment." As he spoke, another man interpreted, which brought smiles and nods all around.

"I suspect this is the first time we have been in a home in many years."

Apparently, the interpreter had trouble with that one, perhaps because he struggled to say something close to his heart, or so Audrey reckoned. From the looks of the others, it was a tender thing to hear.

She felt her heart turn over with that emotion. *I felt the same thing when I returned here last year*, she thought. After Ed's death, there was no home in Boston, which taught her a basic truth: homes need love.

"I'll rev up the truck," Dad said when he could. "Come, gentlemen."

They started moving outside. Audrey looked back to see Heinz fingering the keys one last time, almost as if he feared it couldn't happen again. Time to disabuse him of that notion. "Thank you, Heinz," she said. "Please do this again."

Gerd translated and Heinz nodded and said something that made Gerd shake his head and smile.

"You'd better tell me."

"You don't speak German," he said in a teasing tone. "You realize I could tell you anything I want, and not necessarily what he said."

"I also know you are a good man," she said simply. "Yes, that was hard to say. I was going to hate the lot of you forever."

He took a deep breath, which gave her time to wonder about herself. "What did Heinz say? Incidentally, his English isn't too bad. He's shy. He wanted to know if you would sing a duet with him. He has one in mind. Can you sing?"

"A mediocre mezzo," she said when she recovered from that.

"It's a thought," he said with a shrug. "I know it is months away, Frau Allerton, and the fortunes of all of us can change by then, but we hope to present a Christmas celebration this year. "That is Heinz's aim."

She remembered that camp celebration from last year, and telling her father that she would never attend such a thing. Dad had stayed home, too. Shame on her.

Dad honked the horn, which hustled Heinz from the piano and out the door. Gerd followed and Audrey tagged along, not ready to have the day end, but knowing Walter Watkins awaited with his roster. She had one more question for Gerd before one of the PWs gave him a hand up into the truck bed.

"You're the leader of this group, aren't you?" she asked.

"I suppose I am."

"How did it happen?" Dad honked again. "Coming!"

"I'll tell you sometime."

"You're turning into a gadabout," was Dad's comment as they rattled away.

"I'm surprised."

"And a pretty good piemaker. I'd forgotten."

"I almost forgot, too," she said. She rolled down the window because her face felt flushed and warm. *There is a lot I have forgotten*, she thought. *Nice to be reminded.*

The rain charged the air with the fragrance of ozone and newly turned soil. Audrey wanted to stick her head out the window like Gut Bucket and breathe it all in. Gut Bucket.

"Where's ol' Gut?" she asked.

"Probably in the back with his eleven best friends. I include the guard, of course." He chuckled. "Not much of a guard, is he?"

"No, but we all seem to be making this up as we go along," she observed, which made Dad smile. "Please don't tell Mr. Watkins that we were feeding the enemy."

He was still smiling about that when he pulled into the armory parking lot. They weren't the last arrivals. As others drove in, Audrey noticed that some of the prisoners were soaking wet and shivering, while others must have benefited from the kindness of farm wives with towels.

Dad whistled for Gut Bucket as soon as they arrived. Tail down, Gut jumped from the truck bed and joined him, flopping down with a sigh almost human, which made Dad shake his head.

Audrey squelched her way toward Walter, who held out the roster. "Bad news, or maybe not. Our lovely Major Rheinhold has convinced Captain Gleason that the prisoner count each morning will be held at Camp Veteran itself."

"Why?"

"Maybe he thinks that if I have to drive out to Veteran each morning, I won't do it."

"This will cut into the time you have to help your mother, won't it?"

"It will," he admitted, "and she needs me."

"We have a car in the barn," Audrey said. "It doesn't run, but..." She paused, then told him about the Afrika Korps' best mechanic, currently planting beets in her father's fields. "If he can get that bucket of bolts running, I can take the morning and evening rolls."

"Give it a try. I'll drive to the camp on Monday, Wednesday and Friday, if you can manage Tuesdays and Thursdays."

"We'll need some parts for the auto," she said.

"I can take it out of our budget. Can you arrange for that mechanic?"

"If I can talk to him."

"Find a way as soon as you can. Major Rheinhold is making his announcement now."

Her mind in turmoil, Audrey held the morning's roster as Major Rheinhold strutted up to stand too close to her – drat the man – and announced to the farmers that from now on, they would come to Camp Veteran to pick up their prison laborers, confident, apparently, that Walter Watkins would not drive that added distance to the camp for a twice daily roll call.

"Mr. Watkins," he concluded, with considerable condescension, "You will see that we can somehow manage the calling of names and save you the bother." He clicked his heels together, stared at Audrey's bosom again, and sauntered toward his car, pleased with himself.

Looking not even slightly troubled, Walter called out the PW names by farmers.

She knew what to do when she came to her father's PWs. Walter called out each name clearly and each man came forward to initial his signature from the morning check.

"Gerd Gauss."

"I'm talking fast," she said when she handed him the roster to initial. "We'll get Gut Bucket back to you, so we pick him up at the camp tonight. I need a mechanic to fix that car in the barn. We can talk tonight."

"Distract the major when the roll call is done." Gerd signed his name and walked toward the others, hands in his pockets, the picture of ease.

After Walter called the next farmer's name, Audrey whispered to him, "Gerd can get me a mechanic. I need a distraction about now. I'll explain tomorrow morning." Walter nodded, as if this was something he did every day, and she continued the name check.

When they finished, most of the men milled around in the parking lot, close together and chatting with each other. (Thank you, Gerd.) "Showtime," Walter said to her, and slammed the roster against his leg. He strode to Major Rheinhold and exclaimed, "You are making this job of mine difficult! What will my superiors say when I tell them you are giving counter-orders about this new way we are to track our PWs! Explain that to me!"

Oh, good man. He even forced the major to face away from the PWs. An unhappy Gut Bucket languished alone in the back of the Nolan truck. She quietly called to him, and he jumped down. Gerd whistled softly and the dog, eager to be among his new best friends, disappeared in a sea of blue denim. In no time the PWs were in the trucks, being driven toward Camp Veteran.

"What was that all about?" Dad asked, as she climbed in.

"Make tracks, Dad. I'll tell you."

Dad waited instead, obviously enjoying the sight of modest Walter Watkins chewing out a Nazi. "You're making my job difficult," Walter said. "Mark my words, we'll do that morning and evening head count because it's the law." He swore and stalked toward Dad's truck, the picture of resentment.

"Good job, Walter," she said. "See you at Camp Veteran tomorrow morning? I'll explain this whole thing."

"Please do," he said, then gave her a wonderful smile. "That was fun. I should snarl at overbearing Nazis more often."

Chapter Ten

"I have my doubts that anyone can raise that Ford from the dead," Dad said as they drove toward Camp Veteran after dinner. "Mr. Watkins is so sure that Rheinhold and his super-Nazis are harming those less-fervent PWs?"

"He is. It's on the QT mind you, but he's heard from other extension agents that it's a problem everywhere."

"If you say so."

Audrey heard all his doubt. She gave his shoulder a nudge as they rattled along toward the former Civilian Conservation Corps camp which became a PW camp with the addition of two guard towers and two tall barbed wire fences.

"You enjoyed feeding those Germans, didn't you?" he asked.

"It surprised me, too." Should she? Why not? "I kind of like them. There. I admit it."

"Maybe Gerd Gauss?" Dad asked. "He seemed to have something to say to you over that roster. Something in the spring air?"

"Dad, that is ridiculous," she replied, determined not to be embarrassed. Besides, how nowhere could something like that go? She settled on, "Maybe he's reminding me that my life isn't over."

"I'll thank him for that, then," her father told her, as they came in sight of the camp. "You came back to me so sad and uncertain." He shifted gears to slow down the beast. "I like the Audrey I'm seeing now."

He wasn't one to toss around a compliment. She knew he meant it. "Thanks, Dad."

Locating Gut Bucket was surprisingly easy. The American flag flew over one of the smaller buildings separated by more barbed wire from

179

four long barracks constructed of what looked like wood and tarpaper. By the barracks, some men in denim with towels slung around their necks headed toward another building, probably the bathhouse.

Audrey couldn't mistake it for a Boy Scout camp, not when she looked back at the open gate they had come through, a sentry on each side. And those guard towers. Two barb-wire fences about eight feet apart paralleled each other around the entire camp.

"Can't put lipstick on this pig and make her pretty," she murmured. While she waited in the truck, Dad went inside the office to explain the matter. He came out minutes later with a sheet of paper. "Trust the government. Gut Bucket is now on a list of some sort." He waved the paper at her. "Too many of these and it's probably curtains for our mutt. Out you get, Audie. This nice fella is going to walk us to Block Four."

She nodded at the soldier, who grinned and blushed. They passed another small building with another US flag and a red cross stenciled on the wall. "The infirmary?" she asked the guard.

"Yes, ma'am."

"Is there a doctor on duty?"

"Now and then. The nurse is there all week." He held up a finger with an orange stain seeping through a bandage. "She thinks mercurochrome will cure anything."

They passed a larger building. Audrey heard piano music inside, and wondered if Heinz Dorschel practiced here. "They have an orchestra," the soldier explained. "The Krauts like their music. There's a little stage, too, for plays they write, or concerts. Teachers from the high school teach English here, American history, and French and Spanish in the evenings."

"Pretty posh," Dad whispered to her. "Maybe that stockade is to keep people *out*, who'd like to learn languages and play instruments. I dunno, Audie. I think I understand why some of my friends at the American Legion whine about this place being a country club."

The soldier heard him and made a face. "It's ok for them, but they can't leave." He had the grace to laugh. "I'm stuck here, too, because of the Krauts."

Audrey considered his words. Only a few months ago, she could have made some remark about how the Krauts had ruined any number of lives. Maybe hating all Germans was easier when everything about the war was white or black, and not this maddening gray.

"How many prisoners are there at Camp Veteran?" Dad asked as they walked.

"About two forty. They're mostly from the North Africa campaigns."

"And they're allowed to wear their uniforms?" He pointed to prisoners sitting behind their barrack, dressed in tan or light blue shorts and shirts.

"Yes, sir. That's a provision of the Geneva Convention." The guard stopped before a long tarpaper building with an improbable row of green shoots. "Someone here likes to plant flowers." He grinned. "And apparently steal dogs."

"That's my fault," Dad said. "Old Gut Bucket seems to like hanging around with the guys planting the beets."

"I'll find him for you, sir," the guard said. He opened the door and went inside.

"How're we going to get enough time to talk to the mechanic?" Dad whispered.

She had no idea. The scheme suddenly seemed silly and doomed to fail. What now?

The guard came out. "It seems that everyone decided to play what they call football. It's a strange sport, but they like it." He shrugged. "Would you mind if I pointed you in the right direction? I'm supposed to be on duty by the gate."

Yes! Audrey thought. "I think the two of us can convince our dog that he needs to hang out with better company."

The guard grinned at that. "They're not bad sorts, for Krauts," he said. "Mr. Nolan, just initial the sign-in sheet and post the time of day when you're done. Leave it with me." He left, after indicating the playing field.

There was Gut Bucket, chasing the ball every time someone kicked it. Dad put his fingers to his lips and whistled. Gut Bucket slowly moved toward them, his tail between his legs, ready for a scold. Audrey knelt and scratched his ears. "Don't be silly, Gut," she whispered. "We got you in trouble in the first place."

She stood by Dad's dog, who, in that way of canines, knew he had avoided a scold. He whined, clearly wanting to rejoin his new friends. She thought of breathless newspaper accounts of the mighty men of the Afrika Korps, Rommel's Desert Rats. Here they were, ragged and many in need of haircuts, playing a European sport in a Wyoming prison compound. Gerd waved to her and hurried over with another man she recognized from the sing along.

"Tell us what you need, Mr. Nolan," Gerd said. "We don't dare stand here too long."

Dad looked at the sentry towers. "They're watching us?"

"Not them," he said seriously, reminding Audrey that nothing about this was a game. "Hardly them! Word gets back through others to Major Rheinhold, if you linger long." He knelt to scratch Gut Bucket's ears, too, and motioned toward the tall man hanging back. "This is Dietrich Schopenhauer. He was the best mechanic in Afrika Korps. What do you need?"

Audrey watched as Dad nodded to Dietrich, who knelt, too, to pet the dog. "Dietrich, I need you to get a car running. It's in my barn. My daughter needs it to do the roll call out here on Tuesdays and Thursdays. Mr. Watkins has other responsibilities and can't make it those days." He looked at Gerd. "Will you interpret all that? Maybe I should have spoken more slowly."

Dietrich made a small gesture. "No worries. I spent three years in Detroit, working for Chrysler Corporation, learning about design. *Ja*, I can help." He looked at his hands. "I'm better with engines than beets."

"Thank you," Dad said. "Please check out my auto tomorrow and give me a list of parts you need."

"What about the guard? What about Shep?" Audrey asked. "What if he tells Captain Gleason what is going on? Ten of you are supposed to work in the field."

"No worries," Gerd said, then spoke to her father. "You may use Dietrich however you choose. All Shep knows is that he is to guard ten men." He looked around at the other men, some of whom she recognized from the day's work. "Let us all walk you toward the gate. That way, we can talk a few more minutes." He returned to the pitch, spoke a few words. She heard the laughter, and smiled when six familiar faces joined them, sauntering along as if they did this every evening after work. Gut Bucket, pleased to be the center of attention, darted around like the puppy he wasn't. They were a congenial group walking a purloined dog to the gate.

"About those guards," Gerd began. "Don't repeat this. Some of the boys in Block Two were getting bored. They noticed that the guards in the tower are usually sleeping, especially after the noon meal."

"They're not the best troops in the US Army," Dad said apologetically.

"Not at all," Gerd agreed. "That is why we like them! After dinner on Sunday last week, two of the best infiltrators in Tunisia and Algeria crawled under the wire and climbed into the sentry box. Sure enough, the guard was sound asleep." He laughed and reached down to scratch behind Gut Bucket's ears. "They stole the sleeping man's machine gun, a side arm, and ammunition. Hauled them right down, back through the wire, and hid them in the chapel under the altar."

"Goodness. No one saw them?" Audrey asked, amazed. "What nerve."

"I said they were bored. They left a note demanding a ransom of 5,000 cigarettes, payable in the morning after Sunday Mass."

"And…" Dad asked, his eyes merry.

"There it was under the altar. The guard got his gun back and avoided a court martial – in Germany it would be a firing squad – and we got 5,000 cigarettes."

"How on earth…"

"Did he procure that many Camels? Well, some were Lucky Strikes."

She laughed along with this blond man who liked dogs and who was enjoying this whole thing. So was she. "Gerd, you're trying me!"

"Me? Never! I am a knothead again?"

She rolled her eyes. "What in the world do you do with 5,000 cigarettes? Smoke them?"

"Not I. We use them for barter." He lowered his voice. "If we need to bribe Shep, we can. Cigarettes are more useful to us than money."

"And you will have a safe car to drive, *frau*," Dietrich Schopenhauer said. "Hopefully, Major Rheinhold will hear nothing of this. The repercussion could be frightful."

"It would be," Gerd said simply.

They arrived back at the truck too soon. Dad went into the office to sign out. Audrey opened her door and Gut Bucket jumped in. She climbed in next, not surprised with a boost on her waist from Gerd Gauss. He leaned closer. "I know we can find a way to get a little more sugar to you. Your pie is excellent."

"You are all rascals, you know," she replied as he shut the door.

He looked into her eyes, as if he had more to say. Dad came back and started the truck. Gerd stepped up on the running board. "I am surprising myself," he spoke to her father across her. "I like farming."

"Seriously? Farming is more exciting than flying a Messerschmitt?" Dad asked. Audrey wasn't sure if he was in dead earnest or joking.

"Good question, *Herr* Nolan," Gerd replied. "Maybe I like seeing what develops instead of dealing in destruction." He looked around, as if fearful of detection. "Lufthansa pilots take people to destinations. Messerschmitt pilots don't."

He gave them a cheerful salute, stepped off the running board and joined his friends.

Audrey Allerton was a long time getting to sleep that night.

Chapter Eleven

Wednesday morning, Walter Watkins was late to Camp Veteran and Major Rheinhold looked around in triumph. Captain Gleason turned away, his jaw working, anger written everywhere on his face, along with the great pain that appeared to be his constant companion.

"Captain Gleason isn't up to this," Dad said as he sat in the cab of the beet truck with Audrey.

"He has to do it anyway," Audrey said, even though she felt the same uncertainty. "My boss told me that the U.S. Army officer in charge of the Scottsbluff camp is quite happy for the Nazi officers to control their men."

"That makes some sense," Dad admitted, "but not at the expense of the lives of PWs who aren't Nazi enough."

"Could we even prove such a thing?" Audrey asked. She sighed, thinking of the patient young men from Bavarian farms now planting tiny seeds in Wyoming; the one who recoiled in fear from sudden darkness; the Lufthansa pilot given no choice about joining the Luftwaffe; the music conservatory student. To her surprise but not her comfort, the men had become more than prisoners in denim, because she knew them a little. "If we prove that Nazis are intimidating their own soldiers, would anyone care?"

They looked at each other and knew the answer to that one. To the majority of Americans, men in denim with PW painted so visibly were all Nazis, all the enemy, all to be ignored if anything went wrong with them here. She watched the men milling together inside the gate, amiably chatting with each other, and felt otherwise.

Dad watched them, too. "Audie, you know we'd be a lot better off, you and I, if we didn't have such damned soft hearts."

"I know. What a curse."

185

"I'm glad you're my kid," he said simply.

With a cloud of exhaust that made Dad wince, Walter Watkins chugged through the gate, stopped with a grind of gears and jumped out, roster in hand. "Tallyho," Audrey said, and joined him.

"You're burning daylight," Major Rheinhold said, managing to sound so superior, drat the man. He stood by the admin building, as Captain Gleason leaned against it. "Is not that the expression?" He spread out his hands, the picture of innocence. "I mean, sir, how can you defeat the might of Germany if my men do not plant beets?"

Put that way, their efforts sounded puny and silly. Audrey glared at him, not caring if he noticed. He did, and raised his eyebrows before he bowed elaborately in her direction. "*Frau, guten tag*."

"Burning daylight is the correct expression," Walter replied pleasantly enough but Audrey heard an unexpected edge to the modest man's comment. "However, I believe it is my prerogative, major, and not yours. Good morning, Captain Gleason." He turned to Audrey. "Mrs. Allerton, please ask one of the guards to find a folding chair for the captain."

The grateful look Captain Gleason gave her boss touched Audrey's heart. She did as he asked, and soon the camp's commanding officer sat down with an expression of real relief.

"Audrey, I would like you to read the names this time," Walter said as he handed her the clipboard. "My mother is far from well, and I fear this task, the morning one at least, will fall to you soon."

"I can do that," she replied, not wanting to, wanting no one's eyes on her, the only woman in sight, unless she counted the geriatric nurse in the dispensary, who rarely came out. She inclined her head toward Walter. "That PW I mentioned is going to look over Dad's auto. He is supposed to have a list of parts for me today. I'll hand it off to you."

He nodded, and stepped back, after taking a moment to give the major an impressive glare. *Walter*, she thought with admiration, *the meek aren't going to inherit the earth anytime soon in Goshen County. Good for you.*

She stumbled over a few names, but no one made fun of her except the major, who could roll his eyes most elaborately. *I'll bet you can't pronounce Puyallup, Washington*, she thought, ignoring him with real serenity, *or Natchitoches, Louisiana.*

She found herself enjoying the roll call, especially the names of the PWs headed again to her father's farm. The names had faces now. She nodded to Dietrich Schopenhauer, who was destined for a day in the barn, trying to see if that Ford could be raised from the dead. Gerd Gauss got another nod, but only a small one. No sense in alerting the major.

"Check your cannister for sugar tonight," Gerd whispered, when he came to print his name. "We have been busy."

"For heaven's sake," she whispered back. "If you get in trouble, it's on you."

"More pie?" was his comment as he signed.

"You are trying my patience." That earned Audrey a grin.

She sat in Walter's car as he helped Captain Gleason to his feet and walked with him to the office. *How can this man function?* she asked herself. She watched the two men, and realized she had seriously underestimated Walter Watkins. She wondered if his quiet strength rivaled her own father's, and improbably, Gerd Gauss's. She made herself think how she felt in the company of each man and felt her shoulders relax and calm return. She also decided not to question it, not now, not when there was a deep game underway at Camp Veteran.

"That man is not long for this world," Walter commented as he drove out of the PW camp. "He's convinced he must remain at his post. When I try to ask him about Major Rheinhold's influence, he remains silent."

"What can you do?" she asked. A mere week ago, she wouldn't have thought Walter Watkins would even say boo to a goose. *I've been wrong before*, she reminded herself, then felt that odd sort of calm strengthen within her again. *Maybe I have been wrong about my own grit.*

"I intend to think of something," he said, with an assurance she hadn't reckoned on.

"I will do whatever you require of me, Walter," she said. "Your mother is ill?"

He nodded, his eyes on the road. She watched a muscle work in his jaw. "I know people think I am a mama's boy."

"Oh, but…"

He smiled at the road. "Admit it, Audrey."

"Well…"

When they arrived at the courthouse, he drove into his parking spot, parked, and turned to her, his face serious as usual, except that this time there was something more, a longing, barely masked, that he wanted her to understand him. "I wish I could somehow spread the word that we two, mother and son, are all we have. After my father deserted us in the early days of the Depression, Mama held things together somehow. I always had food. It wasn't prime rib, but I have never really cared for that fatty cut of meat."

Audrey laughed, enjoying this new Walter Watkins. He smiled in that offhand way of his that Audrey understood now was his shelter against deep hurt. "She took in washing and ironing. I collected empty bottles. We did everything we could. When it wasn't enough, we did without, but quietly." He stared beyond her to other days, troubled times. "Now she is ill, and I do not know how much longer we have together ..." His voice trailed off. Again, that offhand smile. "I believe I understand our PWs. I know what it is to feel helpless."

She thought about that all day, as she filed and typed, and edited the make-work flower project. She unnerved herself after lunch by the odd reflection that Gerd Gauss would understand her. She sensed more than knew that he was a man grounded and centered in reality, even as he looked out for others. No wonder the men in Block Four considered him a leader. She allowed herself the tiny luxury (not one under ration by the U.S. government), that perhaps, just perhaps, he was looking out for her, too. She reminded herself that this notion was absurd, but what was the harm of a daydream? This daydream was her business alone and would remain such.

Dorrie and Walter spent some time closeted in the tiny space grandiosely called the Conference Room. Audrey heard low voices, but they came out smiling then sat down beside Audrey's desk, which didn't surprise her, considering the comradeship growing in the office. She liked the feeling and folded her hands on her desk.

"I'm going home now," Walter said. "Dr. Morris called me from the hospital. My mother has been admitted."

"I'm so sorry, Walter," Audrey said and meant every word.

"I'm turning the roll calls over to Dorrie and you, Audrey." He blushed. "I'm reluctant to have you do the count there alone, Audrey. Dorrie agrees."

She wondered how much courage it took to make such a statement fraught with a subtext or two: the unspoken, *You're a lovely woman. There are more than two hundred men at that camp. There is safety in numbers*, went through her mind. She nodded, even though she knew every farmer waiting for his laborers would thrash any of them if someone got fresh with her.

"I'll be taking the extension car to the camp starting tomorrow morning," Dorrie said. She blushed, too, but Audrey sensed a different concern. Dorrie knew she was plain and plump and that her role was to intimidate.

"We will do just fine," Audrey assured her. "Maybe this is audacious, Walter. I know I'm speaking out of turn, but is some way we can, uh, retire Captain Gleason, and...and see someone else appointed in his place, someone who is firm but understanding?"

Maybe she wasn't off the mark, because Walter nodded. "I'll be writing letters with that very idea," he said. He picked up his briefcase but remained seated, as if reluctant to abandon the women. "Even more, I want to see Major Rheinhold removed to that...that camp for super Nazis in Oklahoma. But who will take Captain Gleason's place?"

She knew there was only one answer. "Walter will, won't he, Dorrie?"

Dorrie nodded. "That's right."

"*Me*?"

"None better, sir."

Chapter Twelve

After some stammering and dithering, Walter hurried off to the hospital. Audrey felt a momentary pang, wondering if Dorrie Hatcher was equal to the occasion. Dorrie could read minds, apparently. She favored Audrey with her level gaze and declared, "We can do this!"

And they did. The afternoon roll call went with no hitches, beyond Audrey wondering how much sugar they had stolen from the mess hall, and where it had ended up on the farm. Captain Gleason wasn't there, which meant that Major Rheinhold strutted around with a more pronounced smirk than usual. *Insufferable man*, she thought.

"He irritates me," she whispered to Gerd when it was his turn to initial his morning's signature.

"It's more than irritation," he whispered back. "I think he is planning something."

There was no more time to say anything. Audrey watched him join the others as they waited for the roll call to finish, and return to their barracks.

When Dietrich Schopenhauer came forward to initial his name, he handed her a list of parts. "These are all parts that can be found easily enough," he said. "The only hazard was a wasp's nest in the back seat."

"Poor you," Audrey teased, happy to deal with something concrete she could handle, and not the vague uneasiness from men as powerless as she was. "Dead wasps everywhere now?"

"*Nein, frau* Allerton. I swept out the carcasses," he told her, with lurking good humor.

She assured him they would get the auto parts as soon as possible, which earned her a cheery salute and a moment to reflect on such multitalented men in a Germany without war. But here they were in baggy blue denim, living behind barbed wire, prisoners.

When her father's roster was accounted for, she watched as Major Rheinhold nodded for those ten men to march to their barracks. Then it was back to the next farmer's workers and the next until they finished. She handed the clipboard to Dorrie. "That's all it is."

"That's it?"

"That's it."

Dorrie looked down at the clipboard. Audrey knew what she was going to say before it came out of her mouth.

"Audrey, is there anything to Mr. Watkins's suspicions?"

"I wish I knew," she finally said, hoping that would cover the subject. She saw no point in passing on Gerd's warning.

"Mr. Watkins has enough on his plate without borrowing trouble where there probably isn't any," Dorrie said as she headed toward the car. "Still, we'll do as he requests."

Audrey handed her the meticulous list compiled by Dietrich Schopenhauer of what parts were needed to get the old Ford running, a detail she knew Mr. Watkins had already approved. Dorrie scanned it. "I'm betting Webster's has these," she says. "See you tomorrow."

Both Dad and Gut Bucket were waiting for her in the cab of the truck. "Wait a minute, buckaroo," she said, grabbing at *Herr* Mutt's collar as he tried to follow the line of men moving toward their barracks.

"Nazi collaborator," Dad joked. "He'll probably whine and mope until we're out of sight of the camp."

She laughed because she knew Dad expected it. As she looked back at the line of men as the beet truck rumbled through the gate, Gerd Gauss was looking at her. She wanted to wave. She raised her hand, then lowered it, bothered by the thought that he could never even be a friend, not really.

The thought kept her silent, not that there was anything about the day to share with her father, since it was typing and filing, and working on the plant and flower pamphlet and worrying. Luckily, Dad filled in the blanks.

"Those guys," he said as they rumbled along. "When Shep went back to the house to get their sack lunches, they each pulled out a sock from their baggy trousers and handed it to me."

"*What?*"

"Full of sugar." He smiled at the memory. "I found an empty coffee can and they filled it, Shep none the wiser. What'll it be tomorrow, honey? Pie? Cake?"

"Cake, I think."

"Only if I can lick the bowl."

"Oh, Dad!"

As it turned out, there was no cake or pie on Thursday. Walter Watkins was right.

The morning's weather seemed to match her mood: cloudy with a chance of unease, or in this case, cloudy with bits of snow teasing them, threatening either foul weather by afternoon or sunshine.

Dorrie already stood by the extension agency car, tapping her fingers on the clipboard. "Are we late, Dad?" Audrey asked.

"Nope. There's Captain Gleason today. Lord, but he looks like death on a cracker. The U.S. Army had no business keeping him on duty. Anyone I can complain to?"

"Maybe Mr. Watkins. Maybe the officer who commands the Scottsbluff camp." She sighed as he stopped the truck in its usual spot next to Cal Miner's truck. "You'll fill out a form in triplicate and it'll go nowhere, I have a file folder full of stuff like that."

"Out you get, kiddo." He leaned out the window and looked up. "Don't like that sky."

She joined Dorrie, passing the rows of PWs, conscious of her slacks and sweater, wondering what would happen if someone whistled, which had happened to her a time or two when she walked past a row of GIs outside the armory in Scottsbluff, waiting for a ride to somewhere. Germans were either better mannered or better disciplined. Well, most. She couldn't avoid Major Rheinhold, whose eyes took in every inch of her bosom. She ignored him, disliking him more by the minute.

She nodded to Dorrie, who handed her the roster, and leaned closer to whisper, "Mr. Watkins called the office before I left. His mother is quite unwell."

"Poor man!" Audrey glanced at Captain Gleason. "There is another poor man."

Unsure of herself as Major Rheinhold ogled on, Audrey stepped closer to the PWs and began to call the roll. The men moved to her to sign their name, then joined "their" farmer, the same as usual. When she came to Cal Miner's group of ten, someone in the group called out and pointed. She looked toward the officers to see Captain Gleason sink to his knees, his head down.

Dorrie hurried to help him up, and glared at Major Rheinhold, who just stood there, looking like someone who probably had Master Race tattooed on his backside. One of the prisoners ran for a chair and soon the captain was seated and looking apologetic. "I'll be all right, Miss Hatcher," he told Dorrie, and waved her away. "Just give me a moment to catch my breath." He waved at Audrey to continue.

She did, finishing with Cal Miner's list. She began her father's list, somehow comforted to see familiar faces. Almost all. "Matthieu Bauer," she called, and someone else came forward to sign his name.

Or did he? Maybe she couldn't remember who Matthieu was. Confused, she looked down at the roster. No. Matthieu Bauer had signed his name. "Gerd Gauss?" she called, suddenly unsure of herself.

He stepped forward quickly and signed his name. "Hans Meister just took the place of our Matthieu Bauer. It happened with that distraction. You must call a halt quickly. Now!"

"No. They'll implicate you," she whispered back. "Give me a few more names."

He narrowed his eyes but what could he do? He joined the men by her father's truck. Out of the corner of her eye she saw Dad's PWs whispering together and deliberately distancing themselves from the man who, she realized with a sick feeling, had signed in Matthieu's place.

She took a deep breath and turned to Major Rheinhold, dreading to stand close to him, hating his eyes on her breasts. She held out the roster. "Major, we have a problem," she said clearly. She managed a smile. "I am sure it is my faulty German, but I think someone is in the wrong line." She pointed to Hans Meister, who stood by himself now, as much as he tried to blend in. "Hans, I know you didn't mean to be in my father's line." She looked down at the clipboard, holding it tight to keep her hands from shaking. "You belong with Mr. Miner. Remember?"

She waited, willing herself taller and braver because something was really wrong. Then she saw Matthieu Bauer in Mr. Miner's line, his eyes wide with terror. She looked closer. The left side of his face was bruised and swollen and one of the PWs in Mr. Miner's group had twisted the young prisoner's arm behind his back.

She gave a nod to Dorrie, who joined her. "We have to get Matthieu Bauer out of there," she whispered. "Do you feel tough?"

"I always feel tough," Dorrie said, as her eyes narrowed. "Forward march."

Relieved to have reinforcements, Audrey hurried with Dorrie to Mr. Miner's PWs, who stood ready to climb into his beet truck. She had never cared for Mr. Miner, especially after Walter Watkins tsked tsked at his desk one day about the number of injuries that seemed to happen to men on that detail.

Impervious to stares and whispers that didn't sound gentlemanly, Audrey shouldered her way through the cluster. "There you are, Matthieu," she said, coming up next to him with Dorrie, who glared at the PWs and took the small prisoner by the arm. "This way."

With Audrey on his other side, they walked him to Dad's truck. She saw Hans Meister's eyes narrow and his lips tighten. She thought she saw fear, not malice, on his face, and hesitated.

She turned to Dietrich Schopenhauer. "Mr. Schopenhauer," she began in a clear voice that she hoped carried to Major Rheinhold. "Could you please tell Mr. Meister that he must have gotten in the wrong line? Thank you."

As Schopenhauer spoke in German, Hans moved away because he had no choice. Dad's PWs hustled Matthieu Bauer into his beet truck. Dad was out of the cab now, his hands on his hips, watching Major Rheinhold. He called Audrey over and put his arm around her. "What in the Sam Hill…"

"We got Matthieu Bauer away from Mr. Miner's truck," she whispered. "I have to finish the roll."

"All right, kiddo. We're making tracks as soon as you finish." He patted her shoulder and walked to the back of his truck, watching the prisoners climb in. He raised the tailgate.

Shaken and uncertain, Audrey reminded herself that this wretched assignment wouldn't last forever and finished the roll call. She handed the clipboard to Dorrie. "As soon as I know what is going on, I will telephone you."

Dorrie nodded, then glared at Major Rheinhold for good measure and stalked back to her car.

Audrey let Dad help her into the cab, then relaxed her shoulders as every ounce of courage drained from her body. His expression neutral, he started the engine.

When they were out of sight of the camp, someone banged on the back window. Dad slowed and then stopped. He leaped from the cab after warning her not to move. He came back quickly. "Audie, there's a blanket behind the seat. Hand it to me."

"Dad, what…"

"Mr. Miner's PW detail was going to finish off that little fellow. Open your door and scoot over."

She did as he said. As Dad watched in the rearview mirror, maybe looking for someone from the camp, Gerd Gauss slid into the cab beside her. To her astonishment, he took her hand, raised it to his lips and kissed it.

"You just saved a man's life."

Chapter Thirteen

"What's going on?" Dad asked as he started the truck again.

"It requires an explanation," Gerd said.

"That's what I would like," Dad replied agreeably, as if he spoke to a simpleton. Audrey never cared for that tone of voice, when he directed it at her during a stupid teenage mistake a few years ago. She doubted Gerd cared for it, either.

When Gerd said nothing, Dad stopped the truck. "You're going to tell me everything or I'm driving right back to Camp Veteran and dumping out the whole lot of you! Don't try me."

"I will tell you, sir, but it involves more of an explanation than I can provide in the time it takes to get to your farm," Gerd said hastily. Audrey could tell he was grasping for words. "When …when we arrive, is there a bed for Matthieu Bauer? Will you please call a physician from Torrington? He's already been beaten so badly. *Bitte, Herr Nolan, bitte.* Please."

Dad thought a moment then nodded. He started the truck again. "And you're not going to kiss my daughter's hand again."

"No, sir."

Gut Bucket whimpered. He abandoned Audrey's lap and slid onto Gerd's. "It's good to have a friend," Gerd said as he scratched the dog behind his ears. Touched, Audrey watched the prisoner's shoulders lower. He leaned back and closed his eyes, as if feeling safe for the first time in many hours.

"You need to tell us what is going on," Audrey said.

"I do. I will," he replied. That was all he said until they pulled to a stop in the U driveway, which was fast turning white from those few flakes of snow that were combining into an impressive spring snowstorm to try the patience of ranchers and farmers alike.

"Mr. Nolan, may we please take Matthieu to a bed?" Gerd asked.

"Certainly you may. Audie, open up that room across from you. I'm going to call Dr. Barnes."

"We have no money to pay him."

"That is the least of your worries, young man."

Gerd managed a brief smile. "I have not felt young in many years."

"Join the club. Help him, Audie."

She joined the others at the back of the truck as someone lowered the tailgate and passed Matthieu Bauer down on the blanket. "He's unconscious," she said, alarmed.

"In *der* truck he was barely with us when, pfft, out he went," Heinz piano player said.

Audrey hurried inside and up the stairs, stopping first at the linen closet for sheets and pillow slips. Gerd followed her. She handed him the sheets and pointed to the closed door. The room smelled abandoned. Audrey couldn't remember the last time anyone had slept there. She opened the window, which brought in cold air, but took away the staleness.

Without a word, she and Gerd made the bed quickly. He was tucking in the top sheet when she took two blankets from the cedar chest at the foot of her bed across the hall. She heard Dad directing the PWs up the stairs, the biggest man carrying the smaller prisoner. Gently he set him down, then started removing his clothing. When his shirt came off, Audrey gasped to see bruises around his ribs.

"Why, Gerd, why?"

"Matthieu Bauer, like many of us, is not Nazi enough to suit Major Rheinhold," he snapped, angry, she could tell, but not at her. "I have mentioned this."

"That makes no sense," she managed to say, as a PW gentled the unconscious man out of his shirt. "I'll... I'll get a nightshirt from my father."

She hurried downstairs to her father's room as he came from the kitchen. "I called Doc. He'll be here if the roads are passable. It's getting worse out there. If not, he told me to put warm compresses on his face and keep him propped up."

"Dad, he had bruises like that all over his chest," she said, unable to stop her tears. "Have you a nightshirt?"

"I'll get it." He turned to his bureau and rummaged. "Here." He looked out the window. The snow was falling so hard that she couldn't see the beet truck in the driveway. "I don't think the doctor is coming, and these men aren't going to the field."

"Can you keep them busy today?" she asked, following him to the foot of the stairs, dreading what she would find upstairs. How can a man survive such beatings?

Dad's smile was genuine. "Can I keep able-bodied men busy on a farm? Audie, trust me, I can." He took another look and his expression changed. "I don't think I'm driving anyone eight miles back to the stockade tonight, either." It changed again, and she felt the heart return to her body. "I'm not about to return these prisoners, if it isn't safe. We have a guard. Well, we have Shep. I suppose he'll do." (They both smiled at that one.) "I'll get some warm water and you get some washrags. Find the hot water bottle."

She handed Dad's nightshirt to Gerd, who stood in the doorway upstairs. "*Danke*," he said softly. "He's conscious. Have you any *schnapps*, anything a little strong?"

"Is that a good idea?" she asked, feeling young and foolish and out of her element.

"It is a good idea," he told her. "And while you're at it, take a sip yourself. We'll all pull through this, Mrs. Allerton."

"Audrey," she said automatically.

"Gerd."

She felt too shy to look at him. She took washcloths from the linen closet and went downstairs to see Dad ushering seven prisoners out the door, plus Shep. "We're going to the barn," Dad said, "that Holy of Holies. Lots to do there, including – I am informed by one who knows – dismantling one of Henry Ford's early engines. Mr. Schopenhauer, is it?'

The man she knew as Dietrich only smiled.

"Gerd wants some spirits for Matthieu. Where do you keep it, Dad?"

"I hide it in the cookie jar. Where else? I think you'll find enough eggs and butter in that kitchen for a cake. Just saying. And there's that coffee can full of sugar." He looked at the men watching him. "Gentlemen, let us make an appointment with some manure forks." He winked at her. "Good thing their English is not so great."

"Manure," someone said, then turned to the others. "*Der Düngen, meine Brüder.*"

Dad pointed a warning finger at them as he smiled. "You take care of things here, Audie."

"Yes, *meine Vader*," she teased. "Is that right, Mr. Schopenhauer?"

"Close enough," he said with a smile of his own.

It was the last smile Audrey saw for a long time. She turned her attention to hot water, a bowl, and that hot water bottle, all of it puny first aid again the magnitude of Private Bauer's injuries, seen and probably unseen.

She made two trips before she was satisfied, one trip with a towel slung over her shoulder, washrags and warm water in a basin; the next with a dusty bottle of something looking vaguely medicinal and alcoholic at the same time, and a shot glass. She found another pillow for Matthieu and settled it behind his head, then steadied him as Gerd poured down a small amount of the spirits.

He sniffed the bottle top. "Vile." He peered at the label. "*Herr* Jack Daniels should find another occupation."

"Now you are a critic of American whiskey," she said, striving for a light touch, even as the private gasped from the pain as the other man – was he a medic of some sort? – felt his ribs. "What did they do to him?"

Gerd interpreted the rapid German from Medic Man. "Matthieu told Karl Kreuger here that last night they beat him with..." He thought a moment "...bars of soap in a sock."

"For God's sake why?" Audrey demanded. She sat beside the bed, determined not to leave until she learned something about these men who could just as easily lie to her or tell the truth. "You're all prisoners. You're all Germans. I don't understand."

Karl spoke to Gerd, who heard him out, then shook his head. He said something equally precise in return. Karl shrugged and placed warm washrags on Matthieu's battered stomach.

"We are of two opinions," Gerd said. He sat down on the bed close to her chair. "I believe I can trust you. Karl is not certain."

"Kindly tell him I can be trusted," Audrey said, as she wondered how to get through barriers of language and animosity.

"I know that." He leaned closer, as if to touch her, but refrained. He gestured to the boy in the bed. "Matthieu is a credulous sort – a country boy – who believed the lies, even big ones. You have a word for it?"

"Whoppers," she said. "That big?"

"A weasel of a man named Goebbels speaks on the radio to young men like Matthieu, farm boys with little education and boundless patriotism. He tells them over and over that the Luftwaffe – that would be me and other pilots – has bombed American cities into oblivion."

"That's ridiculous," Audrey scoffed. "The distance...."

"I know. You know." He nodded toward the still figure. "He doesn't, poor boy. His leaders betrayed him and he asked too many questions."

"But..."

Audrey knew there was more, but she heard a door opening downstairs. She went to the landing to see her father, followed by Doctor Barnes, someone who might know how to deal with bars of soap slammed over and over against someone's torso. Wordless with relief, she hurried downstairs, helped him from his overcoat and shook it off on the porch.

"I was already headed out this way. A baby at the Bambergs. Lord, but he came fast! I figured I could keep going another half mile. What is it?"

He winced when Audrey, her words tumbling out even as she led him to the stairs, told him about the soap. "Why in the world..."

"I was only beginning to hear the story from Gerd... from Sergeant Gauss," she said.

"I'll see what I can do," Doc Barnes said, his eyes on the stairs.

She and Dad followed him upstairs. Audrey stood in the doorway of her room while the men went into the room across the corridor. All was silent, then she heard agonized moans. *Please, Lord, let them be gentle*, she thought, *even if Matthieu Bauer is a German.*

As she stood there feeling useless, Gerd came to the door. She beckoned to him and he took her by the arm, leading her toward the steps.

"As we feared, he has a host of broken ribs," Gerd said with no preamble. "The physician is wrapping them now. He said something about internal injuries, and his head...Poor Matthieu. Poor, gullible Matthieu. What they started last night, they were going to finish today."

I don't want to go downstairs, she thought. "Come into my room," she said. "You must tell me more."

After a small hesitation, he followed her into her bedroom. She pointed to the chair by the window, where he stood a moment, watching the snow blow sideways, something Dad, with a straight face, would call a Wyoming Zephyr. "Is this a blizzard?" Gerd asked. "In April?"

"Very nearly. Spring blizzards are odd creatures. Give it two days, and then the snow will be gone, with crocuses poking through," she told him, thinking of other Wyoming Aprils. "The ranchers worry about baby calves, and farmers like my father worry about seeds coming up."

"Will we have to plant again?"

"No. Nothing is above ground yet."

When he sat in the chair, Audrey perched on the end of her bed. "Gerd, you must tell me why this has happened to Matthieu."

He leaned back, enjoying the chair. She felt a momentary pang, remembering Ed leaning back like that and watching her strip to her slip then her panties, in this room. They had made one brief visit here after he received his commission in the U.S. Army, which Mrs. Allerton had insisted come before their wedding, because she wanted to show Ed off to her friends as *Lieutenant* Allerton. Two nights here only, and he sat where Gerd sat now.

When she returned home, a widow, after two years too long in Boston, she asked Dad to put her double bed into the room where Matthieu lay in great discomfort. She dreaded the reminder that someone had shared a bed with her, someone whose body was never recovered from the English Channel. A twin bed suited her now.

But as she regarded Gerd, looking more relaxed as his shoulders dropped and his head went back, she knew she didn't want to sleep forever in a twin bed. *Audrey, where did that come from?* she asked herself, then admitted to herself that she knew very well where it came from. Time to strangle that notion at birth. The more critical angel of her nature took over, jostling her mentally and reminding her that just because she had made delicious love to her husband in her childhood bedroom, it wasn't likely to happen again.

But this man, well-trained by flight and war, was observant, drat him. "Your expression…" he said, ever the interpreter, apparently.

Am I honest or not? she questioned in silence. She could make some excuse, but why? He was a widower under tragic circumstances, same as she. It may have been an exhausted adage, but her father had taught her that honesty was the best policy. How much was too much? She thought she knew.

"Ed – my late husband – sat in that chair once." She didn't know what else to say, even though that came out awkward and clumsy to her ears.

"I can move."

"No need. If I can't get used to someone other than Ed sitting there, I am a pretty poor specimen." She glanced at the nightstand, with its photo of a handsome officer and a lovely bride in slinky satin, cut on the bias. "I have photographs."

She watched *his* face this time, appalled by the bleakness that moved in like a cloud across the sun. "Gerd, what did I say? You have photographs. Please tell me you have photographs."

He shook his head. "I did for a while. Hannelore sent me a little snapshot of the two of them when Stefan was a week old." He tried to smile and failed, which looked more horrible than the bleakness. "Every time I flew, I tucked that photo and my rosary in the left pocket of my flight jacket. When the tail of my 109 was shot away and I glided to a stop in front of the British lines, the Tommies went through my pockets."

"Surely they didn't..." She couldn't say it.

"One rifleman with really bad teeth took that photo – the only picture of my son! – and tore it into small bits before my eyes. *Gott im Himmel!*" He turned away and covered his eyes. His shoulders shook and he wept.

Chapter Fourteen

I have photographs, she thought, horrified at such cruelty. *If I had not miscarried, I would have a three-year-old, and more photos. Dear God, why do I whine? Forgive me.*

Audrey did the only thing she knew to do. She went behind the chair and rested her hands on his shoulders. "We are companions in misery," she said softly, then did something she wondered if she would regret. She kissed his head. "If I had not miscarried, I would have a child. Please tell me you have other pictures somewhere."

He regained masterful control she could only marvel at. "I was captured there and lost everything. For a long time, in that first prison camp in Tunisia, I didn't want to live."

He said no more. Vastly unsure of herself, Audrey found a silly lace handkerchief in her underwear drawer and gave it to him, then returned to her perch on the bed. He wiped his eyes and nose, sniffed, and sat another moment in silence that she knew not to interrupt with foolish words, condolences that could never comfort someone so bereft.

"Your touch felt so good," Gerd said simply. "None of us is touched in kindness. *Frau* Allerton, did you kiss me?"

"I did. I wanted to." She doubted she had ever meant anything more.

"Then I thank you," he said, his voice low. "I have seen how your father puts his arm around your shoulders. It is good."

She thought of her father's casual way of draping his arm across her shoulders, something he had always done, when she was tall enough. Mother never touched her, not even after Audrey dissolved in tears after the awful telephone call in Boston. It took coming home to Wyoming to feel love through touch again.

"It *is* good," she said. "I promise you I will never take that for granted again." *And I will know better than to be so impulsive.*

They regarded each other. Audrey looked away first, wondering how it was possible for someone to have such blue eyes. She liked the way his mouth naturally turned down. In her brief association with Afrika Korps prisoners, she had observed all the deep wrinkles and lines etched there by hot wind and blowing sand. The tans may have faded, but the wrinkles remained like a testament to brutal desert warfare.

What could she do to get them past this boulder of pain? The answer was nothing, but then she knew. "Were Stefan's eyes as blue as yours?"

When he started in surprise, she doubted her wisdom. Then she saw his relieved smile, and knew she was right.

"Hannelore wrote that they were. I could not tell from the photograph. It was such a small one." He looked up, bashful. "Her eyes were brown like yours. Her hair dark, too." He smiled again at the memory. "She was a little woman." His smile faded. "There was nothing I could do for her from Africa, when the RAF dropped bombs every night on Hamburg."

She started to say something, but stopped when he put up his hand. He had more to say. "And there was nothing you could do for your Edward."

"No. You and I are two people out of…millions imprisoned by events we have no control over." Audrey watched his face for anger but saw none. Instead, he leaned over and tapped the corner of the bed where she sat. "And we Austrians are such nice people. *Gemütlichkeit*, as we say."

"Which is…" she asked, as his mood lightened.

"Hard to say in English. Perhaps friendly good cheer. Maybe cozy. The Germans wouldn't understand, but Austrians do."

"There's no word for that in English," she said.

"What a poverty-stricken language you speak," he replied, and she heard the teasing. Gerd Gauss had righted his ship again. She could do no less.

"Isn't it the truth?" she said, keeping her tone light. Should she say a tenth of what she felt? Why not? Another year, maybe less, and she wouldn't see him again. "We can be friends."

"I like that," he replied. "I will tell you more about Major Rheinhold, but it is something your father and perhaps the physician need to hear, too, if they want to get involved and help us."

Help you how? she thought, as he went across the hall. *You're prisoners. We're civilians. We have no control over your situation, either.*

Puzzled, Audrey followed and stood in the doorway. She watched as Doctor Barnes sat beside the PW's bed. He leaned on the chair's armrest, his fist against his cheek, as if wondering what else he could do. He beckoned to Gerd.

"I can't leave him here. He needs to be in a hospital. His skull…internal injuries. I am doubtful." He indicated Kurt Kreuger. "Will you explain that to this man hovering over both of us?"

"I will, if you can tell us how this sort of devilment can end," Gerd said. "This is not the first such incident." He indicated the man lying there. "Matthieu was indoctrinated into Germany's worldwide supremacy before he came here, and saw for himself the lie of what he has been told about America. Now he questions it to our officers, and they single him out for punishment. This is not the first instance."

"You seem to know the lie," Doc Barnes interrupted. "How?"

"I was a pilot for Lufthansa and have flown into New York and Boston, those cities Goebbels declared were bombed." Impatiently, he waved away the comment he knew was coming. "*Herr* doctor, we Lufthansa pilots had to join the German air force, the Luftwaffe, or face a firing squad. Would you call that a choice?"

"No, I would not. I begin to understand," Doc Barnes replied with no hesitation. Audrey watched his resolve seem to strengthen. "And Matthieu? Didn't that very Goebbels say that if someone tells a big lie long enough, people think it's the truth?"

"*Ja*, that very Goebbels, may he rot in hell," Gerd replied in a low voice filled with loathing so deep that Audrey sucked in her breath. He touched Matthieu gently. "Private Bauer saw this country from a train full of PWs like him. He saw the tall buildings in New York. He wondered at the miles and miles of grain fields, corn and cattle, nothing destroyed as Goebbels said. Since his arrival here, he has heard evening lectures from your school here, your… *gymnasium*?"

"High school," Dad interjected.

"Ah, yes. Matthieu began to question the lies, and this is the result. Major Rheinhold rules the camp with an iron fist. Matthieu is not the first to suffer. Please help us." He spoke so urgently and quietly, as if Rheinhold and his goons stood in the corridor listening and ready to carve out another pound of flesh.

"What can I do?" Doc Barnes asked.

"Take Private Bauer to your hospital. Bypass the PW camp. Call the American *Kommandant* in Scottsbluff. We here are a satellite of that larger camp. He can recall Major Rheinhold before he does more damage. The Kommandant will believe you, where he would not believe us. I have tried."

Should she say anything? Audrey looked at her father, who was watching her. He nodded, just a small tip of his head, and she took heart. "Doc, Captain Gleason at Camp Veteran is in no shape to oversee anything, which gives Rheinhold more power. He must be replaced."

"By whom?" Doc Barnes asked, and Audrey heard all his frustration. "I read every day in the paper how manpower is stretched so thin." He sighed. "My own office nurse joined the WACs and serves in France. Audrey, you're asking the impossible!"

"Mr. Watkins in the extension office can fill in." She expected his skeptical look and was not surprised. "Doc, he is *not* the milquetoast too many people think he is. Including you?"

"Well, I...."

She pressed the point home because there was no one else, no other choice. "The whole town thinks they know Walter Watkins, but I see... Dorrie sees... another side. He is capable and he can do this." She watched for the skepticism to fade. When it didn't, she pressed on. "I know Dorrie Hatcher can run the extension office."

"But she's a woman..." Doc Barnes began, but Audrey heard him weaken.

"Doc, half of American ships at sea now are held together with rivets put there by women! Who delivers the mail? Who sorts coal in the mines? When I left Boston, many cabbies were women."

Doc raised his hands comically, as if to ward her off. She had the good sense to see the humor. "Dorrie can do it, and I can help her," Audrey said, wondering if she had any powers of persuasion at all, but remained game to attempt. "Please try."

Doc regarded her with something close to affection. He knew her, from her first breath of life to her return as a widow. He made one last attempt, but she knew his heart wasn't in it. "They're German prisoners of war, Mrs. Spitfire."

"Gerd Gauss here watched British soldiers in North Africa rip up his only photograph of the infant son he never saw, who died with his mother in a bombing raid," she said. "Have a heart Dr. Barnes. That's all I ask."

She heard Gerd's sigh. It was almost as loud at Doc Barnes's sigh. Dad nodded. "I'll add my plea to hers, Doc," he said. "I'll call Scottsbluff, too."

She knew Doc Barnes was not a man of quick decision, unless medicine demanded such. He straightened the sheet around Matthieu Bauer and took his time. "Very well," he said suddenly and decisively, and turned his attention to Gerd. "Uh, you…"

"*Feldwebel* Gauss, sir," Gerd said. "Sergeant Gauss to you, perhaps."

"Sergeant Gauss, get two men to help you and…" he looked at Kurt Kreuger… "this fellow who speaks no English. I don't have a stretcher with me." He glanced out the window. "I've driven through worse."

Everyone went to work. In less than fifteen minutes, Matthieu Bauer lay on the back seat of Doc Barnes's Studebaker, with a PW who spoke rudimentary English by his side. Gerd had been adamant that he remain behind. "It is this way, *Herr Doktor*. I am the ranking sergeant of this little detail. I must have all their interests in mind, not just Bauer's. I stay here."

Doc Barnes buttoned up his overcoat that Audrey handed to him. "Now I will worry about any of you returning to the compound." He glared at Gerd. "Even if you are Germans."

"…Austrians," Gerd said quickly.

"Young man, Hitler was *born* in Austria!" Doc Barnes stated, exasperated.

"Only some Austrians claim him," Gerd added firmly.

"Have it your way!" He nodded to Audrey, who held his hat. He put it on carefully and deliberately. "Years ago, when the earth's crust was still hot" – he winked at Audrey – "I took an oath to Hippocrates to do no harm. None of you are going to suffer like this man if I can help it." He touched his patient, then closed the car door. His gaze went to Dad. "Pete, you better wish for a three-day blizzard! Barring that, hopefully no one of influence in the U.S. Army knows where Wyoming is, so we won't have any soldiers arresting us for treason."

Audrey knew her father. "Even if it clears up tomorrow, they're not going anywhere," Dad assured the doctor. "Doc, they're staying here until I hear from you, or Mr. Watkins, or the bigger feller in Scottsbluff."

"Wish me luck, Peter."

"You have it. First the hospital, then Walter Watkins."

"Thanks, Dad," Audrey said as Doc Barnes started his automobile, the one with the big engine and Wyoming-strength windshield wipers.

"Can he accomplish his task?" Gerd asked, as the taillights dimmed all too soon, courtesy of wind and snow.

"Buncha tough cowboys in this state," Dad said. "And now sergeant, you and your men have a destiny with manure forks."

"Certainly. I have heard and seen a lot of shit shoveled in the past few years," Gerd said, and Audrey laughed.

Dad pointed at her, obviously enjoying himself, now that Matthieu was on his way to better help. "And you, Audie, will bake a cake, the likes of which some of us probably have not seen in years." He looked at each in turn. "We'll get through this."

Chapter Fifteen

Prosaic baked potatoes came first, three pounds of man-sized potatoes in the range, to be slathered in homemade butter because they had a cow. She saw to it that Shep, the prisoners' guard, got them to the barn by noon, along with the puny sack lunches. She watched him go, happy Dad had strung up a rope between the house and the barn.

She was watching Shep disappear in a whirl of snow when the phone rang, two longs, two shorts: the Nolan ring on the party line.

The connection was scratchy, but decipherable. "Doc Barnes. Just listen to me. Don't know how long this connection will hold. Tell the PWs that Matthieu Bauer has a fractured skull. I am very worried. Walter Watkins knows what is going on and he is heading to Camp Veteran as soon as he can. I can't get through to Scottsbluff. Lines must be down. Maybe tomorrow. Walter and I are both trying."

"Thank you, Doc. I'll tell them when they come in for lunch." Scratch, scratch, hollow ping, more scratching, then, "Walter says under no circumstances is Pete Nolan to try to return the PWs to the camp. He's calling the other farmers with the same message. Bed-um down somewhere."

"That's good news, Doc. Thanks."

More scratching, then clear as clear she heard, "Audrey, you're right about Walter Watkins. He already has a plan in place. Now tootle-oo to you, Infant Number One Thousand and Twenty-five. See there? I never forget."

She laughed and hung up the receiver, then leaned her forehead against the wall, breathing as close as she could come to a prayer, considering that the Lord had failed her miserably in the last few years. Perhaps she had been hasty about that.

A massive roast was in the oven and the cake cooling on the table when the storm blew Dad indoors. She helped him off with his overcoat and soon had a mug of coffee warming his hands and then his insides.

"Gonna make that white icing I like?" he asked.

"You bet, Dad." She pointed to the stove with its big coffee pot, the kind Dad said his father used for roundups. "Send in some Germans. I have tin cups and they can haul this to the barn."

"We're swamping out the bunkhouse now. It'll sleep six, and the rest can stay in here. I'll send some in for sheets and blankets." He took another sip. "They've been telling me about Major Rheinhold and two of his lieutenants. You ever heard of the SS?"

She had. "Is that what Major Rheinhold is? I know they're super-Nazis." She thought back to the mimeographed sheets she had mostly read. She doubted that all the farmers had bothered. "Isn't there a special camp for them?"

"It's somewhere in Oklahoma, or so Dietrich Schopenhauer informed me. Sounds like a good spot for our dudes." He set down his cup with more force than Audrey thought he intended. "None of this might have happened, if Captain Gleason was in good health. I can't blame him, I suppose…"

She told him of Doc Barnes's scratchy telephone call. "Go tell them that, Dad. I'll bring bedding downstairs."

"We'll sleep five in the bunkhouse plus Shep in there. How about Gerd Gauss and the piano player in here for sure," he said, and winked at her. "OK?"

"Very well," she said, and tried for dignity.

"You like that pilot, don't you?"

She hoped that didn't require a response, because she had none. She told her father more about Gerd's great loss. "He has not one photograph of his loved ones. At least I have plenty of pictures of Ed and me."

Dad looked away. "There's too much dust floating in this kitchen," was his only remark before he pulled on his coat and went into the storm, hand on the rope, as he felt his way to the barn, with the bunkhouse next to it.

She iced the cake, mounding the extra frosting high on the top. PWs came calling, and she loaded them down with sheets and blankets. She sniffed and noticed the fragrant odor of *der Düngen*, which meant she sent another back with hand towels, soap, a wash basin, and strict instructions she hoped they understood.

Dietrich Schopenhauer wandered through later, looking for paper and pencil. "I have examined your father's Johan Deere," he explained. "I will illustrate my plan to increase the engine power."

"Not too fast!" she joked. "He's fifty-five." She handed him a tablet and sent him on his merry way.

To her surprise and appreciation, two PWs knocked on the back door when she stood in the kitchen, thinking about potatoes to peel and hoping nobody minded more spuds.

"*Bitte Frau*, we are sent here by *Feldwebel* Gauss to…" He paused in thought. "…to achieve greatness here in *die Küche*. Do with us as you see fit."

She set them to work peeling potatoes, and then apples, because her culinary repertory included Jonathans found huddling alone in the bottom of the barrel. Early spring was not a promising time for new produce.

Still, with the introduction of a tablecloth and silverware, the table looked nearly festive. She thought of last year's quiet Thanksgiving, with a roast chicken for the two of them, more everlasting potatoes and gravy, and a pumpkin pie.

"This is better," she said out loud.

"Than what, *Frau* Allerton?" the better English speaker asked.

"Than dinners for two," she told him.

She kept the rest to herself. Despite the spring storm raging outside and howling down the chimney, the uncertainty of Matthieu Bauer's health, and concern over whatever fresh hell awaited the PWs when they finally returned to camp, she felt an odd sort of optimism. She barely understood this little bit of hope. It was hers to savor.

Her company came in as the wind howled, little Corporal Shepherd first, between two strapping Germans who had obviously kept him from blowing away. They shook off their coats on the back porch and followed her into the dining room.

She noticed that no one smelled of manure this time, and their hair was damp and slicked back, their faces clean. She pointed around the table and they sat.

After Dad's blessing on the food – a goodly number of the men crossed themselves, Gerd among them – the potatoes started around, followed by gravy. The roast was next, to great approval. The applesauce was making its circuit when the lights flickered, went out, struggled on again, then went out. Her heart softened when the men seated beside their comrade who had cringed last time put their arms around him until he calmed down.

"I think that's all she wrote for electricity tonight," Dad said from his spot at the head of the table. "I trust you can find the lanterns, Audie."

She could. The dining room was bathed in a half light of dusk as she went into the pantry, followed by Gerd and Dietrich. She pointed to the top shelf. "They already have kerosene, so hold them steady."

Dietrich took two lanterns into the dining room as she rummaged for matches. "Sometimes electricity isn't too dependable here," she said to Gerd as he took down two more lanterns.

"I like the soft glow," he said. He kissed her cheek. "There now. I wanted to do that, but I should have asked first."

"I like surprises," she said. "Did you surprise yourself, too?"

"I believe I did." He looked down. "Maybe it is even a thank you for *your* kiss, which I needed." She could tell he chose his next words carefully. "Audrey, I cannot...explain...how nice not to be your enemy. May I?"

He held out his arms and she carefully came closer. He wrapped his arms around her. "So lovely," he whispered.

She nodded, unable to speak. "We will protect you," she decided on, but that was foolish. "*I* will protect you."

He let her go. "I do not know how this will end."

She took him by the arms, just a gentle touch, wondering what he really meant and too shy to ask. "You and your men can count on us." That seemed safe enough.

"We have to," he said simply. "We must."

Chapter Sixteen

The storm raged as they dined on roast beef, mashed potatoes and gravy, applesauce and rolls. Audrey made the rounds with more coffee, followed by Gut Bucket making his own rounds, getting surreptitious bites of dinner from everyone. Audrey protested, but the PWs laughed when she warned the four-legged opportunist that he would have to go on a strict diet when the war ended.

In his casual way, Dad continued to tease out information about Major Rheinhold's control of the camp. Audrey knew her father well enough to know that he was storing up the details of intimidation, threats and physical injury, details to pass along to someone as soon as this storm abated, someone with power to change matters.

When he glanced at her, probably for reinforcement, Audrey told them what Mr. Watkins had heard from the commander of the Scottsbluff camp that oversaw satellite camps like Veteran.

"Mr. Watkins knows that commanders like Captain Gleason have been advised to let the natural leadership of the camps fall to the highest-ranking German," she said as she rose to prepare the cake. She paused for Gerd's quiet interpretation, and realized how much she liked the soothing, uninterrupted flow of his German, accompanied with gestures, as she spoke.

When he finished and sat back, waiting, one of the prisoners up to now silent spoke in rapid German. Dietrich Schopenhauer interpreted this time. "*Frau* Allerton, he says no one objects to that, and that discipline must be maintained because we are German *soldaten*...soldiers."

She nodded. "An orderly camp is what everyone wants. Tell him that, Dietrich."

213

The automotive designer did, and she saw nods all around.

"We can help you, if it is difficult," Audrey said softly. Gerd interpreted, his voice equally soft.

"C'mon, Audie," Dad said, "let's get that cake in here."

The two of them went into the kitchen. "It was supposed to be so simple," Dad said, keeping his voice low, as he picked up the dessert plates. "These prisoners we're supposed to dislike were just going to work on our farm, go back to their camp, and work until the war ends. We weren't supposed to worry about them, were we?"

"No," she agreed. "You know I didn't want them here."

"I do, kiddo. What happened to us?"

She picked up the cake. "You know as well as I do. They turned into people."

The cake brought an involuntary sigh from all. She set it down with a flourish, then looked at the men, all of them smiling now, even the man who feared sudden darkness. "I couldn't have made it without the sugar you smuggled into my father's house. How did you sneak out all that sugar?"

"In the socks, *Frau*," someone said, and they all laughed.

"Yes, but how?"

The men looked at each other, then at Gerd. She watched in delight as his face reddened. "*Frau*, you tie off one sock and stick it down the front of your trousers."

"Well, maybe *you* do," she murmured, which made Dad laugh.

Someone spoke in German and they all laughed. "I will not interpret that," Gerd said.

"You are all rascals," she said firmly, and waited for laughter after the translation. Satisfied, she held out plate after plate as Dad cut generous slices that went around the table. They ate in satisfied silence, because cake required no interpretation.

Maybe it was all that sugar, no matter its less-then-honest acquisition, but the cake seemed to energize everyone. Three PWs helped her clear the table and wash the dishes, with others drying, all this to the pianist's accompaniment. She found herself answering questions about life in the United States.

"It is this way," one of the English speakers began as he dried another plate. "The professors from the gymnasium – high school you say? –

that come from Torrington, they tell us about America. What do *you* like about America?"

No one had ever asked her that. As she considered the right answer, she knew there were so many responses: the emotional ones, the learned-in-civics classes, the rote answers. To her mind, it boiled down to one thing. "It's my home," she said simply. "I have no profound answer. It's something inside me, hard to explain."

"We feel the same as you," one of the plate dryers said. "Why do we fight?"

No answer. In silence, the dishes were put away. The prisoners of war drifted into the parlor, where the music continued. Audrey draped the damp dish towels on the chair backs, listening as the wind seemed to change directions, as if seeking a way inside, where it was warm.

"Some of us were forced to fight," Gerd said.

She hadn't noticed him standing by the pantry, broom in hand. He swept the floor as she wielded the dustpan. "Then how do you feel about Austria?"

"Betrayed, I suppose," he said, after some thought. "Where were our wise leaders? Perhaps we were not strong enough."

"Will you go back to Austria?" she asked, curious to know what a man does who has lost everyone dear to him and his country is likely in ruins.

"I do not know what I will do, when this war ends, as we know it will." He waved his hand, as if to brush away an unwelcome thought. "I must return, of course. I have no choice in that. But later? I do not know."

They joined the others in the parlor. Dad patted the spot on the sofa beside him and she sat. Was it brazen? She patted the spot next to her for Gerd and he joined her. "What about the pianist? What will he do after the war? Heinz…Heinz.."

"Dorschel. This is strange. He was born in Berlin, but his parents immigrated to Nebraska. His mother was not happy here. She took him back to Germany with his sister."

"You're joking."

"About this? Never. Heinz wanted to write to his father, but Major Rheinhold forbade it. See that scar on his temple? Heinz told our camp nurse that it came from his carelessness making a cabinet. He never asked Major Rheinhold for permission again."

"That's wrong," she whispered back, as Heinz Dorschel moved effortlessly into Rachmaninoff. "Tell him to write a letter tonight and give it to me. I will mail it."

"Bless you, Audrey," Gerd said.

Her heart full, she listened to beautiful music as the storm raged around this quiet haven from war. She had come home in sorrow and defeat. She had seen newsreels of cities in ruins and refugees with few possessions moving here and there in desperation as the Allies slowly made their way north from Italy. There was talk of an inevitable invasion, but from where? She knew feelings had changed in the past year, from unending gloom to a steady resolve that yes, it would end, probably at a greater cost than anyone dared consider.

Heinz Dorschel finished the Rachmaninoff. He looked through her stack of music. "Ah, Brahms," he said. "*Leider, miene Brüden,*" which gave the better voices, including the man beside her, the prompt to sing.

In the dim light, she looked from man to man, some – probably the more recent arrivals – too young to be in anyone's army, others probably too old, but here all the same. Her eyes went again to the scar on Heinz's temple, and she thought of Matthieu Bauer, both strong men, but helpless, if something wasn't done about Major Rheinhold.

"I never thought I would worry about German PWs," she told her father.

"Neither did I, Audie. We'll find a way to make this right."

"I'm counting on you, Dad."

Chapter Seventeen

D ad broke the spell of Brahms. "Gentlemen, my bed awaits me."
He laughed. "Usually I say, 'Audie, let's turn out the lights so these nice people can go home.'" The English speakers chuckled, and Dietrich Schopenhauer interpreted this time.

"Corporal Shepherd, you take five men with you to the bunkhouse. There is water and plenty of wood," Dad said. "Two of you can sleep upstairs here, and a brave soul who isn't too tall can sleep on the…" He turned to her. "Audie, what do you call that fancy sofa in my room?"

"A chaise lounge, Dad," she said, amused that after all these years he hadn't discarded Mother's pretentious couch. It was Audrey's refuge when she was a little girl and thunderstorms frightened her from her own bed. When she outgrew that fear, the chaise lounge turned into a handy resting place for books, magazines, rope, and other bits of farm detritus.

The men looked to Gerd, who assigned everyone a place to sleep. Heinz Dorschel closed the piano lid with some reluctance and left with Dietrich Schopenhauer.

"I want two good speakers of English with Corporal Shepherd," Gerd said. "I will sleep upstairs with our friend who fears the dark." A fleeting smile crossed his face. "My older brother – we shared a bed – used to keep me safe from monsters."

"None in this house," Dad said cheerfully. "Come with me, Anton. You get the booby prize. Can you explain that to him, Gerd?"

Gerd did his best. "Booby prize? I cannot. Anton is resigned to small spaces. He's the bravest tank gunner I know."

"The world is full of surprises," Dad said. "He doesn't look much older than sixteen."

"He isn't."

"This war needs to end," Dad commented. He yawned and pointed up the stairs. Anton followed, and soon the door closed. Gerd sent the last man upstairs and turned to Audrey. "He will cry out in his sleep. I hope he will not bother you."

She shook her head. "He's only here for a night or two. What happened to him? He doesn't look like the rest of you."

"And how do we look?" Gerd asked, obviously amused.

"You put me on the spot," Audrey murmured. "Capable. A bit raffish."

"Thank you! He was a company clerk. During Rommel's push on Cairo, Helmut's task was to catalog the regimental dead and their possessions." He looked up the stairs. "Germans are so efficient, aren't they?" He shuddered, as if a cold wind had suddenly blown across his back and down his shirt. "*Eins, svei, drei, vier, fünf,* and so on. He counts them all, some nights. As you know, he fears sudden darkness."

"Gerd, I don't know what to say." *Never have you been so inadequate,* she heard herself tell herself. She settled on, "This is all so hard."

He gladdened her heart by clapping an arm around her shoulder. "Better times ahead for all of us?"

She nodded, nearly overwhelmed by the simple comfort of his arm. "First order of business is getting rid of Major Rheinhold."

"Indeed. You are going upstairs?"

"Soon. There is always something to finish first."

He gave her a small salute and started up the stairs, only to be followed by Gut Bucket. Gerd stopped. "You don't mind if Schmalz sleeps with me?"

"You'll be crowded. Gut Bucket seriously needs to change his eating habits, which I might point out, were further ruined by you all at the dinner table. Good night."

She finished the "wiferly stuff," as Ed called it during their few months together: making sure the kitchen was neat and the cat either brought in or left out; checking the doors; and standing there, certain she was missing something. She wondered why men didn't do that. When they said they were going to bed, they meant it. "One of the mysteries of life," she said out loud.

She navigated the dark rooms with ease, choosing to stand by the bow window in the parlor for a moment, enchanted, as always, with the odd half light that falling snow created. She remembered other nights like this when Dad stood with her because he knew blizzards made her uneasy. Audrey almost wished that Dad would come downstairs and take away her childhood fear again.

She heard steps on the stairs, gratified that Dad knew her. In a moment someone else stood beside her. Without a word, he put his hand on her shoulder.

"It's just a storm. It blows over. They never come to stay," he said. He gave her shoulder a small shake, as he had done before. This was different. Just the two of them stood in the parlor this time.

"Pardon me, Audrey, but Hannelore used to do precisely what you are doing."

"Roam the house and wonder what little thing remained to do?"

"I can only surmise that this is something women do," he replied. She heard his amusement.

"Yet here you are, too," she said.

He tightened his grip on her and she felt herself relax. "Ah, that is better," he said. "I am here for the same reason you are. You do a final check. I come downstairs, wondering if I should go to the bunkhouse and see if all is well there."

"You're in charge?"

"I am their *feldwebel*. They are my responsibility," he said. "I have never felt so powerless. Our fate is in the hands of others."

"Join the wonderful world of women," she said, keeping her voice light.

Had she irritated him? His silence seemed to indicate such, except that he did not release her. He maintained a loose grip on her, and she knew she could break free, but she felt no such urge. What his presence did was suggest ever so lightly that there would come a time when someone could replace Ed.

"If I have intruded in the world of women..." he began.

"Not at all. You're welcome."

"Well then, I will bid you good night," he said, but she stopped him.

"Not yet. I have some questions." That sounds a little desperate, one side of her brain argued. She ignored it. "Just...just my own curiosity."

He cocked his head toward the ceiling. "Let's sit on the stairs. I left Helmut asleep, but if he cries out..."

"The stairs," she agreed. When they were seated, she turned slightly to face him. "This is probably silly."

He started to speak, then chuckled. "I know enough American idioms to think I should say 'Fire away,' but lately, I do not care for that one. Let me substitute, 'Ask me anything.'"

She put her hand to her mouth to quiet her laughter. No sense in Dad getting suspicious. "It's this: You're a pilot. Pilots are officers. You are a...a sergeant? Why?"

"I was a first officer with Lufthansa, not a full-fledged captain yet. I'm twenty-eight. Perhaps that is why. Answer your question?"

"Well..."

"Not enough of an answer? The other issue was the high command knew I was less-than-enthusiastic, shall we say. Not officer material, perhaps. I know they hoped I would die in North Africa." He shook his head. "After what happened to my one photograph, I did want to die. I don't know why I kept living."

"Living well is the best revenge. Do you have that adage, too?"

"Something like that. What about you?"

"I wanted to live, because I was carrying Ed's child. That didn't end well. I suppose by then I was committed to living. Here I am."

"So you are, and we are all grateful."

What about you alone? she wanted to ask, but that would be utter folly. "There has to be a way to sit out your internment without fear for your lives from within the compound. I believe Mr. Watkins will find a way."

"Excuse me, but he doesn't seem too...too..."

"Forceful? Assertive?"

"*Jawohl.*"

"Looks can be deceiving," she said. "You'll have to settle for that, Gerd, and trust us."

He gave her a long look, as if appraising what was in her mind, or maybe even her heart. The only man who had ever looked at her that way was Edward Allerton. He leaned toward her. She closed her eyes just as the traumatized man in the guest room cried out.

Gerd stood up, his eyes on the stairs, which he took two at a time. Gut Bucket came out of the room whimpering. She followed, wondering if what she felt was great relief or supercharged irritation.

She stood in the doorway as Gerd Gauss, prisoner of war, calmed his comrade, speaking in soothing German. No wonder the great lullabies were written by Germans. What a soothing language, a lover's language equal to French or Italian.

She went into her room and quietly closed the door.

Chapter Eighteen

In her mind if not entirely her heart, that was that, and thank goodness. She knew for certain in the morning, when Gerd and Helmut came downstairs with little Anton from her father's room and set the table for breakfast of bacon and pancakes. They were quiet and respectful, but nothing more.

Almost nothing. In her hurry to get a meal on the table, Audrey forgot to tie her apron strings. She was flipping pancakes when she felt someone come up behind her and tie them. "Germans like order," he said close to her ear. "Austrians admire industry in *others*," he added, which made her laugh and wish him well in her heart.

Thank goodness there was plenty of bacon. Her table of prisoners ate a lot of it and headed to the barn, a most contented lot, so her father observed. "Give a man enough bacon and he is putty in your hands," he remarked to her. "Remember that, Audrey, when you go on the prowl for another husband someday."

"How many prospective husbands will I meet over breakfast, Dad? Really?" She could joke, too, since this peculiar crisis of her heart had passed. "They'll line up here because they covet your acres! That's a bit feudal, but this *is* Wyoming."

They laughed together and went arm and arm to the back door, where he pulled on his coat. "I have plenty for them to do today, but I really hope we hear from Mr. Watkins." He stared into the storm. "This'll wear out by afternoon. We'll have the excuse of digging out tomorrow to keep us here. After that, if I don't return them to Camp Veteran..." His voice trailed off. He kissed her cheek, and grabbed the rope line.

Lunch was roast beef sandwiches from yesterday's monster roast, and more applesauce, plus some canned pickled beets she had no use for because she disliked them, but which met with Germanic approval. Plenty of eggs and cream meant custard pie, apparently so beatific that even Helmut did not flinch when the lights flickered on briefly and then went out again.

She hadn't cooked so much in ages, but it felt good to be appreciated. She cornered Gerd for help as they still sat at the table, "Since you are supreme *feldwebel*" – he grinned at that – "kindly appoint two of your number to corner, kill, and pluck two old hens. Dad will show them which ones. There will be chicken and noodles for supper."

At a look from Gerd, Dietrich Schopenhauer interpreted rapidly. When he finished, there was a chorus of "Ahs," from everyone. Anton, the tank gunner, took Gerd aside before they returned to the barn. Gerd listened and nodded. "Please, Frau, Anton would like to make the noodles."

"I know h… Tell him yes," Audrey said. "And if…if… Heinz the pianist is bored with nothing to do later on this afternoon, please send him in. I work better with music." She leaned in. "Also, he will have time to write that letter to his father in Nebraska."

"He'll be here."

Anton came in when the hens were stewing. He bowed to her and went to work while she made oatmeal cookies. He proved to be a happy taster of the cookies, nodding his approval as he rolled out the noodles to dry. They shared no common language except cooking. She wanted to tell him that he should start a restaurant when he returned to Germany.

When Heinz Dorschel came in and went directly to the piano after stripping off his gloves, she handed him a tablet and Dad's ink pen. "Write to your father first," she said. "Make sure your father knows he can send anything to us at this address." She handed him a smaller paper with their post office box number. "We will see that it gets to you."

"Thank you. This means much to me."

"Heinz, will you visit him when the war is over, or at least when you can?"

"I intend to move here somehow." Sitting there at the piano, he bent over the closed lid and wrote his letter.

She knew he was done when he started playing something so beautiful that even industrious Anton sat down and exclaimed, "Schöne Musik." To make the moment even more magical, Heinz Dorschel sang along.

She dried her hands on her apron and went quietly into the parlor, hoping not to disturb him. He nodded to her but did not stop until the last lovely note resonated into a part of her heart she had never heard from before.

"My goodness," was all she could say. "I know the words. Even a rather poor Episcopalian like me knows them, what is this?"

"It is the Ave Maria from Mozart's opera *Cosi Fan Tutti.*" He pointed to the music.

"Yours?" she asked, when she noticed all the creases. "Yours?"

"I folded it so small that no one found it. Last week when I first saw your piano, I put the pages under my mattress to straighten them. Do you sing, Frau? It's a duet."

"I sing alto. I couldn't do the melody." There wasn't any need for her to add that her talents were puny, compared to his. He had to know it, but the fact didn't seem to bother him.

"I will sing the melody, *Frau.*"

She wanted to hear the achingly lovely aria again and if that was the price, why not? She sat beside him on the piano bench as he kindly played her part through, once for her to hear it, then again to hum it.

"Shall we?"

He played the introduction, and she sang with him. When he finished, he put his hands in his lap and bowed his head over the keys. "I kept this music through so much turmoil. Just thinking about it kept the heart in my chest."

"Let's sing it again then."

By the time they finished, the parlor had filled with prisoners and her father. She hadn't been aware of them as she concentrated on the music, determined not to disappoint the pianist. She looked around in surprise after the "Amen," when the last chord faded into silence.

Silence. Audrey looked up in surprise. The blizzard had worn itself out finally. *Come back,* she thought. *I don't want them to leave.*

"Sing it again, please," Gerd asked, and they did. This time, she managed all the notes, happy to sing with someone who kindly overlooked her amateur attempt. She didn't want to break the spell, but supper bubbled on the hob, and biscuits don't wait well, not with butter ready to melt into the folds and raspberry jam close by.

The men conversed quietly among themselves as they ate. She automatically looked to Gerd to translate, but he did not, beyond telling her and Dad that the men were talking with each other of home, and family. "Music does that," he said quietly.

"Are you thinking of that, too?" she asked, wanting to know.

"I have no family," he reminded her.

Dad surprised her. "You do while you're here," he said, which made Gerd turn away.

"Did I say the wrong thing?" Dad whispered to her, alarmed.

"You said precisely the right thing," she told this dear man who had taken her back, a widow, and restored her to life using the only tools he knew: common sense and deep affection. Maybe he was doing the same thing for the prisoners.

To put a welcome benediction to the meal, the lights flickered, faltered, then came on to stay. Audrey wasn't certain how she felt about that. She also liked the softer glow of the lamps.

Dad looked around the table. "Tonight, let's dig out the path between the barn and back door. Tomorrow, we'll tackle the road to the highway. And after that..." He puffed his cheeks and blew out air, something she remembered from earlier times with Mother when he didn't know what to do. "After that, it remains to be seen."

Audrey stayed indoors with the dishes while everyone trooped out to shovel. When she finished, and as a precaution, she washed all the lantern chimneys, drying them carefully before stowing them in the pantry again. She knew Wyoming; this could happen again next week, or never.

She scrounged up what remained of the sugar the PWs had swiped, added cocoa, milk and cream, plus a dribble or so of vanilla. It was warming on the range when the telephone rang.

She started in surprise, listened impatiently for the requisite party line ring, and lifted the receiver. Through the crackle, she sighed with relief to hear Walter Watkins's grainy voice.

"I am so happy to hear you," she said. She would have said more, but he interrupted (with an apology of course, because he was still Walter Watkins).

"Listen to me, Audrey," she heard, straining against the crackle. "No telling if this connection will hold. I contacted the Scottsbluff camp and told them our fears."

"Good."

"I'm at Camp Veteran right now. Oh, Audrey..."

The connection grew faint and she bit her lip. "I can't hear ..."

Silence, then more clearly, "Audrey, Captain Gleason is dead. Major Rheinhold claims he died in his sleep. The lines have been out two days."

"He wasn't going to say anything until the PWs were back, was he?" she asked, as a chill traveled down her back and up again, a circuit making its own frightening connection. "I wonder what really happened."

"Same here. I called Scottsbluff again. I told them. They'll come here when the roads are passable. Another day maybe." He cleared his throat. "Keep the PWs at your farm. I'll pass the word to..."

The line went dead. She took a deep breath and another, grateful that the prisoners were not at the camp, because there was no telling what Rheinhold would have done before anyone was any wiser.

"Walter, are you safe?" she asked softly, then shook the receiver, as if expecting some response. Nothing.

Chapter Nineteen

Audrey scuffed her shoes into her ugly boots, not taking time for her coat. Some of the men were efficiently shoveling a path almost to the bunkhouse while the others concentrated on the path to the bunkhouse privy.

"Audie, we'll put you in charge of the path to the barn," Dad joked as she ran up to him. He saw her face and sobered. "What gives?"

As the others clustered closer, she told him. "Dad, Walter said Captain Gleason is dead and who knows what Major Rheinhold did!"

"Good Lord," Dad said. "Sounds suspicious."

"Walter said he's staying there in the admin office until the commandant at Camp Scottsbluff gets through."

"I hope your boss has a gun," Gerd said.

The thought of modest Walter Watkins firing anything more deadly than a peashooter left Audrey shaking her head. "He's certainly not the gun-toting type. He did say you and the other PWs at the various farms are to stay put."

His face inscrutable, Gerd interpreted everything. Audrey watched as the PWs conversed softly in German. She knew this wasn't a conversation they seemed willing to share, not with the looks over shoulders that nearly all of them sent in her father's direction; hers, too, if she was honest.

Audrey moved closer to her father. "I don't know what this is about, but it's something they haven't told us, isn't it?"

Peter Nolan was not a gossip or a blabbermouth. He had always kept his own council. She also knew her father to be a man of considerable understanding. No one of her acquaintance could get to the heart of a matter better. "What is it, Dad?"

He pulled her aside. "I have a strong feeling that Matthieu Bauer, our PW now in hospital, is not the first victim of Major Rheinhold and his goons. I do not trust that man. How many PWs who weren't Nazi enough have come and gone to their deaths without Captain Gleason's awareness? I wonder if Gleason accused Rheinhold of...something. I doubt we'll know."

She looked at the prisoners. "A goodly number must have suffered from Rheinhold, I am thinking. Dad, they have to know they can trust us."

"Let's find out." He took her hand and joined the other group. The Germans seemed startled, even irritated, at first, then remembered her own understanding heart. She let go of Dad's hand and gently shouldered her way between Gerd and Dietrich Schopenhauer. She linked her arms through theirs and to her relief, met with no resistance.

"Who else has died because of the major?" she asked quietly.

"No one will believe us," Dietrich said finally, his voice flat. "We are all Nazis to Americans. Even you, Frau?"

"You know me better," she said.

Gerd spoke to the others. Audrey saw their nods. "Three at least," he said at last. "Rheinhold disguised it as illness, or a camp injury and no one questioned him. You saw Matthieu. We have seen other Matthieus, here and in Scottsbluff."

"What do we do, Dad?" she asked. "This might require a little finesse."

"Finesse is not exactly my middle name," he said. "I scoop dung, too, remember."

The English speakers smiled and seemed to relax. Someone interpreted. Others smiled.

"I suggest we see how discreet and quiet we can be in removing Major Rheinhold from Camp Veteran," Dad said.

"How do we do that?" Heinz Dorschel asked.

"We dig out to the highway tomorrow," Dad said promptly, full of purpose. "Maybe a few of you should go with me to Camp Veteran when the road is clear. Audie says Mr. Watkins is there. He might need us."

When she started to shiver, Audrey knew she should have grabbed her coat. "Go inside," Gerd said.

"What else?" she asked.

They were silent. "What else?" she repeated. "We need some ammunition to counter objections from the major or from Scottsbluff."

Dietrich and Gerd looked at each other, as if deciding who should deliver the bad news, or no news at all. "For goodness sake," Audrey said. "We're trying to help!"

"Suppose no one cares that Germans have been murdered here?" Dietrich said, after a glance at Gerd.

"Let's all go in," Dad said hastily. "Audie, did you mention earlier that you were thinking about hot chocolate?"

"It's ready," she said. She tried to pull her arm from Gerd's, but he clamped it to his side. "The path is slick," he reminded her.

"You're hard to dislike," she said as they walked slowly to the house behind the others.

"Perhaps we are shielding you from retribution, too," he said as he opened the back door. "I might call you impossible to dislike."

Suddenly shy, she gave him a little glance to see him smiling at her, despite the turmoil of the last few minutes.

The hot chocolate went around the table and the men were silent, sipping and thinking, from the looks of them. Dad finally broke the silence. "How many of you have been harassed or injured by your own Major Rheinhold?"

More silence, until slowly, slowly one hand went up, then another. Heinz didn't raise his hand, but he broke the ice. "All I have wanted is to write to my father, who lives in Nebraska. I took my plea to Major Rheinhold." He looked like a man holding back tears. "He told me no, that we should not correspondent with American degenerates." He put his thumb and finger to the bridge of his nose. "Pardon me. He also told me that if I petitioned Captain Gleason, he would break my fingers. My fingers!" He pointed to the scar on his head. "This was my warning, but my fingers? Never! What could I do?"

Little Anton the tank gunner appealed to Dad in rapid German. Dietrich blushed, looked away, then interpreted. "Like most of us, and many in the camp, Anton is not a member of the National Socialist Party." He shook his head. "Anton thus informed the major." He paused. "This is hard to discuss."

"Try," Dad insisted. "Let's hear it all."

"Anton was used cruelly by the major's lieutenant. It is not a thing one speaks of."

Audrey glanced at her father and saw the grimness. She knew he was a man of slow burn, but this...

"Who are these monsters?" Dad asked. "They're worse than Nazis."

"They are!" Gerd pounded the table. "They are Schutzstaffel. SS. They wear black uniforms with lightning bolts on the collars. They are here now in ordinary field gray uniforms. They are the worst among us."

"And you, Gerd? You have a story, too." Dad spoke gently, as he teased out secrets that had obviously festered. She stood by the sink, not moving, attracting no attention, wanting no one to shut down because she was there, and a woman.

"The major knows me from North Africa," he said, then took a long sip, as if fortifying himself. He turned slightly toward Audrey. "He's the one who saw to it that I was *feldwebel*, and not a *leutnant*. He doesn't like Austrians, especially unwilling ones. I suppose news of my dismay at being forced into the Luftwaffe preceded me." He held up his hand. "There is more. He had a favorite pilot who claimed kills when there was no other pilot nearby to verify it. I, among others, disputed his claims."

He must have noticed Dad's puzzled look. "It is this way, Herr Nolan: thirty kills, fifty now, earns a pilot a Knight's Cross. You know, glory." He said the word like it was a bad taste in his mouth.

"So Major Rheinhold's pet pilot was a fraud and a liar," Dad said.

"He was. I received my Knight's Cross first and I know it bothered the major and his pilot."

"What happened to the man?"

"Eventually, shot down into the Mediterranean Sea, but not before two other pilots who objected ended up dead because of, ahem, engine troubles." Gerd said. "I suppose I was lucky to escape those, uh, mechanical failures. All the same, a month later my plane was shot from the sky over Wadi al-Azarit. I managed to land, and you know the rest."

"Not really," Dad said, "but that'll do. The major is definitely a nasty character. You both ended up in Veteran?"

"We were in Scottsbluff first," Gerd said. "His goons beat me senseless. My right ear still rings. I asked to be transferred somewhere else, anywhere, before I died, and I was sent to Veteran. To my dismay, Major Rheinhold followed me a month later, and here we are. I know he torments others."

"Can you prove he is SS?" Dad asked.

"*Jawohl*, no matter what he says. Right, Gerd?" Dietrich replied. He raised his left arm and pointed. "Small blood group tattoo here. We'll find him."

"Why does Major Rheinhold do this?" Audrey asked.

"He is SS. There is no explanation needed," Gerd said. "These are terrible men, organized to do the Fuhrer's personal bidding, no matter where, no matter how."

"We'll see what we can do tomorrow," Dad said. "It's late, gentlemen."

Gerd left with the others for the bunkhouse this time, trading places with another, and breaking her heart just a little.

Only a little, Audrey decided. The smart side of her brain was taking a bow, to applause from likeminded, practical brain cells. She knew that was best, but still… No, it was best.

By ten o'clock the next morning, they were through to the county road and met the county plow coming past on the highway, which meant good-natured groans as the prisoners shoveled out the newly reburied portion of their farm road.

Everyone stared when Torrington's entire police force sped by – doing forty miles per hour at least – in one cop car and the paddy wagon. The town's ambulance brought up the rear.

"That doesn't look good," Dad told her when they returned to the kitchen for coffee. "Dietrich. Gerd. Let's go to Camp Veteran. I'd hate to think that Mr. Watkins is barricaded in Captain Gleason's office."

"I'm coming, too," Audrey said, "and don't stop me. Walter is my boss and I may need to get some orders from him to pass on to Dorrie about running the extension office, if he must remain there." She had no idea if any of that sounded plausible, but she wasn't about to be left behind.

Gut Bucket, either. When Audrey opened the door, he hopped in first, eyes bright, tail wagging. "I dunno, GB," Dad said as he climbed in. "You're not too ferocious."

Heinz Dorschel sat next to Audrey, with Gerd, Dietrich and Karl Krueger, the most medical-minded among them, hunkered down in the back of the beet truck. Audrey tossed in some quilts, and received smiles in return.

The camp wasn't far, but the road was barely scraped. "Give it a day and all this will be melted," Dad said as he picked his way carefully through drifts already deepening as the wind blew. "It'll be slicker than snot tonight, though."

As they rode, Heinz handed Audrey the letter to his father. "The address is on a separate slip of paper. Explain all you need to. I hope he can write me back."

"I'll do this first thing," she assured him.

"Please do." He looked out the window, then back at her. "Gerd told me this morning that likely no matter what happens in the next few days, we will be moved from here because we are troublemakers."

"No!" she exclaimed.

"Ah, but yes." He managed a tight smile. "Frau, you have forgotten something. You have forgotten we are German prisoners, and this is war."

Chapter Twenty

When they arrived at Camp Veteran, all seemed normal. Audrey's eyes went first to the guard towers, where she saw, to her relief, soldiers in place as usual. The American flag flew over the smallish building she knew was headquarters. To her dismay, she saw the ambulance by the dispensary, where even now a shrouded figure was being carried out on a stretcher.

"Where is Walter?" she murmured, fearing the worst, because he was no action movie star like Errol Flynn or Gary Cooper, able to defeat Nazis right and left. He was a quiet, ordinary man who made no waves, not ever.

But there he stood at the door to the admin office, pistol in hand, looking tired and triumphant at the same time. Torrington's chief of police stood next to him, grinning. Dad got out of his truck, Audrey and Heinz right behind.

"The camp commander from Scottsbluff called to say he would be here soon, now that the roads are clear," Walter said.

Audrey saw the exhaustion on his face, but she saw something else, a quiet confidence that needed no explanation. She was looking at a different Walter Watkins, and she liked what she saw. This was a man who just might be able to convince the Scottsbluff commander to leave him in charge, that is, if Major Rheinhold was removed.

"Walter, what happened?" she asked. "Please tell us Major Rheinhold isn't..."

"Nope. He and his two lieutenants are locked in the cell. There are cells, you know, in case prisoners are recalcitrant."

Only Walter would use such prissy words, only they didn't sound prissy now. His voice hardened. "In fact, some of the PWs told us – Corporal

Atkins and I. He's in the near tower – that Rheinhold used the cells to torture prisoners."

"And Captain Gleason did nothing?" Dad asked, his voice hard, too.

"He was too ill." Walter gestured toward some of the PWs, who had come out of their barracks, now that more people from the outside had arrived. "These men tell me Major Rheinhold has been running this camp his way for months."

"And no one said anything?" Audrey asked.

"Who would believe us?" Gerd replied. He had draped one of the quilts around his shoulders.

"Why would anyone care?" Heinz added. "We're German prisoners of war."

"So you are," Walter said. He gestured for them to come inside. "What Rheinhold was doing meets not a single paragraph of the Geneva Convention, however." He turned to Audrey. "Dr. Barnes called me this morning. Sadly, Private Bauer died of his injuries last night."

Audrey's eyes welled with tears. Walter touched her arm. "You tried," he said simply. He turned to the PWs. "I want you men to write down all suspicious injuries and deaths in this camp. The dates if you can remember them." He glanced at the clock. "When Scottsbluff's camp commander arrives, we need ammunition against Rheinhold."

"I can show you simple proof," Gerd said. Heinz nodded. "Rheinhold is SS, and the worst kind of German."

"He won't admit to anything," Walter said. Audrey heard doubt creeping in. "I need something concrete."

"You have it," Gerd said. "Take off his shirt. Have him hold up his left arm. Under his armpit you should see – it's small – a tattoo which is his blood group, you know, in case he is wounded and needs a transfusion. All SS have them."

"I wonder why we weren't informed of this," Walter said, more to himself than to Gerd.

Gerd shrugged. "I believe there have been a lot of Germans involuntarily visiting your country." (Walter smiled at that.) "People do get lost in … in…"

"…the shuffle?" Walter supplied.

"*Javohl*, the shuffle. American idioms baffle me," Gerd said, relaxing. He seemed to sense Walter was a friend, or at least not an enemy.

"We'll check." Walter turned to the chief of police, who listened, then nodded and pointed to his own deputy. Two MPs joined them. They conferred, looking back at Gerd and Heinz once or twice. Walter nodded and stood back while they left the office. "We have the men in separate cells. They'll deal with them one at a time."

"Wise of you," Heinz said. "I wouldn't trust them at all. In fact..."

A quiet German conversation followed with Gerd, who gestured to Heinz when they finished. "Gerd and I think you should check all the *leutnants* in the compound." He hesitated, but resolve seemed to conquer discomfort. "I cannot tell you what to do, but this would be wise. Perhaps even the...how do you say?... the sergeants, too."

"*Feldwebel* Gerd Gauss. I will go first." Gerd dropped the quilt, took off his denim shirt and ragged undershirt and held up his left arm. Walter blushed and looked at Audrey, who couldn't help her smile. "Beg pardon, Mrs. Allerton," Walter managed, then took a look. "No blood group tattoo."

Gerd smiled and held up his right arm. "This is just in case you think we are trying to pull down wool over your forehead."

Dad grinned at that. "Close, Gerd, but no cigar," he joked.

Gerd sighed. "*Gott im Himmel*, another idiom?"

"Soon you'll have a lifetime supply," Dad replied. "Put your shirt on before you freeze."

After a word with Heinz, they went outside to stand with the other PWs. Walter stood in the doorway, his hands stuffed in his pockets. Audrey knew he was thinking, because he rocked back and forth on his heels, something he did in the extension office. She waited. She knew her boss.

He turned around. "What with the storm, I'm not certain how many PWs are even here. Mr. Nolan, I imagine most of them are still on the farms, digging out."

"I'm certain of it, Mr. Watkins," Dad said.

"What I want to do is assemble the...the...the men who are here. We'll hand out paper and pencils. I want them to detail any examples of misconduct by their German officers. Do you think they will do it?"

Dad shrugged. "Hard to say. Maybe with their NCOs not present and getting their armpits checked, they'll open up a bit. I think the fear of retribution has a long life in this camp. If only we'd known more about Captain Gleason."

"Walter knew and suspected," Audrey said, which meant poor Walter Watkins blushed even deeper. "Is there a PA system?"

There was. Walter explained to Heinz what he wanted. His voice boomed over the camp as Heinz spoke in German to his fellow prisoners. Most of them were on the farms, but fifty PWs filed from their barracks at the same time two official-looking cars with Nebraska license plates pulled into the compound.

Paper and pencils in hand, Audrey followed the men to the mess hall. Gerd explained what they were to do. "Tell them not to sign their names," Audrey whispered to him. "If this whole enterprise goes south...beg pardon ...If it is not successful, at least no man in particular will be held accountable."

"*Javohl, frau,*" he said. "Goes south. No cigar. Lost in the shuffle."

She laughed and left him in charge, but not without noticing that some prisoners refused to write anything, while others, after looking around, hunched over their paper and wrote.

She stood silent, next to her father, as Walter explained to the colonel from Scottsbluff, an older officer obviously pulled out of retirement, what had happened and how he found things when he arrived at the camp late yesterday afternoon.

"Captain Gleason was dead in his quarters, which are behind this office," he said. He pointed over his shoulder. "No one was in the room."

"Foul play, Mr. Watkins?" the camp commander asked.

"I have no idea, sir." He told the commander what was going on with the ranking prisoners right now. Beyond raised eyebrows, the commander was silent, doing his share of thinking, apparently.

"One prisoner suggested we examine all the officers and NCOs to see if they have that little tattoo."

"If they go, there goes our control of the prisoners," the commander argued. "We rely on them to control their own men."

"But not with threats, intimidation and death," Walter said, to Audrey's mental applause. "Begging your pardon, sir, but we can do better."

"I believe we can, Mr. Watkins. Take me to the NCOs and we'll examine them, too. And any other lieutenants." He nodded to Mr. Nolan. "You should probably go now, sir."

"Not yet," Dad said, in that tone of voice Audrey seldom heard, the one that more-than-suggested he wasn't about to budge. "We've found our group of PWs to be honest and dependable. It would be a shame to have something happen to them if nothing changes here."

"You think I cannot manage this situation?" the colonel said. He was an older man, maybe he had even fought in the Spanish American War, called back to duty and in harness again.

"As one of the beet farmers, I have a vested interest in the well-being of men who are helping plant my crops. That is all." Dad folded his arms and the commander nodded, obviously choosing discretion over further argument.

"Very well, Mr. Nolan, is it? Come with me and we'll inspect armpits."

When they left, Walter nodded to her. "Thank you for showing up, Audrey."

"You're the boss, Walter," she said, striving for a light tone in this place of heavy doings.

"And my friend, I earnestly hope," he said. He did not blush this time. She knew he was serious.

"I am," Audrey replied. She allowed herself one more luxurious thought of Gerd Gauss, and quietly closed that door forever.

Chapter Twenty-one

By afternoon, one more lieutenant and two *feldwebels* joined a stone-faced Major Rheinhold and his two goons in the paddy wagon heading for Scottsbluff this time. They left behind the one bewildered *leutnant* with no tattoo, now in nominal charge of the prisoners. To Audrey's eyes, he didn't look a day over twenty. Standing at almost more-then-attention, his eyes straight ahead, he listened to a warning from the Scottsbluff camp commander that there would be no whisper of intimidation and threat, would there? *Nein, Herr Kommandant.*

To her relief, the Scottsbluff commander left Walter Watkins in temporary charge of Camp Veteran. "This can't be permanent, Mr. Watkins, but you are in charge until further notice."

Using Gerd to translate, the commander went with Walter, Audrey and her father and the police chief to the mess hall, where the men had finished their noon meal. "Prisoners, this is your new camp commander, Mr. Watkins," he announced, and waited for interpretation. "You will do as he says, with no objection. These next few weeks might be difficult. You will obey and follow work assignments." He conferred with Walter, who called over Gerd for a brief conversation. "Feldwebel Gauss will remain here to interpret for Mr. Watkins. That is all. Return to your usual compounds. Dismissed."

The commander took the outgoing mail with him, which included Audrey's typed list, in triplicate, of prisoner complaints against Rheinhold, plus the letter to Heinz Dorschel's father in Nebraska. "I put in a note," Audrey said quietly to Heinz, as Gerd stood by. "I told him he is welcome to correspond with you through us."

"I hope Heinz's father will respond quickly," Gerd said, as Heinz went to help the camp cook with lunch.

"How could he not?" Audrey replied.

"It is this: I strongly suspect that this matter of Major Rheinhold will be dealt with by the removal of all of us to other camps and separated. We are troublemakers because we have called into question the influence of Nazis in the camps."

"Don't think such a thing," she said quickly, surprised how that stung.

"You know I am a realist," he pointed out. He took a long, long look at her. Had anyone else done that, she would have felt uncomfortable. But this was Gerd. "So are you."

He had her there. Dad motioned her toward the truck, but Walter Watkins stopped him. "Audrey, Dorrie is in charge of the agency now, and you'll need to take her spot until this is settled. That means five days a week."

She nodded. She needed to be busier. "We'll do a good job, Walter."

"I know you will," he said with a smile. "Walk me to my car. You, too, Mr. Nolan."

They followed him, and Dad picked up the box of automobile parts. "I found everything on your list, Mr. Nolan," Walter said. "Have your mechanic get that car running. Audrey needs reliable transportation."

"I'll get Dietrich Schopenhauer on it at once." He tipped his hat to Walter and looked at the sun. "I'll keep my PWs busy. Things should dry out fast. Let me suggest that the farmers all keep their PWs until the planting is done, then return them. Knowing you, you'll have order restored by then. A deal?"

"A deal, and thank you, Mr. Nolan." They shook hands.

"Meanwhile, I will have the cleanest barn and outbuildings in southeast Wyoming," Dad joked.

"And perhaps we'll have a few evenings of dinner music, courtesy of Heinz Dorschel," Audrey added, determined to make the best of a situation that was crumbling around her.

"Well, that's a new Walter Watkins," Dad said as they walked toward the beet truck, where Heinz Dorschel and Kurt Krueger waited. "Firm handshake and a steady gaze. This just might work, Audie."

The only obvious objection to leaving Gerd behind at Camp Veteran came from Gut Bucket, who whimpered and whined, followed Dad, turned back, then came back at Dad's sharp whistle, looking deeply abused.

"Gut Bucket, be a good dog," Audrey said as she hoisted him into the cab of the beet truck against his will.

"Need help?"

She didn't have to turn to know who stood behind her, lifting the stubborn dog. "He does weigh a lot," she said, keeping her voice calm. "Thanks, Gerd."

"Anything for you," he said quietly. He gave a little salute and returned to the admin building.

After two days of sunshine, the fields dried out. Dad checked the soil and pronounced it ready for more seeds. By noon, his smaller crew was two-thirds done. By mid-afternoon, Dietrich Schopenhauer washed his hands in the basin on the back porch and invited Audrey for a drive. With an elaborate bow, he handed her the key and climbed in the passenger side.

"Here goes," she said, and turned the key in the ignition. The engine roared to life, sounding more like a race car than a Ford. She looked at Dietrich in consternation. He raised his eyebrows and grinned.

"I may have gone above and beyond the requirements," was all he said.

More cautious, she engaged the gears and away they went, moving smoothly toward the highway. "My goodness," she said. "This is not the same car."

"No, it is not," he agreed. "What did I find in your father's barn but the remains of a Studebaker. A part here, a part there and here we are."

"Dietrich, is this legal?" she asked, enjoying the smooth ride and the sound of meadowlarks in the fields as they flew by at precisely 35 m.p.h.

"Legal? I doubt it," he said, sounding unmistakably proud. "Drive to Camp Veteran."

She did, pleased with the light touch and firm control. The gates were open, so she drove through then stopped in front of the admin building. Dietrich got out and opened her door. "Shall we see how Herr Watkins is doing?"

Walter had matters well in hand. He had moved into Captain Gleason's old office, where she remembered clutter and disorder. The desk was clear of papers. Walter looked up from the typewriter.

"Dietrich got my car running," she said. "This is the test drive."

"And?"

"Success. Should I report to work tomorrow here, or with Dorrie in town?"

"Here," he said. "You can type some letters for me, and take them to Torrington." He clasped his hands on the tidy desk. "In fact, this might be a good division of your labors, if you're agreeable. Here first, then in town."

"I'm in," she said. "Any papers going to town?"

He handed her everything in the Out basket. It was impossible to ignore Walter's delight at his job because it showed in his eyes. *You've come into your own*, she thought, pleased with him. She leaned closer, wanting more privacy, then saw that Dietrich was outside. "Have you heard anything from Scottsbluff?"

"They're still deciding what to do with me," Walter said. "I will tell you this: Rheinhold and his band of merry men have already been sent to a really secure camp in Oklahoma, to languish among their brethren the SS."

"What a relief."

He held out a letter to her. "You might as well read this. I don't think this is necessary, but no one asked me."

She took the letter, with Seventh Service Command stamped in the corner. Her heart sank as she read what Gerd had predicted. A week from tomorrow, the prisoners assigned to Camp Veteran were to be dispersed to other camps in the service command and replaced. She put down the letter, knowing better than to register any emotion. "Will the problems begin again here?" she asked.

"They could," he agreed, "but we know what to watch for." He tapped the letter. "This was forwarded here from Scottsbluff. The camp commander assures me that any new officer-prisoners will be examined thoroughly." His eyes met hers, as if he understood her unspoken objections. But how could he? She was so careful. "We know enough now, Audrey."

"If they keep you here," she said, unwilling to let the army blunder back to the earlier situation, but knowing she had no control.

"Let's hope. One more thing: We have been given permission to attend the burial of Private Bauer in the city cemetery on Friday. "I'll be phoning the other beet farmers with PWs. Tell your father. He can bring the men back here early that morning, so the men can change into whatever remains of their uniforms, then drive them to the cemetery."

She nodded. "Private Bauer is so far from home." She thought of Lieutenant Edward Allerton, unburied, lost forever in the English Channel, and felt her eyes well with tears.

Silent, she took the outgoing mail, clutching it to her breast, and nodded to Walter. Over Dietrich's objections, she dropped him off at the farm and continued alone into Torrington, past the sugar plant, past the courthouse and extension office to the post office. She murmured the usual pleasantries, then rode home in more silence, remembering Ed and mourning how much she was forgetting. She relished the silence, and the big heart of Wyoming.

"I am one of many," she reminded herself as she pulled onto the farm. She watched the PWs in the field with Dad, knowing them by name, even if they mostly had no common language. A new batch of prisoners would thin the beets in six weeks. When cold weather came, Dad would patiently wait for that moment when the air was almost-but-not-quite too cold. The new prisoners would return to pull and top the beets after Dad softened the earth around each plant with a two-pronged plow. Another season would turn, and then another and another until the war ground to a halt, or they all died of old age.

"It isn't fair," she said out loud, wincing because she knew how childish that sounded. "Well, it isn't."

Hohoho, said the gods of war. We don't care.

Chapter Twenty-two

That was Monday. The planting was done by Thursday afternoon. Dad drove the PWs back to Camp Veteran for the first time since the storm. They already knew they were being moved to other camps. As Walter Watkins's handy go-fer, now that she had a functioning automobile, it had been Audrey's job to drive to each farm and leave a mimeographed flyer in English and German, explaining the move, which made no sense to her.

"I don't have to tell them anything," Walter had said the morning before, when he shook his head over the order. "I will, though, because it's the decent thing to do."

She could have told him that war didn't demand the decent thing. These were prisoners from a diabolical regime that had started a terrible war, and who deserved no consideration. But he was Walter Watkins, a man with a moral core the same as hers. Like her, he had come to know them as people trapped in the mess, too. She typed his scrawled note thanking them for their services to the beet and bean farmers of Goshen County, and wishing them well in their new assignments.

When she sat a long time at the typewriter close to his desk, he reached over and touched her shoulder. "We're not very good at this hardboiled stuff, are we?" he asked.

"No, we are not," she agreed. "I'm going to miss them." Then it was too much. "Walter, what is this folly? You've gotten rid of the deadly Major Rheinhold and his henchmen and made this a safe place. Are they being transferred to hellholes where the whole thing will repeat itself? Why?"

He sat back but did not turn away, or blush beet red as Walter Watkins of a month ago might have. "I asked Colonel Dempster at Scottsbluff precisely that." He rolled his eyes at the memory. "He glared at me and said I'd be replaced as soon as possible. 'You're too soft and these are Germans,' he told me."

"We're a couple of chumps," she said, which coaxed a smile out of him. "I don't intend to change. Do you?"

"No. I don't have it in me. Meanwhile, I'll do the best job I can, as long as I can."

So will I, she thought. All the beet planting was done, so she stood with him as the farmers returned with the crews they had lodged and fed for a week, until the storms of both weather and flagrant abuse had passed.

Walter called the names and the PWs came forward to sign the roster. Audrey knew she was no good judge of people she barely knew, and Germans at that, but she sensed a relaxation among the crews. They all knew what had happened. They stood easily – not at attention, eyes forward and shoulders back under the eyes of Major Rheinhold – but carefully casual, if watchful, because the hated SS were gone. As she observed them, Audrey wondered if any of them, herself included, would ever again feel the joy of carefree times. Maybe that would be the birthright of the next generation.

I would like to raise little ones in better times, she thought. Without considering the matter, she looked at Gerd Gauss to see him observing *her*. When he nodded slightly, she hoped his linguistic talents didn't include reading minds.

Before Walter dismissed them to their barracks for showers and then supper, he gestured Gerd forward to interpret. "Tomorrow is the funeral for Private Matthieu Bauer," he said, and waited for Gerd. "Colonel Dempster of the Scottsbluff Command has given us – you – permission to attend. This is your choice." He looked at the farmers. "We have a few transports here, but a few more beet trucks would be good." He counted the raised hands, Dad's among them. "Good, then. Tomorrow at 10 a.m., please. You are dismissed."

Dinner at home that night was chicken pie served to Dad and a morose Gut Bucket, whose heart wasn't in the meal. Head between his paws, he moped, and gave Audrey the royal side eye when she tried to feed him a tidbit from the table. "I suppose you're used to being the center of attention," she told him. *So was I*, she thought.

"I probably shouldn't tell you that he now answers to both Gut Bucket *and* Schmalz, should I?" Dad teased.

She laughed because she had to, then excused herself to do the dishes in silence, missing Heinz at the piano each night, someone usually singing along – something besides the rustle of Dad's newspaper, and then his snoring when it put him to sleep after a long day in the field. There was no one to help dry the dishes or sweep up. The silence of earlier months had helped her healing. The silence now got on her nerves.

Buck up, Audrey, she scolded herself. *There will be other crews for thinning, weeding and the harvest.* She frowned, remembering the directive from Scottsbluff that came a few days ago, with the information that henceforth, crews might go to different farmers every day. There would be much less opportunity for mischief. Or understanding, she wanted to add.

It was still on her mind in the morning as she dressed in black for the funeral, the same dress she had worn to Ed's service, an odd ritual with no coffin and no trip to the cemetery. The dress that hadn't seemed black enough three years ago was too black now. She added a red and blue scarf around her waist and straightened Dad's tie when he came out of his bedroom.

He held up a chain with a ring on it. "Anton must be frantic without this." He put it in his pocket. "Nice kid. He didn't complain when I snored."

"Oh, Dad!"

There was only a grave waiting for Matthieu's coffin in a far empty corner of the cemetery, but it was surrounded by at least one hundred of the PWs. It was a shock to see many in their field gray uniforms, some in good shape, others showing the wear of battle. These were the uniforms she had seen in many a newsreel. The Afrika Korps troops were even more distinctive in their yellow/tan shirts and shorts, with the ball caps with extra-long bills to keep off the desert sun.

"You can almost tell where they were captured," Dad whispered to her. "Some must have been in offices – that's a pretty nice olive drab uniform on Heinz – and then there's Gerd, with nothing but what he was wearing when his plane went down."

"He told me the Tommies took his leather flight jacket," she whispered back. *And his rosary, Knight's Cross and photo of his wife and son*, she didn't say. She looked away from Matthieu's simple wooden box covered with a German flag, someone's possession. Maybe the Scottsbluff commander had the right idea. The less anyone knew about these men, the easier it was to hate them.

"But why put Matthieu out here in the back forty?" Dad asked her as the young acolyte swung incense and many of the men crossed themselves.

"Walter said there is every possibility the dead will be repatriated someday, or at least moved to another cemetery," she whispered, her eyes on the priest as he prayed.

Dad nodded. "He could at least have the company of our neighbors."

On Gerd's quiet orders, the men who planted Dad's beet fields lowered the casket into Wyoming ground and shoveled in the dirt, all of them taking turns. Dad walked to Walter for a word, and she crossed her fingers, hoping her boss wouldn't object to a few minutes at the farmhouse for cake and coffee. Dad also handed the ring on the chain to Anton, who clutched his arm in gratitude.

"Walter said it's fine, as long as we invite him, too," Dad said when he returned to her side. "I like *this* Walter Watkins."

So do I, she thought, pleased she could serve cake one last time and show Gerd, Dietrich, Heinz, and the others that someone else was thinking of Matthieu. If she was honest, she wanted to say goodbye to these friends. "Let's go home."

The sky was deep blue and the day warm, as if trying to make up for any hard feelings after last week's blizzard. Maybe it really was the last blizzard of the winter. She longed for green fields and new calves and lambs with their stiff-legged strut in the neighbors' fields.

"Another season, eh, Audie?" Dad asked, interpreting her thoughts.

She started to return some comment when she noticed a tall man with a suitcase beside him sitting on their front porch. "Who..." she started to say as Dad brought the truck to a stop. She stared in amazement as she heard a shout from the bed of the beet truck and saw Heinz Dorschel leap out and run with arms outstretched. The two men grabbed each other.

"Dad...Dad...Could that possibly be his father?" she asked, astonished, as the other prisoners leaped out, too, and surrounded the father and son.

"He must have read Heinz's letter you mailed and got right on the train," Dad said. "I'll be damned." He motioned to Walter, who had stopped his automobile and stood staring at the scene.

"What in the world...." Walter began, then grinned. "Audrey, what're you up to?"

"I probably broke a rule," Audrey told her boss, feeling no contrition. "Heinz's father farms near Hastings. So close! He wanted to send him a letter, and Major Rheinhold would never allow it. I...I... said I would mail it."

Walter didn't even try to look stern. "Mrs. Allerton, I think you and I are going to be busted back to extension agent and clerk, if Scottsbluff gets wind of this." He grinned. "Oh, well."

Heinz let go of his father and gestured to her and Dad. "Frau Allerton, Herr Nolan." He put his hand in her father's hand. "I can hardly think in English."

"You're doing fine," Dad said. "Mr. Dorschel, is it? Come inside, all of you. There's cake and coffee."

Everyone went inside except the Dorschels, who sat on the porch swing and alternated between talking in rapid fire German and staring at each other as years of separation and war dropped away. Audrey served everyone in the dining room, then took cake to the father and son, not wanting to interrupt them, but somehow needed to see the glimmer of a happy ending for someone, if not now, then later.

"How long has it been?" she asked, after she served them.

Mr. Dorschel – Josef – looked across the newly planted field. "Fifteen years? Heinz was ten when my wife decided to return to Berlin." He shook his head. "I had a farm here. I was a citizen of two years." His voice broke. When he spoke again, his voice was low and filled with pain. "She promised me Heinz could visit. Promised me! And then there was Hitler and trouble, and no one visited."

Heinz put his arm around his weeping father and spoke softly in German. She left them together. They needed no one but each other.

She stood by the piano, looking down at the keys, already feeling hollow inside, knowing these prisoners who had become her friends would leave tomorrow for other camps. *I should have stayed in Boston, where I could drink tea with ladies, talk about nothing, and roll the occasional bandage*, she thought, then rejected the idea immediately. The war right here was a better war.

She held her breath at a hand on her shoulder, and closed her eyes. Better just enjoy the moment. She inclined her head toward the hand. Gerd turned her around and kissed her, a slow, probing kind of kiss that made her stomach sink to her knees. Her arms went around him, and she savored every single second of the experience of holding a man too close. One Mississippi two Mississippi three Mississippi four Mississippi.

The kiss ended before five Mississippi. It had to. Men were laughing in the dining room, and the Dorschels were deep in conversation on the porch, but anyone could pop in. Gerd Gauss had no business kissing her, and she certainly knew better. He held her off and she studied his amazing blue eyes, knowing she would never see the like again.

"I don't want to go tomorrow," he said. He touched her forehead with his. "This is a problem with no solution."

He was right. After only crumbs remained of the cake, the PWs piled into the beet truck. Walter took her aside. "I'm doing the wrong thing now, but it's the right thing," he told her, his voice low. "Heinz and his father are staying here tonight. Bring both to camp at six a.m. tomorrow. Drive right up to the admin building. Let him out and take Mr. Dorschel to Torrington. He can catch the train back to Cheyenne, with no one the wiser."

Could I keep Gerd here tonight? Oh, pretty please, she wanted to ask. "Yes, boss," she settled on. "No one will know about the Dorschels."

She shook her head when Dad opened the cab of the truck for her, not trusting herself to remain tearless if she came along for this final ride. Audrey ushered father and son inside the house. Standing alone on the porch, she waved Gerd out of her life.

But there he was and she couldn't look away, not yet. He put his hand to his heart, and she did the same. She watched him until the truck was dust on the road.

Chapter Twenty-three

No one ever knew. After leaving Heinz at the admin building in the morning, she dropped Mr. Dorschel off at the depot in Torrington. He kissed her hand and said he would stay in touch. Walter had given her a pile of correspondence to type in town, so she banged away on the Underwood, taking out her irritation at the U.S. Army, the Seventh Service Command, SS thugs, and an Austrian she had no business kissing.

She finished the letters by ten o'clock, and read them over carefully, dry government letters to other dry government offices. As agitated as she was over the PWs leaving – oh, be honest and admit it was Gerd Gauss leaving – she had to smile to see what she had typed instead of "gasoline rationing should satisfy local demands." Maybe only a sharped-eyed secretary would notice "gaussoline rationing," but she couldn't count on that.

The error brought her up short and she laughed inwardly. No need to let Dorrie, whose office she shared, even suspect what an idiot the extension agent's clerk/typist was.

In the course of two hours, Audrey mentally resigned four times so she didn't have to see any more PWs ever (overlooking, of course, that her father needed PWs to plant and harvest and she would have to run away to interior Canada to get away from the world). Twice she imagined the excuses that she needed to return to Boston to help her mother (who practically tripped over her servants and never needed help), or her mother-in-law (who probably still wondered what her darling Edward had ever seen in the little hick from Wyoming). They were lame excuses; she discarded them.

Before lunch time, she resolved to resign and move to the nearest cloister, one that took a vow of silence, if the nuns could overlook the fact that she never went to *any* church after Ed died because she still thought that monumentally unfair of the Almighty. Which also meant that by noon, she had cajoled herself back into the reality that she had fallen in love with the wrong man, he was gone, and life was going to go on anyway.

She typed, inwardly whining and complaining, with Dorrie none the wiser. At least she could pull the tattered shreds of her dignity around her and tell no one how foolish she was.

Or not. As she stared at the calendar, Dorrie cleared her throat. "Audrey, you haven't heard a word I said."

All manner of apologies and denials came to mind, but Dorrie was right. "Not a word," she admitted. She pointed a thumb at her chest. "Here sits the stupidest female in Wyoming. I fell in love with a PW and now he's gone."

"Gerd Gauss?" Dorrie asked, not hiding her smile.

Audrey threw back her head and laughed, because she could now, since she'd raked herself over the coals and was done with him. "Jeepers, I was that obvious?"

Dorrie clasped her hands on the desk. "Only to someone who fell in love with Walter Watkins."

"Dorrie, what on earth are we ever going to do?" Audrey said, when she could speak.

"Soldier on. That's what Gerd is doing," Dorrie said quietly, "and you must, too. I'm used to soldiering on."

"I will not whine so much," Audrey told herself in the silence of her souped-up Ford, as she drove to Camp Veteran with letters ready to sign. She wondered how many years Dorrie Hatcher had been pining after the equally shy Walter Watkins, her boss. Everyone has a story. Her war story was one to tuck away and remember now and then, if she wanted to.

Her resolve lasted to the admin building, where she found a letter addressed to her in unfamiliar handwriting. She recognized European handwriting, and she tucked it in her purse. She tapped on Walter's door and stuck her hand in to wave around letters to sign. She set the letters on his desk and decided that even if her dreams were silly and best forgotten, she could still do some good for Dorrie.

"Walter, never fear. The extension office is in excellent hands," she said. "Dorrie is on top of everything." She held up a manila folder. "I have homework. I am to go over these lessons for ladies cooking on rations. You know, how to sauté ration books until they reach the proper tenderness and then make a white sauce out of motor exhaust to coat them. I'll do more of her job, so she can do more of yours."

"I know she can handle anything I throw at her," he said. "Audrey, go forth and teach the women of Goshen County, who will listen attentively, then do as they darned well please."

Maybe she could slide in an unobtrusive comment. "That note on my desk. Do you know who left it there?"

"It was the PW who changed your Ford into a Duesenberg touring car," he teased.

He grinned and waved her out of the office. She put the note in her purse, wondering why Dietrich Schopenhauer would leave her a note. She looked into Walter's office again. "By the way, you're certainly keeping up the good work here. Is your mother feeling better?"

The smile left his face. "She passed away before the blizzard."

Audrey felt her heart turn over. *Just when we think we know everything,* she thought. "You never said a word. Oh, Walter."

"There was too much going on here. I sat with her to the end, though." He tapped the papers before him. "And I…we…can help others. It's what she always did. I can, too."

As Walter returned to his work, Audrey knew, with a force that filled her, that it was time for her to really, truly, grow up.

When she got home, she thought about throwing away the letter. She held it over the burn barrel, telling herself she didn't want to read it, which was a lie. She *did* want to read it, but what good would that do? None. She set the letter from Dietrich in the burn barrel.

The prisoners remaining in Camp Veteran were put to work policing the grounds and sprucing up the individual barracks. This included laying down fine gravel and spreading it around on the walkways. The surprise of the week came when she started her day at the office in the courthouse instead of Camp Veteran, getting there before Dorrie, who was never late, at least until this morning.

Audrey looked up from her typing when the office door opened, and gasped in amazement. Dorrie Hatcher was in tears, Dorrie who never flinched when ranchers or farmers got right in her face and yelled at her over some new government regulation.

Audrey came around her desk, eyes wide, her arms open, and Dorrie collapsed against her, weeping. "Oh, Dorrie, Dorrie, did someone die?" she asked. "Tell me who it was. May I help?"

Dorrie took the handkerchief Audrey held out to her and wiped her eyes and nose. She sank down at her desk, her eyes stark and disbelieving. Audrey knelt beside her, "Please, Dorrie!"

Dorrie clutched her hands. "I was passing by the depot. The patrolman stopped us and let the line of new PWs cross to the trucks." She shook her head in disbelief. "They're so young! I doubt half of them are over fourteen. What's the world coming to?"

Maybe the god of war will not be satisfied until every mother's son is in a grave, or missing, or shellshocked, she told herself as she held competent, stalwart Dorrie Hatcher as she wept.

She saw the prisoner-boys herself that afternoon as she took mail and more correspondence to Camp Veteran. The new arrivals had finished the clothing issue. The smaller among them staggered under the weight of too-large trousers, shirts, a belt, one pair of shoes, drawers, stockings and undershirts, an overcoat, and on top, the camp uniform of blue denim.

She saw them next in the mess hall as they obediently lined up in front of the one lieutenant remaining and an NCO. She saw relief in some eyes, fear in others, as they listened to the lieutenant tell them something or other in German. He seemed as unsure of himself as they were, and not much older, but at least he was not SS.

"We're going to miss our interpreters," Walter whispered to her. "These boys are just off the farm. Where are Gerd, Dietrich and Heinz when I need good interpreters?"

I need Gerd worse, she thought, then gave herself a mental shake. *No, I don't need him. That's silly.*

The lieutenant finished, gave a half-hearted Heil Hitler, which still startled her, and pointed to the table where she and Walter sat. No one smirked or laughed when Walter mangled their names, but stepped forward obediently to sign then print their names, ages, and place of birth. She smiled at the young soldiers, her heart breaking, then pointed them toward the steam tables where the few remaining older camp residents serve their first meal, the one she fervently hoped reassured them that no one would starve in Wyoming.

She saw some of these young prisoners working in her father's beet field the next week and the next. (Walter had never seen the point in assigning them to different farms every week.) As summer warmed the land, Dad patiently demonstrated how to thin the beets, stripping off the smaller shoots and leaving the biggest to thrive and grow and eventually turn into sugar. Audrey watched them grow more assured as they did what was asked of them.

She felt her own assurance grow when she knew Doc Barnes had insinuated himself into Camp Veteran at Walter's quiet request, to check everyone weekly for signs of beating or other mayhem. He found none, and Audrey let out her own sigh of relief, even as she allowed herself the tiny luxury of thinking about Gerd and hoping he was safe, too.

She was home with a cold and slight fever on Tuesday, June 6, idly listening to Tommy Dorsey at midday when an announcer interrupted with news of a massive Allied landing on the beaches of Normandy, France. The connection was scratchy with news a world away of GIs wading ashore under heavy fire from the cliffs, many dying in the surf, but others moving forward doggedly, seeking shelter under those cliffs, and Rangers climbing under withering fire to silence pillboxes. Planes buzzed around, some dropping bombs and other strafing, but Allied soldiers kept coming in waves, relentless, not to be dislodged from Fortress Europa. D-Day.

Her head throbbed, but she dressed and went to the field, signaling to Dad, who hurried over, followed by Shep, the same corporal guard, the only other familiar face because this time she was determined not to get to know these youngsters.

She told them the news. Dad motioned to the PWs. "We are all going to the house. It is lunch time," he said, and waited for the one lad who knew a little English to explain. They trooped in together, ready for lunch, that baloney sandwich and apple, and unauthorized baked potatoes and butter that her heart knew they needed, no matter her determination to ignore them. Well, two potatoes each and more butter, with homemade bread, because Audrey was Audrey.

They sat and ate, smiling at the milk she poured, as Dad and the corporal guard listened to the radio, staring at it, as if someone was going to materialize and make everything plain. At the urging of the PWs, the lone English speaker did his best to interpret. Lowered eyes and headshakes told Audrey that they understood enough. She saw some tears, but more hope.

Ed was on her mind that night as she prepared for lonely bed. She did what she usually did, and talked to him, telling him about the day's news of the beets, and the extension agency run so competently now by Dorrie, who still cried over the young prisoners. She told him of her talks to women's church groups, and men's clubs, and school children about conserving this, and re-using that, and turning cardboard sleeves with slots for nickels and dimes into war bonds. More than one member of the Elks Club had told her last week that she was the prettiest speaker they'd heard from in donkey's ages, which made her blush.

"Ed, they assured me I would find another husband when the war ends and the boys come home," she told her late husband. "I wish it were you, even if I know that is impossible."

Tonight, she mentioned D-Day, which broke her heart. Why wasn't Ed still alive to hear the news himself?

And lately, since it was her private time, and no one was listening, there was that small moment, that little luxury, when she thought of Gerd's hand on her shoulder. Nothing more than that. She ended the small thought with her hand on her heart. It wasn't much, but everything was rationed, even love. Only heartache had no limit.

Chapter Twenty-four

The summer of 1944 turned into fall and winter, with news on all fronts of advances bought dearly with Allied blood. More PWs came to Camp Veteran and all the camps of the Seventh Service Command. For the most part, the prisoners were a serious lot, once they overcame the initial fear of retaliation in camp, or starvation. More and more attended the evening classes in English, basic hygiene, world literature and current events that high school instructors taught after their own classroom days were done.

Mostly they were *heer*, or the army units of the Wehrmacht. The glamorous Desert Rats of the Afrika Korps were just a memory. Tobruk, El Alamein, Kasserine Pass and Gazala became names for the history books. The foot soldiers slogged on in Europe, moving closer to Germany itself, with its younger and younger soldiers, and old men drafted to fight for the Fatherland.

As the months passed, Walter remained in charge of Camp Veteran. No one objected. True to his modest nature, Walter told her in a brief moment of candor that he'd spent a lifetime being overlooked. For form's sake, Audrey tried to protest, but he waved it off. "I know who I am," he told her. "I'm a background man. In this case, let's hope Camp Veteran comes to no one's attention, the same as I."

Audrey nodded her agreement, aware that her boss Walter Watkins was probably the best leader in all of the Seventh Service Command. "Walter, you're a peach," she said. "Argue all you want, but it's true. You're saving lives."

"And changing my own," he added. *And mine,* Audrey thought. *Whatever happens, I hope this war has made me better.*

One bittersweet moment was seeing Corporal Shepard off to war. Plain and simple, the army needed him more in Europe than in Wyoming. He was no taller than before, and she worried, but there was no wattage in any bulb brighter than Shep's smile at his good news. "I'll miss you, Mr. Nolan and Mrs. Allerton," he said on his last afternoon of guarding PWs who didn't need to be guarded, and weeding beans this time.

Guard duty had always been misnamed, but this was their little secret, apparently. For the year she had known him, Audrey smiled to see little Shep planting, thinning and weeding alongside the prisoners. He was quicker than the PWs when it came to topping off the beets during the harvest, and almost wriggled like a puppy at Dad's high praise.

"Audie, I don't think he had much family back in Arkansas," Dad said, as they saw him off from Camp Veteran. "I told him he's welcome to work for me fulltime when the war's over. I could use a foreman. Maybe I'll get some cattle again. It's been a while and prices are finally good."

"I was hoping you'd make Shep an offer, Dad."

"I did and he agreed. We can turn that bunkhouse into a nice place for him."

The brighter spot came at the end of the beet harvest when the air was cold and snow predicted any day now. The beans had long since made their way to market, but beets demanded cold weather to bring out the sugar. Soon the factory in Torrington, also staffed by PWs, would stink, hum and whine to the business of turning beets into sugar.

With his own harvest of beans, potatoes and corn in Nebraska silos and on its way to American stomachs at home and abroad, Josef Dorschel sent them a letter, and then to their delight, added a visit. He called from the depot, and they drove to town to get him.

The worried concern of his first visit had been replaced with something Audrey saw as calm assurance. He knew where his boy was. "He is in Benkelman, and he is allowed to write. I'm thinking I can finagle – good American word, eh? – a short visit with him in December."

He shared unwelcome news over pot roast and mashed potatoes. "Everyone knows the war will end soon, maybe even before Christmas," he said, the worried look back. "Heinz wrote that rumors say all PWs will have to work a few more years in France or England, repairing that which mad Hitler destroyed."

"The Allies have the power to do that," Dad agreed. Audrey passed the rolls around again. "Thanks, Audie. You know, Josef, you should write to your senators and representatives."

"Executive, legislative and judicial," Josef recited. "How I studied for that citizenship test all those years ago!"

Audrey laughed and passed the strawberry jam. Dad leaned closer. "Really. Write to them and explain your special situation – you know, how your former wife took your little son back to Germany, and how he had no say in the matter. Offer to sponsor him."

"Sponsor?"

"Yes. Vouch for him. Assure the government that Heinz Dorschel will never be a drain on the government's resources and that your son will make a fine citizen."

"I can *do* that?"

"Absolutely." Dad glanced at Audrey. "It's been on my mind. Some of these boys are good workers, aren't they?"

"*Ja.* I have several PWs, myself." He sat back as Audrey cleared the table. "I can do that. Right now, I have a little news for you."

Dirty dishes and all, Audrey sat down. "Please, Mr. Dorschel, what do you know of the others?"

"Not much. That pilot is in Fort Robinson, near Chadron. I believe they are training war dogs. The man who fixed your car is somewhere near Omaha – two camps there." He shook his head. "Helmut, the man afraid of the dark? He killed himself."

Dad sighed for them both and took her hand. "I wish they had left him here. We could have helped."

"*Ja,* but no one listens to us." Josef brightened. "The man who helped with poor Matthieu?"

"Kurt Krueger," Audrey said.

"Heinz says he is working as a dispensary aide in a camp near Lincoln." Josef held up his hands. "And that is all this man knows. Tell me your news."

They had no other visitors that winter, except for the unwelcome visitor that came in the form of more news, this time of serious battle in Belgium, an unexpected last gasp by the dwindling army and Luftwaffe that gouged out a bulge in Allied lines stretched to the limit.

This news traveled everywhere, including Camp Veteran, where silent prisoners sat around radios in each barracks, burning more coal against a winter more bitter than usual, maybe wondering how their own families would manage when the Allies finally broke through, as everyone knew they would, and continued their steady pace toward the heart of Germany. PWs from eastern Germany wore longer faces, certain of terrible retribution at the hands of Soviet forces coming closer, as well. It was going to be a race to Berlin.

Other disturbing news meant changes in camp life, and not for the better. As the Allies advanced, they came upon concentration camps, where Jews, gypsies, and other malcontents suffered, starved, and died by the hundreds of thousands, perhaps millions, all in the demented name of racial purity, and anti-Semitism on a scope unheard of. Audrey took no pleasure in going to the movies occasionally with Walter and Dorrie, who had grown closer together in their own shy way. The newsreels of gaunt men and women stared back at her through barbed wire, unable to comprehend liberation after years of terrible abuse. And the stacks of skinny corpses? Audrey avoided the movies.

The liberation of *stalags* changed American opinion about German prisoners. GIs and Tommies alike, some as gaunt as concentration camp survivors, told their stories of abuse and trouncing of the Geneva Convention, which called for humane treatment of prisoners of war.

One morning Audrey came to work to see a letter from Camp Scottsbluff on her desk, already initialed by Walter. She read the chilling words of cutting back rations for prisoners of war in the United States, because there had been no such kindness ever shown to imprisoned Allies. The gloves were off. No more kindness was the lot of PWs now. No more Fritz on the Ritz.

"All the good we did was for nothing, apparently," Walter said, as he watched her from his own office.

"But we're feeding growing boys here in camp," she said in feeble protest, but they both knew there was no arguing with government policy. "You know, those boys we want to send back to Germany healthy and thinking kindly of America as they rebuild a new Germany."

"I know. You know. Dorrie knows." He waved his hand to include Goshen County and maybe the Rocky Mountain West. "The government commands, and we must obey." He held up another mimeographed sheet. "Here are the new dietary requirements."

"The government commands, indeed," Audrey told Ed's photograph that night as she turned out the light. She lay there, well aware that her short time with her husband was already fading from her mind. "We never planned on war, did we?"

Not for the first time, or even the fiftieth, she wondered if anyone ever really won a war. She took all the small satisfaction she could from Dad's reaction over breakfast to the reduction in meals for the PWs who quietly and obediently worked in his fields and those of his neighbors.

"I'm a dab hand at making a pretty good stew, Audie," he told her. "If it just happens to be bubbling merrily away when the boys come in for their skinny sandwiches, who is going to know?" He gave her an arch look. "And if someone I know and love feels like turning out a pound cake with strawberry jam on it, or mounds of gingersnaps, I'd call that an amazing coincidence."

"Dad, we'll be fraternizing and collaborating with the enemy again," she teased.

"I know. Ain't it grand?" His expression changed. "I can't do that until the planting season, though. Now my farm workers are holed up in their barracks and hungry."

Let it end, she thought. *Let it end.*

Chapter Twenty-five

But when? Bloody advances in the Pacific, ditto in Europe could be read no other way. Audrey looked for bright spots (they all did), and surprised herself with a few.

Or rather, her father did. She knew he fretted that "his" boys were stuck in the compound, eating stingy rations, during winter with nothing to do because he didn't need them until April. She knew it weighed on his mind each evening when he picked up his fork and stared at the Swiss steak and mashed potatoes she cooked, or frowned over brownies. She sighed when he stomped off to the parlor to glare at the newspaper.

She was finishing the dishes one night when she heard a loud, "Hah," from the parlor, followed by Dad reaching for his coat in the kitchen. "Audie, put on your coat. I have a brilliant idea."

Curious, she followed him out the back door and into Wyoming wind. He tugged her along purposefully to the bunkhouse, unused since last year's memorable blizzard. He had brought along a flashlight, which he shone on the shabby interior.

"Better warn Dorrie that I am showing up in the extension office tomorrow with a request for at least six prisoners."

"To remodel the bunkhouse?" she asked, then kissed his cheek. "You're going to make this sow's ear into a silk purse, aren't you?"

"Yep. Didn't I tell you I wanted to turn this bunkhouse into nice quarters for Corporal Shepard when the war's over and I can hire him?"

"Dad, you are a brilliant man." Audrey kissed his cheek then laughed. "Of course, they'll be stumbling over each other in this tight space."

"That's our little secret, Audie, isn't it?" When she nodded, he added, serious now. "And they'll eat better."

259

Dorrie, acting extension agent, heard him out the next day, and sent the application through proper channels to Lt. Colonel Dempster in Scottsbluff. In two weeks, he had his crew and the crew had food – beef stew, chicken and noodles, roast, meatloaf, and cake.

"You know, they may be young, but I believe they are smuggling our leftovers into camp," Dad said a week later with real satisfaction, to find that the remains of a good-sized roast had vanished. "What happened to that other pound cake?"

"Beats me," Audrey said, and they laughed together.

The extension agency returned to what passed as normal when Walter found himself replaced by a young lieutenant who had lost his left arm at Normandy, but none of his fight. Lieutenant Christopher made himself at home in the admin building and developed a surprising rapport with the equally young *leutnant* left in charge after what Audrey called "the overdue SS purge" of Major Rheinhold and his fanatical ilk. Between the two of them, Camp Veteran became a little less bleak.

Walter's return to the extension office meant some adjustments. Audrey reverted to Mondays, Wednesdays, and Fridays, and Dorrie returned to her desk. To Audrey's delight, Walter, the quintessential late bloomer, discovered two things: Dorrie had done a fine job as extension agent, and he loved her. They were married during the first week of beet seed planting in April. Audrey sang "Oh, Promise Me," and wished Heinz Dorschel were there to accompany her.

She picked the tune out in the parlor, rolling her eyes at the sentimental lyrics, all of which seem to rhyme in time-honored fashion, not quite moon, June, croon, and spoon, but close, to her critical dismay.

"Really, Audrey," she murmured. "Can you sing this with a straight face? I mean, take your love to some sky where you can find sweet violets of early spring? Violets in the sky? Who writes this stuff?"

She did sing "Oh Promise Me," though, with all her heart in the First Presbyterian Church, and happily waved off Mr. and Mrs. Watkins to a too-brief honeymoon ninety miles away in romantic Cheyenne. It wasn't so hard after all. She loved them both.

Back the sheet music went to the piano bench where she rummaged a little more, hunting for "Passing By," that achingly lovely Elizabethan ballad she couldn't sing when Heinz Dorschel held it out. She gave the fading pages the one-handed treatment, both loving and dreading it because it was the song she had sung to Ed, and he to her.

She hummed first, steeling herself for a wave of sorrow, except that it wasn't there this time, replaced instead by the sweet memory of Ed's love and his kindness. *I did but see you passing by*, she thought, wondering at four and a half centuries of love and heartache, wondering how many had sung this in war and peace, all gone now like Ed. Could she sing it? She could try, changing the words as she had done before, singing them to her husband.

"'There is a good man dear and kind, with never a face so pleased my mind,'" she sang, but softly. This next part would be hard. "'I did but see him passing by…'" Oh, the biggest test. "'And yet I'll love him till I die.'"

She stopped playing, waiting again for sorrow or regret. Again, there was none, only a great gratitude that her love had been with Ed Allerton to the end. Death had come far too soon, but that was the fault of war during his allotted time on earth. She looked at the next verse and something changed inside her.

"'His gestures, motions and his smiles, his wit, his voice my heart beguiles.'" She hummed the rest of the verse, thinking this time of Gerd Gauss, and waited for that to ring hollow, weird, or silly. It didn't, to her relief more than her surprise.

She knew what came next and stopped, her hands still poised over the keys, wanting to sing, but certain she couldn't and think about Ed, or even about Gerd, the man she knew she had to forget because some things simply couldn't happen, not ever. The page blurred, but she read the words in silence. "Cupid is wingéd and doth range, my country, so, my love doth change. But change ye earth or change ye sky, yet will I love him till I die."

The unfairness of her situation smote her like a sledgehammer against her back. She gasped and leaned forward against the awful pain of knowing she would not see either man again. They were both gone, and she was bereft in a terrible way. She covered her eyes and sobbed.

"Audie? *Audie?*"

She thought Dad was in the barn, tinkering with the tractor. Now he sat beside her on the piano bench, holding her close, letting her weep into his old tractor-tinkering coat. Unable to stop herself, she sobbed out her whole misery, first her anger at Ed for dying, which made Dad hold her tighter. Next came her anger at war for killing the man she loved.

Dad wiped her soaked face with his red bandana, something which used to make her laugh and wonder how he could be such a goof. "Oh, Dad, it's worse," she managed to gasp out when she could speak. "You'll hate me."

"Not a chance, Audie. Tell me everything."

She did, blurting out her love for Gerd Gauss, a Messerschmitt pilot whose Luftwaffe brethren had cut down Ed in his prime. What was she *thinking*? Their talk on the stairs, and that final kiss right here, when they couldn't possibly have stood together any closer. About how if the house had suddenly emptied out, they still never would have made it upstairs to a bed. That wasn't something to admit to her father, but she held nothing back.

Dad chuckled, so Audrey allowed herself to think that he still loved her, even if she was indiscreet and in love with someone so inappropriate that even Ivan the Terrible seemed like a better choice.

"You don't hate me?" she asked, after another application of the hopeless damp rag of a red bandanna.

"Not a chance, Audie," he said. "I watched the two of you, believe it or not." He left the piano bench and returned with a dish towel. "Here."

"I'm hopeless," she said simply. That wasn't enough. She needed to berate herself further. "Then I did something really stupid, I mean, well, maybe not as dumb as falling in love, but something I regret."

"Better tell me, even if it's so stupid that I couldn't possibly still love you, kiddo."

"Dietrich Schopenhauer, of all people, left me a note before they were sent to Scottsbluff. I took it home, stared at it, and tossed it in the burn barrel." The tears came again, except this time she could lean against Dad's shoulder and weep. "He and Gerd were friends. Now I have nothing."

"Don't be so sure about that," he said, when she had subsided to hiccups. "Wait here."

He took the stairs two at a time, something she'd never seen him do, and was back in record time. He handed her the same letter she had tossed in the burn barrel, smudged from those ashes, but still unopened. Open-mouthed, she stared at the letter. "Why, Dad?"

"I was about to burn a bunch of newspapers, but I saw that first," he said. "I couldn't burn it." He sounded less assured, and more like a person who was picking his way through life the same as she was, life with its twists and turns and dead ends and astonishing surprises. "I'll leave you to it."

He started to rise, but she took his arm. "Stay with me, please."

She opened the note, spread out the sheet, noting the decidedly European handwriting.

Dad squinted at the close words with the quaint curlicues. "I'll read over your shoulder." She nodded and held it closer.

"Dear Frau,

I am stepping entirely out of bounds by writing to you. You have never solicited my advice, nor do I ever expect you to. You cannot respond to this letter, even if you wish, because I have no idea where I am going. All I know is that we are being dispersed throughout the Seventh Service Command.

Hopefully, you do not object to the extra power I installed in your vehicle. As a designer of engines, I could not resist. That said, be careful on curves and do not assume an air of invincibility behind the wheel.

Audrey smiled at that. "Dad, he was so proud of that auto."

To the matter at hand: You will likely never receive a letter from Gerd Gauss. We have argued about this, and he is not a man easily dissuaded. Know this: He loves you. He told me. I suggested that when war ends, he might contact you, but he said no, because he has absolutely nothing to offer you.

He told me this last night. "Dietrich, I have nothing – no home, no employment, no family, no status. I am not German, but I am to Americans who see me and hear me. I cannot burden her with such a dark stain."

"Stubborn man," Audrey said. She ran her finger lightly over the words, *He loves you.*

Frau, to attempt an American idiom, the ball is on your pitch. Gerd is my friend I cannot help. No man, German or otherwise, likes to feel powerless, but we are precisely that. Whatever remedy there is must come from you, if you are so inclined. And your inclination is not my business. I will never tell Gerd I wrote to you.

I have intruded long enough on your circumspection. Please believe me that getting to know you and your father was a bright spot in my particular war.

Yours sincerely,

Dietrich Emmanuel Rudolf Schopenhauer

She put the letter in her lap, speechless. They sat together in silence, the clock's tick the loudest noise in the room. They both jumped when it chimed on the half hour.

"What are you going to do, sweetheart?" Dad asked at last.

"If I'm smart, I'll forget him."

"Are you feeling smart?"

She shook her head. "Not particularly."

Chapter Twenty-six

The remodeling of the bunkhouse was completed right before spring planting began, the work done by youngsters with more enthusiasm than skill, which meant Dad spent more time helping out. Audrey cooked for them, making everything she wanted to, hang rationing and decrees.

"Just don't tell our neighbors," she said to Dad after he returned from driving them back to the camp one night.

"Our neighbors are way ahead of us," Dad replied. "I ran into Petersen a week ago while I was returning my crew. He told me in confidence that his crew was building a machine shed he didn't need, because Angie Petersen was going to give him what for if she couldn't find a way to feed *her* boys."

"We're hopeless."

The beet planting began in mid-April as usual. She joined her father in the field, listening to his patient explanation of the process, watching him kneel in the soft earth, and watching each man in turn imitate him. In moments like that she regretted that he had no son to pass on his farming skills to, only a daughter indecisive and unsure of herself.

She thought back to last spring's planting, and her introduction to the man she knew she loved, the man living behind barbed wire, working near Chadron, if Josef Dorschel was right. It might as well have been on the moon.

She couldn't explain to herself why she felt better and braver when Gerd was around. His hand on her shoulder, nothing more, had somehow put the heart back into her frame. Now her life was just office work and cooking. Coming into the field this morning had felt right, until she let herself remember that there were no guards anymore. Lieutenant Christopher still commanded their little branch camp and had watched most of his guards being funneled to other assignments. She doubted they had ever been needed.

Fewer guards now reminded her of their guard, Corporal Shepard, a cheerful worker so pleased to be sent to the "real war," as he put it. She hadn't expected him to write, but his one Vmail to them last fall, full of misspellings and enthusiasm to be in the fight at last, cheered them both. She had received no answer to her prompt reply, putting it down to the chances of war.

They wouldn't have known about his death at Remagen if she hadn't been delivering letters to Lt. Christopher and glanced in his In box, with its memo from Camp Scottsbluff, listing casualties of interest to the Seventh Service Command. She didn't ask permission, but picked it up to stare at, then turn away.

"Did you know any of these men?" the lieutenant asked. "Scottsbluff sends me stuff like this every week."

She pointed to Corporal Shepard's name. How could she explain Corporal Shepard to Lt. Christopher, that quiet, unassuming, hard-working young man who probably never had a girlfriend, or much of anything. Shep had told her once how excited he was to get to see Nebraska and Wyoming, which told her all she needed to know about his modest world.

"We knew Corporal Shepard," she said quietly. She cried on the drive back to town, cried for the first time since her deluge at the piano bench, happy, oddly enough, to know that she could still feel something, even if it was sorrow. Poor Shep. Poor everyone.

Dad had taken the news with a start, and then a nod, followed by a long moment standing on the back porch looking at the former bunkhouse. Audrey had planted zinnias, but they weren't up yet. His voice strained, his back to her, he told her to plant flowers there every year. "You know, for Shep."

It would have been a simple matter to close the door on Shep and the bunkhouse, but Audrey didn't. After work the next day, she bought enough blue and white gingham at Woolworth's to make curtains for the front room and bedroom. She was off on Thursday, so it was no big deal to run up those curtains on Grandmother Nolan's treadle machine. She borrowed a willing PW to install the grooved wooden blocks another PW had made in the camp's little woodworking shop. He ran a dowel through the gingham panels and hung them, stepping back to admire the effect.

"Who lives here?" the PW asked.

"No one. I wanted curtains. I have enough material left for a tablecloth," she said quietly, seeing this effort for what it was: normalcy rising from the chaos of war, a brave blue and white phoenix. She couldn't have explained it to anyone, but she knew she was healing from the loss of her husband and maybe even the loss of Gerd. Time would tell.

"There's no table yet," the PW pointed out. He was young; in a few more years he might meet an amiable *fraulein* who understood that there would be a table and chairs, then a sofa and a bed. He only needed a little direction, like some men.

She sewed the tablecloth, and there was material left over for blue and white napkins. Feeling foolish, she ironed them, folded them, and left them on the unused kitchen counter.

The zinnias poked their heads above ground the week in May that Germany surrendered to Allied forces. By then, the PW farm laborers were weeding the beans in Dad's fields. "Look at them. Their world will change soon," Dad said to her. "I'll call them in. You turn up the radio."

Silent, their faces betraying next to no emotion, the PWs listened to the death throes of Berlin as the Russians, besiegers for many weeks, burst upon it with predictable violence, rape, and wrenching mayhem. Silence, then surrender, first to Allied forces on May 7, and then to the Russians two days later. The war in Europe was over.

She and Dad drove into Torrington that night, wondering what they would find, after listening to jubilation on the radio, broadcasting from New York City's Times Square where a city of millions went mad with joy. Torrington's celebration was more subdued. Not for them the sight of thousands of GIs and sailors passing through since 1941. Torrington's war was prisoners, first the proud and suntanned Afrika Korps, and a few Italians that everyone liked. They were followed by lesser *soldaten*, at least in the eyes of Rommel's arrogant troops, whose suntans had by then turned sallow or faded completely. Then came the frightened barely men/mostly boys, proof of the Third Reich's desperation to field an army, any army.

The streets were quiet as usual, but the bars were full of thoughtful men like Dad. Audrey had her first beer in the Silver Dollar Saloon that night, sipping it slowly because she didn't care for the taste. Her father and the other farmers and ranchers sat in companionable silence because they knew each other, their conversation centered mainly on when their own boys would be home.

One of the ranchers, a middle-aged widower who had been coming to the extension office mainly (she suspected) to look her over, nodded to her and raised his glass. She smiled back. He was a nice man and he had a good ranch. Mother would be disappointed, but Audrey knew she didn't belong in Boston.

She drove home, because Dad surprised her by drinking more than he usually did, which was almost never. When he went upstairs, she stayed in the parlor. She went to the piano and pulled out "Passing By." She played it through without a qualm this time, remembering Ed, who would always be in her heart, and thinking of Gerd and wondering how life would treat him, back in Austria.

What would she do? The war was by no means over, with every effort concentrated now on the Empire of Japan. She hadn't worked herself out of a job yet, especially since Walter had told her that Lt. Christopher was probably moving on to more responsibilities, and he would be back in charge of Camp Veteran. Besides that, Dorrie needed her in the office. There were still crops to harvest by autumn, and it would take months to sort everyone out and send them home to an exhausted, bombed-out Europe. Their fate in Europe? Problematic, at best.

Nothing was going to change right away. Maybe everyone could gradually get used to no ration books, new cars, and blessed nylon stockings again. The veterans would come home, and the prisoners go away.

Thoughtful, she turned out the lights and went upstairs, smiling a little at the thought of her circumspect father's hangover in the morning. She left her tears downstairs, not precisely certain who she had cried for. Surely not for herself; that was selfish. She had cried so many tears for Ed already. Her tears couldn't be for Gerd, wherever he was, and what might have been. Surely not. The very idea.

Chapter Twenty-seven

Like most events in life, if allowed to take root, the end of war in Europe settled into a pattern of sameness, simply because there was more war to be won. No one was going anywhere, with the exception of Lieutenant Christopher.

All apology to Walter Watkins, Art Christopher announced that he had put in for more active duty, not thinking in his wildest imaginings that the U.S. Army would find a spot for him closer to the war. "Believe this or not, but I am going to be an ADC to General Bradley, well, one of several," he told them when he summoned them to the camp. "I'm going overseas."

Audrey could tell he wanted their approval at his good fortune. "I'll miss you, but you're ready for this," Walter said. "Don't you think so, Audrey?" She nodded.

"Do you really think so?"

There was no need to fib, just to make the one-armed lieutenant feel good. "I really do," Walter answered. "You've done a fine job here."

And so he left, not before asking Audrey if she'd like to correspond. "I'll be going back to Denver eventually," he said a few days later, as she dropped him off at the depot. "It's a nice place." He looked around. "Torrington probably seems a little slow to you, since you lived in Boston."

"Oh, a little," she assured him, because he seemed to think she needed to know there were other places more in tune with the times. He didn't know that Goshen County suited her right down to the ground. However, a few Vmails to the lieutenant wouldn't hurt.

Red of face, Dorrie finally admitted that she and Walter were expecting. Hardly surprised (everyone in town suspected), Audrey still managed

269

wide-eyed amazement, even as she smiled inside. "What a delightful turn of events! When?"

"The middle of January," she replied. "I'll work here as long as I can, but I think the extension work will fall to you until the PW camp closes."

Camp closure was on every prisoner's mind. As acting camp commander again, Walter made himself available to any of them with enough fluency to inquire. He had the courage to hand out bad news as soon as he learned it. The War Department was already deep in conversations with corresponding governments in Europe, including those still in exile. He told them this one afternoon as the planting concluded, the land warmed and the next task in a few weeks – no one's favorite – would be weeding acres of beans.

"We have been informed that the United Kingdom, France, Belgium and The Netherlands have already approached President Truman about using your labor to clear away bombed out buildings and rebuild roads and highways." Audrey watched the fine lines deepen between his eyes and saw the toll of war in them, even if poor eyesight had kept him from the armed forces. Walter Watkins had faced no foe worse than zealous Nazi prisoners, or grasshoppers and too much snow, but war had aged him, too. "It's been a long six years of destruction."

Audrey saw the restless movement of the PWs; so did Walter. He raised a placating hand. "I know you will continue to be a credit to your countries, no matter what lies ahead."

And they were, but with an added spark in the summer of 1945 that delighted Audrey and reminded her how much she would miss these young men in a strange land, these youngsters she had vowed not to care about too much. The guards were gone, except for a few MPs to patrol the perimeter and stroll the streets of the tidy camp. She even noticed PWs driving tractors in the field. No one in town seemed to bat an eye when they showed up in town, a few at a time, to watch a movie. Everyone enjoyed *National Velvet* and *State Fair*; the newsreels not so much.

Farmwives, and she included herself, abandoned all pretense of keeping these growing men on a limited diet. Even then, there was the mystery of the disappearing eggs. Dad usually collected the eggs each morning after she left for town or the camp. "I won't say our hens have gone AWOL, but there's been some dereliction of duty," he informed her over supper one night in early August, when it was just the two of them.

"Maybe they're on strike," Audrey joked as she cleared the table, well-acquainted with that glint in Dad's eyes.

"I think our boys have something to do with this. Audrey, can you think of a German dish that requires lots of eggs?"

She couldn't. "Crepes is French, isn't it?" she asked, then remembered a lovely stroll in Boston with Ed, and a visit to a French restaurant. It seemed years ago, so many years ago. "It's French." She hesitated, then told Dad about that afternoon with her husband only two weeks before she saw him no more. She didn't add that was when she informed Ed he was going to be a father. Some moments remained hers alone.

Dad was no slouch. At lunch the next day, when the boys trooped in, hands and faces clean, to sit down to porkchops, hash browns, and tomatoes, he trained that gallows smile on them that Audrey knew well from her own scheming teen days. "Gentlemen," he announced, "is there a particular favorite German recipe that uses a lot of eggs?"

Although Audrey hid her face in her napkin so no one would see her smile, she couldn't overlook the guilty glances. She heard the murmured interpretation and wondered what would come next. These PWs were not slow of thought.

"Hmmm?"

"Herr Nolan, there is *senfeier*," Rolf announced, testing the waters by offering no more information.

"Lots of eggs?"

"*Jawohl*. A plethora. And wine," Rolf added, after a glance around the table, as if to see how deep he needed to dive.

Dad went for the kill. "Where do you get your wine?"

Rolf fell right in. "We make our own and hide it under the altar." The others nodded, then looked at each other, as if in silent agreement to say no more. No one mentioned the eggs.

"We're aiding and abetting a bunch of hardened criminals," was Dad's only comment when he returned from taking them back to camp after work. "I still want to know where the eggs went. They can't fly."

She found out two days later when Dorrie didn't feel up to a drive to Camp Veteran, and Audrey delivered the mail. Walter met her at the door of the admin building, an MP on either side of him, all of them smiling.

That was odd. She didn't think it was in the MP code of conduct to smile. Then she heard a chorus of peeps coming from Walter's office.

Keeping a straight face, she walked past her boss and peered into a pasteboard box filled with one, two, ah yes, a dozen newly hatched chicks, some still sporting a jaunty bit of eggshell on their heads.

"Did you by chance find these in that same barracks where Gerd and the others lived?" she asked when she stopped laughing. "We are missing a whole clutch of eggs."

"Sergeant Clancy held a barracks inspection this morning," Walter said, gesturing to the more fearsome of the two MPs, who struggled to contain himself. "He found these noisy little beauties under the floorboards in Compound Four."

"That's the place. I think they were going to make *senfeier,*" she said, and decided then not to give away their other secret of homemade wine. "I'll take these home to Dad. I hope you won't punish them." No heads rolled.

The matter went no farther, and she had a good story to write to Lieutenant Christopher, in Paris now. She wrote how Dad found the whole thing amusing. "He told me this: 'I look at it this way, Audie,'" she wrote, "'no harm, no foul. That's f-o-w-l.'"

She sent the Vmail to Art Christopher, even as she wished she could send a similar one to Gerd, who had vanished from her life. She knew he had her address. She also knew from Dietrich's letter that he would never write.

August 15, a Thursday when she was working at Camp Veteran, the radio in Walter's office that he usually kept on low, crackled to life as he exclaimed and turned it up. She left the filing cabinet where she was purging files and hurried into his office. The two of them stared at the radio with the news of the surrender of the Empire of Japan. Last week, they had learned of two shockingly powerful bombs, one detonating over a Japanese military garrison, and the other on a seaport three days later.

"That's it," Walter said, his voice subdued and almost disbelieving. "It's over, Audrey." He put his forehead on his desk. Audrey touched his shoulder then quietly left his office, closing the door behind her.

She walked into the tidy gravel street and looked toward the dispensary next door, where the old nurse had left her office, too, as well as the prisoner she had been treating for a stubborn case of hives. They were joined by the MPs, and the prisoner-cooks, then all the men who weren't on various farms. No one said anything.

She drove home in silence an hour later, pulling up before she reached the house, where she saw Dad's boys sitting on the porch. She turned off the Ford and leaned back in the seat. "It's over, Ed," she whispered. "I wish to God it had never started." She dug a little deeper into the quiet part of her heart where she stored bits and pieces that she shared with no one. "It's over, Gerd."

Chapter Twenty-eight

Japan formally surrendered on September 2 in Tokyo Bay on the battleship *Missouri*, attended by Allies from nine different nations. The war was over.

Over for some but not for others. Walter shook his head over the growing mound of paper on his usually neat desk, because that was Walter. "I predict it's going to be hurry up and wait until after the new year," he said. "There are crops to harvest, aren't there?"

The seasons reigned supreme again as the frightened teens from Fortress Europa who had grown into confident, suntanned men in Wyoming harvested the beans first, then the beets. When the work was done, they left the fields for the final time.

"I'm going to miss them," Dad said, when he met her at the camp that last day. Gut Bucket had come along for the ride, something he seldom did, since his usual job was to prowl the grounds, sniffing for men long gone, then whine about it, something Audrey wanted to do, but couldn't. "So is Schmalz," he added. "Let's go home."

Dad had a knack. He knew the first snow of November would come that week the beets were on their way to the factory. She stood at the window in the parlor, watching the snow, wondering where Gerd was.

She wondered through November, when word came that transporting prisoners to Europe was going to continue for weeks, maybe months. Unwelcome but inevitable news followed: prisoners in the middle of the nation might languish longer.

So they did. The only bright spot came when Dad received permission for their latest batch of PWs to come to their farm for Christmas dinner. As much as she wanted a turkey or a ham, Audrey settled on family beef yet again, personally disappointed, but confident that hungry men would be happy with anything.

And one other entree: She visited Magdalena Haupt with a request. Magdalena still cleaned offices in the courthouse, including the extension office, even though she and Bruno Haupt had sold their farm and lived in town now.

She made a point to be there early in the morning to catch Magda before she went home to fix breakfast for Bruno. "Mrs. Haupt, could you cook something for me for Christmas?" she asked. "We're having our Germans over for dinner and I'd like to serve them…uh…sigfine?"

Magda only looked mystified for a moment. She set down her mop. "I think you mean *senfeier*, Mrs. Allerton."

"That's it! I have plenty of eggs but no wine. I am happy to pay whatever you ask."

Magda took Audrey's hand in hers. "Bruno and I have been here since before the Great War." She raised her chin and Audrey saw all the pride. "We are good American citizens, but my heart goes out to the boys of Camp Veteran. *Senfeier*, it will be." She looked away, as if envisioning a Germany in ruins, far removed from the lovely land she and Bruno had left. "They are just boys and they must go back to devastation. No payment needed, Mrs. Allerton."

They enjoyed Magda's reminder of home. After the roast beef, mashed potatoes and gravy had gone around the table, and butter melted into the rolls, Audrey went to the kitchen and returned with Magda's dish. She breathed deep of the eggs cooked in mustard sauce and wine, and smiled at their stunned expressions, followed by their laughter and a *sehr gut* or two.

She glanced at Dad, who struggled, even as she did. He took the first serving from Audrey, then held the dish. "I could never have raised any crops if you, and the men before you, had not helped me with such diligence." He swallowed and waited for the interpretation. "I…we…will miss you." His lurking good humor returned, especially since Audrey, through amazingly blurred vision, saw sudden long faces around the table. "You still owe me one dozen eggs, and don't you forget it!" Everyone's laughter healed an amazing number of wounds.

One last surprise that Christmas was for her, and Dad was in on it. They left her with the youngest PW and the dishes, and hustled out of the house. She sensed a plot immediately, because the prisoner left to wash while she dried spoke no English, so she could weasel out nothing beyond a huge grin.

"Frau Allerton," one of the more fluent speakers finally announced from the back door, "you must now be folded with a blind...no...no blindfolded."

Never mind that it was her own damp dishtowel. Dad helped her into her coat and took her hand. "I'm being led astray," she teased, as he held tight to her hand.

The bunkhouse door opened. Someone had lit a lamp because she smelled the kerosene. The fold of the blind came off and Audrey stared at a table and two chairs, the table covered with her blue and white tablecloth.

"We made it for you in the woodworking shop, *frau*," the interpreter said, then included her father in his kind gaze. "We used some of those canteen chits we earned for working in your field, *Herr* Nolan. We will miss you both."

Two weeks later, a week into 1946, the word came from Scottsbluff, and the word was time to leave. Walter called her into his office after he hung up the receiver. "That's it. We're to have them there by seven o'clock tomorrow morning. Good thing the roads are clear."

"Good thing you don't need me along," Audrey said. She could spend time later (maybe when she was an old lady in 1976 or so and depending on how her life went), either reminiscing, or wondering if remaining behind had been her wisest decision ever.

"We'll be fine." Walter looked around the little office in admin. He had already packed the contents of the filing cabinet, per a request from the War Department. All else that remained of his time as the perfectly right commander of a prisoner of war camp could be dumped into a smaller box. "Audrey, we did our best."

"We did. It's over and we can get on with life."

If that was so, why did she wander around the parlor that night, sitting at the piano, then getting up, then staring out the window – wouldn't you know it – in the direction of Camp Veteran? It was as if some cosmic monster, maybe war itself, had ripped out her heart, stomped on it, thought better of the matter, apologized, and tried to stuff it back in her chest, where it didn't fit anymore.

"It's hard, isn't it, sweetheart?"

"I thought you were asleep under that newspaper, Dad," she said and sat beside him. "What happened to me?"

"You grew up. You left home. You married a good man. He died in the war. You came home so sad. You ended up dealing with those very people who killed Ed. You saw beyond it." He took a deep breath, as if wondering if he should say more. She finished for him. "I fell in love again. I don't know what to do about that except move on. Dad, is there someone out there for me somewhere?"

"Without a doubt."

She hoped he was right. She read in bed a long time that night, mostly reading the same two pages over and over. When she couldn't keep her eyes open, she turned off the light.

The phone rang at some point in the early hours, two short rings and two long ones over and over: their party line. As she hurried downstairs, Audrey knew it couldn't be personal. Ed was long dead, and Mother unlikely to call anyone in Wyoming ever.

"Yes?"

Walter talked fast, his words tripping over each other. "Dorrie's water broke we're at the hospital you have to go to Scottsbluff with the PWs the big folder is on the table in my office be there at seven o'clock good luck." Click.

She turned on the light in the kitchen. Four o'clock. She looked out the window on a clear night, one with stars so close, Wyoming's specialty.

"What's up, Audie?" Dad asked from the stairs. She told him. "You need any help?"

"I can manage, Dad. No sense in both of us losing sleep over this."

She knew the road well, remembering all the trips in Dad's beet truck, and then in her souped-up Ford. Maybe when Walter was coherent and a father, she could ask him what use the little community of Veteran would find for the buildings. Maybe the barracks and smaller structures would disappear in that way of unused buildings, and gradually begin new lives as machine sheds, or barns on nearby farms and ranches. She couldn't see much use for the two guard towers.

"What do you think, Gut Bucket?" she asked the dog beside her. He had insisted on the trip, pawing at her until she paid attention.

All the lights were on at Camp Veteran. One of the MPs opened her car door for her. "No Mr. Watkins?" he asked solicitously. He chuckled when Audrey described the early morning telephone call, and the nearly incoherent conversation. She retrieved the necessary papers from Walter's desk and rejoined him, looking around to see all the PWs assembled, standing next to their duffels, the ones given to them when they arrived here, frightened and wary. She noticed with some sadness that the wary look had returned.

And why not? When she came home to Wyoming, it was always with joy to see her father again, and friends, and maybe just the way the land stretched on for miles, with hills in the distance. Goshen County held none of the stunning grandeur found on the other side of the state in Yellowstone Park, or among the Tetons, but it was home, and she loved it.

These young men were going home to ruin, rubble and devastation, maybe even a worse fate behind Soviet checkpoints. She knew some had never received any letters from home. Some didn't know where their families were, or even *if* they were. On top of that, many of them, maybe all, were headed first to the ruin, rubble and devastation of Allied countries prostrated by six years of Hitler's war. They were trading American farm labor and good noontime dinners provided on the sly by farmwives, for European skinny rations and loathing, still far from home. She didn't envy them.

She called their names on the roster one last time as each man initialed his entry and climbed onto waiting trucks. She smiled at them all, wanting to reassure them. To her delight, the two PWs who built the table and chairs kissed her cheek.

Gut Bucket beside her, she climbed into the first truck. They drove forty-five miles on dark Highway 26 to five miles beyond Scottsbluff to the old airport, where a substantial prisoner of war camp had been built in record time. To her eyes, every building now looked temporary and shabby. Soon there would be no evidence of war. She couldn't help her sigh.

"Hard to believe it's over, isn't it, Mrs. Allerton," the driver said. She knew him as Camp Veteran's general all-around handyman.

"Sure is."

"What're your plans, if I may ask?"

Plans? What were her plans? "Maybe I'll visit my mother in Boston," she said, knowing she would do no such thing. "I might stay right here."

"A pretty lady like you?"

She laughed. "Yes, a pretty lady like me."

They joined other trucks, idled briefly, then became part of a convoy to the Burlington-Northern Depot. When they stopped, her driver pointed out Col. Dempster. "He'll take your forms. The MPs will get the men out."

With Gut Bucket by her side, Audrey joined a small group of branch camp leaders from all over Nebraska, some of whom she had met during Walter Watkins's months as acting camp commander. They chuckled when she explained her presence instead of Walter's. The colonel took her papers, looked them over and thanked her.

The sun rose. She watched the Camp Veteran trucks disgorge their PWs. All around her were Germans standing in blocks, not at attention, but orderly, as she had come to expect. These were the men she should have hated to her dying day, but didn't. Most wore at least some fragments of their original uniforms under their US Army-issued overcoats. Here and there she saw the long-billed ball cap of Rommel's Afrika Korps.

She wondered if these were prisoners from all over the state, because there were so many. "What happens now?" she asked one of the other camp commanders.

"It's the train east and then a troop transport to Europe." He shook his head. "Can't say I envy them, going home to ruin." He brightened. "We did what we could here."

"We did," she replied, and felt a quiet satisfaction. "Is our war over now, too?"

The commander smiled and tipped his hat to her.

"All right, Gut Bucket, there's our driver," she said, and bent down to pat her dog. "Let's go home."

What happened next happened quickly. A familiar voice shouted, "Schmalz!" Gut Bucket looked up, alert. He sniffed the air and darted between the ranks of Germans, who cheered him on, some reaching out to pat the fast-moving dog, and some to give her low whistles of appreciation. Men.

Her heart in her throat, she hurried after Gut Bucket, and there they were, *her* men of the Afrika Korps, opening their little circle to give her room – Dietrich Schopenhauer, Heinz Dorschel her pianist, Kurt Krueger, little Anton. She looked for the frightened man, then remembered his death by suicide. And there was Gerd Gauss, who had watched over them all.

Without a word, her PWs gathered around, linked arms and faced out as Gerd grabbed her, held her close and kissed her in that circle of momentary privacy. Same wonderful kiss, same strong body. The man she loved in spite of everything, maybe because of everything. She couldn't hold him any closer or tighter – damn these winter overcoats anyway – as he buried his face in her neck.

"Help me somehow," was all he said. "Please help me. I love you."

"I promise I will, Gerd. I promise."

Chapter Twenty-nine

August, 1949

Perhaps she had been hasty in declaring more than three years ago that she would never return to Boston. Audrey hadn't expected to owe an unpayable debt to Mother's third husband, William Peabody (no Peabody was ever called Bill, of that she was certain). To say that Mr. Peabody was a well-placed and hugely connected lawyer was to understate the matter.

But that seemed like years ago. Each day that passed since her final view of Gerd Gauss, holding her close in the circle of his friends, seemed more terrible than the one before. She had no way to find him, not in a world where so many displaced people wandered. If he was still a prisoner somewhere in Europe, no source gave her information. No doors magically opened. She had no address in Austria. In bad dreams, she sent letter after letter to a mound of Viennese rubble, until the stack of unopened letters was taller than the concrete.

She arrived at some acceptance, because to stay sane, she had no choice. Gerd had her address, if it hadn't been taken from him like the photo of his wife and son. If he was alive, it was his choice to write to her. If he was dead, she would never know. She did know that little people like Gerd Gauss and Audrey Allerton were multiplied by millions in a restless, post-war world where the shooting may have stopped, but nothing had returned to normal.

Helpless, but quietly so, she felt herself withdrawing into a shell, where the daytime Audrey Allerton did her duty at the extension office with smiles and diligence. The nighttime Audrey stared at her bedroom ceiling until exhaustion wore her out and she slept. She was certain of one thing: she longed for Gerd Gauss.

How long that could continue, she did not know until the day when the postman finally delivered a letter to her postmarked Wien, Österreich. Had Dad not quickly pulled out a kitchen chair and guided her into it, she would have landed on the floor. Dear God, he was alive. Her hands shook so badly that Dad had to open the letter.

She nearly held her breath from "Dearest Audrey," to "Love, Gerd," reading a distressing story of a year spent shoveling rubble and starving in France. When he was finally allowed to return home, Austria was no better. Soviet meddling and mayhem in his country came with more hunger during the winter of 1947-48. "Tell your father I have lost all my Wyoming girth," he wrote.

What followed was the huge difficulty of finding employment, any employment. She sighed to read of his getting a job shoveling coal instead of rubble, which became increasingly difficult to do as he and Austria starved together. "I eat when there is food, and remind myself that I have a job, which makes me luckier than some. Oh, but the children."

She smiled, just barely, when he wrote of an unusual bit of good fortune, brought about because those Tommies back in Tunisia had swiped his leather flight jacket. "I confess I did like that jacket. We Desert Rats of Rommel took a certain pride in being flyboys," he wrote. That was then. He wrote of former pilots still wearing their flight jackets who were hounded from town to town, beaten, and never given jobs, because Austrians and Germans blamed the Luftwaffe for raining down Allied bombs on *them* in retaliation for the London Blitz. "It is the peculiar madness of war," he concluded. "Had I worn my long-gone flight jacket, such would have been my fate, too."

She memorized his last paragraph, in which he wrote of his unfailing love for her, even if he might never see her again, or find a way to make a life with her…somewhere. When she finished the letter, she handed it to Dad, who objected at first, calling it for her eyes only. "No, Dad," she replied simply. "This was your war, too, and I am your daughter. You know my pain."

Letters went back and forth, never quickly enough to suit either of them. It distressed her to learn that Dietrich Schopenhauer, her auto design engineer, was stuck behind Soviet borders. Amazingly, Kurt Krueger was picking his way through life in Berlin's Western Sector, working as a hospital orderly, but with bigger plans. The others? Lost to the times.

Except for Heinz Dorschel, and she learned of him through his father in Hastings, Nebraska. Only two months before she got on the train to Boston, Josef Dorschel paid them a surprise visit. Seated beside him in his truck was Heinz himself, who grabbed her, swung her around and gave her smacking kisses on both cheeks.

Everyone talked at once, but the story came out. "I did as you said, Herr Nolan," Josef said, as they sat on the porch and Audrey poured lemonade. "I contacted my senators and representatives, wrote pleading letter after letter." He looked at Heinz with more love than generally seen anywhere. "Three years almost, but here he is. I sponsored him."

They stayed overnight, Heinz describing his long year in England, clearing rubble in Coventry and enduring the hatred. "I despaired," he said simply. The return to Berlin was no better, his mother dead and his sister finally driven to suicide by Russian gang rape. "I shoveled more rubble there and cried many tears." He looked at his father with pride and love. "Now I am where I belong. I will become a farmer."

The sweetness returned when he sat at the piano and took out the Mozart. "Do you remember?" he asked. How could she forget? They sang the lovely Ave Maria duet again. He found "Passing By," and questioned her with his eyes, but she couldn't.

She wrote all this to Gerd. She lived for his letters.

Dad surprised her a month later. The beets had been thinned and weeded, and he decided to run electricity to the bunkhouse, still empty, since no one could really replace Corporal Shepard. She found Dad out there after she returned from the extension office.

"Whatcha doing, Dad?" she asked. She flicked some dust off the blue and white gingham tablecloth then patted it as she thought of Shep, buried in France.

"Since we live in the twentieth century, I thought it was high time to electrify this little place, too. Shep's zinnias look fine, as usual."

"Always."

"Take a look in the other room and tell me what you think."

"Think? Four bare walls?"

Dad smiled. She opened the door on a double bed that hadn't been there last week or any week, and a big dresser that she knew had come from the attic. The rocking chair looked new.

"Dad, what're you up to?" she asked. "Did you find someone to take Shep's spot?"

He nodded, looking for all the world like a man who wasn't quite sure what to say. He finally settled on, "Audrey, I did something monumental. Took me three years, but I did something. Sit down."

She sat on the bed, mystified. Dad was not a great man for subterfuge. What you saw was what you got with Pete Nolan. "Dad?"

"Audie, I didn't want to get your hopes up, but going on three years ago, I took a page from Josef Dorschel's book and wrote our senators and rep."

She held her breath.

He waggled his hand. "So so, but then I got smart. I thought of the man who could really help: your mother's third husband."

"Dad!"

"Ol' Peabody has some pretty astounding State Department connections. He remembered you, of course. After he got over the initial shock of my idea, he said he'd get right on it."

"Dad."

"You'll need to come up with a better word, Audie. Call Gerd an early birthday present."

Mother's maid knocked on the door and reminded Audrey that it was nearly time to go to the dock. After she curtseyed and left, closing the door so quietly, Audrey couldn't help a laugh – quietly, this was Mother's house – as she thought of all the times Dad had stood at the bottom of the stairs in their farmhouse and shouted up to her to get a move on. That would never do in Boston in any house belonging to William Peabody, attorney with those State Department connections.

She got a move on, putting on the proper summer dress for a widow – sedate but not too sedate – on her way to the dock to meet the freighter *Jolly O*, out of Portsmouth, England. "I know your father could have paid for passage on a liner," Mother complained.

"He could have," Audrey agreed, "but Gerd has his pride and this was cheaper." *How much coal did you shovel, my love,* she asked herself. *I suspect you're working out part of your passage shoveling more on the Jolly O.*

"You couldn't find a regular American? Mrs. Allerton has declared she will never speak to you again."

Others might not either, Audrey thought, *until they get to know Gerd.* "I wish it were otherwise, but that is hers to deal with."

"You're going right to the courthouse?"

"We are. Gerd proposed in his last letter."

Not precisely. Was a proposal between a widower and a widow ever simple? This was the letter where Gerd Gauss, *feldwebel* who watched over his men in Compound Four, unburdened his heart to her. He laid it bare, this man with nothing in the world except, apparently, the same crazy optimism infecting her. It was love crossing borders and death and disappointed hopes.

In his letter he asked, *Do you know why I always patted my heart? The inside pocket of my flight jacket held my rosary, and each letter Hannelore wrote. I thought I patted for good luck, but I patted that final letter with the photograph of her and our son after I knew they were gone. Audrey, I did it for love, not luck. I know that. Now it is love between me and you. I have discovered that mine is a generous heart with room for you and our children. I have nothing else to offer. Is it enough?*

Yes, she wrote back. *Room and to spare. I'll marry you.* She knew Gerd hadn't specifically asked, but she knew him, and she loved him. He never was the enemy.

That was more than Mother needed to know. "Thanks for marrying William Peabody," she settled on. "He's already started the courthouse paperwork. I never met a man with more influence. He astounds me. Three days, he assured me."

Audrey didn't mind that Mother couldn't unbend enough to actually meet a freighter at Boston's less-then-genteel docks. That was Mother. William Peabody didn't mind shepherding her out of the Rolls and to the dock to stand protectively by her side as she watched the *Jolly O* tie up and the gangplank come down.

As sweet as this moment, Audrey remembered yesterday's sweet moment, a visit to one of Boston's oldest cemeteries. She walked the familiar row of Allertons, an old and distinguished New England name. She stood more than a moment in front of Ed's memorial, a tombstone with name, birth and death dates, but an empty grave. As his son's widow, Ed's father allowed her to choose a remembrance in the stone. She read it out loud, not certain if she would ever return to this sacred spot: "His was a life of service and sacrifice for his country."

Had things been different...but they weren't, she reminded herself. "Dear Ed," she whispered, and touched the plain marker. "Dear Ed." She stood another moment, head bowed, then left the cemetery without looking back. A door quietly closed as another opened.

She recalled herself to the moment, to the anticipation of the people on the dock and the people at the railing, everyone intent. It took a moment to spot Gerd. William Peabody had told her that the Statue of Liberty had nothing on Boston's harbor, where others yearning to breathe free made their way to the USA. This was now the American century. Audrey knew she was gazing into the future.

There he was, her future, looking for her. He was shockingly thin, but regular meals in their little house behind Dad's place would change that. The usual down-droop of his lips rose when he spotted her. She waved and blew him a kiss.

He patted his heart.

Epilog

October, 1950

Who wouldn't relish waking up on a cool Wyoming morning to see a lovely woman, cuddled close, sleeping so soundly? Gerd knew he could end that sleep with a kiss and a lot more, but not this morning. It was enough to lie there and think about his wife, his three-month-old son who slept all night now – *Lobe Gott im Himmel* – and the work coming next week in the beet harvest. Harvest was always hard, but he had enough to eat now.

His father-in-law told him that this year, they would also help with the sugar beet and bean harvest on the Gardiner place to the north. "Carl Gardiner's arthritis is so bad that he can't do it. We other farmers will," Peter told him last night over dinner.

We others. Maybe this was part of what it meant to be an American, where everyone pitched in and helped. Maybe it was also livestock auctions to raise money for an addition on the Veteran elementary school, and listening to the Gettysburg Address on the Fourth of July. Maybe it was also that peculiar feeling that rose up from his toes when their son was born. His second thought, after thanking God for a safe delivery, was *Here is my first American child*. Whatever that feeling was, he liked it.

He turned his attention to the lovely woman beside him. *Schöne Ehefrau, but you have long eyelashes*, he thought, as he watched Audrey, the dearest person in his challenging, far-from-simple life. How was it a woman could get more beautiful in one year? Even when her belly was so big with their son, she was still beautiful. Maybe it was the way she looked at him and her eyes softened. He liked her laugh, a full-blown laugh he remembered in France where he labored as a PW and starved, and nearly two more years in Austria, where he starved some more. Was he famished for food, or that laugh and the woman who came with it? Not so hard to tell.

Once married, they never held anything back from each other. He asked her about that once, how a circumspect, modest woman could be so... oh, there was no word in German or English. She blushed and massaged him and he forgot the question.

She was kind. So was he, especially on the anniversaries of the deaths of their first loves. Only a few weeks ago in September, he had respected her silence and the faraway look in her eyes. He knew she was remembering Edward Allerton. She respected his silence in May, as he spent time alone walking the fields and thinking of lovely Hannelore and Stefan.

He still would have given the earth for that final photograph of Hannelore and Stefan, the one ripped to shreds in front of his eyes after his capture in Tunisia. He told Audrey only last week that he would always think of himself as the father of two sons, which made her say, "As you should, my dearest. You are."

He smiled to think of Peter Otto Gauss, sleeping in his bassinet in the front room, probably on his stomach with his bottom pooched up. Audrey had suggested they name him after their fathers, which suited him. *Vader* would be amazed if he could know how happy his son was as a farmer, and not an airline pilot.

Thinking of that, Gerd looked at the clock and turned on his side toward Audrey, giving his good ear the chance to listen for the 6:48 a.m. sound of an airliner high overhead, but not too high, since the takeoff was from Scottsbluff and the plane small and incapable of great altitude. Ah, there it was.

Audrey opened her eyes. "Is it on time?" she asked, which made him laugh quietly, not wanting to wake up little Pete.

"To the minute."

"That's a relief. I'd hate to have you stew about it all day," she said, which meant he had to nuzzle her with his nighttime growth of whiskers, then cover her mouth with his hand so she wouldn't shriek and wake up Pete.

"Wretch," she teased, then got down to business, cuddling closer because the air was cool, and they had left the window open last night. "What do you think about Dad's offer? He'll expect an answer today."

"*Ja*, let's do it," he told her. "We need the room. After the beets, we can add *die Toilette* on this house and then move. Not before."

"And he'll be invited – ordered – to eat with us in his big house." She chuckled. "Dad isn't much of a cook." She put soft hands around his neck. "When was the last time I told you I loved you?"

He may not have been a German, but he was precise. "About two o'clock this morning, when you grabbed me out of a sound sleep. My defenses were down."

"I didn't notice," his wife said. They laughed together.

He didn't need his good ear to hear their son tuning up in the front room. "You or me?"

"You. I'll get ready."

Audrey unbuttoned her nightgown. He retrieved their small son, who was sucking on his fist now, already a gut bucket like the one who slept under his bassinet. The dog was no fool. Soon enough this littlest Gauss would be dropping food from his highchair.

He handed his son to Audrey who snuggled their baby as he sucked. Gerd lay down again and closed his eyes, the happiest man in America.

Author's Notes

For some time, I had wanted to write some World War II stories. Earlier this year on Facebook, I asked readers to share how their folks met during World War II.

One meeting, in particular, caught my eye. Reader Arsula Shumway wrote that her parents met on a Greyhound bus. Her father was a U.S. Army Military Policeman transporting a prisoner. This was all I needed. What follows in "All My Love," was my invention, and is entirely fictitious. Thanks, Arsula, for telling me about your parents.

The second story, "Yet I Will Love Him," comes from an experience I had when I lived in Torrington, Wyoming. One of my jobs as a ranger at Fort Laramie NHS was to be the fort's liaison with the Goshen County Historical Society. This meant I attended the society's monthly meetings.

One meeting many years ago, I chatted with a lady who told me about an experience she had relating to a local prisoner of war camp. The lady said she was driving by the armory when a policeman stopped traffic to let some new German POWs cross the highway.

She told me, "They were just boys. I sat there and cried because they were so young." I never forgot that. It shows up in my story about one of those PW camps (Incidentally, the preferred term then was PW, rather than POW.)

By war's end, there were some 435,000 prisoners here, many of whom became farm laborers for farmers who had lost their hired hands to wartime service. It's not a well-known story, except in those communities which ended up as destinations for prisoners.

To learn more about America's POW camps, I recommend Arnold Krammer's, *Nazi Prisoners of War in America* (Scarborough House

Publisher, 1979). It's the only book I know of with such detail. My other sources included state histories.

My thanks to Don Hodgson, retired history professor at Eastern Wyoming College in Torrington, Wyoming, and a personal friend. I asked Don if he knew of any old fellows still alive who might remember the POW camp in Veteran, Wyoming, about 16 miles from Torrington.

He put me in touch with David Eddington, a retired farmer well into his 90s now, whose family's farm abutted the POW camp, which was a former Civilian Conservation Corps camp.

Dave was a wealth of information. He told me about the labor-intensive beet crop, and said the Germans were meticulous and efficient in the fields. "They liked to work, and they were nice guys," Dave said in our telephone interview.

I did incorporate Dave's dog into my story. "He stayed over at the camp about half the time," Dave remembered. "The prisoners liked him."

My thanks also to my editor Jennifer McCord, and my daughter, Liz Carter, who both looked over these stories with the editor's eye, catching my more boneheaded errors.

The historian in me has a request for readers: If you haven't already, please write down your parents or grandparents' World War II, Korean War or Vietnam stories. You'll be glad you kept alive their part in our American history.

About the Author

A well-known veteran of the romance writing field, Carla Kelly is the author of forty-five novels and three non-fiction works, as well as numerous short stories and articles for various publications. She is the recipient of two RITA Awards from Romance Writers of America for Best Regency of the Year; two Spur Awards from Western Writers of America; three Whitney Awards, 2011, 2012, and 2014; and a Career Achievement Award from *Romantic Times*.

Carla's interest in historical fiction is a byproduct of her lifelong study of history. She's held a variety of jobs, including medical public relations work, feature writer and columnist for a North Dakota daily newspaper, and ranger in the National Park Service (her favorite job) at Fort Laramie National Historic Site and Fort Union Trading Post National Historic Site. She has worked for the North Dakota Historical Society as a contract researcher.

Interest in the Napoleonic Wars at sea led to numerous novels about the Royal Navy, including the continuing St. Brendan Series. Carla has also written novels set in Wyoming during the Indian wars, and in the early twentieth century that focus on her interest in Rocky Mountain ranching.

Readers might also enjoy her Spanish Brand Series, set against the background of 18th century New Mexico, where ranchers struggle to thrive in a dangerous place as Spanish power declines.

You are welcome to contact Carla at https://carlakellyauthor.com